5

BLOSSOM IN WINTER - FROST IN SPRING

Lucidus Smith

authorHOUSE®

AuthorHouse™ UK Ltd.
500 Avebury Boulevard
Central Milton Keynes, MK9 2BE
www.authorhouse.co.uk
Phone: 08001974150

First published by AuthorHouse 9/2/2010

ISBN: 978-1-4520-5388-2 (sc)

DEDICATION

My love, my life, my gift from God;
My bride, my help, my sparkling wine.
Your smile delights me every day,
My own sweet dancing, Banffshire quine.

29th June 2010   LS

Contents

INTRODUCTION

April 1948 – the Second World War had been over for two and a half years and the country was getting back to normal; well, as much as rationing, bomb sites, shortages, unemployment and hardship allowed it to.

One man's life was much like another's; glad to be alive and free, but beset by guilt and sadness of everything that happened in the war and filled with bitterness about the way they had been treated since it ended.

Arnold Smith is typical of a soldier who eventually came home, but could not settle back into the old routine, although he had tried hard to, for the last two years. When his sweetheart gave him the bad news that she had found someone else, it was the final straw, so he packed a few things in a bag, got a bus to Paddington railway station and bought a ticket for the next train out. He was not even too sure of where it was going, but he was just pleased that it was going somewhere new!

CHAPTER ONE
TICKETS PLEASE

"Tickets please – tickets please, c'mon there! Give that chap sitting next to you a nudge for me son, he may be asleep, but I'm not certain," the ticket inspector said to the lad with the cap, who was sitting next to Arnold Smith, in the crowded carriage.

While Arnold came too, the tickets of the other occupants were carefully checked and the old man with the parcel was asked to pay the extra fare to Banbury, since his ticket only went as far as Princes Risborough.

"Come on sir, I haven't got all day, where's your ticket? I'm beginning to lose my patience mate, give me a ticket or pay the fare."

"I can't find it," said Arnold, as he searched through his pockets, "I've been asleep since Paddington. I was the first person in the carriage; I put my bag in the rack up there and just nodded off. My bag!! That's gone too. Someone's pinched my ticket and my bag and my wallet!"

"Very touching sir – either pay up now, or you are in serious trouble," replied the ticket inspector.

Arnold stood up and proceeded to carefully check all of his pockets again and then appealed to the rest of the carriage as he sat down again, "Did anyone else get on

1

at Paddington and see me sleeping here, with my army rucksack up there in the rack?"

A middle-aged man in a business suite, sitting in the far corner spoke up, "Well actually I did. I was the third person in the carriage at Paddington. You were asleep in the corner, another young fellow was next to you and there was a bag in the rack; but I didn't notice that it was a rucksack. I assumed you and the other man were friends since he was sitting close up next to you in an empty carriage, which is unusual, as normally the corner seats are the first to go!"

The elderly lady sitting opposite to Arnold then added that when the man next to him got off the train at Princes Risborough, he had said to her that since his friend was still sleeping would she mind telling him that he would meet him in the usual place next Tuesday for lunch and that he had picked up the rucksack and taken it with him.

Arnold looked stunned and said, "But I didn't get on with a friend and I bought a one way ticket to Birmingham and I most certainly do not have any plans to return to London. He must have taken my wallet and ticket while I was sleeping and I don't have any more money on me apart from a few coppers in my pocket."

The ticket inspector took out his note pad and pencil and made a few notes and then spoke to Arnold, "Well I'm sorry son, but I have to put you off the train at the next stop. If you care to give me your name and address, we will contact you if your rucksack turns up, but frankly I don't rate your chances. I don't suppose anyone else here would care to pay for this man's ticket to Birmingham?"

The other passengers started to look at each other and whilst feeling genuine concern for Arnold, did not feel they could afford this unplanned expenditure, but were put out of their embarrassment when Arnold spoke up; "To be honest, it really doesn't matter where I get off, as I have no real plans for the future. I just needed to get out of London, so the next stop is as good as anywhere else, thank you. I assume it will be Bicester."

"The next major stop is Bicester, but we are making a special stop at the Army Depot before then, which is very near to the villages of Upper and Lower Style, so I will give you a choice of Bicester or the Styles," replied the inspector.

Arnold sucked his lip and thought for a moment and then replied, "It may as well be the Styles, perhaps I can find some work locally, who knows, my luck has to change sometime!"

At which point in the conversation, the train started to slow down and as it came to a halt, Arnold got out of his seat and opened the door. He looked down at the elderly lady and thanked her for speaking up for him and as she reached out to shake his hand she slipped a half crown into it and suggested he might need a cup of tea. He smiled and nodded his thanks and jumped down onto the platform. A porter came rushing across and started to say that he could not get out here, but the ticket inspector jumped down as well and took the porter to one side while he explained what had happened. He then climbed back into the train which slowly gathered speed and continued on its way to Bicester and beyond.

The porter walked across to Arnold and said, "Rotten luck mate, being robbed like that. I was about to have a brew, do you want to join me?" Before Arnold could reply he turned and walked across to a small hut at the end of the platform where a kettle was on the boil and took out a couple of mugs from a cupboard. "Milk and sugar?"

"Just milk", replied Arnold, "Oh no, he's only gone and pinched my fags too!"

"Don't worry mate, I've got some tobacco if you don't mind a 'roll your own'," and with that the porter passed a tin of Old Holborn and a packet of cigarette papers to Arnold.

While he rolled himself a cigarette the porter made the tea and then passed a mug over to Arnold. "The inspector said you were on your way to Birmingham, but you sound like a Londoner, so I assume you weren't going home. My name's George by the way." George held out his hand and Arnold took it and said, "My friends call me Digger and thanks very much for the tea and fag. You're right, I do come from South London and to be honest I have no real plans, just had to get out of London, you know how it is, it was time to move on, do something new."

"Oh ho, sounds like woman trouble to me," smiled George, "well if you want some work and don't mind what you do, there is a brick works just outside Upper Style and they are looking for fit and healthy men and I'm sure you'd get somewhere to stay in the village, might be worth a go. If you get really stuck you could always sleep in the air raid shelter at the bottom of my garden, it might do for a few nights while you get sorted. We live in the middle of the block of cottages at the end of Station Drive, you can't miss it."

"That's really good of you mate, which way is Upper Style and how far from here?" asked Digger.

"Go down the drive and turn right at the end and the village is just over a mile away."

The men chatted for a bit longer while they finished their tea and then Digger got up and after saying good bye headed off down the drive. He had just reached the end of the road when he came across a middle aged lady standing at the side of her black Morris Eight looking down at a very flat offside rear tyre.

"Looks like you've got problems there love," said Digger.

She turned on him and snapped, "I am most certainly not your love and I didn't need you to point out to me that I have problems. I have to be in Aylesbury by 2:00pm and there is no way I can change a tyre in these clothes."

Digger was about to snap back, but was reminded of the kindness which George had just so recently shown to him, so he 'bit his tongue' and said instead, "Would you like me to change the tyre for you ma'am?" She was obviously taken off guard by his civility and after coughing a little, replied that she would be most grateful.

Digger took his coat off and laid it on the bonnet and then went round to the boot and took out the jack, spare wheel and wheel-brace. Unfortunately the dirt road was still wet from the overnight rain and positioning the jack in the correct place meant getting his trousers covered in mud, this was definitely 'one of those days'! Not having changed a wheel since his army days, Digger forgot to loosen the nuts before jacking the car up, so he had to let it down again, loosen the wheel nuts and then jack the car up to get the wheel off. He put the spare wheel on and guessed it was not as well inflated as the other three wheels, so said to the lady, "This tyre is a little flat, but will be quite safe if you take it easy. I suggest that you go to a garage in Aylesbury and get it pumped up and also ask them to repair the puncture. It looks like a tack has gone straight through the tyre and punctured the inner tube, so it should not be difficult to repair."

"Thank you, I will do that. I am sorry about the state of your clothes Mr err, I didn't catch your name."

"Smith," replied Digger, "and don't worry about the clothes, with all that's happened to me today, I'm just waiting for the lightening strike."

"I didn't think I recognised you from around here, are you just passing through?"

Digger gave her a quick synopsis of his day so far, finishing up by telling her that he was going to the Brickworks to look for work.

"Well Mr Smith, it seems that you and I will both remember the 5th April 1948 with something less than affection."

"The 5th April!" blurted out Digger, "Oh no, I had lost track of the date. Is there a church in the village, I must get to a church this afternoon?"

"Yes of course, St. Luke's, it's almost the first building you come to as you enter the village. If it happens to be closed, the vicarage is next door, I'm sure the vicar would open it for you. If you have a problem, just mention my name, Mrs Duffy-Smythe. You will also find a lane down the side of the church which brings you out to a large building called Millstone House, which is where I live. You say you are looking for work, well my handyman cum gardener has had to go away on family business and there are quite a lot of jobs that need doing. If you would like a few days work call at the house and ask for Mrs Black, I will telephone her from Aylesbury and let her know you might be coming."

"Well thank you ma'am, I appreciate that and I may well take you up on your offer. I will just put all the tools away and we can both get going." With no more ado, Digger put the tools and punctured wheel back in the car, Mrs Duffy-Smythe got behind the steering wheel, started the engine and headed off down the road. Digger turned the corner onto the main road and walked the mile to Upper Style.

He passed the gatehouse to a large estate and walked a bit further until he reached St. Luke's. The church door was open and he went in and sat down in a pew about half way down the church.

Well Ginger, he thought, its four years now and as he closed his eyes the memories and images came flooding back. His throat started to go dry and he could feel the lump forming there and slowly it got bigger and bigger. The tears started as a trickle but soon turned into a flood and the sobs got louder and louder as the pain and the loss just took over his whole being. Just when he thought he had got it under control another wave of sadness just burst over him and he heard himself crying out in anguish. "Oh Ginger, I'm so sorry mate, forgive me for being so stupid;" with which he just seemed to be immersed under a mountain of sadness and hopelessness.

The first he knew that he had company was when he felt a hand on his shoulder and the big man sat down beside him. "I didn't want to disturb you in your anguish my friend, but I didn't want you to be all alone either," the vicar said.

"Hello padre, I'm sorry if I was disturbing you, I didn't mean…." But he got no further and the two men just sat there for another ten minutes without saying a word.

The fact that he had called him padre confirmed what the vicar had suspected that this was an ex-soldier remembering a fallen comrade. "It's all right son, I lost good friends too, I understand the pain you must be feeling. Do you want to talk about it or just have a cup of tea and leave it to another time?"

"The tea sounds good, I'm too choked to talk now, but if I stay around here, perhaps another time eh," said Digger.

The two ex-soldiers rose and went to the door, the vicar leading the way across to the vicarage just thirty yards from the church. They went into the kitchen where his wife Mildred was washing dishes in the sink, "Tea for two, please love," said the vicar and motioned Digger to the wooden chair at the end of the table. "I would normally offer you an armchair, but in view of the state your trousers are in, you will forgive me if we stay in the kitchen. Have you taken a fall in the mud or something?"

Digger explained what had happened to him and apologised for his muddy condition, while the vicar's wife served tea and a large slice of fruit cake to both of them. After he had finished speaking she said, "Well you can't go for a job looking like that, I have a pair of trousers that belonged to our son which I am sure will fit you, I'll go and get them." She returned shortly with a pair of corduroy trousers along with an army shirt and jumper and showed Digger to the bathroom where he was able to wash the mud off himself and try the clothes on.

The shirt and jumper fitted fine and the trousers were Ok, if a bit tight!

"Leave your clothes here and I will wash them for you and you can pick them up in a day or two," said Mildred "do you have anywhere to stay yet and what did you say your name was?"

"My name is Arnold, but all my friends call me Digger. The porter at the station has offered me a bed for a couple of nights, while I get fixed up, so thanks, I would be most grateful if you could wash them for me. I don't know whether to try the brickworks first or take up Mrs Duffy-Smythe's offer, what do you think?"

The vicar cleared his throat and was about to reply, when Mildred got in first and said, "There is no competition in my mind. Millstone House itself is a large building and there are also outbuildings which I am sure you could easily sleep in. As for that handyman she talked about, I just don't think he will be coming back. It must be well over six months since he went and no-one has heard a word from him."

"Thank you dear;" said the vicar quickly, "I'm sure that Digger will take that into account when he makes his decision. But time is getting on and he needs to do something today."

"You know, I think your wife is right, I'll give Mrs whats-her-name a try first. She said to call and ask for a Mrs Black, do either of you know her?"

Mildred again jumped in quick with her reply, "To be honest we don't, as she doesn't come to church; unlike Mrs Duffy-Smythe who is a very regular member of the congregation. But she does have a reputation of being a bit prickly, some of the women in the village work there occasionally and a young girl, Sissy, is maid there and is always complaining to her mother about Mrs Black; not that I put a lot of store in what young Sissy has to say."

"Ah well, forewarned and all that, I'll wander down there and see how it goes. Thanks ever so much for the tea and fruit cake, I can't remember the last time I had home-made fruit cake, and thanks also for the loan of the clothes. I will come by in a couple of days and pick my things up. Bye for now and thanks padre for being there for me."

The vicar smiled and as they shook hands he said, "Good luck Digger and don't forget my offer for a chat, when you're ready. Millstone house is about a five minute stroll down the lane at the side of the church and watch out for muddy puddles!"

Digger left the kitchen and crossed back past the old church and onto the lane. It was barely wide enough for one vehicle but had tracks which showed it was regularly used by something a bit bigger than the Morris Eight. After a while he heard this strange noise which seemed to be coming from behind him and imagined for a moment that he was being followed. He stopped and the noise stopped, he started walking and the noise started again. He checked his shoes in case he had stepped into something unpleasant and found they were still muddy but not fouled. He tried a quick run and the noise got faster and suddenly it dawned on him that it was the trousers. They were still quite new and the ridges of the corduroy were rubbing against each other and here was him imagining all sorts of possible solutions. For the first time in several weeks, Digger heard himself laughing and it felt good. Of course he was disappointed with Sarah for the way she had treated him, but life must go on and he had to live it for himself, if only one day at a time. Sure enough one person had robbed him, but many more had been kind and helpful and he owed it to Ginger to live a full and active life.

"Let's go and see what this Mrs Black has to say then," he thought to himself, as he walked up to the front door and knocked twice.

CHAPTER TWO
LOOKING FOR WORK

Digger waited for a minute and as no-one answered he knocked again a bit louder; which was his second mistake! The door burst open and a lady in her thirties, with a face as forbidding as he had ever seen, stood there glaring at him.

"Can't you read?" she thundered.

Digger looked at her and remembered the warning which the vicar's wife had given and realised she had not overstated the position regarding Mrs Black, whom he presumed, now fumed before him. He decided that if he was going to work here, at Millstone House, for a few days, he needed to establish himself with this lady, right up front, so backing down and being polite was just not an option.

"Of course I can read," he replied and pointing to the doorbell, said "it says push and I did, but it didn't work, so I used the knocker, which probably says knock, if I cared to study it!"

Mrs Black may have been slightly daunted by the unexpected response, but was far too enraged to show it, instead she stepped out of the doorway, forcing Digger to step back and pointed to the sign at the side of the door which announced, "Tradesmen are to report to the back door please."

"Assuming you are not an invited guest, or a friend or neighbour who is calling in, this means you! So might I suggest that you do what it says and go round to the back and try again." With that, Mrs Black stepped back into the doorway and firmly closed the door behind her.

Digger looked at his watch and saw it was well after five o'clock and there was little opportunity to find somewhere else to spend the night, apart from an air-raid shelter, at the bottom of someone's garden, so telling himself that he gave as good as he got with Mrs Black, decided to do as she had suggested and try again round the back. But where was the back?

He remembered that he had seen a rickety old farm gate and driveway at the side of the house, which seemed to go round some outbuildings, so he decided that this must be the way to the back and that he should check it out. He did consider knocking on the door once more and asking Mrs Black which way he should go to get round the back, but thought the answer would give her far too much pleasure.

The farm gate was open and Digger walked through it and down the drive for about twenty five yards and followed the road as it went round the end of the buildings and came to an abrupt stop at a pair of heavy, six feet high, entrance gates. He turned the handle, thinking by now that Mrs Black had had plenty of time to nip out and lock them, but found that it turned with ease and he went in, closing the gate behind him. Just then a young girl came rushing down the path and said to him, "Hello, while you're here give me a hand opening them, will you, as I find them so heavy."

Digger smiled and helped the girl open both gates and fix them back in position.

"I'm Sissy, I work here, are you the man who is coming to do some work for Mrs Duffy-Smythe?" Digger was about to reply when another voice rang out from the house, "Sissy, you stop your nattering and bring the young man over here, Mrs Black will see him in the kitchen."

"That's cook, she just never gives up, moan, moan, moan all day long. I don't know why I bother to stay on here! Come on then, I'll show you where the kitchen is. Would you like a cup of tea?"

Sissy took Digger into the kitchen, which was not overlarge, but was warm and friendly, so he sat down on a chair and waited. The door opened and another lady entered carrying a mug which she put down on the table by Digger. She looked a very fit sixty something and although she didn't smile, appeared to be of a pleasant disposition, "Help yourself to sugar, love, she won't be a minute. I'm cook, what's your name?"

"Hello cook, I'm Arnold Smith, but all my friends call me Digger, nice to meet you and thanks for the tea, I'm parched."

"Well to be honest love, after the bad start with Mrs Black, I don't think you will be around long enough for us to become friends, so I will call you Arnold." With that she turned round and left the room. Digger was not sure whether her last comment was a joke or a warning, but he liked it here and decided to try and be pleasant at the next interview.

He looked up and saw Mrs Black standing in the doorway. "Oh do please make yourself at home, shall I ask cook to find some slippers for you? Mrs Duffy-Smythe rang and told me to expect a knight in shining armour named Smith, is that you?"

Digger nodded, it was safer than speaking.

"Well Smith, I don't much like the look of you, I doubt if you've done an honest day's work in months have you? Drink your tea and get out, we don't have any work for the likes of you round here."

Digger jumped out of the chair and stood in front of her, making her step back a pace. "Well Black, I don't much like the look of you either, I was expecting to work for a lady, not for some bad tempered old bag of a housekeeper whose only claim to fame is her volume and limited vocabulary." He was about to get started on her looks and dress sense, when he noticed another lady standing outside the kitchen door. Mrs Duffy-Smythe had arrived home from Aylesbury and was standing quite still and smiling to herself.

"Oh, good evening ma'am, I was just going," said Digger, somewhat shamefacedly, "your housekeeper tells me there is no work at the moment."

"Just listen to him, Florence, housekeeper, I'll give him housekeeper!" But that was where Mrs Black stopped speaking, in mid sentence; some line had been crossed which Digger could not understand, for she just apologised to Mrs Duffy-Smythe and quickly left the room.

"My sister has her good days and bad days, Mr Smith, and this is a bad day. She is not my housekeeper, but lives here and runs things for me so I am free to do the things that I need to do. So whilst I understand that you and she might never get on, blood is thicker than water and I will not have you speak to her like that again. Is that clear?"

"Yes ma'am," said Digger, "so there is some work I can do?"

"Most certainly and to start with you can reverse the car into the garage for me and I will go and talk to my sister. I suggest for tonight you find somewhere in the garages to sleep and we will look at things afresh tomorrow. I expect you are hungry so I will ask cook to bring some food to you. There is a sink and toilet in the garage, is that all right with you Mr Smith?"

"Yes ma'am, thank you, that sounds fine. I'll go and put the car away," and with that Digger left the house and walked back down the path. It was quite dark now and it was starting to drizzle, so even a draughty garage was better than sleeping rough under a hedge somewhere, or a damp and draughty air raid shelter.

The car started easily and was soon safely parked in the garage, he left the lights of the car on to help him find the light switch which was just inside the door, the only problem was that none of the lights came on! He walked back down the path towards the house and spotted cook coming out of the first door of the outbuildings, "Excuse me cook, you don't by any chance have a spare light bulb do you?"

"I must be a mind reader Arnold, I was just getting you one, but that's all I have, if you put it in the light fitting in front of the wash area, it will give you enough light for tonight and I will get some more tomorrow. If you knock at the kitchen window in half an hour I will give you something to eat." With that she passed him the precious package and a newspaper.

"Many thanks" said Digger, "I haven't read a paper for several days."

"Oh it's not for reading Arnold," she said and went back into the house.

Digger put the bulb into the suggested light fitting and was immediately blinded as the light came on; he had forgotten to turn the switch off. He turned the car lights off and closed the garage doors and then proceeded to inspect the whole garage area. There was a large dusty work bench against the corner wall by the toilet and some shelving ran above it and along the back wall. A cupboard under the bench had an assortment of tools and tins and such like and what looked like a field mouse nest in the corner, for something small scampered away as he opened the door. In the middle of the back wall between the two windows was a table and chair, which were again very dirty but seemed sound and a cupboard in the far corner contained some working clothes, a pair of Wellington boots and an assortment of hats and gloves. Down the far wall were positioned various pieces of gardening equipment, including a large robust yard broom.

About this time a very strong call of nature hit him and he moved quickly to the toilet. It was filthy, like everything else in the garage, but to his relief the old wooden seat was intact and he wiped off the worst of the dirt with a cloth he found in the cupboard. Just in time he realised that there was no toilet paper on the holder and smiled as he remembered cook's words about the newspaper. He retrieved this from where he had left it and settled down to read the paper, leaving the toilet door open for light.

Meanwhile, Mrs Duffy-Smythe had gone upstairs to her sister's room and gently knocked at the door. "Amanda, can I come in please?" she called, "we need to chat about what has just happened downstairs with Mr. Smith."

"Of course you can come in, I'm not sick just upset with myself," she replied.

The two ladies sat opposite each other in the two armchairs, neither quite knowing what to say, so Amanda started by saying, "I know you think I acted badly towards that man, but I was in the study dusting your photographs when he knocked on the door. I must have been dreaming, because he made me jump and I dropped the photo of mummy in the silver frame and managed to damage the frame and break the glass. I know how much you treasure that photo and I was so cross with him and with myself for being clumsy."

"I noticed it down there and wondered what had happened," Mrs Duffy-Smythe responded, "but I am sure we can easily get it fixed and the photo was not damaged."

Amanda sighed with relief and said, "That's good, I'll take it with me when next I go to town. Anyway, that obviously put me in a bad mood and when I got to the door and saw him standing there wearing army clothes, it just threw me completely and I didn't want anything to do with him. You didn't mention he was wearing army clothes when you rang. I just couldn't bear to have him anywhere near me. I'm sorry, but you know what I have been through!"

"I didn't mention it because he was not wearing army clothes when he helped me with the car. He just got himself covered in mud, helping me. I called in at the vicarage on the way home, since he had said he wanted a church and I had told him about St. Luke's and wanted to see whether he had actually gone there or was just trying to create a good impression with me."

"Why did he need a church, what did he want to confess?" queried Amanda.

"Well to start with the vicar wouldn't say anything about him and pointed out that I would not appreciate him discussing me with others. I explained that I thought I might be able to offer Mr Smith a few weeks work, but was nervous at having a strange man living on the property and would value the vicar's opinion of him."

"Tell me you aren't serious," cried Amanda, "a soldier living in our house!"

"I never said in the house, did I? I said on the property, we have the old chauffeur's cottage sitting there empty, I thought he could use that. Anyway, the vicar told me that his wife had seen someone going into the church who looked a bit dishevelled, so he went across to investigate. When he got there, he found Mr Smith sobbing his heart out, obviously grief stricken over something. Eventually he went up and they chatted and discovered that it was the anniversary of a comrade's death from the war. He took him into the house for a cup of tea, where his wife noticed he was covered in mud and offered to wash his clothes and lend him some of her son's clothes."

"I didn't know they had a son, does he live away?" asked Amanda.

"The son died in 1942, she just can't bring herself to get rid of his things, so it was a pair of her son's trousers along with an army shirt and jumper she lent to Mr Smith. He was only dressed that way because he had helped me, it is not his normal way of dressing and he can get his own clothes back shortly."

"Did the vicar give you an opinion about him then?"

"He said he thought Mr Smith was a decent chap and we should not be fearful. He said it was his wife who had persuaded him to work for us, rather than the brickworks, which he had also been considering. She noticed that his hands did not look like labourers hands and thought he would be better working for us. She confirmed what her husband said about him and thought he seemed a very nice man."

"So it's all settled then, regardless of what I might think," said Amanda.

"For goodness sake Amanda, nothing is settled; we just have a heap of work, with no-one to do it. We can't find anyone in the village to do jobs for us at a price we can afford to pay and the place is starting to look very shabby. All I am suggesting is we give him a chance. We let him stop here for a couple of days and see how he does with the jobs we give him. Surely you can agree to that?"

"OK, two days, but if I'm not happy, he goes – all right? Where have you put him tonight?"

"I told him to sleep in the garage, at worst he will use the car, I suppose."

Amanda started to smile, "You did warn him about the plumbing and not to use the toilet and basin."

"I don't know what you are talking about dear. What is wrong with the toilet and basin?"

"I must have told you surely, I had to turn the water off at the mains last year as all the valve mechanism had rusted away and the water just poured over the top of the cistern. Or perhaps I didn't, it was while cook was visiting her sick brother and you were up in London for the book launch."

"This is the first I have heard of it, I will go and let him know, goodness is that the time already?"

Unfortunately for Digger, Cook had remembered Mrs Black telling her that she had turned off the water supply to the garage and assumed that this had been to prevent any of the pipes freezing up during winter. Being the good natured soul that she was, she went out of the kitchen and into the first room of the outbuildings, which happened to be the old dairy and was now used as a laundry room. It also housed the downstairs washroom and toilets and was where all the stopcocks were located. She found the stopcock for the garage in the small white cupboard in the corner and proceeded to turn the tap in an anti clockwise direction, until it was fully open. She then returned to the kitchen and continued with her chores.

Digger was engrossed with yesterday's news or more particularly how Chelsea had managed to lose yet again, when he heard the gurgling sound above his head. After a minute or two he heard the water running down the pipe and started to get nervous. Deciding it was time to leave post-haste he received the first few drops of rusty water on his head and down his neck. Whilst making a hasty exit from the doomed closet, he fell over his own feet and clothes and ended up stretched lengthways on the floor in front of the basin. It was at this point that he realised what the other sound had been, that had been worrying him for a while now. It was the sound of water cascading from the sink onto the floor; the tap having been left in the open position and the plug hole having been filled with rubbish. It may have only been a minute or two since cook had kindly turned the water back on, but mayhem was breaking out all around Digger.

Mrs Duffy-Smythe had been quite calm when she had told Cook about the plumbing problems in the garage. Cook on the other hand had turned slightly pale and had rushed out of the kitchen door. Both ladies arrived at the garage just in time to hear the cry of pain as Digger slipped and fell quite awkwardly on the wet floor and opening the door were amazed to see him improperly attired on the floor, with water flowing over the sink onto his head and the toilet cistern cascading further streams of water down the wall.

It is of course at times like this that the true differences between people can be observed. Cook held her apron to her face and just laughed till she cried and had to lean against the outside wall to save herself from falling over, whilst Mrs Duffy-Smythe first checked to make sure the car had not been involved with any of these happenings and then tried to speak to poor Digger on the floor, but discovered that she too had erupted into uncontrollable mirth and had to join cook against the wall.

Luckily for them all, Mrs Black had thought to turn the stopcock off before joining the ladies outside, so although the spectacle was not quite what it had been, she too had to give in, to the overwhelming desire to shriek with laughter at Digger's unfortunate situation.

By the time the three ladies were in control of their emotions again, Digger had risen from the floor, adjusted his attire and had walked over to the chair and table and sat down. Somehow his trousers had stayed reasonably dry but his shirt and jumper were soaked, so he removed them. Cook suggested that the others return to the house while she offered to mop up the mess and attend to Digger. She asked Mrs Black whether she might have anything suitable for Digger to wear in place of his wet clothes.

Apart from bruised knees and elbows, Digger was not badly hurt and felt a lot better after a hot meal and several mugs of tea in the kitchen. Mrs Black did find a large woollen sweater that he wore over his vest after it had been dried in front of the fire. Cook suggested that he spend the night in the laundry room, which happened to have a large old armchair where the back let down flat, so you could use it as a bed. She found a couple of old blankets and a pillow and bid him goodnight.

Mrs Duffy-Smythe and her sister, were still chuckling about it later in the evening and had to admit that it was the funniest thing they had seen in many a year.

Digger eventually got to sleep about midnight after churning the events of the day over and over in his mind. He was reminded of something Ginger used to say when something strange happened, "There's nought so queer as folk!"

"Well, you certainly got that one dead right Ginger," he said to himself.

Millstone House
Artist - Malcolm Henry Sales

CHAPTER THREE
A FAIR DAY'S LABOUR

"Ooh, that doesn't look very comfortable," said Sissy as she walked into the room where Digger was snoring heavily, "I couldn't sleep on that old thing if you paid me. Cook says you are to come for your breakfast right now or you will have to go without."

Digger woke suddenly and found his head was off the back of the chair-bed, his arm was stuck out through one of the sides and his left leg had managed to fall through between the webbing straps of the seat. "What did you say Sissy, about breakfast, what time is it anyway?"

"Its half past seven and if you don't come straight away, you won't get any. So you'd better get a move on. Bye," and with that she bounced out, closing the door behind her.

Digger manoeuvred his way off the chair, put his trousers and jumper on and after a quick splash in the sink made his way to the kitchen.

"You've only just made it Arnold," said Cook, "just remember we eat breakfast at 7:00am in this house and if you are late then you go without. I'm going to the shops later, if you give me some money I will get you some washing gear, as you don't seem to have any with you."

Digger was about to say that he didn't have any money when he remembered the half crown the lady in the carriage had given him, so he passed it across to Cook. "This is all I have, so please get what you can with it. Do I just help myself here to what I want for breakfast?"

"Well I'm certainly not going to wait on you," she snapped back at him.

"I don't mind helping him," said Sissy and moved across to the range, where the egg and bacon were frying.

"You'll do no such thing my girl, I've given you your chores for the morning, he's big enough and ugly enough to help himself, although after last night's antics, I'm beginning to wonder about that!" Sissy shrugged her shoulders and pulled a face and lifted the lid of the rubbish bin and took the inner container outside in order to empty it into the dustbin.

"That's not fair," answered Digger, before he noticed the grin on Cook's face, "so, I guess it's time to stock up for the day. Do you happen to know what jobs they want me to do?"

"Mrs Black will see you after breakfast, Arnold, but my guess is she will get you to start on those filthy garages."

"That's a really posh name is Arnold, I don't know any other Arnolds," interjected Sissy as she walked back into the kitchen.

"My friends call me Digger, so perhaps you would prefer that Sissy."

"Oh no, if Cook calls you Arnold then so will I. I'll get started on cleaning the bathrooms then Cook," and she turned to Digger and whispered, "see what I mean, she knows I hate doing the bathrooms, so what's the first job of the day?"

"I heard that Sissy," said Cook, "any more of your cheek and I'll ask Mrs Black if she wants the upstairs windows washed as well! Now, get on with your work."

Sissy went to the laundry to get the cleaning materials, mop and bucket and Digger munched his way through two eggs, four rashers of bacon, a large sausage, umpteen tomatoes and mushrooms and three slices of toast, butter and marmalade, oh and two large mugs of tea.

He was just finishing his final slice of toast when Mrs Black came into the kitchen. He braced himself for the first crossfire of the day and was surprised when she sat down and asked if he had managed to sleep in the chair and whether he had hurt himself in the fall. At which point she put her hands to her face and started laughing.

Digger replied that he had slept fine and apart from a few grazes had not hurt himself and was fit and able for work.

They went outside into the garden, although at this stage Digger considered it looked more like a wilderness and Mrs Black stood and looked around her for a while and then walked over to the garage. "I expect there will be a fair bit of mess to clean up from last night, would you mind opening up both sets of doors so we can see what state things are in."

Digger opened the doors in front of the car first of all and fastened them back in place. He then tried the other two doors and managed to open one about a foot and the other a bit less. "These hinges are rusted solid, I will try soaking them in oil and see if it frees them up," he said.

The morning light flooded in and both of them stood there staring at the mess that the escaping water had made, along with the dirt and muck that had accumulated from all the months of neglect.

"Do you want me to try and fix the cistern or are you going to leave it shut off?" Digger asked her. "It's just that if you do leave it shut off, I will need to use the facilities in that other room where I spent the night."

"I really think they are past saving, for the moment use the other washroom and toilet, I will let Cook and Sissy know. Spend the morning on the garage and see what difference you can make. We are virtually out of wood and the coalman has forgotten us again, so we are desperate for something to burn. Somewhere in all this mess, there should be an axe and saw and there are plenty of dead branches at the edge of the Manor's wood over there," pointing to somewhere beyond the garden wall. "We are allowed to just help ourselves to what we want. We used to have a wheelbarrow, but I have no idea where it is now. Lunch will be at twelve and Cook serves it on time, I have to go into town, so if you need anything, ask Cook. Here are the keys to the car, bring it round to the front of the house for me please."

With that she headed back into the house and Digger unlocked the entry gates and then drove the car round to the front, just as Mrs Black appeared in the doorway. He realised that the original tyre was now back in place and was pleased that his advice had been followed.

He returned to the garage and found an old beer crate which was just high enough to stand on to wash the windows inside and out, which considerably improved the natural lighting, so armed with the large broom he tackled all the dirt and muck.

At the back of the bench was an old oil can he had spotted yesterday and somewhere on a shelf he found a can marked 'Machine Oil', so putting the two together he soaked every hinge, bolt and lock he could find, as well as the hinges on the two large entry gates that he and Sissy struggled with the previous evening.

"Elevenses Arnold, where are you?"

"I'm down by the bench Sissy, but don't come in as I have bits and pieces all over the floor, I will come out." With that he emerged covered in cobwebs, dirt and oil into the sunlight. "Goodness, is it eleven o'clock already? Well it must be for Cook is never late, I'm told."

"She's not here, had to go the village for some shopping, so I have made the coffee, hope you like it, but it's that bottled stuff and I never know how much to use."

"If the washroom is free, I will wash my hands first, any chance of some cake then, if you are in charge?"

"How could you eat cake after all that breakfast, you're as bad as my brother Tom, my mum says he must have worms or something! I'll get you a piece."

While Digger washed his hands Sissy raided the pantry and returned with a large piece of jam sponge which she handed to him, "Cook will go mad when she finds out I have given you this, she was saving it for herself, serves her right for giving me all those rotten jobs," she laughed.

Since he was already into his second bite, there seemed no point in making any honourable gestures regarding the cake, figuring that Sissy could take care of herself and where would they find another maid round here anyway?

The rest of the morning soon passed and the garages were looking a lot better and even the stubborn door had started to budge a bit, so it received another visit form the oil can. The log saw and axe were among the garden tools and both were in a very sad state of repair, but the prospect of carrying all the chopped wood from the trees to the garden did not fill him with relish.

He found Sissy and asked her if she happened to know where the wheelbarrow was and she, without thinking, said yes, her dad had borrowed it. They agreed that if the wheelbarrow was back by tomorrow morning, there would be no need to inform anyone else of its temporary vacation.

"Anyway," she said, "why don't you just drag some of the bigger branches from over there to over here and use the chopping block in the corner, that's what I do when I need firewood."

"Out of the mouths of babes," thought Digger as he went off to rummage again through the cupboard with the work clothes. He found a set of working men's overalls, a bit like he had seen the railwaymen use, a couple of flat caps, a gabardine type of waterproof jacket and several pairs of old gloves from which he was able to make one and a half useable pairs. There was also a pair of Wellington boots that fitted him snugly with a pair of socks inside that just needed a bit of darning. He took everything out and shook out most of the dust and found the overalls fitted well enough and being in the cupboard, were not as dirty as he had expected.

Being equipped with rubber boots and working clothes, he filled the bucket with warm water, from the tap in the washroom and washed all the floors and walls with soapy water. He was very pleased with the difference he had made and sat down on the chair by the table to admire his handiwork.

"What a difference you have made Mr Smith," remarked Mrs Duffy-Smythe, "you know I don't ever remember those other doors ever being opened."

"Good morning ma'am," replied Digger, "judging by the amount of oil it is taking to free up the hinges, I am not surprised. I see you got the tyre repaired yesterday, did they have to replace the inner tube or just repair it?"

"I told them to replace it, mainly because they had one the right size and who knows when that might happen again, but I said to repair the old one and leave it with the spare tyre. Waste not want not! Did my sister mention that we normally eat lunch at twelve o'clock?"

Digger nodded that she had and Mrs. Duffy-Smythe continued, "Well, it will not be on time today, like you, I was up a bit later than normal, so I have put it back to one o'clock. Cook should be back soon from the village and we normally have cold meat or a pie or something, nothing too heavy. I see you have looked out the saw and the axe, we desperately need fuel for the fires and kitchen range, so please make that your next priority. I might see you later, but I am immersed in a new book and tend to disappear for days on end, while the inspiration flows." She smiled and then walked back to the house and Digger decided to find out where this supply of wood was located.

The rear wall was surrounded by a meadow and about one hundred yards beyond that was the wood. He walked along the edge of the wood for a couple of hundred yards in each direction and noted all the dead wood lying around. Selecting a large branch at random he proceeded to pull it out of the wood into the meadow. Following Sissy's advice he started to drag it over to the gates and then through into the corner of the garden, at which point he staggered into the garage and collapsed in the chair. Looking at his watch he noticed it was now twenty past one and realised the whole operation had taken more than ninety minutes.

"I warned you at breakfast Arnold, we serve meals on time in this house and you are late again, this is not a good start," said Cook, "and here are the things you needed from town and you owe me sixpence and a ration book coupon."

"It's nice to see you too Cook and I will have to owe you the sixpence as I won't have any money until I get paid. By the way, when is payday around here?" asked Digger.

"Sissy and I get paid on Friday afternoon so I expect you will be the same, I can wait till then. There is some food ready in the kitchen' come and eat something, not that you will be very hungry after eating my piece of sponge cake!"

Lunch was simple, a piece of cold meat pie, beetroot, pickles, cheese, bread and tea to wash it all down.

"I bumped into Mildred, you know the vicar's wife in the village and she gave me your things which she had washed and ironed for you, they are on the dresser over there," turning in her seat she pointed to the far wall where an old welsh dresser filled most of it. "She said you could keep the clothes she gave you if you wanted to, as you didn't have any others, wasn't that nice of her?."

"What a lovely lady, there aren't many like her around these days," replied Digger, just slightly chancing his arm. "Sissy will be pleased to know that I have followed her advice and dragged a branch into the garden, all I have to do now is saw it up and chop it into logs. The saw I found doesn't seem too bad, but the axe is in a terrible state, is there anywhere round here I can get it sharpened?"

"I can't think of anyone round here who does sharpening. We haven't had a smithy, if you'll excuse the expression, for years, so I cannot help you with that one."

Sissy, who had been quietly peeling potatoes, piped up, "What about that Bertie who lives down by the lake, my dad says he has all sorts of tools in that shed of his, perhaps he could sharpen the axe and we're desperate for some wood."

"I think the girl could be right this time, it's certainly worth a try. If you follow on down the track past the house for about a quarter of a mile, you will see a path going off to the left, straight into the trees. Now I know his house is down that path somewhere, but you will have to find it yourself. Folks say he is a nice old chap but I find him sarcastic and awkward, so it's up to you," suggested cook.

"Well I certainly can't do anything with the axe the way it is, so I will take a walk and see if he can help us." With that he wandered back outside, picked up the axe and headed off down the road.

It was a pleasant walk and he easily found the path cook had mentioned. After walking through the wood for about a quarter of a mile, he emerged into a large clearing with a cottage squarely situated in the middle of it. A boundary wall seemed to circle the cottage and a varnished gate sat in the wall, with a wide path behind it leading to the front door. Here we go again thought Digger, as he knocked twice on the door. No-one came, so he knocked again and then heard a voice calling out, "I'm round the back, come round the back."

Following the voice round to the side and then to the back of the cottage, Digger stopped at the edge of a beautifully kept lawn and searched the garden for the voice's owner.

"I am over here son, to your left and forward fifty feet."

Digger obeyed the instructions and then spotted an elderly man sitting on a bench in the corner, hidden by a mass of flowers and bushes. His hair was short and he had a beard and held a book in one hand and a glass in the other.

"Good afternoon sir, I hope I'm not disturbing you, would you be Bertie by any chance, I don't know the surname I'm afraid."

"Goodness me, the last time someone called me sir, I was a skipper of my own boat, but all I skipper now is that model on the pond, but yes I am Bertie and who might you be young man?"

"Digger Smith at your service, I have been taken on at Millstone House for a few days to do some odd jobs and was wondering if you could help me with this," he said, lifting the axe for Bertie's inspection.

"That my boy, has had its day, I will be pleased to help you bury it, get me a spade from the shed," he replied, pointing across the garden.

"Well actually I was hoping you might be able to help me sharpen it, it's all I have to chop up some wood for the fire, before we all freeze to death over there."

Bertie put the book and glass down on the bench and walked towards Digger, he held out his hand and the two men shook hands and smiled at each other, as they each recognised a kindred spirit.

"I was working in the shed this morning, so I'm afraid it's a bit untidy at the moment, but somewhere in there I do have a small grindstone."

As Digger looked in the shed door, he noticed a few shavings on the floor and a couple of chisels on the bench, apart from that it was immaculate. Every tool and tin and bottle had its own place and pieces of wood were all piled according to size and purpose, he whistled slowly, "If you think this is untidy, you should see the garage over at Millstone, this is a palace."

"Flattery will get you everywhere, my young friend, pass me down that red and gold box on the second shelf, will you please."

The box was duly passed down and opened and a small hand grindstone wrapped in an oily cloth was taken out. Bertie clamped it to a piece of wood, which he then clamped in his large woodworking vice.

"Have you by any chance used a grindstone before Digger?"

"No never," said Digger, "I have not had much experience with these sorts of tools, but I am pretty good with engines, not that that's relevant right now."

"You turn the handle and I will hold the axe and we will see what we can do."

There was silence for the next ten minutes, apart from the quiet cursing when Bertie caught his finger on the grindstone.

"It isn't brilliant, but it's a lot better than it was. We sometimes get a travelling knife sharpener through here and he has a big grindstone which is what this axe really needs, if I see him I will ask him to call, but I know last time he had a run in with your Mrs Black, so he may need some incentive. Thirsty work eh, do you fancy a beer?"

"That's a big improvement, thank you," said Digger, as he tested the edge with his thumb; "Is it OK if I call you Bertie?"

"Of course it is, just don't call me 'late for lunch'."

"I would love a drink, but nothing alcoholic for me, a cup of tea would do fine. Do you think I could use your bathroom Bertie, I'm busting a gut at the moment."

"That is completely out of the question," he then paused for effect and continued, "mainly because I don't have one. But you can use my toilet which is the green door on the end. I'll put the kettle on."

The green door opened on to a room with a large sink, with a single tap and a smaller door leading to the WC. Hanging on the wall was a large tin bath, presumably for bathing and next to it, a smaller one, presumably for soaking clothes.

After washing his hands, Digger started to walk round the garden admiring the colours and their incredible neatness, not a weed in sight!

"Tea up Digger," called Bertie, "I'll take it over to my seat. No need to rush, we will let it brew a bit first."

The tour completed, Digger wandered over and sat down. "What are you reading?"

"Oh this is a very old novel called 'He would be a Gentleman' by Samuel Lover, "I must have read it twenty times over the years, it's a great story, you can borrow it when I have finished, if you like."

"Thanks, I would like to, but I'm not sure how long I will be staying at Millstone House. There is enough work to keep me going for weeks, but I had a run in with Mrs Black yesterday and I am certain that she would throw me out today if she could."

"I presume you are cutting up logs and splitting them with the axe, what state is the saw in, as its very dangerous to use a rusty saw, it might just break on you? You can borrow mine tonight if you wish and get yourself a new blade for your own one tomorrow. The Ironmonger's in the village stocks blades, if I remember correctly."

"Well if you don't mind, I will do just that and return your saw tomorrow, it will give me an excuse to escape the women for an hour or so."

The two men nattered for a bit longer and then parted; Digger carrying the saw and the axe back down the pathway, returning to Millstone, just as Mrs Black drove into the garden.

"And where have you been, may I ask, I thought I left you with a day's work and here I find you have been out for a stroll. What is that you are carrying?"

What is wrong with this woman, thought Digger, who just ignored her and walked over to the branch he had left in the corner of the garden.

"Did you hear me Smith, I just asked you what you were doing?"

"I told you yesterday, it's Mr Smith, Mrs Black, and if you ask a reasonable question, I will give you a reasonable answer," replied Digger, struggling not to raise his voice.

"I have been to get the axe sharpened and have managed to borrow a saw from your neighbour down the road, who has advised me that it could be dangerous for me to use one with a rusty blade, which is exactly what your saw has!"

"What do you mean my neighbour down the road? Not that old fool in the woods, I wouldn't take his advice too strongly, if I were you," with which comment she turned and headed for the house.

Digger spent an hour sawing and chopping and was very pleased with the pile of logs and firewood he had created. Cook showed him where they were stored and then the two of them sat down to dinner.

"I have to tell you that you are in the bed chair again tonight Arnold, but that if they decide to offer you a longer stay, you will be able to move into the chauffeur's cottage, at the end there. The two ladies are discussing you right now and will speak to you tomorrow at lunch. If it's any consolation, Arnold, I told Mrs Duffy-Smythe that I thought you were a good worker and should stay here for a while, but it's not up to me."

"Thanks Cook that was kind of you, obviously no hard feeling over the sponge cake, which was undoubtedly the best I have ever tasted. I hope Sissy did not get into trouble over it and is there any left?"

"Don't push your luck, young man," she said, but got up anyway and produced a brand new sponge she had baked that afternoon.

After dinner he bid goodnight to Cook and went back outside and cleaned the tools thoroughly before putting them away. Since it was a nice dry evening he decided to go for a walk into the village and check out what was there.

Bertie's Cottage
Artist - Lynnette Lilley

CHAPTER FOUR
MAN'S BEST FRIEND

When Sissy got home and told her dad that the wheelbarrow had to be back at Millstone House the next morning, she was very glad that she was 'the apple of his eye', for otherwise she would have felt the full force of his anger.

"What do you mean, 'Arnold says he won't report me if I have it back by the morning'! I've a good mind to come round there and have a word with Mr la de da Arnold," he thundered.

"No Tom, you won't, half the folks in the village still refuse to talk to me after the last time you had a word with someone; I'm sure young Tom won't mind wheeling it round after tea, will you dear?" interjected his wife.

Young Tom knew better than to say no, so discreetly replied, "Where do you want it left Sissy?"

"If you leave it in the long grass down by the side wall, no-one will ever know Dad had taken it," she said.

"I didn't take it, I requisitioned it. It was during the war and ours was broken, I just never got around to taking it back, so let that be an end to it," which meant heaven help anyone who ever raised the subject again.

Glad for an excuse to get out for an hour, without being asked endless questions, Tom got the barrow from the back garden and headed off through the village, past the church and down the lane, only to meet Digger coming towards him.

"Hello mate," called Digger, "are you connected to Sissy by any chance?"

"Err yes, I'm her brother Tom, are you Arnold by any chance?"

"Got it in one, nice to meet you Tom," and the two men shook hands. "My mates call me Digger, I don't really like Arnold, if you don't mind."

"I know what you mean Digger, they call me 'Young Tom' round here, because my dad's name is Tom as well. If he lives to be a hundred, I'll still be 'Young Tom' at seventy. Isn't Digger an Australian name, you don't sound like an Australian, more like a Londoner?"

"It's a long story which goes back to school days that I won't bore with you; you are right though, I am a Londoner."

"It must be great growing up in a big city, with lots of things to do and see, not like this place where there is nothing to do and you can see the lot in ten minutes. My Auntie took Sissy and me to London at Christmas once, when we were young. We got the train into town and then caught a bus to where the big shops are and she took us to see Father Christmas and his grotto, it was great, even got a present to bring home. I think the shop's name had a 'P' in it, but I'm not sure," said Tom.

Digger thought for a moment then said, "The only shops I can think of are Derry and Tom's and Harrods,"

"That was it, Harrods, I remember now. Do you want to take over this barrow, then you can put it where you like, I was going to leave it in the long grass down the side of the wall, only I thought I would pop round and see if my friend was in."

"Yes sure, leave it there, I'll pick it up on my way back, I was just out for a leg stretch down to the church and back."

The two men strolled back towards the village and parted company at the church, Tom heading for the pub and Digger sitting down on the seat by the wall.

"Is that you Digger?" a voice called out from the church doorway.

"Evening padre, you must have cat's eyes to have recognised me from there. The old army training eh?"

"Well actually I recognised your voice; I was up in the bell tower and can hear everything that goes on from there, so be warned! How are you settling in at Millstone?"

"Pretty mixed if I'm honest. Cook and Sissy seem to like me, Mrs Black can't stand me and Mrs Duffy-Smythe hasn't shown a leaning one way or the other, but I'm the only help she has to get things sorted over there, so I am hopeful they will ask me to stay for a few weeks. Please thank your wife for washing and ironing the clothes and I would like to hang on to the ones she lent me for a while, if that's OK."

"You hang on to them, it will help her to know that our son's things are being used by someone who needs them. Have you ever done any campanology, by any chance?"

"Now at a guess you are expecting me to make some stupid comment about tents and living under canvas, which I do have plenty of experience of, but I know we are discussing 'Bell ringing' because an old army mate of mine, 'Big Dutch', was a keen campanologist. The way he described it to me, it sounded better than ballroom dancing, but not as good as football and no, I have never done any. Why, are you looking to start or do you already have a team?"

"Well, yes to both questions, let me explain. I put all the ropes away at the start of the war, apart from one, in order to have one bell that we could use as a signal; so all the ropes are still in very good condition, as we bought a new set in about 1938. There are still a few members of the old team in the district, but we could do with some new blood, would you be interested in taking part, assuming you are around for a while?"

"That's a pretty big assumption at the moment, but yes, I would be happy to give it a go, anyway I must be wandering, don't forget to thank your wife for me for the clothes and the warning," with that he waved his goodbyes and headed back down the path and retrieving the barrow walked down the side of the long wall and upturned it in the grass. Sleep came a lot quicker on this second night, something to do with all the sawing and chopping and that life had started to get better again.

For some reason he woke promptly at 6:30am, washed and shaved and reported sharply at seven for breakfast. Something had obviously upset Cook, for all she said was "Help yourself" and walked out, never to re-appear.

He ate on his own and at seven thirty decided he would start work on the firewood again, after retrieving the barrow from where he had left it last night. Taking the saw, he walked down to the wood and did a thorough investigation of the immediate area. He found an overgrown track which he had not spotted yesterday and this led to a clearing where a great pile of sawn wood had been stacked for drying, obviously this was to be used on the manor estate and was not for burning. To the side of this was another large pile of smaller branches and broken ends which he presumed was for burning. Sawing the longer bits into about four foot lengths he was able to lay them across the barrow and by elevenses, had managed to transport enough wood, to last several weeks, from the clearing back into Millstone's garden.

Once again Cook was uncommunicative as she poured his tea and offered him a biscuit, so he felt obliged to enquire, "Have I done something to upset you Cook?"

"No Arnold, you haven't," she replied and just sat there, staring at the wall.

He finished his tea and was rising from the table when she spoke again, "Sissy's mum called in to say she wasn't well and wouldn't be at work today. That girl has had more days off work in the last six months, than I have had in the last six years."

Digger wondered if it was something to do with returning wheelbarrows and her wondering if he had dropped her in it, but he said nothing.

"And does anyone here offer any help," continued Cook, "of course not, everyone just expects me to cope, as usual. I'm not blaming you Arnold, but you seem to be having a very unsettling effect on our Sissy!"

What on earth does she mean by that, thought Digger, women!

"There is one thing though, I want to hang some washing out and the grass needs cutting where the clothes lines are, would you mind cutting it for me please as your next job?"

"Of course I will, except I haven't found a mower yet."

"And you won't, because it's mine and I hide it, I don't want that father of Sissy's taking that as well." Rising from the table she walked out into the garden and down to the end door of the outbuildings and proceeded to unlock it and go in. A few seconds later she emerged pulling a mower behind her, complete with grass box.

Digger cut the grass under the clothes lines as requested and was pleased with the marks the roller left on the lawn. Not perfectly straight, but not bad he thought. Cook came out to inspect and then told him to clean the mower and leave it by the end door and she would put it away. This he did and then continued sawing the branches and chopping the wood for the rest of the morning.

He stopped work at five to twelve and washed up, ready for lunch at twelve sharp. "This is it," he said to himself, "a 'Black' and white situation!" With that thought he sat down where Cook indicated and waited for events to unfurl.

Mrs Duffy-Smythe arrived first, smiled and sat at the head of the table, followed by Mrs Black, who scowled at him and sat down on the same side as Digger, but well apart and Cook sat opposite them, in the middle, almost like an umpire.

Digger wondered whether he should offer to stand whilst they passed judgement, but considered he had a fifty-fifty chance of staying there, so sat quietly on his seat.

"I won't beat around the bush, Mr Smith," said Mrs Duffy-Smythe, "this is not a unanimous decision, but we would like to offer you work for another two weeks. You can live in the chauffeur's cottage for the time you are with us and we will give you your food and basic drinks and pay you twenty five shillings a week. Before you answer, my sister will give you some idea of the work we want you to do."

"We want enough wood cut, chopped and stacked to last us at least three months. The picket fence round the front of the house needs painting, all the windows and doors in the outbuildings need painting and the broken panes of glass replaced and the holes in the roof repaired, unless you have a fear of heights of course," she added sarcastically.

Cook then plunged in with her list of jobs, "I want the vegetable garden dug over and potatoes, peas, cabbages, runner beans and marrows planted and the soft fruit bushes pruned and sprayed. Then I want all the fruit trees down the side of the wall pruned and retied to the wires."

"Thank you Cook, well Mr Smith, what is your answer?" asked Mrs Duffy-Smythe.

Digger was quickly going over the list of jobs in his mind and decided that it was probably more like four weeks rather than two weeks work and he was feeling surprisingly good about himself after a day and a half in the fresh air.

"Thank you Mrs Duffy-Smythe for the offer of work, which I am pleased to accept on the terms you specified," replied Digger.

"Good grief man," snapped Mrs Black, "a simple yes or no would have done!"

"Shall I serve lunch now," interjected Cook, who went to the dresser and moved the food onto the table, where everyone tucked in.

Digger continued, "I have to be honest and tell you I have not done any painting and decorating, nor have I fixed roofs and broken panes of glass, but I am happy to give it a go. The other thing, which I realised yesterday, when visiting Bertie, the chap who sharpened the axe for me, is the right tools make a lot of difference and quite frankly I am not sure we have the right tools here."

Mrs Black could not contain herself any longer, "What did I say to you, he admits he can't do any of the jobs we want him to do and he complains about the tools, why are we bothering?"

The frustration of dealing with her sister's intolerance and awkwardness finally overcame Mrs Duffy-Smythe's self control and she turned on her sister, "I have just about had enough of this negative and hostile attitude Amanda. You have managed to upset everyone who has come to visit us from the village and even the doctor told me that the next time you are ill, to call someone else in. Mr Smith will be here for another two weeks and I am sure he has enough intelligence to find out how to do any job he hasn't done before, don't you Mr Smith?"

"Yes ma'am," he replied and was surprised to find himself felling sorry for Mrs Black!

They ate their lunch in silence and Mrs Black was the first to leave the table. After she had gone conversation started up again.

"I don't suppose the vicar's wife mentioned my Ration Book to you, when she gave you my clothes back," he asked Cook.

"No Arnold, she just gave me your things, why, where did you leave it?"

"It was in the back pocket of my trousers, I don't think it got pinched with my wallet, but I don't remember taking it out either. As regards tools, Mrs Duffy-Smythe, I only borrowed the saw from Bertie for a day or so and really should return it to him. He thinks the shop in town might have a spare blade for the log saw I found here. Do you mind if I go and check and do you have an account with the shop, as I don't have any money and am already in debt?"

"That was subtly put, I guess you want paying for these two days to get you started, here's ten shillings, get a receipt for anything you buy in town and no, I don't have any accounts with anyone, that's not my way! Cook has a key for the cottage, so I suggest you get the saw business sorted and then clean the cottage up, as it is in as bad a condition as the garage was, I'm afraid."

Digger took the money and he and Cook went outside and walked down to the cottage door. "Thanks Cook," he said, "I appreciate that your vote probably made the difference as to whether I stayed or went. I will try and get started on the vegetables sooner rather than later."

She unlocked the door and turned back towards him, "You can put the mower in the garage now, but guard it with your life. Don't be too hard on Mrs Black, Arnold, she has not been the same since her husband got killed, she used to be a really nice pleasant girl when she was younger, it's such a waste."

Digger went into the cottage and took the mower from the middle of the floor and put it in the garage. This place needs a week's work on its own he thought, I'll get the saws sorted and then come back and start cleaning it out.

He picked up the two saws and headed into the village. The Ironmongers was in the middle of the shops opposite the village green on Thame Road, 'Tanner & Son Ironmongers' is probably what gave it away, but the metal dustbin and garden tools stacked outside probably helped as well.

"Good afternoon," said Digger to the middle aged man behind the counter, "I am reliably informed that you may be able to help me with a new blade for this saw."

"Well I might be my friend, who on earth gave you this information?" asked Mr Tanner. "Are you by any chance the man who got robbed on the train the other day and is working at Millstone House?"

Digger was contemplating the difference between Military Intelligence and Village Intelligence and knew which he considered to be better organised, "Let me see, Bertie gave me the information about the shop, yes I did get robbed and am working at Millstone and just in case it is not already known, my inside leg measurement is twenty eight and a half inches."

"Not according to Mildred, who washed your trousers for you, she said, let me see," as he pretended to look at his note book, "ah yes I have it, twenty nine inches. Don't look so surprised my friend, what else do people round here have to talk about, it's just the way villages are."

He took the saw and went out the back returning a few minutes later with a new blade already fitted. "You are in luck, that's one I had in stock before the war, not a very common type, like gold dust these days, nine pence to you, please."

Digger passed across the ten shilling note and waited for his change, "May I have a receipt please." The shopkeeper wrote out the receipt and Digger left the shop and went into the Post Office where he bought five Woodbines and a box of matches. Walking back the way he came, he crossed the main road and knocked at the vicarage door. Mildred answered the door and smiled a greeting at Digger.

"Hello Digger nice to see you, we were just about to have a cup of tea, do come in." Digger followed her into the kitchen where the vicar was just filling the pot, he looked up and said, "These ex army chaps can smell a brew from a mile away you know, nice to see you, how's it going?"

They chatted for a while and discussed who was best to ask for advice re roofing and glazing. The vicar said he had replaced a lot of windows in his time and was happy to come and help when Digger got to that particular job, but the roof tiles on the outbuildings were years old and he didn't know of anyone in the area who might be able to help, but would keep thinking about it.

When Digger got up to leave, he thanked Mildred again for the washing and loan of the clothes, at which point she gasped and ran out of the room, returning a few seconds later with his Ration Book. "What must you think of me Digger, I found it in your back pocket before I washed the trousers and it had a five pound note folded up inside," and she passed both items across to him.

He looked perplexed and then remarked, "My sister normally looked after the book and got supplies in for me each week. When I told her I was leaving London for a while, she gave me the book and this must be the balance of the money she was holding for me. Good old Vi, I must write and tell her she has rescued me from poverty."

With a spring in his step, which had been missing for quite a while now, Digger headed down the path and kept on going past Millstone House until he reached the track to Bertie's cottage. Sitting on a wall at the side of the track he took out the cigarettes and lit up, being careful to blow out the match and return it to the box.

He managed to set off again without the saws, which he had left at the side of the wall, so after about two minutes of walking, had to come back for them. He was almost through the wood when he heard a wailing sort of sound, coming from the dense undergrowth away to his right. He tried to ignore it but it sounded like something was trapped and he wondered what on earth it could be. He started to push his way through the tangle of bracken, brambles and hawthorn until he felt that he too was getting caught up in it. Not really knowing what to do, he stood still and listened and thought he now detected a whining sound like a dog would make, so he whistled as loud as he could and waited. "Woof woof, woof-woof, howl." He looked in the general direction of the barking and could just make out a black shape, totally caught up in the undergrowth. "Hold on fellow," he shouted, I will go and get some help and come back for you." "Woo-oooof, woof," came the reply back.

Digger retraced his steps back to the path and sprinted the remaining distance to Bertie's cottage, where he found the owner busy in the front garden.

"Hello son, you didn't have to run to bring the saw back today, tomorrow would have done fine. Why all the hurry?"

"Hi Bertie, I was hoping you could lend me something to break my way through the undergrowth over there," pointing in the general direction of the wood, "there's a young dog all caught up and I fear it will try and follow me and tear itself to shreds."

"A young dog you say, I wonder whose that can be? Anyway, I have the very thing, hold on a jiffy." He disappeared round the back and returned with a couple of pairs of gardening gloves, a pair of shears and a machete. "I acquired this on my travels in the far east, nothing quite like it for dealing with heavy undergrowth, come on lets go find this poor animal."

Finding the dog was the easy part, extricating him from the undergrowth took a lot longer. "He looks a friendly dog, Digger, but keep the gloves on anyway and see if he will let you pick him up; if we let him walk, he may run and get caught up again."

The dog seemed quite happy to be picked up and showed his appreciation in the usual doggy way, by profusely licking Digger's face. The dog was carried into the garden and the gate firmly closed behind them.

"Put him down and see what he does, I'll go and get a bowl of water," said Bertie.

The dog ran round the garden, introduced himself to a few trees and then came back and started drinking from the bowl of water, which he finished at one sitting.

"Not only is he thirsty, poor thing, but judging by his thinness, has not eaten properly in days. I have some dry biscuits in the kitchen, I will get them for him."

"There are some marks on his back Bertie, they look like old scars, I think someone has beaten the dog with a strap or something. No wonder he ran away. He can't be more than three or four months old, can you think of anyone local who has dogs like this?"

"The gamekeeper at the manor has Labradors and he is a pretty unpleasant person when it comes to humans, but I know he treats his dogs well. I don't believe this young fellow is local, I think he has travelled quite a distance to get here. I have some scissors, you hold his head and I will try and cut all the burrs and bits of bramble out of his fur, or he will tear himself to pieces, doing it himself."

It took another half hour and another bowl of water and a further handful of biscuits before they finished and the dog was not going to win any prizes at dog shows for quite a while. Digger kept an eye on him while Bertie made the tea and then broached the subject of ownership.

"Since you found him Digger, it's up to you what happens to him next. I can't offer to help you as I am asthmatic and allergic to dogs and cats, so it really is your problem my friend."

"You know Bertie I used to dream of having a dog when I was a kid and promised myself that if I would have one when I grew up, I think it's time to honour that promise; we certainly don't want to return him to his previous owner just to get beaten again."

"What about the folks at Millstone, what do you think they will say about him, not everyone in England is a dog lover, just most of them. You also need to think about the cost of keeping a dog, there's the license fee and food and leads and bed, lots of other things to think about."

"You know Bertie, I really don't care what anyone else thinks. This dog needs me and if we have to face the wide world together, so be it. You couldn't lend me a piece of rope could you?"

"Well said, I'm proud of you, a man after my own heart, let's see what we have in the shed."

They crossed to the shed and found a leather strap about fifteen inches long, which they used for a collar. A piece of rope about three feet six was attached and the dog was walked round the garden.

"You have forgotten the most important item Digger."

"I'm sure Cook will have some old bowls I can borrow, if that's what you mean."

"Wrong! The dog needs a name and some basic training, judging by the way he is pulling on the rope. Now my daughter Deborah, who works in London, is heavily into the R.S.P.C.A. so I am happy to speak to her and see if she can get hold of any dog training material, but the name is down to you."

"Mac, his name is Mac. That's what I would have called him when I was a boy, so Mac it is. But we must be going, dinner is in half an hour and I have a cottage to clean out before bed time."

"Oh, they're keeping you on then, how long have they offered you?"

"They have offered two weeks, but listed at least a month's work, so assuming my new buddy here is accepted, we will be around for a while."

"Pop by tomorrow and let me know how it went. If they kick you out, you can sleep in the shed for the night."

Digger waved, Mac woofed and they set off back to Millstone House.

It's funny how things we expect to be a problem are not and vice versa of course, even Mrs Black welcomed Mac to the house and cook produced a proper collar and lead which belonged to her old spaniel, 'Trevor'. A large bowl of food scraps was provided and he was even allowed to lie on the kitchen rug, while Digger and Cook had their dinner. After dinner he gave her the precious Ration Book and asked if she would mind it for him.

In view of the late hour, the cleaning of the cottage was left till the next day and an old blanket found for Mac to sleep on. The new friends slept in the laundry together, Digger experiencing the pleasures of the bed chair for the third and last time.

CHAPTER FIVE
BEHIND THE WHEEL AGAIN

Mac was whining by the door at 6:15am, so Digger was awake early, only to discover that it was pouring with rain. He opened the door and let the dog out into the garden, marking the spot where it stopped to squat. Obviously Mac didn't like the rain either, as he headed straight back to the door and barked loudly to be let in. Digger put some water in the bowl that cook had given him and the dog lapped it up.

After washing and shaving he sat down and played with the dog and thought about all the jobs he had been asked to do. Since it was pouring with rain, he assumed no-one would object if he spent the day cleaning out the cottage, and wondered what furniture, if any, he would find. The garden was massive and had not been dug in years, so it was important to make a start, especially since Cook had been so supportive. The fence had to be at least a hundred and twenty feet long and had a lot of broken and missing boards, but Mrs Black had this as a priority, so he needed to make a start on this as well.

"Right," he said to himself, "decision time. Start off with gardening until elevenses, wood chopping until lunch, the fence after lunch until afternoon tea and the outbuildings until dinner." In that way, he thought, I reduce the risk of pulling something, from overdoing any one activity and everyone's job will be started and after two weeks, they will each be about half way through, so I will get the month here that I really want.

He wasn't quite sure what to do with Mac during breakfast, but when he turned up without him, he was sent back to fetch him and Cook had some titbits all ready for him. When Sissy arrived she was just besotted with the dog and showed no lingering symptoms of the previous day's sickness.

Mrs Black came into the kitchen as breakfast was ending and said that Digger was free to sort the cottage out in the morning, but they were expecting a visitor to arrive on the 12:45pm train in Oxford and since both she and Mrs Duffy-Smythe were busy today, he would have to go and collect him in the car.

"But what about insurance, am I covered?" he asked.

"I would not have asked you to drive the car if you were not covered by the insurance. Assuming you have a licence and are actually able to drive the car properly, you will meet the train and pick up this gentlemen, Mr Masters," and she showed him a photograph of a bald headed middle aged man with a moustache.

"Just to put your mind at rest, I have driven everything on wheels that the army possesses and at least half a dozen different motor cars, as well as several motorbikes! So I am sure I can manage to get to Oxford and back, provided you have a map."

She stood there staring at him and then said quietly, "You were a driver then, during the war. There's a map under the dashboard. You need to allow at least forty minutes for the trip," with which she turned and left.

"What happened there?" asked Digger.

"It's all right Sissy, you can start on the bedrooms today, off you go," instructed Cook. When the girl had gone, she turned to Digger, "Mrs Black's late husband was also a driver in the army, she still hasn't managed to get over it, I'm afraid your being here is going to be a constant reminder for her. You need to avoid her Arnold, if you can and for goodness sake stop getting so hot under the collar every time you speak to her. You can leave the dog here while you are cleaning the cottage, don't want the poor thing getting all that dust in its lungs, do we."

By the time Sissy and Mac brought him a cup of tea for 'Elevenses' he had managed to sweep and wash the whole of the downstairs of the cottage. The room by the front door was a kitchen with a sink and built-in dresser and he moved the table and chair from the garage to join the other kitchen chair that was already there. The stairs went up the middle of the house and another room, which had been used as a parlour had a door just at the foot of the stairs and filled about three quarters of the back of the cottage. The other quarter being a toilet and hand basin which had a door the other side of the stairs. The kitchen had a fireplace equipped with an old iron range, in the wall by the garage and the parlour had a fire with an open grate.

The parlour was not small, but it was 'cosy' and possessed a couple of old horsehair armchairs, a chaise longue, a side table, a book case and another built in dresser.

After receiving the official 'Guided Tour' Sissy said she was impressed and then told him that Cook would have a sandwich for him before he set off for Oxford.

Checking his watch, he decided that the upstairs would have to wait until he returned from the trip, so he washed and changed into the clean clothes Mildred had laundered for him and got the car out of the garage. He found the map under the dash and studied the route.

"Are you comfortable with this trip Mr Smith?" asked Mrs Duffy-Smythe.

"Mr Masters is my agent and I promised him the first draught of my book today and I am still completing it. With my sister's help we should have it all typed up by the time you arrive with him, but please don't rush, we need all the time we can get."

"As I mentioned to Mrs Black, I am an experienced driver and appreciate the trust you are showing me with your car. It will be good to get behind the wheel again and I will make sure we are not back too early. Will the gentleman be returning to Oxford tonight?"

"He normally stops one night and goes back the next day, so I will take him tomorrow. Anyway, you need to leave soon and I need to get on. See you later."

Digger had his sandwich and then climbed into the car and headed for Oxford. He almost made it on his own but got lost after turning down St. Aldates and had to ask a policeman, who looked at him in a very quizzical fashion and made an entry of the car's registration number in his note book.

The train arrived on time and several middle aged gentlemen disembarked and two had moustaches! Digger looked carefully at them trying to remember the fleeting glimpse he had seen of the photograph and approached the man in the trilby hat. "Excuse me sir, would you be Mr Masters?" enquired Digger.

"No I'm not, stop bothering me – go away."

"Charming!" thought Digger, let's try the other chap, second time lucky.

"Excuse me sir, would you be Mr Masters?"

"I most certainly am and you will be Mr Smith, nice of you to come and pick me up. I assume Mrs Duffy-Smythe is still finishing the book off as we speak?"

Digger did not know what to say, so he just smiled.

"No need to be embarrassed Mr Smith, all these writers are the same, if I didn't come and collect it myself, she would still be completing it next week. I assume you have been instructed not to rush, so why don't we have a drink before we set off. There is a really excellent tea shop not far from here."

The two men chatted while they walked to the tea shop and to Digger's relief Mr Masters made it clear it was his treat, so coffee and cakes for two were ordered, served and devoured, while the men chatted about life, the war, the state of the country and of course football. Mr Masters had been a lifelong Arsenal supporter, whereas Digger had always supported Chelsea; Mr Masters commenting on his loyalty and fortitude.

The drive home was leisurely and it was a little after three thirty when they drew up outside the house and Digger was not at all surprised when the front door flew open and Mrs Black raced out and demanded where on earth he had been!

Mr Masters turned on the old world charm and explained he had been delayed on a confidential matter in Oxford and had enlisted Mr Smith's assistance for which he was extremely grateful. Thus mollified, she escorted him into the house, whilst ordering Digger to put the car in the garage, a course of action which he obviously would not have considered on his own.

Mac gave him an enthusiastic welcome and had to be restrained from jumping up and putting muddy paws on his clean clothes. Cook provided tea and cake and then with Sissy's assistance, interrogated him as to the afternoon's events and surprised Digger when she told him that she had only been to Oxford once, since moving to Millstone House with Mrs Duffy-Smythe in 1943.

As Digger got up from the table, Sissy asked him if he had been in the cottage yet and he replied he had not and asked her why?

"Oh, you'll see!" she said, and grinned at Cook.

With the dog running at his heels, Digger headed for the cottage, intrigued at what had been going on. At first he noticed nothing and then realised that someone had put a tablecloth on the table and that the old stove had been cleaned, lit and a large black kettle was keeping warm on the side of the stove.

The parlour now sported a pair of curtains and a rag rug had been put on the floor in front of the fireplace and an old picture of London Bridge, hung on the wall. The toilet area had been cleaned, the window opened and chemicals sprayed liberally around, with a pile of newspapers left on the window shelf.

Digger checked upstairs, but this was in the same state he had left it in, so returning to the kitchen he found Cook and Sissy, pretending to work, but actually waiting for his return.

"What can I say to you both, it looks fantastic, that was really kind of you to take such a lot of trouble on my behalf. Thanks just doesn't seem enough!" With that he walked up to cook, put his arms round her and gave her a big kiss on her cheek.

"That will be quite enough of that Arnold, whatever next," said Cook, but didn't instantly try and escape his hug.

"Hey, I helped too," said Sissy, "where's my kiss?"

Digger turned and kissed her on her cheek as well and then said, "I really appreciated the picture of London Bridge, I used to work quite close to it and often used to walk over it during my lunch hour and just stand in the middle and watch the barges going up and down. Anyway I had better get changed and start on the bedroom, I don't fancy another night in that chair!"

"I have looked out some sheets and blankets for you, but I suggest you hang that old mattress over the line and use the carpet beater in the laundry on it," suggested Cook.

Changing into his working clothes, he started to work on the bedroom. This room occupied the whole of the upper floor and was set in the eaves, with only a short wall of a couple of feet and a small section of ceiling. A dormer window was the only source of natural light and this gave a great view out over the fields and woods to the village beyond. Whilst there was no fireplace, the chimneys from downstairs did run up the garage wall and he could detect some warmth from the fire burning in the kitchen stove. Between the two chimneys was a heavy wooden door, which was firmly locked.

The room contained a four foot bed, with a chipped chamber pot underneath, an old padded chair, which had definitely seen better days, a chest of drawers and a wardrobe. An empty light socket hung from the middle of the ceiling and a large trunk stood by itself against the end wall.

To his surprise, he found some items of clothing in the chest and wardrobe and the trunk, which was firmly locked, was very heavy. The springs of the bed seemed to be intact, although a bit rusty, so lifting the mattress off the bed, he carried it down stairs and hung it over the clothes line. He found the carpet beater and gave it a good beating, which produced clouds of dust, as had been suggested earlier.

"Dinner in half an hour, Arnold, how are you doing?" asked Cook, as she walked across the grass to where he was standing.

"Well it's not perfect, but I guess it will do. I managed to open the sash window in the bedroom about two inches, so some fresh air will help. Funny thing, though, but I found a whole load of clothes in the chest and wardrobe and a large trunk, a bit like sailors use, was in the corner, obviously full of stuff, but locked tight. Any ideas who they might belong to? I assume the previous chauffeur owned them."

She walked a bit nearer and then said quietly, "There was no previous chauffeur. Shortly after we came here a wounded soldier we knew from London came here to stay and recover. While he was here, he stopped in the cottage, did a few jobs around the place and maintained the car. Unfortunately, his wounds did not heal properly and he had to go back to hospital, where he died several months later. Mrs Duffy-Smythe was heartbroken as she had known the man for years and they were good friends, I will ask her what we are to do with his things. Dinner now in fifteen minutes and don't be late."

Taking the mattress back into the cottage, he discovered a pile of sheets and blankets along with a couple of pillows had been left on a kitchen chair. He just had time to make the bed before going to the kitchen for dinner.

"Liver and bacon, with onions and mashed potatoes, you must have known this was one of my favourites Cook and it's Thursday too, my mother always served this on a Thursday."

Cook smiled, "Let me guess, you also had 'Shepherd's Pie' on a Tuesday or Wednesday and 'steamed fish' on a Friday."

"Very close, we had a fish and chip shop at the bottom of our road and they did the best 'Rock Salmon' in the area. By the way, are you happy being called Cook, or would you prefer I use your name?"

The air around the table suddenly took on a distinctively chilly nature and putting down her knife and fork she looked straight into his eyes and spoke slowly, "If I had wanted you to use my name, I would have told you my name. Employers and staff in the houses I have worked have called me Cook for forty years or more, is that clear?"

Digger was dumbfounded, why on earth would anyone get so upset over such an innocent question? "Cook it is then!" he said and ate the rest of the meal in silence. The tinned pears and custard were also consumed in an unpleasant silence, which was only broken by Mrs Black coming into the kitchen and saying, "The vicar rang for you earlier, Smith, something about a camping practice at a quarter to eight tonight."

"He probably meant a 'Bell Ringing practice'. I said I might be interested."

Mrs Black put her hands on her hips and walked up to the side of his chair. "I really don't give a fig what you plan to do in your spare time, but I think I would have detected the difference between camping and Bell Ringing, don't you?"

Enough is enough thought Digger and turning in his chair he replied "Quite frankly Mrs Black, I don't think you could tell the difference between-" but he got no further.

"Digger my young friend, there you are," interjected Mr Masters, who had just entered the room, "come outside and join me in a cigar, I would value your opinion on something," with which he hustled Digger out the door, into the garden and headed for the door to the cottage.

"Why don't you get us a couple of chairs Digger and we can sit quietly and enjoy the cigars."

Digger brought the chairs out and the two men sat down and lit up. "I owe you one Mr Masters; I was just about to get the sack when you interrupted me. That woman has real problems with men, or maybe it's just me."

Mr Masters did not reply immediately, just sat there enjoying the cigar. "This brings back memories eh Digger, sitting out under the stars having a smoke with your mates?"

At this point the dog suddenly appeared and stood panting between the two chairs.

"So this is the fabulous Mac, you were telling me about, hello boy, where did you come from?" asked Mr Masters, showing he was well used to handling dogs.

"I see what you mean about his back, someone has used a heavy strap on him, you will have to be very careful how you train him, lots of affection and rewards. No heavy handedness with this dog."

Digger looked at his watch and said, "Not sure I want to do this Bell Ringing, but the vicar is a good bloke and I need to get away from here for a few hours, so I think I will wander down there. Would you mind taking the dog back into the kitchen with you when you return, he seems to be the only male around here that is welcome in this house!"

When Digger reached the church he could see the vicar with several other people just making their way to the bell tower. "Hi there Digger, glad you could make it. There are only four of us tonight but we can run through the basics, let me introduce you to the famous Davy Jones, who has been ringing bells for over seventy years and has won more competitions than any other man alive."

An elderly man shook Digger's hand, "Nice to meet you Digger, welcome to the team. I gather you have not done this before. Have you met Moira yet, our district nurse?"

"No I haven't, nice to meet you Miss," he said, looking into the shadows where he could see she was hanging up her coat.

A young woman in her twenties, emerged from the gloom and spoke in a gentle Scottish lilt, "Good evening, it's good to know I am not the only beginner here tonight. Your reputation has gone before you Mr Jones; a patient of mine was telling me all about your past successes today."

"Well who was that I wonder, anyway with your permission vicar, we will get started," said Davy, who now took control of the proceedings.

"Firstly for my methods to work, we all need to be regular to practice and on single name terms, so it's Davy, Digger, Moira and vicar, is that Ok with everyone?"

They all nodded their agreement and the first 'post war' practice of the Upper Style 'Bell ringing' team, got under way.

Around nine o'clock Davy called a halt to the practice and they all went across to the vicarage for tea and cake. Davy and Moira left together with Davy trying to find out who had been talking about him to her.

Mildred came into the kitchen carrying a wine bottle, "Would you like to try a glass of my home made Rosehip wine," she asked Digger.

"Thanks for the offer Mildred, but I don't drink anything alcoholic these days. I assume it does have a kick in it."

She smiled, "This is not very potent, you should try my three year old elderberry, that really does have a kick. Would you like some more tea then?"

He thanked her as she filled his cup, but declined a second piece of cake, "I'm feeling tired tonight, so I'm off to bed, night Digger, night love."

The vicar got up and kissed his wife and sat down and sipped his wine. "Can I ask what made you become Tea Total, if it's not too personal?"

Digger looked up and thought a second and then replied, "No, I don't mind telling you. It is all connected with the loss of my best mate Ginger, the chap whose death I was remembering last Monday. About a week before he got shot, the lead lorry in the convoy had hit a landmine and the driver had been killed and several other blokes badly hurt. The driver was quite new to our unit and had become a friend of Ginger, Big Dutch and me. We had got to know him quite well in a short time and the 5th was the first time we had been able to have a few drinks in his memory. You were in the army, you can imagine what happened."

The vicar nodded and waited for Digger to continue.

We sat down behind one of the lorries, and I got out the fags and passed them round. Although I had drunk a few beers, I wasn't drunk, just a bit light headed and it made me careless. The first match went out as did the second, so with my last match I lit my own first, to make sure, you know, I could light the others from mine; then I lit Dutch's then Ginger's. A single shot rang out and Ginger fell back. A sniper must have worked his way round to our flank somehow and he caught Ginger square in the chest. He died in my arms and it was all my fault vicar, I should have known better, if I hadn't been drinking I would never have lit the third cigarette and Ginger would not have been shot. That's why I don't drink today, but it's too late for Ginger, isn't it. I can never forgive myself for causing his death."

The vicar lifted his bible from the table and turned to Matthew chapter eleven and read verse twenty eight to Digger, "Come unto me, all ye that labour and are heavy laden, and I will give you rest. When Jesus spoke those words, Digger, he wasn't just talking about physical labour and physical burdens, but anything which might be conceived to be weighing us down, including guilt from our past. Similarly, when he talks about rest, it isn't a temporary respite from our burden he means, but a permanent removal of the load we are carrying. Do you mind if I pray with you about this?"

Digger nodded and the vicar prayed, "Heavenly Father, I ask now, to remove the terrible burden that this man is carrying and to release him from all the guilt that is wearing him down. You know how much he regrets what happened and I pray that you will forgive him and let him know that he is forgiven, so that he can put this tragic incident behind him and get on with the rest of his life. Amen."

"Thanks padre, I'd better be going," with that he walked across to the door and went out.

"Bye Digger, see you Sunday morning," the vicar called after him.

The lights were all off as he walked past the house and down the side to the rear gates; he let himself into the garden and through the cottage door. Mac came bounding up and made a big fuss of him, he spotted a note had been left on the table, which he picked up and read, it was from Bertie, "Hi there Digger, I came round to invite you to have dinner with me tomorrow night, say about seven. Should have some dog training literature by then!! Bertie."

He also noticed some cheese and biscuits had been left on the dresser for him and assumed this was a peace offering from Cook, what a strange day, he thought to himself as he climbed the stairs, why can't women be good blokes like Mr Masters and the padre and Bertie?

CHAPTER SIX
BERTIE'S FOR DINNER

"Ah, pay day, that should be another ten shillings, at this rate I can retire in another one hundred and twenty six years," thought Digger, "I wonder how everyone will be today."

Cook appeared to be in a good mood and greeted him cordially as he entered the kitchen, "Good morning Arnold, how did you sleep last night, it being the first night in a proper bed and all? Are you hungry?" enquired Cook, as she filled his plate with breakfast.

"Famished and I slept like a baby. Probably the best night's sleep I have had in weeks thank you, that old bed was surprisingly comfortable and to wake up with that view over the fields, was just great. Did you speak to Bertie, by any chance last night?"

"He came round just after you left, he said he would leave you a note, did you find it?"

"Yes, he has invited me to dinner tonight, so I won't be dining in this evening, thank you. He didn't mention why he was inviting me did he?"

Cook shook her head, "If we don't get the potatoes planted soon, we will miss the crop this year, how far have you got with my vegetable patch?"

"I have dug two rows, as you asked, about twenty feet long and was going to do another this morning, will that be enough?"

"Let me think," she said, "two rows of twenty feet, planted two feet apart is twenty plants and I have about three dozen potatoes to put in, make it four rows and I will space them out a bit more. If you can turn over the compost heap as well, there should be enough compost to put some in the bottom of each of the rows. My old dad always put compost in the bottom of his potato trenches."

Digger completed digging the trenches after breakfast and Cook came out with the seed potatoes to oversee the planting. The trenches were then covered over and small mounds made over the potatoes. While he was working, Mrs Duffy-Smythe and Mr Masters came out and while she drove the car out of the garage, Mr Masters came over to bid Digger goodbye.

"Well Digger, you look busy today so I won't detain you; I hope you enjoy your stay here and if ever I can be of help, just give me a call, here's my card," with which he passed him his business card.

"Thanks a lot Mr Masters, it's been good meeting you and thanks for the cigar and intervention last night." They shook hands and parted company.

Sissy arrived a bit later with his morning tea, "Hello Arnold, Cook told me to bring your tea over, as she says it will be raining shortly and you'll want to get the digging finished." With that she turned and walked away, calling the dog after her.

Within half an hour, the weather proved Cook right, just as Digger was finishing the mound over the last potato trench the shower started, so he made his way to the kitchen.

Cook informed him that Mrs Black had also gone into Oxford, when he asked, so he told her he was going into the village to see if he could get some sandpaper for rubbing down the woodwork in the outbuildings. Getting some money from the cottage, he started to stroll into town just after the rain had stopped again.

As he neared the end of the track and approached the main road, he glanced down to his left and saw someone sitting by the roadside with a bicycle on the road beside them. He wandered over to see if the person was hurt and realised it was Moira from the Bell Ringing team. "Good morning Moira, is everything all right?"

"Oh, hello Digger, I was riding along without a care in the world, when my front wheel got stuck in that rut and over I went. No harm done, just a bit shocked."

He helped her to her feet and went over and picked the bike up. "You can't ride this, I'm afraid, the wheel has been buckled. Do you know where the nearest bike shop is around here?"

"Oh dear, I use one in Aylesbury, I still have half of my round to do today, it will take me forever!"

"The tyre seems to be OK, but the front wheel is very badly buckled and I doubt if it is repairable. Hold on though, we do have an old bike in the garage and I am pretty sure that the front wheel is the same size as this one. If you can manage to walk, why don't I carry your bike to Millstone House and I can see if I can detach it from the frame and change the two wheels over."

"That would be terrific, if you're sure you don't mind."

"We Bell Ringers have to stick together," said Digger.

While Cook and Sissy attended to Moira's grazes, Digger got the old bike down from the rafters and took the wheel off. It was a bit rusty, but spun freely on the axle, so he then checked to see that it would fit the forks of Moira's bike. Having taken the tyre and inner tube of the buckled wheel he carefully fitted them to the new wheel and pumped the tyre up. He then triumphantly wheeled the bike out into the garden and tried it up and down the drive. He decided that both tyres were a bit soft, so he pumped them up a little before parading before the ladies, who had come out of the kitchen to see his antics.

"If you leave the wheel here Moira, I will ask Mrs Black to take it to the cycle shop the next time she goes to town, perhaps they will be able to fix it for you" said Cook.

"Thank you ever so much, everyone, but if you will excuse me, I need to finish my round," replied Moira, "I am most grateful Digger and hope I haven't spoilt your day's schedule." She got onto the bike and rode off down the lane towards the village.

"Right, I will try again, won't be long," said Digger.

The Ironmonger's had sandpaper, in three grades, rough, medium and smooth, a two inch paint brush and some wood primer and putty, in case he had to fill any holes. He obtained a receipt and headed back. Although there had been no more showers, the sky was still a bit overcast, so he decided to start indoors, reasoning that the outside woodwork could still be damp.

By the end of the day he had rubbed down all the windows in the cottage and garage and had applied a coat of primer as well. As the rain had stopped completely now, he sawed up a few logs and made sure that the firewood box was full. Only now did he remember the fire in his own stove, which had gone completely out. It took him about twenty minutes to light it and he was determined to keep it going throughout the day in future. Since it was not as big as the kitchen range he went and chopped some wood especially for it, which he brought into the cottage and stacked by the side of the grate.

He looked at his watch and saw it was six o'clock and tried to remember what he had done with Bertie's note, then realised he had used it to get the fire going. "What time did he say, was it six thirty or seven?" he asked himself. "I will just get there for twenty to, then I will only be ten minutes late or twenty minutes early, no harm done."

He got himself ready, bid Cook goodbye, called Mac to him and the pair set off for Bertie's cottage and dinner. Mac was careful to walk very close to Digger through the wood, but bounded ahead when they reached the clearing. The evening sun was bouncing off the different colours of the thatch in the roof and smoke was coming out of the end chimney. There was no sign of Bertie so Digger called out his name, but still no answer.

"Come on boy, he must be inside, let's go and find him."

Opening the door, Mac bounded in and headed for the fire and almost immediately started barking. Digger followed the dog and then stopped short as he saw the old tin bath full of water, in front of the fire, with Mac and someone else in it.

"Get out, get out, daaaad, there's a black dog, come and get him, get out blast you!"

Digger just stood there, mesmerised, staring at a woman, in her early thirties, attempting to get Mac out of the water.

"You're not Bertie!" was all he could think to say.

She had been so busy with the dog she had not seen Digger approach and immediately changed from throwing the dog out, to holding him close to protect her modesty.

"Ahhh! Daaaad, there's a man here, staring at me, get him out, quick."

Digger did not move, just stood there with his mouth slightly open, when a missile, which later turned out be a new bar of Lifebuoy soap, hit him with some force in the left eye.

Stepping back several paces, he trod on Bertie's foot, who was now advancing towards him and the pair fell in a heap on the floor.

"Between howls of laughter, Bertie was able to say, Digger old chap, you're early. I see you and Mac have met my daughter Deborah."

"Get out the lot you, this isn't funny, get out!" shrieked the enraged daughter.

The two men and the dog, retreated outside and immediately went round to the washroom, where a cold flannel was put on the eye. "This is going to be a right shiner," said Bertie.

"I am so sorry for bursting in like that. I managed to destroy your note and wasn't sure if you said six thirty or seven o'clock, so I figured twenty two, was a good compromise. I honestly had no idea your daughter was in the bath. What must she think of me? If you would rather Mac and I went back home I quite understand."

"Nonsense, the best of us make mistakes and lose notes and things, she's big enough to get over it. I will just go in and explain things to her; you keep the cold flannel on that eye a bit longer and hold on to Mac."

Bertie went back into the house, calling out as he went, "Deborah, where are you, Deborah, it was an innocent mistake, can you hear me."

71

He returned after about ten minutes and asked Digger to help carry the bath of water outside. They did this, with only minor spillage and upturned the bath on the front lawn. They went back into the cottage with Mac finding a place by the fire and the three humans sat down, evenly spaced round a circular table.

"Right," said Bertie, "let me formally introduce you to each other."

"What do you mean introduce us," shrieked Deborah, "this moron and his dog attacked me in my bath. You should be ringing the police and having them arrested, not serving roast beef."

Bertie smiled and continued, "Digger, may I introduce you to Deborah, my favourite daughter."

"Favourite, my foot, I'm his only daughter," she commented.

"Thank you Deborah; and this is my latest friend, Digger – say hello to each other."

"Hello Deborah, it's a pleasure to see you, err meet you," said Digger as he held out his hand across the table.

"You rat!" cried Deborah, as she picked up the serving spoon and whacked him across the knuckles with it. "Dad, he's humiliating me, tell him to go."

"Ah, she's broken my hand," wailed Digger, as he got up from the table and put his hand under the cold tap.

"For goodness sake Deborah, stop it, surely you can manage to be nice for just once, it is my birthday!"

Deborah looked chastened, but said nothing, whereas Digger responded, "Bertie, I had no idea, many happy returns of the day. You should have said it was a birthday dinner and I would have got you something. I feel really mean coming empty handed."

"The moron has feelings, whatever next, joined up writing perhaps?" enquired Deborah.

"Please," pleaded Bertie, "let's just eat and chat. Deborah has found a dog training manual in London, which she has brought down for you."

"Except now, I'm giving it to the dog, you need training more than he does," she said.

Digger sighed, "I am truly sorry Debbie, I"

He stopped abruptly, as Deborah's right foot caught him squarely on the left shin.

"Never call me Debbie, do you understand, I hate being called Debbie," she hissed through clenched teeth.

The rest of the meal passed without serious incident and a sort of truce was agreed, although nothing was actually said. The merits of various dog training methodologies were reviewed, with Digger taking a neutral stance, this time. After the meal he limped over to an armchair, well away from Deborah's feet or hands, but recognised there was still a danger from missiles.

For a birthday present she had managed to find an ounce of his favourite tobacco which he enjoyed by the fire and Digger smoked the last of his Woodbines. To his surprise, it turned out that Deborah rode an old Indian motorbike, which they went out to inspect, but were not allowed to touch.

When he asked how the book was going, Bertie said he had finished it and offered to loan it to Digger, which he accepted, with Deborah affecting a shocked expression and asking if he realised it had words and not pictures.

Digger and Mac left the party at around ten thirty and slowly walked back home and were surprised to see the car sitting outside the garage. Since the keys were in the ignition, he assumed he was to park it in the garage, which he did. Deciding that he did not wish to give lengthy explanations regarding his assorted injuries, he left the keys in the car and went to the cottage. He gave Mac some water and made himself a cup of tea, which he took through to the parlour. Settling into the old armchair, he opened the book Bertie had lent him and started to read.

Several hours later, he realised that his eyes were sore from a combination of reading the book and the bar of soap. He experienced some difficulty climbing the stairs and then having to undo buttons, but finally got to bed and fell instantly asleep.

CHAPTER SEVEN
RONNIE BLACK

It was with great difficulty that Digger rolled out of bed, some time after nine thirty, as he could only see out of one eye and his left shin was bruised and sore and the knuckles of his right hand were swollen and painful. He changed into his working clothes and hobbled down the stairs and into the kitchen and opened the door to let Mac out into the garden for a run. The fire in the stove had gone out and the water in the kettle was cold, so he had to shave with cold water again, vowing to remember to keep the fire going through the night in future.

The left eye slowly opened after bathing with the cold water and the hand responded to the same treatment, but the shin remained very sore.

Digger entered the kitchen with Mac at his heels and sat down at the end of the table just as Cook returned from getting some flour from the larder.

"What on earth has happened to you Arnold, have you been in a fight or something," she asked?

Mrs Black and Mrs Duffy-Smythe had been quietly discussing a matter over a cup of tea and looked over to see what Cook was talking about, Mrs Black then commented, "Isn't that typical of a man, he can't even go to a friends for dinner without getting into trouble!"

"What about 'Innocent until proved guilty' then," responded Digger and then felt obliged to relate the whole incident, to the utmost amusement of the three ladies.

"Well don't think we are going to pay you for a day's work when you are obviously incapable of doing anything, apart from feeling sorry for yourself," snapped Mrs Black.

"For a start you still owe me for Thursday and Friday and for the tools I had to buy out of my own money and no I don't expect you to pay me if I am not able to work," said Digger, "and I'm sorry that your husband is dead but you don't have to take it out on me, just because I was an army driver like him. A lot of good blokes died in the war and I understand how you must feel."

Mrs Black could contain her bitterness no longer, "You understand nothing. For a start my Ron was not a good bloke, he was a pig and he got what he deserved, he lied to me and he deceived me and I hate him for it."

The pain coming from her across the table to Digger was palpable and he just sat there as the words raced round his brain, and his eyes filled with tears, until finally he broke the silence. "Ronnie Black, your husband was a driver, you are talking about Ronnie Black whose lorry got blown up by a landmine in France in March 1944." He said it as a statement not a question, but Mrs Duffy-Smythe nodded her agreement to him.

"I don't know why you should hate him Mrs Black, but Ronnie was one of my mates, along with Ginger and Big Dutch, we were all corporals in the same unit. Ronnie got caught with the landmine and Ginger was shot by a sniper and only Dutch and me are left. Ronnie was without doubt one of the nicest men I have ever known and he thought the world of you, he was always singing your praises and telling us how much he loved you and the great plans you had both made for after the war. He didn't have a deceitful bone in his body, he was a man of integrity and honesty, why on earth do you have such a low opinion of such a great bloke?"

"Such a great bloke eh? Well how come a day after I got the telegram telling me he had died, there was a letter from his CO telling him to report to the Guard House regarding his arrest for brawling in a French brothel. He loved me so much did he, couldn't wait to see me again, so why did he get arrested fighting over some French tart in a brothel! He betrayed me and all we held in common, he defiled our marriage bed with another woman – and you think you have the right to defend him and judge me!"

Digger looked across the table and quietly said, "I know this is not true Mrs Black. After we landed in France we were all very busy and confined to camp. We only got one night in town and the four of us decided to go for a drink. We found a small café where they had some local wine and served a great meal with local cheese to follow. We all walked home together about midnight and played cards for a couple of hours, when the call came through saying we had to provide a driver for the CO. We cut the cards and Ronnie lost and he went off and drove the CO to a meeting at HQ. He waited there for the CO and when the meeting finished he drove him back to camp, getting there just in time to join the rest of us as the convoy left on its mission. We never went into town again and Ronnie was dead two days later."

"That's a great story Smith and your loyalty is commendable, but how do you account for the letter from his CO, the one he was supposed to be with, explain that away if you can," said Mrs Black.

"I can only guess at what happened, unless you still have the letter. The Army Admin was prone to make mistakes and get things wrong. There were three other Smith's in the unit and I got to know them all pretty well as we regularly got each other's mail, payslips and orders. When Ronnie joined our unit, just before we left Dover, there were several other men who joined us as well. One of them was a Corporal Ray Black, who was a very different bloke all together. He was dishonest and always in fights and went missing after that night in the town.

I would guess that the office sent the letter to the wrong Corporal Black and if you still have it, it should have his Service Number as well as his name and rank on it."

Mrs Black got up from the table and left the room, Mrs Duffy-Smythe turned to Digger and said, "Was that all true Mr Smith, or were you just being loyal to a friend?"

"What I have just said to Mrs Black is the absolute truth and I am happy to give you my friend Dutch's address and you can write and ask him to verify it. If she has kept the letter, she will know for herself and hopefully start to grieve her loss. He was a good man, a man who died bravely for his country and was faithful to his wife, right to the end."

Mrs Duffy-Smythe got up and left the room, leaving Cook and Digger and Mac, reflecting on what had just happened. "Well Arnold," said Cook, "you must be starving, would you like me to cook you some egg and bacon?" Digger nodded and smiled at her.

"I don't like the look of that hand either, you should pop round and let the doctor take a look at it, I will give him a ring and see if he can see you this morning. His house is next to the Church Hall on the Princes Risborough road. Help yourself to tea, the pot is freshly made."

While Cook prepared breakfast for Digger they chatted about his exploits the night before and decided that Deborah was to be avoided but that dog training should start right away. Cook thought that Mac had both Collie and Labrador in him and would respond well to being trained and offered to help Digger in the task. After breakfast he went back to the cottage and tidied the bedroom and got the fire going in the stove and brought in some more wood from the pile of branches in the corner of the garden, not wanting to take any he had prepared for the house. He then picked up the book that Bertie had lent him and settled down to read.

In the meantime, Mrs Black had gone to her room and was busily searching through a box of papers when her sister knocked on the door and called out, "Amanda it's me."

"Come in Florence. I know it's in here somewhere, I just can't find it. I want to believe what Smith said, but I don't trust him."

Mrs Duffy-Smythe walked in and sat down in the chair by the window. "You won't find the letter in there Amanda, because if you stop and think what you did when you got it, you will remember that you screwed it up and through it in the bin."

"Oh goodness, you are right, now I will have to write to the Army and that could take weeks to get a reply."

"Well, luckily for you, I took it out of the bin and have it here and it has a service number on it, do you have a record of Ron's number anywhere?"

Mrs Black held up a pay slip and the two ladies compared the number on the letter to the number on the payslip. "Oh Ron, forgive me, how could I have ever doubted you. All this time I thought he had betrayed me with a prostitute and he was innocent, Ron I'm so sorry my love." For the first time in four years Mrs Black wept for her dead husband and all the bitterness and hurt was washed out of her and she was able to grieve for the man she had loved.

"Florence, I can't face Mr Smith today, but would you mind thanking him for me for giving me back my Ron."

"Of course dear, if you will be all right, I will go and do it now," with which she left the room and went downstairs to the kitchen. Cook turned towards her and asked,

"Was he telling the truth about Mr Black, was there a mix up?"

Mrs Duffy-Smythe sat down and replied, "It was exactly as he said, there was a different service number on the letter. I never believed it at the time and wanted to write then, but Amanda refused to let me and I did nothing. Four years of misery for an admin error. Where is he now, as I need to thank him?"

"I think he is in the cottage, will you let him know that the doctor will see him at twelve forty five, I was worried about that hand, I think that Deborah may have broken a bone or two. Vicious little minx!"

Digger was engrossed with the book and missed the first tap on his door, but responded to the next louder knock, "Come in Cook, the door's open," he called out.

Mrs Duffy-Smythe went in and was surprised how clean and tidy the cottage now looked. "Mr Smith, where are you?" she asked.

Digger jumped out of the chair and immediately wished he hadn't, as his ankle gave way and he fell onto the parlour floor. Mrs Duffy-Smythe heard the crash and went through into the room, to find Digger using the chair to get himself up.

"What is it about you and our floors Mr Smith, have you hurt yourself?"

He turned to face her and then sat down again, "No Maam, my ankle just gave way, but I'm fine thank you. Excuse me for sitting down, is there something I can do for you?"

She sat down in the other chair before replying, "Firstly, Cook asked me tell you that she has arranged for you to see the doctor at twelve forty five, but I don't think you will get there on your own, so I will drive you in the car. Secondly, on behalf of my sister and myself, we want to thank you for clearing up the matter of Ron and the letter about the charge, I really believe that my sister will be her old self again and I am so grateful for what you said to her, Ron was such a nice man, he deserves to be remembered with love and respect, not hatred. Lastly, I need to pay you for the rest of the week's work and for the tools you have purchased, may I have the receipts please."

Digger gave her the receipts and she paid him what he was due, she then looked at her watch and suggested he met her outside in fifteen minutes, for the drive to the doctors. As she was leaving, she turned and said, "My sister has been hurting so much these last few years and has shut all memories of Ron out of her mind, but I am sure that she will now want to talk to you about him and his last days, would you mind?"

"No, that would be fine," said Digger, "he really was a great bloke and his death was a tragedy, I would be happy to talk to her about him."

When Mrs Duffy-Smythe returned to the kitchen her sister was having a cup of tea with Cook and when she mentioned that she had offered to drive Digger to the doctor's, Mrs Black said she would do it for her and went upstairs to change.

Digger opened up the garage and started the car, but didn't want to risk driving it, considering the state he was in. He was surprised when Mrs Black appeared and sat behind the wheel and told him to get in, but he meekly obeyed and sat next to her in the front. She never spoke until they actually stopped outside of the surgery and then with obvious difficulty she spoke quietly and gently to him, "Mr Smith, do you mind if I call you Arnold? I have re-read the last few letters that Ron sent me and I couldn't understand why you were not mentioned. He talked about Ginger and Big Dutch and an Aussie chap he was really friendly with, but not you!"

Digger smiled, "Because I was called Digger, Ronnie assumed I was Australian and Ginger was terrible at winding people up, so he just led Ronnie into thinking I was an Australian and kidded him that I had grown up in the Outback and kept sheep and kangaroos. We just never had the chance to tell him the truth."

She sighed to herself and said, "He was a bit gullible, but he told me how much he liked you all and how you had made him so welcome and I now feel so rotten at the awful way I have treated you. I am so sorry Arnold."

"Mrs Black, I am so pleased to have been able to put things right between you and him and I fully understand why you behaved the way you did. Anyway, I must go, thanks for the lift but please don't wait as I want the exercise of walking back. Bye." With which he got out of the car and went into the doctor's.

The waiting room was the front room of the doctor's house, but Digger found it empty. "Hello, anyone at home?" he called out.

"The door facing you Mr Smith, come right in," called out Dr. Bloom.

Digger entered the consulting room and sat down in the chair at the end of the desk.

"Goodness me Mr Smith, whatever happened to you and how does the other chap look?" asked the doctor, with a big smile.

Digger went over the story of the fireside bath, the birthday party and Deborah while the doctor checked out his various injuries.

"The good news is that the eye and leg are not seriously damaged and will be all right in a couple of days. Exercise the leg but don't overdo it. I will give you some drops for the eye which I want you to use for a week or so. The fingers are another matter; she must have hit you with tremendous force to cause an injury like this. I am not sure if this middle one is broken or just badly bruised, so I will have the nurse strap it up so you can't use it and come and see me on Monday at the same time as today, by which time I should be able to make a better diagnosis. Unless of course, you would rather get yourself to Oxford for an X-ray."

"Monday will be fine, thanks doctor, I feel so stupid about being hurt by a woman, please keep this to yourself or I will be a laughing stock in the village."

The doctor put his pen down and looked straight at Digger, "Mr Smith, you have two minor injuries and one serious injury, by rights you should report this assault to the police. Just because they were inflicted by a woman does not reduce the seriousness of the matter. The next man she attacks may not be so lucky; you could have lost the sight in your eye! My nurse should now be in the room next door and she will bandage your hand. Good bye, I will see you Monday."

Leaving the consulting room, Digger turned to say goodbye and almost knocked the nurse over as she was carrying supplies into the medical room.

"Hey, mind out, you almost knocked me over," she cried, "why Digger what are you doing – my goodness how did you get that shiner?"

"Sorry Moira," he said, "it's a long story. The doctor suspects I may have a broken finger and wants me to have it strapped up for a couple of days, I guess that's your department."

"You're in luck, I normally finish at eleven but was running late today. Let's have a look at that hand."

They went into the medical room where she strapped his fingers and put some drops in his eye, whilst extracting the full story of how he got his injuries.

"This is going to affect you for a few days Digger, you really should let Davy Jones know regarding Bell Ringing practice. He only lives round the corner, I will take you there now if you like, I was just leaving," she offered.

"Thanks Moira, if it's not out of your way that would be great," he replied.

They left the doctor's surgery and walked round the corner and Davy Jones' Locker was the second cottage on Jobs Rise. Moira lifted the latch and opened the front door and called out for Davy, who appeared from the kitchen and told them both to come in. He was obviously pleased to see them and invited them to stay for lunch, "I was just about to have some leek and potato soup, you will both join me wont you, I have a great big pot-full and freshly baked bread."

They sat down to the table in the kitchen and admired Davy's gleaming copper pots and discussed the finer points of Campanology. He told them that he had persuaded the railway porter George and his wife Daisy to join the team and their son Georgie would come as well. Digger said he had already met George and commented what a nice chap he thought he was. The next practice was Monday evening and Davy suggested Digger should come, even if his damaged hand meant that he was unable to participate, as he wanted to teach a modified technique to everyone and for them then to learn a simple ringing sequence.

After lunch they walked round the garden and fed the fish in the pond and finally bid Davy goodbye at about two thirty. Since the post office was now closed Davy decided he would walk to the pub and get some cigarettes, "Which is the shortest way to the pub Moira," he asked, "I am out of fags."

"Well I am sure they don't do you any good Digger, they seem to make people cough a lot, but it's your life I suppose. If we carry on down Jobs Rise, we can come out on The Green just down from the Stag.

They chatted about the village as they walked to the pub and Moira told him that she had only been there since the previous October after finishing her training as a district nurse in Bristol and that she rented a house from the brickworks and lived just two doors away from Sissy and her family. Although she had grown up in Inverness, she had trained as a nurse in Aberdeen and worked in Edinburgh for a while, before deciding to be a district nurse.

Having purchased his cigarettes they strolled across the village green and stood on the corner of Oxford Road and Tower Street chattering away until Moira finally said, "Goodness, is that the time, I have to wash and iron my dress for church tomorrow, how is your leg now, is it still hurting?"

"My leg, oh, I had forgotten all about it, I think the exercise has done it good. I guess I need to practice eating soup left handed judging by the soup stains down my front and thanks again for strapping my hand for me. It's been really good chatting to you."

"My pleasure," she said, "are you not coming to church tomorrow?"

"To be honest, I am not a regular churchgoer, but the padre, or should I call him the vicar, and his wife have been so kind to me, I had thought about going, so I will see you there then, bye."

With a spring in her step, Moira went home to wash and iron her best dress and to write and tell her mother of the week's activities and of the new man in the village.

Digger called in at the vicarage, ostensibly to find out what time the service was on Sunday, but allowed himself to be persuaded to come in for a cup of tea and a piece of cake, which had to be cut into small squares for him, for ease of eating. He got back to Millstone House around four thirty and checked with Cook what time dinner was on a Saturday. "Dinner," she said, "I still have your lunch sitting on the table Arnold, if you are not going to be in for meals, you might have the good manners to let me know. We eat dinner together at seven thirty on a Saturday, don't be late."

Mac was very boisterous, so Digger took him for a walk along the path around Manor wood where Mac managed to scare a few young rabbits. He ended the walk by going past the pile of wood he had found and managed to bring some smaller dry branches back with him which he put on the fire and then read until dinner.

Mrs Black was a different person that evening and discussed all the jobs that needed doing around the house and garden and of a trip she now wanted to make, to visit Ronnie's parents who lived in Worcester. She said that she had not been in touch with them for over three years and wanted to go and see them and to try to make amends for her rudeness . Digger mentioned that he would like to have their address in order that he could write to them, if Mrs Black didn't object. She said she had no objections and would look it out for him.

When he finally put the book down and went to bed, he found some pyjamas had been laid out for him. They were a little on the large size, so he knew they were not Ronnie's and wondered who to thank for them. Looking out of the window, he could make out some of the village houses and found himself wondering if one was Moira's and what a nice person she was.

"Funny old day!" he said to himself.

CHAPTER EIGHT
SUNDAY BEST

The fire in the kitchen was on its last legs when Digger opened the small door to take a look. He rolled up some newspaper and added a few twigs and gently blew the fire into life. The remaining embers started to glow and he added some large pieces of wood and soon had a warm glow coming from the fire. The kettle quickly boiled and he was able to wash and shave in warm water for the first time in over a week.

He took Mac for a walk in the woods, but had to cut it short as his leg was still sore, but was pleased to note that his eye was functioning properly again, although it was still a 'shiner'. Whilst walking he remembered to collect some more wood for his own private store and filled up his log box in the kitchen. After a quick look at the 'Canine Obedience Training Guide' which Deborah had given him, he took Mac outside into the garden and started on basic obedience training, starting with the 'Sit' command.

Both man and dog were ready for food when they heard Cook's dulcet tones informing them that breakfast was ready and that they should come at once. Mrs Black made a fuss of the dog and gave him the scraps that Cook had put aside for him and everyone chatted as they ate breakfast.

"Mrs Duffy-Smythe, Mrs Black and I have to go out today Arnold," said Cook, "so I have left some cold meat and salad under that cover on the dresser. Just help yourself to what you want. We will not be home until late, so leave the garden gate open for us and if you have to go to bed, then lock the back door for me and leave the key in the laundry room under the mat."

"Right-o Cook, no problem, going somewhere nice?" he asked.

"Where we are going is our business Arnold, you just make sure you do as I have asked," she snapped back.

He carried on with eating his breakfast and had a second cup of tea, before getting up from the table and heading for the door. He had decided to say nothing more as she was obviously in a bad mood again, but as he reached the door he turned to her and smiled and said, "Safe journey and could I borrow the boot cleaning brushes and polish?" She nodded and he lifted the box out of the larder and walked out to the garden. Checking his watch he saw it was nine thirty and decided he should sort out his things for church.

He cleaned his shoes, washed and changed into his own clean clothes and read some more of the book. At ten forty he said goodbye to Mac, leaving him in the kitchen and slowly walked to the church. There was a queue of people at the church door, all being greeted by a man in a suit who shook everyone's hand and welcomed them to the service. The man introduced himself as Mr Taylor and said he was the local school teacher and asked if Digger was meeting anyone in church. Digger mentioned Bertie and Moira and was told that whilst Moira was in the choir, Bertie normally sat about half way down on the right hand side, but had not arrived yet.

He was handed a hymn book by a middle-aged lady who was standing just inside the door and wandered over to the right hand side of the church. "Goodness," he thought, "is it only six days since I came in here to remember Ginger, what a lot has taken place since then." Finding an empty pew about half way down the church, he sat down and looked around at the rest of the people gathered there. The old organ was gently playing a soothing piece of music and he was deep in thought when Bertie appeared and sat down beside him. After shaking hands and smiling at each other, Bertie asked how he was and informed him that Deborah had returned to London.

Their conversation was cut short by the appearance of the choir and the vicar who was resplendent in a gleaming white surplice over his long black cassock.

The service proceeded without having much effect on Digger. He had managed to catch Moira's eye and she had smiled at him and Sissy had waved from the other side of the church and he had waved back. As he had stood up to sing the next hymn, he suddenly became aware of the tune the organ was playing and realised it was one of the hymns they had often sung in the army church services he had attended. He looked down at the hymn book and read the familiar words of the first verse:

> Courage, brother! Do not stumble,
> Though thy path be dark as night;
> There's a star to guide the humble:
> 'Trust in God, and do the right.'

As he thought about the words and closed his eyes he saw Big Dutch, Ginger, Ronnie and himself standing side by side, singing for all they were worth and realised it was the last time they had worshipped together before Ronnie had died.

He became aware that the music had stopped and Bertie was pulling at his coat and telling him to sit down, which he did. Once seated he continued to think of that time and the conversation they had all had afterwards. It was about courage and death and dying and how Ronnie had told them that because he was a Christian, he was no longer afraid of death, as he believed he would go to heaven and be with God, although he hoped it would be many years in the future. How wrong he was!

Digger rose at the end of the service and slowly filed out of church behind Bertie and shook hands with the vicar who hoped they had enjoyed the service. Bertie was in the process of inviting Digger back for lunch when Moira joined them, looking very pretty in her best dress. "Hello Digger, Bertie, it's good to see both of you today, how are all your injuries doing," she asked Digger?

"They're much improved, thank you nurse and may I say how pretty you look."

"Why thank you kind sir," she said "and what have you two been hatching up?"

Bertie replied, "I was telling Digger how lonely I was, now that my daughter has returned to London and have just invited him to come to lunch. Would you care to come along as well Moira?"

"I would love to, are you sure you have enough for us all?"

"Cook has left some cold food out for me, which I could collect when I go to pick Mac up from my cottage, why don't

I go off now and I will meet the two of you in half an hour at your place Bertie."

"That's splendid," said Bertie, "I love impromptu get-togethers, Moira and I will take a stroll to the cottage and get the kettle on in readiness for you and Mac."

Digger left the church yard and was just stepping onto the track when a man wearing an old tweed jacket and smoking a pipe called out to him, "Hey you, yes you with the limp, I'm looking for a woman called Florence Stall, I'm told she lives round here somewhere."

Bad manners had never impressed Digger and as a South Londoner, he did not always feel kindly disposed towards those who came from the north of the Thames, which is what he construed from the man's accent. He turned and called back to him, "That's nice mate, good hunting." With which he turned his back and strode out for Millstone House.

He arrived back at his cottage to find Mac anxious to get out and visit the trees, so after putting some wood on the fire he went along to the kitchen and inspected the food that Cook had left for him. He found a carrier bag in the larder and managed to put all the food in it and decided that he would make up Cook's fire, to try and get into her good books again.

By the time Mac and Digger reached Bertie's the table was laid and the tea brewing nicely. The contents of the carrier bag were laid out on the table and the threesome set about enjoying Sunday lunch.

During the conversation Bertie told of the very rude man who had accosted them outside church and demanded of him where a certain Florence Stall lived. The man would only accept that she did not live in the village when Moira told him she was the district nurse and knew everyone in the area and could state categorically that no-one of that name lived in either Upper Style or Lower Style. Digger said that he too had met this gentleman and had decided that he would not have told him of the woman's whereabouts even if he had known who she was.

After lunch the things were cleared away and the dishes washed and Bertie lead a very pleasant stroll along the bank of the lake to the top end by the Manor House and back again. When they returned to his cottage he suggested a game of cards and proceeded to teach them how to play Canasta. Needless to Say Bertie won quite easily but the other two slowly picked up the tactics of the game. Around five thirty Moira announced she needed to leave and get things sorted out for a new week, so Digger gallantly offered to escort her home, just in case the rude man was still in the area.

They thanked Bertie for his hospitality, packed up the remains of Cook's cold dinner in the carrier bag and set off with Mac back to the village.

It took almost forty five minutes to reach Moira's house during which they compared growing up in Inverness to growing up in London, discussed the effects of the war on the British way of life and started to touch on future hopes and aspirations. Moira thought about inviting him in for tea, but noticed the odd curtain was moving in the street and decided against it. They bid each other goodbye and said they would meet again for the Bell Ringing practice Monday evening.

For reasons he couldn't explain, Digger found himself whistling on the way back to Millstone and hadn't noticed that the car was in the garage when he walked into the kitchen with the carrier bag.

"So that's where all my food went, when I told you to help yourself, I did not expect you to feed the whole village," complained Cook.

Ignoring the complaint, Digger placed the contents of the carrier bag on the dresser, put the bag in the larder and turning to the three ladies seated round the table said, "Good evening ladies, I trust you had a pleasant trip. My day has been excellent, thank you Cook for asking, my faithful friend and I will now retire and leave you in peace."

"One moment Arnold," said Mrs Black, "the car was not running at all well on the way back from St. Albans, would you mind having a look at it first thing tomorrow as we may need to make another lengthy journey in the near future."

"Certainly Mrs Black, but I do not have many tools here, so I am limited with what I can do, but I will check it out first thing for you."

Mrs Duffy-Smythe then looked up and asked, "You didn't happen to notice any strange faces around the village today did you Mr Smith."

"Not that I can think of. Maam," he replied, "well apart, that is, from a guy who was looking for a woman called Florence Stall. He asked me and Bertie and Moira about her. I just ignored him, but he was more persistent when he spoke to them and only stopped bothering them when Moira told him she was the district nurse and assured him there was no-one of that name living round here. Rude, rough looking man he was."

"A big man, mid forties, London accent."

"That's right, why do you know him?"

"I should, he's my husband. You didn't say anything about my sister and I living here?"

"No, certainly not. I had no reason to, anyway, I thought your surname was Duffy-Smythe not Stall and your sister I know to be Mrs Black and I don't know Cook's surname. Why are you so frightened of him, you're shaking?"

Mrs Duffy-Smythe put her head in her hands and started to weep, while Mrs Black comforted her and Cook put the kettle on.

Mrs Black looked at Digger and spoke quietly, "This man, Tom Stall, is not a nice man. He drinks, he gambles and when he's drunk and losing, gets violent. During one of these violent bouts, he beat up Penny so badly, she had to go to hospital for two weeks to recover. Ron and I went to the police and he was arrested and sentenced to three years in prison. He already had a history of violence before this incident. While he was serving his three years, Penny disappeared. She changed her name several times, moved house a dozen times or more and changed careers from being a journalist to being a writer. Finally in 1943 with Ron away in the army, we all moved here into the village and Millstone House.

Today we have all been to a memorial service for an old friend who has died and his daughter told us that Tom had telephoned her to find out about us and told her that he knew where we lived and wanted to speak to Florence. So now he knows and it will only be a matter of time before he turns up on our doorstep and the nightmare starts all over again!"

Digger looked stunned and said, "I really don't know what to say, I'm sorry this man has turned up again, but I guess this is not the right time to discuss what we can do about it, but be assured that no-one will come in here and hurt your sister while I am in your employ. Goodnight." With which he and Mac left the kitchen and after walking round the garden and locking the gates, went back to the cottage.

Cook poured tea for everyone and then sat down at the table. "We have all been hiding from this man for ten years and it's time it stopped. Let him come, there are three of us and Arnold and the dog. He is ten years older now, we know he is overweight and has had heart problems, together we can beat him. We just need to be prepared. I refuse to let him spoil one more day of my life. For goodness sake, we have just been to a memorial service for a man who was playing golf two weeks ago and today is dead and gone. Life is for living and each day is precious."

"You are quite right Cook," responded Mrs Duffy-Smythe, " your loyalty to me has cost both of you a lot and I appreciate it and agree, it's time to stop running and hiding and time to start preparing ourselves for defeating him. With Mr Smith living at Millstone House and the three of us, Tom Stall will have a fight on his hands this time round!"

CHAPTER NINE
THE ACCIDENT

Mac had never been so agitated before and barked so loud that Digger thought the cottage must be on fire or that intruders had entered Millstone House. He jumped out of bed, pulled on his trousers and boots and picking up a large stick that was lying by the front door, rushed out into the garden, with Mac at his heels, still barking loudly. He quickly scanned the garden and garage and noticed that the gates remained locked and there were no signs of flames. He looked towards the house and everything was in order, which left him perplexed as to what Mac was so excited about.

Realising that the dog had raced off to the woodpile in the corner of the garden, he followed in pursuit and arrived in time to see Mac biting a large rat on the back of its neck and then tossing it to one side as he dived in, after another. Digger realised the rat was not quite dead, so dispatched it with his large stick and watched as the dog disposed of four others, before returning to Digger to get his master's praise.

They both returned to the cottage for a drink and a biscuit and as it was now almost ten to six, Digger decided to wash and dress and read a bit before breakfast. Since the bandage on his hand had got dirty from the stick he had been holding, he took it off and exercised his fingers. They were certainly bruised but he doubted they were broken, but thought it was still worth getting the doctor to check them out.

Everyone was present for breakfast and Cook demanded to know what had set Mac off barking enough to 'wake the dead'? The story of the rats in the woodpile was listened to with relish and all the ladies commended the dog for his courage and made a big fuss of him, whilst instructing Digger to put down some rat poison, which he could buy in town.

The subject of Tom Stall was raised and what precautions could be taken against his next visit to the village. Mrs Black said she would take a drive to Lower Style and then speak to the police constable who was based there and Mrs Duffy-Smythe said she would speak to the vicar as he was often a point of call to strangers to the village and asked Digger to mention it to the doctor when he went for his appointment. Cook advised against saying anything to Sissy, unless they intended the whole village to be informed by the following day.

They were just getting up from breakfast when Sissy arrived, full of the joys of Spring and dying to tell them the latest village gossip. She said that yesterday, her dad had nearly come to blows with a stranger he met outside the pub, who was asking about a woman he was looking for, who was supposed to live in or near to the village. Her dad had told the man that he didn't know anyone by the name the man had said and the stranger had the cheek to call him a liar. Her dad was furious and took a step towards him to thump him one, when the man bent over holding his chest, saying he could hardly breathe. Her dad thought he was putting on an act to get out of a thumping, but when the man sat down on the pavement, having turned a bright red, he wasn't so sure and just walked away. Her mum was so pleased that he had not got into trouble again.

Everyone was dumb-struck and did not know what to say, until eventually Digger asked the question that was on all their tongues, "So what happened then Sissy, did the man stay or leave?"

"Dad said he managed to get up after a while and slouched over to his car and get into the driver's seat. He said it was an old Rover Ten and looked in good condition; dad likes cars and has always wanted one of them. Anyway, dad says when he came out of the pub; the car had gone, so assumed the man was well enough to drive away."

"Talking of cars," said Digger, "you asked me yesterday to have a look at yours, so I will be off, see you all later," with which he got up, grabbed the last piece of toast and left the kitchen and went over to the garage to inspect the engine of the car.

Mac went out with him and scampered over to the woodpile but found no more rats, so wandered back to the kitchen door to see what titbits from breakfast would be offered. Cook and Sissy discussed the jobs for that day and the two sisters went into the study to mull over Sissy's new information.

"It's a pity Sissy's dad didn't give him a good thumping," said Mrs Black, "that might have been an end to our troubles, mind you, Daphne said that she thought he sounded unwell when she spoke to him on the telephone, so maybe he really did have an attack of some sort."

"I don't know what to think, Amanda, I have never wished anyone ill, but I just dread having to see Tom again after what he did to me. There must be some way of ending this nightmare!"

"Well let's get on with the practical matters, if Arnold has fixed the car, I will drive down to Lower Style and you ring the vicar and arrange to see him. We need to keep ourselves busy and stop thinking the worst."

Mrs Black entered the garage to find Digger cleaning the plugs and points whilst whistling one of the hymns from yesterday, "Almost done Mrs Black, just have to put everything back together again and I'm sure it will be running a lot smoother for you. Perhaps next time either of you go to Aylesbury, you could pop into the garage and buy a new set of leads as well as some spark plugs and points. I could also do with a set of feeler gauges as I am having to just guess the various gaps at the moment."

Mrs Black carefully noted down what Digger had asked for in her note book and then said, "I can drop you off at the doctors before I go to Lower Style if that is any help Digger and would you mind getting some rat poison since you are going close by the shop. I have a real fear of rats, both the four legged and the two legged ones."

With all the electrics back in place, the engine burst into life and after dusting himself down, he got into the passenger seat next to Mrs Black and she drove him to the doctor's surgery.

After a thorough inspection of his eye, leg and hand, the doctor pronounced him fit for work but advised him to avoid bars of soap and ladle wielding Amazons in the future. He was almost out of the door, before remembering to tell the doctor about Mrs Duffy-Smythe and Tom Stall. He made a note of the name and the man's condition as described by Sissy that morning and remarked that he should not have been driving a motor car in view of the severity of the attack he had suffered and that they should notify the police in case there had been an accident.

The rat poison was purchased at the Ironmongers and he was warned of the danger to dogs and other animals and not to leave the tin lying around where children could get hold of it. The shopkeeper then said he had some new putty and glass in stock and advised Digger to reserve some now before it all went.

"Just out of interest," said Digger, "how on earth did you know that I had been asked to repair some broken windows?"

"That's easy and I am prepared to reveal my sources, this time," replied Mr Tanner. "Your Mrs Black called in here the other day and asked me to keep my ears open for second hand roof tiles, like the ones on your outbuildings and asked if we had any glass or putty; so I had a walk past Millstone House after church and noticed at least six broken panes of glass and somewhere around three dozen broken or missing tiles. The glass is easy, but the tiles are unusual, I know I have seen some like them somewhere round these parts, but can't remember where yet. Give me time, it will come to me."

"I'm impressed Mr Tanner, you're wasted here! I'll speak with Mrs Black about the glass and let you know the when and where – bye for now," with that Digger left the shop and wandered down to the Post Office to buy cigarettes and a paper, before walking back to Millstone for lunch and an afternoon in the garden.

The policeman was out when Mrs Black arrived at his house in Lower Style, but his wife assured her he would not be long and invited her in for a cup of tea. The two ladies got on well and were soon discussing the intimacies of a policeman's footwear and the cost of aprons and were deeply engrossed in conversation when he arrived home for his lunch.

"This is Mrs Black dear, from Upper Style, she wants a word with you privately, why don't you take her into the front room," his wife suggested.

"Right then Mrs Black, let's go through to the front," he said and led the way into the next room. He took out his pad and pencil and made notes as she outlined the problem and the trouble Mrs Duffy-Smythe had gone to in order to avoid her husband.

"So they are still married then?" he asked, "that makes things a bit more difficult, I will need to speak to my sergeant about what options we have. He is based in Aylesbury and I know he isn't around today, but I will speak to him first thing tomorrow and come and let you know what he says. Here's my phone number, you ring me if he comes round and I will come straight over, day or night. But do make sure you tell that young man you mentioned, not to take the law into his own hands or it will be him who finds himself in trouble. Now if you will excuse me, I think my lunch is ready. Goodbye Mrs Black."

"Goodbye constable, we will see you tomorrow morning then, thank your wife for the tea for me please."

It was raining when she got outside and had to make a dash for the car, it started first time and she could see that Digger had cleaned the windscreen, which had gotten splattered with mud the previous day. "No wonder Ron thought so highly of Arnold and his friends and to think I almost chased him away, what a mistake I would have made!" It was still raining when she got back home and was surprised to find her sister was still out visiting the vicar, so she rang the rectory and arranged to come and pick her up to save her from getting wet.

Once home Mrs Duffy-Smythe described her meeting with the vicar and his suggestion that perhaps it might be better to arrange to meet with Tom on neutral ground with a mutual friend or associate present to mediate if necessary. Although at first she had pooh-poohed the idea, she was beginning to see it as a viable option and asked her sister and Cook for their opinions. Whilst several doubts were raised by the other ladies, the consensus was that it might be worth a try, but that they would wait to see what the police constable had to say when he called on Tuesday morning.

During lunch it was decided that since Digger could not work in the garden because of the rain that he should make a start repainting the interior of the laundry. The paint was flaking off the walls and the window frames were virtually bare and several panes of glass were cracked or broken and one of the door hinges was coming loose. Digger and Mrs Black made a list of all the items they required to fix everything up and she rang through to the Ironmongers with her order and arranged that one of them would pick everything up the next day. This left Digger with the job of washing everything down in the laundry and wire brushing the loose paint off the walls and woodwork.

Conversation was pretty much dead over dinner, so they decided to put the radio on and listen to a programme on the Home service that Cook had suggested.

Digger borrowed an umbrella to go to the church for the bell ringing practice and was pleased to renew his acquaintance with the railway porter, George and to meet his wife Daisy and their young son. He walked Moira home afterwards who mentioned she had been asked by her parents to visit her great aunt, who lived in Buckingham, this coming Saturday. She was celebrating her seventy fifth birthday and would otherwise be on her own, so she said she had agreed to go and asked Digger if he would like to accompany her, to which he readily agreed.

The rain had stopped by the time he reached his cottage, so making sure Mac was indoors, he put some of the rat poison in places the dog could not possibly get in to, before stoking up the fire and going to bed.

When he woke the next day, he realised that the rain had been heavy throughout the night and noticed that one or two drips of water were coming from the ceiling and falling on the floor and on him and his pillow was soaked. Once he was up and shaved and dressed, he went into the garage and found a couple of tins which he put on the floor to catch the drips.

He mentioned the leaking roof to Mrs Black and his conversation yesterday with the Ironmonger about second hand roof tiles and the fact that their ones were a very unusual type.

"That's a coincidence," said Mrs Duffy-Smythe, "the vicar told me yesterday that a farmer from Brill, who used to live in the village, had telephoned to say that they were pulling down some old farm buildings and was the vicar interested in any of the roof tiles, as the farmer thought they were the same as those on the vicarage. Well, the vicar checked and rang him back to say that all his were intact but it might be useful to have half a dozen as they were very unusual. Now I have a feeling that the vicarage and Millstone house were built at a similar time, so it might just be worth checking this out Digger."

"I'll go over after breakfast, if you like and check if the vicarage tiles are the same as ours and if they are, I can ask the vicar to ring his friend and say we could be over later in the week to collect them," suggested Digger.

"Why don't you take the car Arnold and collect all the goods that we ordered from the Ironmongers," said Mrs Black, "as my sister and I need to be in for a visitor this morning."

"While you are in the village, would you mind getting a few things for me Arnold," enquired Cook, "I was going myself but you can save me a trip."

The car battery was flat since Mrs Black had put the lights on to come back in the rain yesterday and had forgotten to switch them off. The starting handle was discovered under the carpet by the rear seat and after almost wrenching his arm out of its socket on the first swing, Digger managed to bring the car engine to life with the second. Deciding that the car needed a run to re-charge the battery, he drove for about five miles down the Oxford road and back again, before stopping in the village for his shopping. He used up virtually all his money in the two shops and made sure he got receipts for everything. He parked in front of the vicarage and got out to inspect the roof tiles.

"Hello Digger, what interests you in our roof then?" asked the vicar who had been trimming his roses in the front garden.

"Sorry vicar; didn't spot you there. Mrs Duffy-Smythe mentioned the phone call you got from your farmer friend at Brill about second hand roof tiles, so I thought I would come and see if yours happened to be the same as ours."

"From memory I do believe they are," said the vicar, "come round the side and I think you will get a much better view from there."

The two men strolled round the side of the house and Digger could make out the distinctive shape of the tiles and asked the vicar if he would mind telling his friend that they would be interested in some.

The vicar made the phone call and then reported back, "Well the good news is that they are still there and you can have as many as you want at a sixpence each. The bad news is that you will have to go on the roof to get them yourself and the building is coming down soon, as it has been condemned as unsafe."

"Did he say exactly when the building will be coming down?"

"It appears he has scheduled it for Wednesday of next week, if it hasn't fallen down on its own by then, so I suggest you get over to Brill as soon as you can."

"Thanks vicar and I will get you half a dozen as well, when I get ours. Bye"

Digger parked the car in the garage and unloaded all the decorating supplies straight into the laundry and carried cooks supplies into the kitchen to find the three ladies and the policeman seated round the table in deep conversation.

"Oops, sorry to interrupt, I'll go out again," said Digger.

"No stay, Arnold, the constable has just informed us that my husband was very ill when he left here on Sunday having suffered a heart attack. He was travelling back down the A40 to London when he lost control and the car went off the road and hit a wall. Mercifully no-one else was involved but he is seriously ill in High Wycombe hospital. They don't think he will last more than a couple of days."

"I see," said Digger, "I hate to say it, but this does solve the problem for you at least, Mrs Duffy-Smythe. There is no need for you to be fearful of him finding you any longer if he only has a few days to live."

The policeman nodded his agreement and then got up from the table and said, "That is certainly true and we can consider this case closed, so if you will excuse me ladies, I need to be on my way, good day to you all."

"Thank you constable for coming and for the trouble you have taken, we are most grateful to you," said Mrs Black, who rising from her seat opened the door to allow him to leave.

"Well good riddance to bad rubbish, I say," said Cook, "he got what he deserved and we can all rest secure now."

"He wasn't all bad Cook. We did have some good times together, he wasn't always violent," interjected Mrs Duffy-Smythe, "I want to go and see him, I need to go and see him, I think it will give me closure. Arnold would you mind driving me to High Wycombe hospital, I don't think I could manage it on my own at the moment?"

"Of course I will Ma'am, when do you want to leave?"

"Let's all have a cup of tea and lunch and we will go after that," she replied.

Lunch was a quiet affair during which Digger reported back on the roof tiles and the need to go to Brill to get them themselves. He said that he thought it was worth asking Bertie to go with him, as it was a difficult and possibly dangerous job and Bertie was a man of great experience and sound judgement. Cook snorted, but the others agreed to the suggestion and that the sooner he went the better, if the building was unstable.

Digger and Mrs Duffy-Smythe arrived at the hospital about three forty five and agreed that whilst she went to see her husband, Digger would go and get some petrol for the car and then return to pick her up just after four fifteen. He mentioned that he was out of cash due to the morning's purchases so she gave him a ten pond note and said that they would settle up that evening.

He was in a private room just off the Male Ward and the sister had warned her he was in a very poor state of health. She sat down on the wooden chair by the side of the bed and spoke quietly to him, "Tom, Tom it's me, Florence, can you hear me?"

He looked up and tried to smile but was obviously in a lot of pain and reached out to hold her hand, "Ello Florence, I thought you might come when you eard I was a goner. I knew you was in that village somewhere, I could sense your presence. I've been looking for you since I came out of prison, but you just disappeared, I guess that's what you wanted, eh.?"

"Yes Tom, that's what I wanted, I just couldn't face you again, after what you did to me. You hurt me so badly Tom, I needed over twenty stitches and you broke my arm in two places and I really thought you would have killed me if Cook had not come and intervened."

"Florence, there's not a day gone by since then, that I haven't regretted what I did with all my heart. It was madness. You're the only woman I have ever loved and I still do, I still love you Florence, honest, there's never been anyone but you for me and to think that I hurt you and frightened you and made you hide from me!"

She sat there silently while he wiped his eyes and then continued, "Night after night I just sobbed because I had lost you. Remember what my dad used to call you 'Blossom', you were my 'Blossom in Winter'. You made my dull grey days into something beautiful and lovely; you made me come alive. Just like a tree in Blossom on a winter's day brightens up everything about it and makes it seem like Spring, that's what you did for me Florence."

She felt like screaming at him, but her reply was said quite calmly, "How can you say that Tom, knowing what you did to me. If I was so important to you, why did you get drunk so often and gamble and then come home and treat me so badly. You were always fighting and in trouble, long before you turned your anger on me."

"Just think for a moment Florence, I was never angry or violent with you when we first met, was I. Think back. Yes,

I always enjoyed a drink with the boys and sometimes there was a fight, but that was just the way we were. No-one ever got badly hurt and we were all mates again the next day. And yes, I admit that I gambled at the dogs and the races, you knew that right from the start, but I never lost more than I could afford and never got into debt with the bookies."

"What are you trying to say Tom? Are you daring to suggest that all that violence and aggression was somehow my fault? Are you!"

"I never said that and anyway fault is not the right word. Each of us was responsible for our own actions and I have to take full responsibility for what I did to you; but yes, I am saying that you were the cause of my anger Florence."

She stood up and this time she did lose her self control as she shouted, "I don't believe this Tom, I came here today to say goodbye, because I heard you were dying, not to listen to this ridiculous accusation that I am responsible for all the evil you did."

"Florence, please sit down, hear me out, just for once. Every time I ever tried to have this conversation with you, that's exactly what you did, you walked out on me. I told you, I take responsibility for what I did, but you did cause it Florence, you did. I married a sweet, charming, gentle, polite, gifted young woman, that I adored and worshipped and would willingly have died for. And that's what you were most of the time, except during your monthly period. Then you changed personality. You became spiteful and hateful and insulting. You made fun of me in front of our friends, you shouted and ordered me around like a servant, you treated me like I was rubbish, you really hurt me, month after month after month."

The ward sister had heard the raised voices and walked into the room; she looked at the two people staring at each other and decided to leave again.

Florence sat down and Tom continued, "While we were courting, I never saw you like that, you always had something on during that time of the month, you deliberately hid your other side from me. I was a young man, I was stunned, I didn't know what to do, I didn't know how to handle it, or even know if the way you behaved was normal. My mother was never like that and I didn't have any sisters so I had no idea if your behaviour was common to other young women, men just don't talk about this sort of thing! With no-one to speak to, I just found it easier to go to the pub and get drunk. The rest you know."

"How dare you blame me, you monster? My mother always said you were not good enough for me and she was right."

"Your mother was a snob who looked down on me and my parents because we were working class and she had never done a day's work in her life, miserable old cow!"

"That's it, look at you, look at your fists, you would hit me now if you could. I have heard enough Tom. I am going, goodbye."

"Florence, before you go, I really am sorry for what I did. I loved you so much and I hurt you so bad. Please tell me you forgive me. Let me die in peace. Please."

She got up from her seat and without looking at him walked towards the door. As she turned the handle and opened the door, she heard him say one more time, "Florence, say you forgive me." As she left the room she heard him cough so she informed the sister on the way out, that he had taken a turn for the worse and that she would not be coming back.

He died two hours later.

CHAPTER TEN
FLYING OBJECTS

Digger had managed to find a garage and fill up with petrol, but had taken a wrong turning and found himself a mile down the road to Amersham before realising his mistake. He stopped at a small shop and bought a stick of Barley-Sugar and some matches and got directions back to the hospital from a very attractive young lady behind the counter. He parked the car in front of the main building, which gave him an excellent view of the entrance lobby and then turned the engine off. As he was expecting a long wait he wound the window down and lit a cigarette but had only been sitting there a few minutes when Mrs Duffy-Smythe rushed down the steps and got into the passenger seat beside him. He could see she was very upset, so without saying anything to her, he just started the car and headed for home.

She sat quietly for the whole journey with her head hung low and when he dropped her off at the front door she barely managed to say thank you to him. He drove round the house to the garage and parked the car in its usual place and was still closing the garage doors when Cook appeared beside him with a tray of food and with Mac close behind her proudly holding a very large bone in his mouth.

"Hello Arnold, I think it would be better if you and Mac ate your dinner in the cottage tonight, as we three ladies have a lot of things to discuss and to be frank, we can't do it if you are there. Oh and Mrs Black told me to say 'thank you'," said Cook.

"Fair enough," said Digger, slightly relieved that he would not have to share their company over dinner. "Is Mrs Duffy-Smythe OK, she seemed to be very upset when she left the hospital?"

Cook completely ignored this question and went on to say, "Oh, another thing Arnold, we had a phone call from the farmer who told the vicar about the tiles. He wanted us to know that the building they are on was now coming down on Friday of this week and suggested that you should go there tomorrow, if you want to get some before they all get broken. I have written down the directions he gave me to get to the farm and I told him that weather permitting; you would be across tomorrow morning."

"Right you are, thanks, I had better go and see if Bertie is free to come and give me a hand, that roof sounds like it is about to collapse at any moment."

The three ladies had no sooner sat down to dinner when the telephone rang. "Would you mind answering the telephone Amanda, I have a feeling it might be the hospital, I left our number with the sister as I was leaving and she promised to let me know if there was any developments."

Mrs Black picked up the telephone and spoke to the sister who was in charge of Tom's ward, "I see, yes, thank you, his father you say, yes, well, I will tell my sister, do you have an address, just a moment while I get a pen. Right go ahead, thank you. Goodbye."

She sat down again and turned to her sister, "Tom died about fifteen minutes ago. It seems he had another attack just after you left and never recovered. It appears his father arrived shortly after you left and was with him at the end. The sister has given me his address as Tom had put him down as next of kin."

"I hardly recognised him this afternoon; he had lost a lot of weight and looked so old. He was badly injured from the accident and had bandages round his head and had received terrible internal injuries from the steering wheel. When he spoke, his voice was faint and weak, but it was the same old Tom, he had not changed at all!"

"What did he say to you," asked Cook, "why was he looking for you now, after all this time?"

"His doctor had told him that his heart and liver were in a bad state and that he only had months to live. He said he wanted to find me to say sorry. He realised he had been a brute and done a terrible thing to me and wanted to apologise. Needless to say I was speechless, I sat there thinking to myself, 'what on earth did I ever see in this man, this brute who almost killed me' and would you believe it, he then started to get belligerent with me, because I just sat there quietly."

"Oh I believe it all right, a leopard doesn't change its spots and Tom Stall was always a bully," snapped Cook, "let's be grateful he is finally out of our lives and cannot come back and bother us again."

"Hold on Cook, the man has just died and you did say that he expressed regret for what he did, we have to assume he was sincere, if those were virtually his dying words, were they Florence?" asked Amanda.

"Err, yes, he said something so quietly I couldn't quite make it out, but at the end I believe he was genuinely sorry for the way he hurt me. His poor father must be heartbroken though, to have lost his only son, they were so close. I will speak to our solicitor tomorrow about sending a note to him; I think it would be hypocritical to send flowers though."

Meanwhile, Digger had finished his tea and Mac had buried his bone and after seeing to the fire and tidying the cottage, the pair set off down the track to see Bertie. Although it was quite dark, they both knew the path and got there safely just as he was sitting down to listen to the radio.

"Hello Digger, Mac, it's good to see you both, can I tempt you with some Ginger Beer while I drink the real thing."

"Thanks, I'd enjoy that, did you make it yourself?"

"Afraid not, but I am assured this is good stuff though," replied Bertie.

The two men sat down by the fire and started to chat about their respective days.

"You know I haven't been to High Wycombe in over ten years," observed Bertie, "I don't suppose you noticed if there was much war damage to the town."

"To be honest I got lost and ended up chatting to this young woman in a shop who gave me directions and only just managed to get back in time to meet her coming out of the hospital, so didn't notice much at all about the town."

"And you say her husband is probably dead now, the chap we met on Sunday! What a difference a few days can make eh!"

"To change the subject Bertie, do you have any experience of roofs and tiling," asked Digger; who then went on to recount the story of the vicar's farmer friend at Brill and the opportunity to get some tiles to replace the broken ones over his bedroom.

"I have had very little to do with roofs, they do not figure too prominently aboard ships," he joked. "My advice Digger is to wait until the building falls down and pick up the ones that aren't broken from the ground, a much safer option! Some of them are bound to survive the crash. The chances of you picking up a serious injury on that rickety old roof seem pretty high to me."

"I take your point, but I was thinking that if we went across there tomorrow morning for a look see, at worst we have a pleasant morning out and at best we get some tiles for the roof, so my bed won't get wet the next time it rains."

"I like your logic," said Bertie, "provided you agree not to take any stupid risks I will come with you. I may have some rope in the shed that might come in useful and a pair of plimsolls that might fit. Tell Cook that I will come to Millstone for breakfast tomorrow morning and that will be my fee for assisting you."

"That's great Bertie; we eat at seven sharp, I'm sure Cook will be delighted."

When Digger finally got back to Millstone House it was after eleven o'clock, so he just left a note for Cook on the table, informing her that there would be an extra person for breakfast.

Digger woke suddenly at six fifteen, something had moved the furniture downstairs and it didn't sound like Mac. He crept downstairs and noticed the door was ajar and a seat had been moved outside. He looked through the crack of the door and could see Mac on his back with his feet in the air, with Bertie, who was sitting on the chair, scratching his belly for him.

"What time do you call this Bertie, I said seven not six, I thought I had burglars."

"This is the best part of the day Digger, I had no idea you were such a sleepyhead! I have been up for an hour already to watch the animals drinking by the lake and to hear the birds singing. I have managed to get some life into your fire and the kettle should be boiling by now and I could really do with a cup of tea please."

Digger made the tea and then got washed and dressed and tried on the plimsolls that Bertie had brought. Not a perfect fit, but they would do.

"The only other thing I could find in my shed that I thought might help, is this," he said, and produced a metal tool almost two feet long that was flat with two hooks at one end and a heavy metal handle at the other end.

"What on earth is that, another weapon from your dim and distant past I would guess?"

Bertie smiled and swung it around his head, axe like, "Well it could be, but actually it's very British, it's called a 'Slate Ripper'. You slide it under the slates, hook it round the nail head that is holding the slate in place, then hit the handle here, with a hammer, and the nail is cut through and the slate can slip out."

"That's ingenious, are tiles held on with nails in the same way as slates then?"

"Well not quite. Whereas every slate would be nailed in place, most tillers only nail every fourth row down, or where a tile has been replaced or is in a particularly vulnerable position. I have also made you some wooden wedges so you can raise the upper tiles, which might be broken and release lower ones which are intact."

"Thanks Bertie, you are a real star, let's go and eat."

Mrs Black and Cook were chatting in the kitchen when the two men entered and Mrs Black immediately welcomed Bertie and thanked him for being prepared to assist Digger with the tiles. She also said that Cook had requested to go with them as she had never been to Brill and had been told it was a very pretty village and had superb views over the surrounding countryside, provided the men had no objections, of course.

The men readily agreed and when told that cook had prepared a hamper to take with them in case they were out all day, the strained atmosphere round the table changed to one of relaxed cordiality, especially when Bertie started to tell one of his seafaring stories about pirates and when he was skippering a boat in the Bay of Bengal.

Breakfast was cleared away, Sissy given her orders for the day and the car loaded with tools, rope, old blankest (to protect the car from the tiles), food and a first aid kit, 'just in case'. Mrs Black gave Digger the instructions she had taken down the previous day and told him that the farmer had said that the building in question was to be found not far from the old village windmill. She said that she would telephone the farmer and arrange for someone to meet them there at around nine thirty.

They set off on the Bicester road and found the side road to Brill just outside the village of Oakley. It was a beautiful spring morning and as they climbed the winding road up the hill both Cook and Bertie turned round to enjoy the view of the Oxfordshire countryside as it spread out behind them. Digger parked the car in The Square just down from the cross and they all got out and started to look around for a windmill.

"It's not like it is something small," said Digger, "it's got to be here somewhere. There's a post office over there, I'll pop across and get directions from them."

He walked across to the Post Office and explained what he was looking for and was told where to find the windmill and where the postmistress believed the building in question might be. He called the others over and they all got back into the car and he drove once round The Square, since they were pointing the wrong way and turned first left after the large red brick house, in the general direction that the postmistress had indicated.

"We should see the Windmill any minute now," Digger informed them, "and we need to take a track which goes down the side of it. Ah, here it is, hold on to your hats, this is going to be bumpy."

They drove for another twenty yards, which seemed a lot longer, when Bertie cried out, "Stop a minute Digger, there's a man waving at us over here. Do we know the farmer's name?"

Cook and Digger both shook their heads as Bertie wound the window down.

"Good day sir, are you the farmer with the roof tiles?" Bertie called out. The man nodded and pointed to a level piece of ground just beyond where he was standing. "Digger, I think we need to drive through that gate and park where the farmer was pointing, be careful though, as there are some large ruts in the track," said Bertie.

They parked the car and everyone got out and stared at the dilapidated building in front of them.

The farmer came over to where they were standing and mopping his forehead with a large blue handkerchief said, "No trouble then in finding us, that's good. That old stable there, (pointing to the single story building that they had been looking at) is the one we are pulling down and you are welcome to all the tiles you can take. Did the vicar mention that I am charging a shilling each?"

"He told me on the phone that it was sixpence," interjected Cook.

"Sixpence if they are chipped, a shilling if they are not chipped," stated the farmer.

Digger moved in front of Cook and said that a shilling was fine for whole tiles and mentioned that the vicar wanted a few for himself as well.

"I am away on business for most of the day," said the farmer, " but my wife is around the farm, you can pay her for the tiles when you leave. I have to warn you that the building is in very poor condition and you do this at your own risk, I hope that is clearly understood. Rather you than me, I hate heights anyway."

"We understand that, thank you. Do you have a ladder we can borrow to get up on the roof," asked Digger.

"There should be one just inside the stable along with some lengths of timber that might be useful, but I say again, that's an old roof so do be careful," replied the farmer, with which he said goodbye and left.

"If you and Bertie want to get started Digger, I will go over and say hello to the farmer's wife and see if I can organise a cup of tea," suggested Cook.

"Good idea Cook," said Digger, "mind you it looks like we could be in for a hot day, so it might be worth buying some lemonade or suchlike from that shop we passed. Come on Bertie, let's inspect this stable and decided the safest approach to this job."

They circled the stable completely and found that the end wall nearest to the car was intact and sound but the back wall was badly cracked and bowed and the other end wall had large chunks of it missing, like someone had driven a large vehicle into it. The front of the building had lost all of its doors years ago and had just been used as a store for hay and straw. Although the roof sagged badly in a lot of places, most of the tiles were in place, although a large number were damaged.

When they went inside they spotted the ladder and the timber lying by the end wall and were surprised to see that a large number of the roof beams were missing and most of the remainder had large cracks in them, where they had struggled to hold the weight of the roof.

Digger turned to Bertie and said, "What do you think we should do? I could climb up inside over there and try and break a hole in the roof and take the tiles off from inside, or rest the ladder against the outside of that sound end wall and work my way in from the top."

"If you want my honest opinion Digger, I think we should climb back into the car and drive home. That roof is a death trap, there is no way you can risk working inside, for if it collapsed on you, I don't think you would survive. The strongest part of the roof is in fact the end by the other wall and if we were to wedge a couple of pieces of that timber under that section there (pointing to the roof about ten feet out from the end wall) if it did give way, it would take enough of the weight to allow you to get down safely."

They agreed that this was the best approach and proceeded to wedge two stout poles under the ridge beam, tying them in place with the rope. They then took the ladder outside and found a safe piece of wall to rest it against which would allow Digger to climb up onto the roof.

"I guess the next question is how do I get them down from the roof. I need to work quickly and don't want to make a pile of tiles as they might slip or the weight might be too great."

"The ground in front of the stable is wet and boggy," replied Bertie, "if I spread some of that straw on top of it, I reckon you could slide them down the roof and if I don't manage to catch them, they will land in the straw and probably be all right. I have my gardening gloves in the car, I will go and fetch them and the tools. Why don't you count the sound tiles in that area and see if it will be enough."

Bertie got the tools and gave them to Digger and then spread some bales of straw in the area he had suggested. By now Digger was on the roof and slowly working his way along the ridge.

"Tell me when I am over the supported part Bertie, as I don't need to go any further than that. If I start two rows down from the ridge and just take off all the tiles from about back there to the wall on this side, it will give us enough for our needs and also the ones I promised the vicar."

"That will do, you are right over the support poles now. Look, there is a broken tile near your foot, if you can ease that one out with the wooden wedges I gave you, it will give you a good start to get at the rest of them."

To his surprise the tile lifted out quite easily and he slid it down the roof. Bertie caught it and put it down to one side. Although a large piece of it was missing, he was surprised how heavy it was and told Digger to make sure he called out, every time he slid one down the roof to him.

The first row of tiles was off in about thirty minutes and safely stacked to the side of the stable. Digger was feeling stiff and was glad to climb down and stretch his legs.

They both went inside to inspect the roof and were pleased to note that there was no movement in the supporting beams that they could detect.

"Those cross beams look strong and should be able to support your weight, because you will not be able to remain seated on the ridge for the next row. It is probably best to get out to the supported section again astride the ridge, but you will need to test that first beam for your weight. Mind you, if it carried those tiles, it should carry you all right," commented Bertie.

"One of those ridge tiles is loose. I wasn't sure whether to pull it off or leave it in place, I am fearful it will come off completely - with me on top of it. Right, let's get cracking again. I was hoping Cook would have been back with a drink by now, probably nattering to the farmer's wife somewhere."

The next hour passed quickly with both men knowing what to do and working well as a team. They had more than enough good tiles stacked ready for loading into the car when Cook arrived with a drink for them. Digger carefully got down from the roof and stretched himself and rubbed the stiffness out of his legs and arms and Cook commended the pair for all they had achieved that morning. She admitted that she had not made it to the shop having found the farmer's wife to have been a very pleasant lady with a similar background to herself, having originally come from the Yorkshire Dales.

They packed some of the tiles into the boot and back seat and were putting the tools away when Digger remembered he had left the slate ripper wedged under a tile on the roof. Wanting to impress Cook with his skill and agility, he climbed back onto the roof and worked his way down the ridge, while she stared at his antics in horror. He held the tool firmly and tried to pull it free, but for some reason it was wedged solid. He decided to give it a little twist on his next attempt, which did free the tool but the tile itself shot into the air and then started its descent of the roof. He sat there mesmerized watching it cartwheel down the roof and only at the last minute did he think to shout a warning to those below.

Cook gasped and tried to move, but her feet were stuck in the mud and she was right in the tile's path. Had it not been for Bertie reaching out and diverting it with his gloved hand, it would certainly have struck her on the forehead. As it was, he was unable to catch it and all he managed to achieve was to divert it onto his own head. It caught him just above the right ear and he went down like a sack of potatoes. Fortunately the cap he was wearing had taken some of the blow and prevented his head from being split open.

Digger quickly climbed down and ran to his friend. He was out cold but he was breathing, so it was agreed that Cook would stay with Bertie while Digger went to the farmhouse to summon help.

A telephone call to the pub, up from the windmill, ascertained that the doctor was having his lunch and he arrived, quite breathless about five minutes later, with some of the men from the pub. Together they carried him to the surgery, where to everyone's relief, Bertie came to and asked for a drink.

The doctor then checked him over and realised that he was seeing double but was otherwise all right. He said that Bertie must not be left alone until his vision was back to normal and his own doctor had pronounced him fit.

Cook asked if she could use the telephone and the doctor directed her to the room next door. She returned a few minutes later and announced that Mrs Duffy-Smythe had agreed that Bertie could use the guest room until he was better, which would mean they could all keep an eye on him.

Bertie, of course protested that this was unnecessary, but Cook put on her 'I'm in charge here' look and told him it was all agreed and that she would never forgive herself in anything happened to the man who quite possibly saved her life.

They took a slow drive home, calling in on their own doctor on their way, who said he would speak to the doctor at Brill and come and visit Bertie a bit later in the day. While Digger went to pick up Bertie's things from the cottage and make sure everything was in order, Cook and Mrs Black helped him up the stairs to the guest room.

The doctor duly came and gave him a thorough examination and said that they should try and keep Bertie awake for as long as possible, so they all took turns in chatting to him, except for Mrs Duffy-Smythe who was still very upset over the previous day's events.

When Mrs Black asked how much the tiles had cost, Digger explained the price mix up and that he had forgotten to pay for them in view of all that had happened and that most of them were still stacked by the stable. She then telephoned the farmer and after giving an update on Bertie's condition, apologised for not paying for the tiles and arranged that she and Digger would return for the remainder of the tiles on Thursday morning, when she would personally settle all that was owed to him.

CHAPTER ELEVEN
GREAT AUNT MARY

The doctor called to see Bertie after surgery on Thursday morning and was pleased to announce that there was no lasting injury for him to worry about. He said that he should be able to get up and walk around a little today and would be fit enough to return home on Friday.

Cook felt obliged to recount his heroic actions to the doctor, who shared her opinion that he had certainly saved her from a very serious injury and noted the subtle change in her demeanour, that the whole incident seemed to have occasioned.

In their own conversations, a certain warmth had crept into their discussions and Mrs Duffy-Smythe was astounded to hear Bertie refer to her as 'Victoria' rather than Cook.

Mrs Black and Digger had left for Brill right after breakfast and had enjoyed the ride along the country lanes and the opportunity for Digger to tell her a little about the life he and Ron had shared overseas in the army. They first drove to the farmhouse and paid the farmer's wife for the tiles and then down to the old stable where they collected the tiles and carefully loaded them into the back of the car. They then called to thank the doctor who had been so helpful yesterday in patching up Bertie and returned to

Millstone House in time for lunch. Digger was delighted to see his friend was up and about and commented to Sissy that Cook seemed different somehow.

"You don't know the half of it Arnold," she said, "she's hardly left him alone all morning and been really pleasant to me, when she has been downstairs. I said I didn't want to clean out the laundry today and she said I could leave it for another day if I wanted. That has never happened before!"

"How strange," replied Digger, "I had the impression that she really didn't have much time for Bertie before yesterday."

Their conversation was interrupted by Mrs Black who had just walked into the kitchen, "I have just heard the weather report Arnold and we are in for bad weather tomorrow and Saturday, I was wondering if it would be worth replacing some of those broken tiles on your roof this afternoon."

"Good idea Mrs Black, I could do with some help though, those tiles weigh a ton."

"My brother's home today, he's been up on our roof a few times, I could go and see if he'd help, if you like," interjected Sissy.

Mrs Black smiled at her, "An excellent idea Sissy, tell him I will pay him three shillings for an afternoon's work, if he can come at once."

Sissy grabbed her coat and hat and ran out of the house to find her brother and talk him into coming, hoping that she would make at least sixpence out of the deal for herself.

"That's bad news about the weather though, Moira was hoping to visit her great aunt in Buckingham on Saturday and asked me to go with her," commented Digger.

"Buckingham, that's quite a difficult place to get to from here. You could get a bus from Aylesbury, or even Bicester come to that, how had you planned to travel?" asked Mrs Black.

"That's a good question, perhaps I will pop round and see her later on, you don't mind if I am out all day Saturday, do you."

"Of course not, but bear in mind, if getting there is difficult, getting back could be even worse. I might well be able to give you a lift in the morning to Aylesbury, but you will probably need a taxi back in the evening and that is going to be expensive."

Sissy turned up with 'Young Tom' in tow and he and Digger discussed the best way to tackle to roof. They decided that they could best get out onto the roof through the window in Digger's bedroom but soon realised that the roof was too steep to walk on without some sort of support. They found a short length of ladder in the garage which they were able to get onto the roof and tie in place using various hooks and projections that they found. It was a slow job, but they worked well together, conscious the whole time that an accident was just waiting to happen.

During the course of the afternoon, they managed to replace seven broken tiles and a further eight that were missing completely and became adept at walking across the roof and moving the ladder to where it was needed.

By five o'clock they had both had enough and decided to call it a day. At least Digger thought that his bed should stay dry, the next time it rained. They left the ladder tied down on the roof and made their way back through the window.

Tom received his three shillings from Mrs Black and he and Sissy walked home while Digger took Mac for a walk in the wood and collected some more fuel for his own fire, he thought he just about had time to wash before dinner, when there was a knock at the door and Mac barked excitedly.

"It's me Digger, don't let him jump up, I'm still a bit groggy on my feet," said Bertie.

Digger held onto Mac's collar while Bertie came in and sat down.

"Victoria asked me to tell you that dinner would be a little later tonight, about fifteen minutes. So you have time to make an old man a cup of tea and keep me from over-zealous females."

"I assume by Victoria, you mean Cook?" asked Digger as he lifted the kettle off the range and filled the teapot with water.

"The very same, I gather it is some sort of an honour to be allowed to call her by her proper name."

"Honour in deed old chap. I once made the mistake of asking her name and she barely spoke to me the rest of the day. One lump or three?" asked Digger. He made the tea and passed a cup to Bertie.

"I was just about to wash before dinner, I'll leave the door open so we can chat."

Digger removed his working clothes and went into the washroom, taking the kettle with him. He washed and shaved and also washed his hair as it was covered in moss and dirt from the roof, but found conversation was difficult as Bertie was obviously playing with the dog. His head was immersed in the big white towel as he emerged from the washroom and realised that Bertie had company, apart from Mac.

"Hold on Digger, ladies present," called Bertie.

He lifted his head from the towel to find Cook and Moira both standing next to where Bertie was sitting, "Oh sorry, I didn't hear you come in. Just turn your backs please while I go up and change." With which he scooped up his clothes and retired to the safety of his bedroom. When he came down stairs again, the room was empty, so he filled the kettle and put it back on the range and then walked down to the kitchen.

Cook was standing by the stove stirring a pot of soup, "Mrs Duffy-Smythe has decided we are all to eat in the dining room tonight, Arnold and since Moira called in to see how Bertie was, she has been invited to join us. If you can pour the soup into that tureen for me and then follow me, I should be obliged."

Digger did as he was told and then followed her through the house into the dining room. This was a fairly large room with two big windows that overlooked the garden. Everyone was seated around a large oval table and Cook indicated that he should take the chair between Bertie and Moira. No-one spoke while Cook served the soup and then Bertie, unable to contain himself any longer, turned and said, "Well it's good to see you with some clothes on again Digger!" at which the whole table erupted in laughter to Digger's obvious embarrassment.

"Mrs Black has said she will take us to Aylesbury on Saturday morning Digger, isn't that kind of her?" said Moira. "We can easily get a bus to Buckingham from there and I spoke to George at Bell Ringing on Monday and he says that there is a train from Bicester on Saturday evening which stops at Upper Style Army Depot Station, so we can do a circular route."

"That's great Moira; I assume we will be able to get a bus from Buckingham to Bicester OK? What time is the train from Bicester?"

"George said it normally runs at five past eight, but in order to make certain we catch it, he says we should arrive before seven forty, as it can leave up to twenty minutes earlier, if the mainline train has been delayed."

The rest of the meal passed pleasantly and Digger and Mac walked Moira home afterwards and then returned to the cottage. He put the kettle on made a drink but since there was no obvious sign of Bertie around the kitchen area, he and Mac drank alone.

The forecast rain arrived overnight and much to his relief, the new tiles did the trick and kept his room dry, although there were several leaks in the garage and laundry which would need fixing in the near future.

At breakfast, Bertie announced that he was going home and Cook insisted on escorting him there and asked Digger to carry a large hamper of food she had prepared for him. The rain had stopped when they set off and Bertie seemed his old self again. Digger dropped the hamper in the kitchen and left Bertie and Cook to sort things out, while he returned to Millstone for a day of woodcutting and painting with a little bit of gardening, thrown in for good measure, in the late afternoon.

The postman called in the morning with a package for Cook, who arrived back at Millstone just in time for lunch, looking a little flushed, which she explained was due to the fact that she had been rushing. She left the house again in the afternoon, with the package but did not say where she was going, but instructed Sissy to prepare a cold buffet for everyone to eat in the evening.

When the time for Dinner came, Cook was still absent, so Digger and the two ladies helped themselves to the cold buffet and proceeded to eat. No sooner had they started, than Cook arrived and apologised for being late and explained that Bertie had started to feel giddy during the afternoon and she had not wanted to leave him, but he was all right again now.

When Digger suggested that he might pop round after dinner to check up on him, she almost bit his head off and said that all Bertie needed was to be left alone and to enjoy a good night's sleep in his own bed.

Digger was about to make some comment about whose friend Bertie really was, but decided against it and just finished his meal and went back to the cottage.

Mrs Duffy-Smythe was the first to speak, "That outburst was quite unnecessary Cook, Arnold was only concerned about his friend, but he need not be, need he? There was nothing wrong with Bertie, was there?"

"I don't interfere in your affairs and I'll thank you not to interfere in mine," snapped Cook.

"Well for a start you do interfere, as you put it, in my affairs, but I prefer to think of it as the concern of a real friend, which is what I am endeavouring to do for you, right now. I watched your face as you undid the parcel and read its contents, earlier today. You looked like you had seen a ghost. But if you do not wish to talk about it, then that is your affair."

"Good," said Cook, "well that's all settled then. It's a confidential matter which Bertie has kindly been helping me with this afternoon and as soon as it has any bearing on my position here, I will inform you. He did feel a little faint this afternoon and is fine now, but it had nothing to do with the accident!" She smiled at them both and got up and went to her room, leaving them to clear away the dinner plates and dishes and to do the washing up.

"Well Amanda, what did you make of that?"

"In all the years we have known her, Bertie is the first person ever to be told her name apart from us and we really know nothing about her life before she joined us. Maybe something or someone, has come back from her past and she finds it easier to discuss it with a stranger than with us.

I wonder though, what exactly she meant by 'any bearing on her position here'."

Breakfast was a quiet affair and straight afterwards Mrs Black and Digger drove off into the village and picked up Moira. She was standing at the window when they arrived and jumped into the back seat. She said that her great aunt loved flowers, so she intended to buy some at Aylesbury to save the risk of them getting damaged on her bike, yesterday.

Mrs Black dropped them off at the bus station and then went on to do some shopping while the two young people investigated the timetables. The next bus was due in thirty five minutes so they went off to buy some flowers and get a cup of tea, which Digger paid for, having been paid for his work and reimbursed for his expenses that morning.

When they returned to the bus stop, there were already a dozen people in the queue and it was starting to drizzle again, so everyone made a dash for the bus when it arrived. Moira sat by the window about halfway down on the pavement side of the bus and Digger slid in beside her. This was the closest he had been to her and to any woman for that matter, for quite some time and as he looked out of the window, he could not help but notice what lovely clear skin she had and how nice her hair was looking and suddenly he felt good about himself.

"Now you paid for the tea, Digger, so I am paying for the bus fare and no arguments."

Just then the conductor came along and Digger asked for two singles to Buckingham,

"Is that the stop on the outskirts or in the centre?" asked the conductor.

"The centre please," said Moira and gave him the fare. "We need to travel to Bicester this evening; can we get the bus from the same stop?"

"Yes, Miss, twenty past the hour and the last bus is nine twenty."

She thanked him and then took a packet of Polo's out of her pocket and offered them to Digger, who took one and said, "My friend Ginger held the unit record for keeping a polo intact in his mouth, have a guess how long."

"Ten minutes." He shook his head. "Twenty minutes." He shook his head again. "An hour." He shook again. "Oh, I give in. If he lasted longer than an hour he must have been cheating."

"Very good, you are right, he did cheat, he kept it wrapped in silver foil and it lasted a day. We had all bet a shilling, but the rules didn't preclude wrapping, so we all had to pay up. He did take us out for a meal though."

With such light-hearted chatter the journey soon passed and they arrived in the centre of the county town of Buckingham about ten minutes after the rain had stopped and alighted from the bus. "My aunt's little house is this way," said Moira, leading him through a maze of streets to the gate of an old timbered cottage, with the most impeccably kept front garden. Moira knocked at the door and an elderly lady, grey haired but erect answered the door.

"Moira dear, how lovely to see you and this must be your young man Arnold, that you mentioned on the telephone, do come in both of you, it's grand of you to come and see me on my birthday."

She took them into her front room where Moira kissed her and gave her the flowers. The room was full of furniture and ornaments and pictures, but somehow, it didn't look crowded or untidy. Since it had been a cold wet morning and she knew they were one of Moira's favourites, she had cooked 'Stovies' for them, which were eaten around a roaring fire with large mugs of tea.

"These are delicious," said Digger, after his second plateful, "I've never had these before. Have you been down here very long err, I'm sorry, I don't know what to call you."

"Well Arnold, to answer your questions, I have been down here for over forty years and you have a choice as regards my name. My students called me Miss Ballater and my friends call me Mary, which do you prefer."

"I prefer Mary, if that is OK. What did you teach?"

"I taught history, art and music and more recently I have been teaching the piano to aspiring young musicians. Do you play an instrument at all?"

"I was allowed to play the bass drum in the Boys Brigade band, but that is the limit of my musical achievements."

"The BB Arnold, well that will impress Dod, Moira's dad. I assume you know he is a Boys Brigade Captain."

"No, I didn't, well I'll be!"

"So what did you buy Moira Arnold, or am I not allowed to know?" asked Aunt Mary.

Digger looked puzzled and then spotted Moira smiling to her aunt, "Is there something I don't know here Moira."

"Oh you bad cruel girl, fancy not telling him it was your birthday as well as mine. Shame on you, imagine how he must feel."

"Aunt, we have only been friends for just over a week, how could I say it was my birthday, it would not have been fair."

"Arnold, there is a sweet shop at the bottom of this road and this young lady loves home-made fudge and I happen to know that they have some in today, if you would like to get her some," suggested Aunt Mary.

"Thanks Mary, I will do just that, excuse me ladies."

The bottom of the road, was in fact almost a quarter of a mile away, so by the time Digger returned, aunt Mary had gleaned all the necessary facts and feelings on the matter of the boy friend, from her great niece and proceeded to spend the rest of the day enjoying their company and deciding on the worthiness of Digger.

They said goodbye to the old lady at seven o'clock and slowly walked down to the bus stop, and caught the bus for Bicester, which arrived at the bus stop just after twenty past. They purchased their fare and told the conductor that they were catching a train to the depot on the Princes Risborough line and he advised that they should alight at the Bicester North railway station, which they did, arriving there with fifteen minutes to spare. The ticket office was closed, so they walked onto the platform and sat down in the waiting room.

No-one else came into the waiting room but there was some activity on the other platform so Digger walked across the bridge and spoke to a porter.

"Excuse me, are we on the right platform for the train to the army depot near Upper Style?"

"You are on the right platform mate, but you are twelve hours early, the train leaves five past eight tomorrow morning, not tonight," replied the porter.

"But how do we get home tonight then?" asked Digger.

"You could catch the last train to Risborough, but then you would still need to get a taxi from there, if there are any around at that time of night. Your best bet is to get a room in the hotel and catch the train tomorrow. At least you know that's certain."

Digger thanked the porter and walked back over the bridge to where Moira was anxiously waiting for him.

"We have a problem Moira. George got his train times wrong. It leaves at five past eight in the morning, not in the evening and from what the porter just told me, I don't think we can get home tonight."

"What did the porter say, are there any alternatives?" she asked.

They discussed their options, including going back to Aunt Mary's in Buckingham and in the end decided they could just about afford a couple of rooms at the hotel between them, so they walked into town.

The receptionist smiled and checked her book, "We have one double room, what name shall I say?" she asked.

"No, you don't understand," said Moira, "we need two rooms, not one, we are not married, just friends."

"Well, I am sorry Miss, but the rest of the rooms are taken, I am sure the gentleman can sleep on the floor. It looks like someone else is coming in, so make up your mind quickly please."

"We will take it please, the name is Leith, Miss M Leith," interjected Digger. "Miss Leith will need a call at six forty and breakfast for two at seven fifteen, will that be alright?"

"Yes sir," she replied, "room eleven it is; first floor, turn right and the second room on the right, the stairs are over there. Have a pleasant evening."

She handed him the key and Moira signed the register and he led the way into the foyer where they both sat down in the corner seat.

"You just listen to me Arnold Smith, I don't know what kinds of girls you are used to, but if you think I am going to spend the night in this hotel with you, then you are sorely mistaken, do you understand me?"

"Well Miss Leith," he replied, "I am used to decent girls, just like you and it never crossed my mind that you would consider spending the night with me in this hotel. This will not be the first time I have spent the night in a station waiting room, but it may be the last, so here is the key to the room, I will see you at breakfast tomorrow morning, downstairs at seven fifteen. Goodnight Moira and thank you for a lovely day."

As he started to rise Moira threw her arms round his neck and gave him a big kiss. "Goodnight Digger, I am so sorry that I doubted you, thank you for being such a gentleman, this has been the best birthday ever." She then kissed him again and went upstairs to her room.

It was just starting to rain again when he left the hotel, so he set off at a good pace for the station. The fire in the waiting room had gone out when Digger returned, but the room was still quite warm and he had it all to himself. The wooden bench was just about long enough for him, so he collected up some newspapers which were lying around the room and laid them out on top of himself. It took him a while to drop off to sleep as he ran the day's events over in his mind and was still sound asleep when the London express thundered through the station at around five thirty, the next morning. He freshened up in the washroom and managed to scrounge a mug of tea from the early morning porter when he arrived for work and then took a slow walk back to the hotel.

He and Moira enjoyed the sausage and egg breakfast and found conversation to be both easy and enjoyable while eating toast and drinking tea. They pooled their finances and were able to pay the hotel bill with enough left over to buy some cigarettes at the corner shop they passed. The walk back to the station was soon completed and they arrived in good time to catch the train, which left dead on five past eight.

When they arrived at Upper Style, George was nowhere to be seen and although Digger called his name out loud, several times, George did not appear. "I bet he knew he had made a mistake and given us the wrong time, he has deliberately kept out of our way," said Digger, "you wait till I see him at practice, I'll give him what for."

"We all make mistakes," said Moira, "no harm done." They both laughed and then slowly walked down the road to the village, past the church and on to her home.

In thinking about it later, Digger was not sure at which point he held her hand, or she held his, but they both knew that a romance had started and when they arrived back at her house, she felt very comfortable at inviting him in for a drink.

CHAPTER TWELVE
COOK'S PACKAGE

Moira and Digger freshened up at her house and arrived in church with just a few minutes to spare. When they sat down together in Bertie's usual pew, they were virtually announcing to the whole village that they were now ' going out' together.

The vicar's wife made a point of speaking to them after the service and invited them both to dinner, which they were pleased to accept. Since Cook was not in church, Digger asked Mrs Black, who had attended the service with her sister, to make his excuses to Cook, explaining that they had been invited out to dinner elsewhere.

It was a traditional roast lamb dinner, with roast potatoes, parsnips and cabbage, followed by apple pie and custard. While the ladies did the washing up, the men cleared the table and discussed the football results.

Meanwhile, at Bertie's cottage, he and Cook were discussing the contents of the package she had received on Friday.

"For goodness sake Victoria, either you take me into your confidence and tell me the whole story from start to finish or you and this package can leave my house right now.

How can I possibly give you any sound advice, when I only know half the facts of the matter!" said Bertie angrily.

"No-one outside of my own family knows the whole story Bertie and it's not going to be easy for me, because it will bring back too many bad memories, but you are right and I would like you to know about my past," she answered. "Let's sit down by the fire and we can chat."

Bertie poured them another cup of tea and they made themselves comfortable.

She began, "I was born in a small cottage a few miles from Penrith in the Lake District. My father was a farmhand and my mother sometimes helped out picking potatoes and such like. We were poor, but so was everyone else in the area, life was hard but it was good. My elder brother and I went to the local school and it was there that I met Dick who was the son of the game keeper on the local estate. We were lifelong friends and always knew we would one day be married, as indeed we were on my eighteenth birthday. Dick was just a few months older than me and worked with his father on the estate. When we got married he was allocated an estate cottage and we set up home and had four blissful months of wedded life together."

"Do you mind if I ask the odd question, Victoria, just to clarify things in my own mind?" enquired Bertie.

"To be honest, I would rather just tell the whole story at one go, for if I stop, I may not get started again. Save your questions to the end please Bertie," she answered.

"Anyway, one day Dick was asked to help with a shoot on a local estate and his dad said it would be a good chance to earn a few bob extra, so he agreed. I packed his lunch as usual, kissed him goodbye and that was the last time I saw him alive. They said it was an accident; they said that he walked in front of the guns; but he would never have done that. Dick had been out with his dad at shoots since he was a boy, his father had drilled into him how to behave at a shoot and where you should stand to be safe from the guns. We all knew it was just not true, it was just a cover up. There wasn't even an inquest; they just said it was his fault, 'a hunting accident'!"

"Oh Bertie, I loved him so much, it still hurts deep down whenever I think of him, my lovely husband, my wonderful handsome man, shot down like that!" At which point she just broke down and sobbed.

Bertie walked over to her chair and sat on the arm and put his arm around her and just sat with her, what could he say to someone who was still grieving the husband she lost over forty years ago.

She finally stopped sobbing and went to the washroom while Bertie made the tea and cut some bread, which they toasted over the fire. It was almost an hour later when she felt sufficiently recovered to continue with the story.

"The funeral for Dick was held the following week and the Estate Manager came to see me shortly afterwards and told me I had to get out of the cottage. I was given two weeks to vacate my home, as they wanted it for another family. I went to stay with my brother who now worked at a Saddlers in Penrith, but they were almost as poor as we had been and could not afford to keep me, so I got a job working in the local grocers. The shop was owned by a Mr Owen who was a widower with a teenage son called Howard. I was beginning to get myself together again and thought everything was going well until my sister-in-law became pregnant and my brother asked me if I could find somewhere else to live before the baby was due."

She stopped for a drink, so Bertie took the opportunity to ask whether her brother was still alive and she told him that he was and that he still lived in the Lake District, but was not in very good health.

"My employer got to hear of my predicament and asked if I would consider marrying him and becoming the second Mrs Owen. To be honest I was still in shock over Dick's death and was surprised that Mr Owen had made this proposal, I had no idea he had such warm feelings for me. I asked my family what they thought about the offer and was amazed to discover that my parents thought it was a very good offer and that I should accept his proposal. My brother thought it was too soon and that I should say no, but his wife, who was pregnant, wanted me out of her house and she supported the view of my parents. To cut a long story short, we got married the week before my sister-in-law had the baby and I moved out of their house and into the Owen's house which was directly next door to the grocers. And then my troubles really started!"

"I can't believe you were encouraged to marry someone you didn't love, just to get a roof over your head. They must have realised that you were still grieving for your late husband and were in no state to make such a decision," said Bertie.

"Oh don't tell me, I know! If I had been able to think straight, I would never have married him, but don't get me wrong, he was a good kind man and always treated me well, it wasn't him, it was the son, Howard. While I was just working in the shop, he was quite civil to me. Oh, he could be a bit stuck up, because his dad was someone in the town, but once I became his stepmother, he was just intolerable, he made my life hell on earth!"

"Surely his father dealt with it, he didn't leave you to handle him on his own, did he?" asked Bertie.

"He tried, but Howard lied and said I was making it up and his father was not strong enough to deal with him. I endured this for five years and then Howard went off to join the army and my life changed once again. As I said, my husband was a good man and treated me well and although we didn't love each other in the way that Dick and I did, we did respect and care for each other and to be honest, I enjoyed the 'middle class' way of life, it was certainly a lot better than being working class and living in poverty." She stopped and drank some more of her tea and then continued with her story.

"Howard would come home on leave every now and then and we would tolerate each other for these short periods, but there was never any love lost between us. I somehow managed to get pregnant once, but had a miscarriage and it never happened again.

We lived together for another fifteen years after Howard left to join the army and then my husband became ill. He lost almost five stone in a year and I had to watch him slowly waste away. He died on New Year's Day1925. When the solicitor came to read the Will, I discovered, that despite what he had promised me, he had never changed it from when his first wife died. The son got the shop, all the stock, the house everything and I got nothing."

"That's terrible," said Bertie, "you say that he had promised you something, did he give you any idea what it would be?"

"He always said he would leave me a fifty percent share in the shop and everything else and I am certain he meant it, he just never changed his Will. I had virtually run that shop for him, unpaid, for all those years and Howard knew this, but true to form he lied about it and said his father had always promised it to him. In the end I was handed One Hundred Pounds and given two weeks to leave and since I had nowhere to go, I had to give up all rights to the furniture and everything else that was mine, apart from what I could carry with me."

"Is Howard still there then, is that why you have been asked to visit this solicitor in Kendal?" asked Bertie.

"No, he sold the business, the house and everything in it. After that, he left the army and disappeared with the proceeds; I had no idea what happened to him and neither did I care. But look, I really don't want to go to see these people in Kendal on my own Bertie and my brother is just too sick to come with me; would you come with me please?"

"Hold on a moment, I think I heard something outside," said Bertie and as he got up from his chair, the front door opened and Mac came bounding in, closely followed by Digger.

"Hi Bertie, how are we today, Mac get down, bad boy!" said Digger, holding the dog's collar so that he could not jump up on the chair.

Before Bertie could reply, Cook was up out of her chair and standing in front of Digger with her hands on her hips and a face like thunder, "How dare you come bursting in like that on a sick man, I told you yesterday not to bother him, he needs rest, why must you always be so rude and inconsiderate, get out Arnold and take the dog with you, Bertie needs to rest," with which she went across and opened the front door, indicating that they should leave now.

Bertie and Digger stood there looking at each other speechless and then Bertie got up from his chair and walked across to Digger and said quietly in his ear, "Let's go outside my friend, we need to talk in private."

As they walked through the door, Cook was about to say something else, but the withering look that Bertie gave her made the words freeze on her lips. Once outside Digger started to apologise but Bertie interrupted him, "Digger my friend, I think I have made it clear that I enjoy your friendship and that you are welcome any time, without formal invitation, to drop into my home to see me. I can only apologise most sincerely for what was just said inside and I assure you that the sentiments expressed were definitely not mine. She has insulted a good friend in my house and although there are extenuating circumstances I am not able to discuss with you, I will advise her of that fact straight away, so for the moment I would be grateful if you would leave us alone, so that I can do just that."

"I am sorry Bertie for causing a problem between you and Cook, but she often snaps at me like that, I guess we just don't get on. Anyway, I am glad to see you are looking so much better and I was wondering if I could borrow your ladder tomorrow. There is heavy rain forecast for the rest of the week and there are still some tiles to replace over the garage and laundry."

"Of course you can, if you come round tomorrow morning, I will give you a hand with it, but if you will excuse me for now, I have some important issues to sort out."

They shook hands and Mac and master walked back to Millstone and Bertie slowly walked indoors.

"Of all the cheek, barging in like that on a sick man," began Cook, but she got no further-

"Sit down Victoria, we need to chat; sit down please Victoria, I don't want to ask you again," ordered Bertie.

She sat and waited while he got his thoughts together, "You have just insulted a friend of mine, in my home. Friendship is the most important thing in the world to me, life is about our relationships with other people. I have toured the world in my time and seen many wonderful sights, the Pyramids, the fjords of Norway, the sunset over the Indian Ocean, Sydney Harbour Bridge, the palace of Versailles, I have had wealth and lost it again, but the thing I treasure most is a good friend and that's what young

Digger is becoming, a good friend. What you just did had absolutely nothing to do with me being sick, it was plain unadulterated spitefulness. He happened to arrive at a time that was inconvenient to you, so you just launched into verbal abuse on someone who had just came to visit a friend. My great uncle Harry used to say, 'spitefulness and bitterness are like *Frost in Spring*'. As a late frost indiscriminately kills all the young shoots and destroys the blossom on the fruit trees, so a spiteful and bitter person affects everyone they come into contact with."

He walked over to the window and then came back and stood in front of her, "I know you have had a hard life Victoria and have not been treated fairly, but that should make you more sympathetic towards other people, who have problems of their own, like Digger. Earlier you asked me if I would go to Kendal to visit the solicitor with you and I was about to say yes, before you revealed this other side to your nature. I suggest we both think about it for a few days, because I am not so sure I want to get involved with your affairs now; if you are not able to control your resentment, then I don't think I will be able to help you."

She got up, picked up her package and walked to the door and opened it, as she was leaving he made his final remark to her, "By the way Victoria, I expect you to have apologised to Digger, before we talk again. Goodbye."

As she walked home, the lump in her throat got bigger and bigger and she only just made it to the safety of her own parlour before she broke down and wept. "Why does this keep happening to me," she asked herself, "why can't I meet someone for once to look after me and care for me, why did Bertie have to be so horrible to me and he expects me to apologise to Digger, never!"

Breakfast on Monday morning was a do-it-yourself affair, as Cook was not feeling well and had remained in bed. Young Tom turned up with Sissy, just after eight thirty so he and Digger and Mac went to Bertie's to get the ladder. When they arrived at the cottage, Bertie was out in the garden, feeling his old self again, which was just as well as Mac was in a distinctly playful mood. They had a cup of tea together and then got the ladder out from behind the shed and Tom and Digger carried it back to Millstone.

The two men worked well together and by late afternoon had all the remaining broken and missing tiles replaced and were able to return the ladder to Bertie. Since Mrs Black had already paid Tom he went off home and Digger and Bertie sat in the garden just chatting and catching up with each other. Neither mentioned the previous day's incident, but both were pleased that it had not affected their friendship.

Mrs Duffy-Smythe knocked on Cook's door at around nine thirty and said, "It's only me, I have brought some breakfast for you, how are you feeling today?"

She went in and put the tray on the bed but got no response from Cook, so she left again. When she went back in at ten p.m. the breakfast had not been touched, so she sat down on the bed and just sat there to see if Cook would speak to her.

"I don't want to talk, leave me alone please," said Cook.

"Would you like me to ask the doctor to come round and see you?"

"No thank you, I just want to be left alone, my head is sore."

"I will bring you some water and an aspirin, perhaps that will help," said Mrs Duffy-Smythe, with which she took the tray back to the kitchen and returned five minutes later with the glass and tablet which she left on the bedside table.

When she went through to the study, she found her sister making up her shopping list, "I was going into Aylesbury this afternoon Penny, is there anything I can get for you?"

"You might take that broken picture frame with you, I am sure that the little jewellers on the corner that we sometimes go to, would be able to sort it out. Cook is still in her bed and says she has a headache!"

"Goodness me, that must be the second one in fifteen years then! She has been in a strange mood ever since that parcel came and what was it she said to us, about changes to her position here! Something is going on, she was pacing up and down and crying during the night, she woke me up several times with her noise and this house is so quiet normally," replied Mrs Black. "We need to have a talk with her whether she likes it or not, if she is going to leave us, we need to start advertising for someone else and in this area it could take a long time to find someone suitable."

"Well, as you know, I told Arnold to go and ask Bertie if he could borrow his ladder yesterday and he appeared to be in a very subdued mood when he returned. I asked him how Bertie was and if everything was alright and he said Bertie was fine but that he and Cook had crossed swords again, but did not understand why and that Bertie had intervened on his behalf. There is something about Arnold that definitely seems to upset her, which is a real shame, for he is doing such good work here that we really don't want him leaving just yet," said Mrs Duffy-Smythe.

"You are, after all, her employer Penny, why not have a talk with her while I am out this afternoon and if she is going to leave we have the right to know why and when."

When Mrs Duffy-Smythe took in a cup of tea and a biscuit after lunch, Cook was sound asleep, but still sitting up in bed with a newspaper open in front of her. She was surprised to see that it was the 'West Australian' from December 1947 and was open at the farming page.

Someone had put a circle around the recent cattle sale article, which stated that a Mr H Owen had sold five dairy cows at the Pinjarra Saleyards, she also noticed a photograph lying under the paper of a teenage boy's birthday party and a lady, who looked like a younger version of Cook, holding a cake. Written on the back were the words '1906 Howard's 15th birthday'.

She was suddenly aware that Cook was awake and looking at her, she turned towards her and said, "This is you, isn't it? What is this all about and who is the youth in the picture? Why the Australian paper, I need to know what is going on here and I am not leaving until you come up with some answers."

"Very well, sit down and I will tell you the whole story as far as I know it. That is me in the picture and that is my step-son, Howard, on his birthday," replied Cook.

"Your step-son, well I'll be, but you don't look much older than him yourself."

For the next hour, Cook told her the same story she had told Bertie the day before, but this time there were two people weeping over the death of her first husband Dick. On leaving Kendal after the death of her second husband, she went to Lancaster and worked in a hotel for about three years. A regular guest at the hotel was a businessman from London and one day he asked her if she would like to be his housekeeper, he lived in Epsom and travelled to London each day on the train. She remained with him for two years, until he was transferred overseas to India, when she then went to work for an associate of his, who was Mrs Duffy-Smythe's father.

"And the rest you know, until that package came the other day," she said and pointed to the wrapping paper lying on the bed. "It contained a letter from a solicitor in Kendal asking me to go and visit them in order to 'hear something to my advantage' along with the picture of Howard on his fifteenth birthday and the Australian newspaper with the article you saw, circled. I can only assume that the Mr H Owen mentioned in the paper, is the very same obnoxious person that made my life a misery and stole what was rightfully mine."

"Do you need someone to go with you to Kendal, or are you happy going on your own?" asked Mrs Duffy-Smythe.

That simple question was the cause of another bought of weeping and a further hour of conversation, when the events of yesterday afternoon, were explained and discussed in great detail.

"Well I hate to say this Coo!! Look I am tired of calling you Cook, your name is Victoria and that is what Amanda and I will call you in the future, is that understood?"

Cook nodded her agreement, so Mrs Duffy-Smythe continued.

"Well I hate to say this Victoria, but if you care for Bertie half as much as I think you do, whatever the rights and wrongs of the situation, you are going to have to apologise to Arnold and tell me, why is it he seems to upset you so much?"

Cook didn't answer, but opened her bedside drawer and took out a photograph of her and Dick on their wedding day and passed it to Penny.

"Oh my goodness, the similarity between Dick and Arnold is striking, no wonder it has been so difficult for you. But the fact remains, it is still not his fault Victoria, but anyway, it has to be your decision and if you need Amanda or I to go with you, then you only have to ask."

The evening meal was an awkward disjointed affair and Digger was pleased to get back outside and take Mac for a walk in the woods. He also managed to carry back some of the logs from the pile he had made, and drop them in the corner of the garden, for sawing up in the morning. He washed and changed his clothes and then went over to the church for Bell Ringing practice, where he and Moira pulled George's leg endlessly about the train timetable mix up. After practice, he and Davy and Moira walked back to the village pub where they all enjoyed a drink and a game of darts, before Digger escorted Moira back home.

Mrs Duffy-Smythe related all that Cook had told her during the afternoon, to her sister and they both agreed that if Victoria needed someone to accompany her on the trip up to Kendal, then they would both go with her.

"Perhaps if we drive up there, we could take a few days holiday ourselves, I have always wanted to explore the Lake District, they say it is very beautiful." said Mrs Black. "We could always send Cook, err, I mean Victoria, back here by train while we travel down to Worcester and say hello to Ron's parents. To be honest, even if she doesn't want us to go with her, it would be lovely to have a few days holiday, so let's do it anyway. I feel that I want to get to know Ron's parents a bit more now and I would like to see where he grew up. Arnold was telling me a little bit about Ron's army life and I have so many un-answered questions, that I need to get a few answers to them now."

CHAPTER THIRTEEN
TRAVEL ARRANGEMENTS

Although Cook was up bright and early on Tuesday morning, she managed to be occupied the whole time that Digger was having breakfast, which suited him fine. He agreed with Mrs Black that he would use the car in order to go into the village to pick up the glass and putty from the Ironmongers, so he could fix all the broken windows. The vicar had agreed the previous evening that he would come over for an hour in the morning, to show Digger how to safely remove the broken panes and to replace them with the new ones.

They then went outside to the front of the house and discussed the picket fence and the reasons why the progress on this particular job had been so slow to date. Digger took a screwdriver out of his pocket and proceeded to push it through several of the upright pieces of wood, like a knife through butter.

"I am afraid that most of the fence is similar to this," he said, "but the supporting posts seem to be in good order. To be honest Mrs Black, it would be so much easier and quicker, to buy some new wood for the worse affected sections."

She asked him to make a list of what he would require so that she could ring the timber merchants and get an estimate of the cost, before discussing it with her sister.

Digger drove the car into the village and after buying some Polo's and a newspaper, picked up all of his supplies from the Ironmonger's. He then called in at the vicarage and after only a brief chat with the vicar's wife drove back to Millstone House. After the regulatory cup of tea with Cook, the two men set to work on the broken and missing panes of glass in the garage and other outbuildings. As with most handyman jobs, Digger soon discovered that the real art lay in the preparation, so removing the old panes of glass and cleaning the frames ready for the new, took a lot longer than putting in the new glass. Having said that, he also discovered that getting the putty in and achieving a neat and even finish was an art all of its own and after the vicar had demonstrated a few times he had a go himself. The first pane took just under an hour to do, as the putty fell out twice and he cracked the glass tapping in the nails, but he slowly got the hang of it and was managing to do them in just over five minutes each, by the time Sissy arrived with a tray of tea and some biscuits. The men sat down outside the cottage and had a ten minute break, after which the vicar looked at his watch and decided he had better get back home as Tuesday morning was when he first sat down in the quiet of his study and produced a first draught [*draft*] of his sermon for the following Sunday.

Digger offered to drive him back home, but he said that since it was such a nice morning that he preferred to walk home, so the two men shook hands and parted company.

Sissy, Cook and the two sisters sat in the kitchen for their morning tea and biscuits and using 'coded conversation', so that Sissy could not fully understand what they were discussing, the sisters questioned Cook about her plans.

"Have you decided how you are travelling, yet Cook?" asked Mrs Black.

"Oh, I didn't know you were going somewhere," said Sissy.

"I wasn't aware I had to get your permission before I made a trip," snapped Cook.

"Pardon me for breathing," replied Sissy and standing up, took her tea into the garden, along with a few biscuits.

The two sisters sat and looked at Cook and just waited.

"It was none of her business, it will be all over the village by tomorrow, I expect. But to answer your question, I would really like Bertie to come with me, although I did appreciate your offer."

"Does that mean you have spoken to Arnold, then?" asked Mrs Duffy-Smythe.

"I haven't had a chance yet, but I intend to later. He's been busy with the vicar, repairing the glass all morning, although why he needed help with such a simple job, I really don't understand," Cook responded.

"Amanda and I have decided to take a few days holiday anyway; it has been ages since we had a break and the change will do us good. We thought we might spend a few days with my old school friend in Derbyshire and do a bit of walking and then cross over to the west and maybe visit Worcester and Somerset. I am sure that Sissy and Digger can look after things for us here, even if the three of us are away together," said Mrs Duffy-Smythe.

"That's very trusting of you, leaving a complete stranger in charge of your home and possessions," observed Cook. "We still know absolutely nothing about him, apart from the fact that he used to live in London and claims that he got robbed on the train."

"We know a bit more than that Cook, he was in the army with Ron and according to Ron's letters, which I have been re-reading, was a very decent and responsible chap and it appears was offered a commission, but chose to be with the ordinary men," said Mrs Black. "Besides which, he could have stolen the car any number of times and has not done so, has he? I really do not want to hear any more negative comments please and if you want my advice, which I am sure you don't, I would be honest with him, show him the photograph of your first husband and explain the difficulty his presence has given you. He is a reasonable man and has also suffered loss and I am sure he will understand what you have been going through." With which, she got up and went to the garage to get the car.

Cook and Mrs Duffy-Smythe just looked at each other and smiled. "If someone had told me a fortnight ago that your sister would be defending Arnold, I would have thought them insane. What a difference a few days can make!" observed Cook.

When Digger came in for lunch, he was surprised to find Cook was there on her own and the table laid for just two. He had been keeping Mac out of her way since Sunday and was pleased she made a proper fuss of him, when he came in with Digger.

"Where are the others today?" enquired Digger.

"Mrs Black has gone into Oxford, Mrs Duffy-Smythe is writing and Sissy's mother wasn't too good today, so she has gone home to look after her. Please sit down Arnold, I have cooked a meat pudding, which I know is one of your favourites. Would you like some orange juice to have with it?"

"Thank you Cook, that would be lovely," he said guardedly and sat down at his usual place.

While they were eating and making small talk about the house and garden in general and the vegetable patch, in particular, Cook suddenly got up and went across to the dresser and took something out of the drawer. "I have something I want to show you Arnold," she said, "it will explain why I have had a problem in our relationship."

She sat down and passed it to Digger. It was the photograph of her first husband Dick.

He looked at the picture in silence, stunned by the likeness of the man in the photograph to himself. "That's incredible, it could be me or my dad when he was younger and my mother had a photo very similar to this. Who is he?"

Cook gulped and cleared her throat and then said, "That's my first husband Dick, on our wedding day, we were both eighteen. Within five months of that picture being taken he was dead, killed in a hunting accident. I have just never got over losing him – every time I see you Arnold, you just remind me of him and it brings all the hurt and sorrow back."

"I'm so sorry Cook, I had no idea, it must be absolutely awful for you. I will finish off what jobs I can this week and leave the house at the weekend, I'll let Mrs Duffy-Smythe know," with which he got up from the table and walked towards the door.

Cook was very surprised by his response and she too got up, walked over to him and put her arms around him and started to weep. Mrs Duffy-Smythe heard the commotion and rushed into the kitchen and was amazed to find the pair standing there, just holding each other. Digger smiled at her with tears in his eyes and she backed out of the room again.

After what seemed like hours, Cook finally disentangled herself and went over to the stove and put the kettle on. She made a cup of tea and they both sat down again.

"Arnold, I want to say how sorry I am for the way I have treated you, especially for the other night at Bertie's, but when you came into the room with your hair having been blown in the wind and your cheeks red with running after Mac, it could have been my Dick standing there and I just lost control. I am so sorry dear," she said.

"That's all right Cook, of course I understand. If I ever see a bloke who reminds me of my friends Ginger or Ron, it still give me a funny turn, so I do understand, but as I said, I will speak to Mrs Duffy-Smythe and let her know that I will be moving on."

"No Arnold, don't do that. It's funny, but as we were holding each other just now, it was as if it was Dick holding me and I was being given the chance to say goodbye to him; the pain has gone; it's as if I have finally let him go, I feel a real sense of peace. Thank you Arnold, please don't go, at least, not on my account."

While Digger was sawing logs and counting fence posts in the afternoon, Cook took a stroll over to see Bertie. She found him in the garden in his favourite seat, reading, or rather he had been, until he had nodded off. She gently took the book off his lap and sat down beside him and put her arm through his and closed her eyes and she too fell asleep.

On waking, Bertie was surprised to see Victoria beside him, but when he looked at her, he realised how much she had come to mean to him, in such a short time. He tried to move without disturbing her but failed in the attempt and she came too with a jump.

"Oh Bertie, I must have dozed off. I haven't slept too well since Sunday. I talked with Arnold today and showed him the photograph of my husband and even he was shocked by the likeness. I told him I was sorry about the way I had been with him and for what I said the other night. He was really good about it and even offered to leave; he's such a nice man when you get to know him and it's funny, but I feel a real peace now, like I have said goodbye to Dick and let him go."

"I know what you mean Victoria, it took me a while to do that with Deborah's mother. I am pleased for you," said Bertie and squeezed her hand.

"With regard to my trip to Kendal, please say you will come with me; I don't think I could face the solicitor on my own."

"I will be delighted to accompany you to Kendal Victoria, is there any time limit that we have to abide by stated in the letter?"

"It doesn't give a time limit but it does say most urgent. I could ring them when I get home and arrange a date for us to go there, do you have anything else coming up in the near future, or are you free?"

"I have kept my diary completely free to be at your disposal," he said, in a very posh voice. "But as my great Uncle Harry always used to say, 'strike while the iron is hot' so let's get up there as soon as we can, I am sure Digger will keep an eye on things for me, here. I do believe that there is a coach from Oxford to Carlisle several times a week, why not ring the coach station and check if I am correct, before you ring the solicitor. You can then choose a day after the coach arrives to give us a chance to refresh ourselves and while you are on the telephone, ask them to give you the name of a local hotel we could stay in and suggest they book it for us. After all, the letter did say that they would pay all your expenses and that of a friend to accompany you, didn't it?"

Mrs Black and Digger were in the kitchen discussing the quotation from the Timber Yard when Cook returned and asked if she could use the telephone for a long distance call.

Mrs Black told her to use the study as her sister was lying down upstairs with a headache.

She first of all phoned the Coach Station who informed her that a coach for Carlisle left every Thursday and Monday at ten past ten and passed through Kendal at approximately six thirty at night and that passengers were able to leave and board the coach in Kendal.

She then rang the solicitors office and was lucky to catch the senior partner who happened to be working late. He was aware of the letter, although he was not handling the matter himself and confirmed that his colleague would be able to see her at eleven am Friday.

Cook then asked Mrs Black if it would be alright for her to have a week or so off, starting this Thursday and was there any chance of a lift into Oxford Bus Station for nine thirty Thursday morning for her and Bertie. A quick conversation between Mrs Black and Digger, confirmed that he could give them a lift and pick up the wood from the yard on the same trip, so that was all settled. After dinner Bertie arrived to see how things had gone and agreed that Thursday would be fine by him to head north. While he and Cook retired to her parlour to discuss their trip, the two sisters telephoned their friend in the Derbyshire Dales to see when they could visit her. The friend said that she worked three days a week as a laboratory assistant at Sheffield University and suggested that they drove up this Friday afternoon so that they could spend the weekend and Monday/Tuesday together.

Mrs Black then wrote a short letter to Ron's parents, telling them that she and her sister would be in their area towards the end of next week and would it be convenient if they called in to say hello.

While all this was going on, Digger decided to walk into the village and found Moira clearing weeds and rubbish from her small back garden. He helped her for a while and then waited while she washed and changed before they took a short walk to the pub for a drink. Over a shandy and a packet of crisps, he brought her up to date with everything that had been happening over at Millstone.

"That is just amazing," she said, "that you should so strongly resemble her first husband. You don't have any family links with that part of the country, do you?"

"Not as far as I know," he replied, "but my sister is the family historian, I will have to ask her next time I speak with her."

"And then you say Cook hugged you and cried on your shoulder and said that she wants you to stay at Millstone House. So, let me get all this straight. Mrs Black thinks you are wonderful, Mrs Duffy-Smythe called you a knight in shining armour, my aunt considered you to be a nice young man and now its Cook's turn! Tell me Arnold Smith, do you always have this effect on all the ladies you meet, wherever you go, or is it just to those you find in small rural communities?"

CHAPTER FOURTEEN
COMMUNICATION PROBLEMS

When Cook realised that Bertie didn't own a white shirt any longer, she insisted that Digger give them both a lift into Aylesbury to purchase one for him. Mrs Duffy-Smythe gave her approval for the trip and Mrs Black gave him her shopping list and a request to call in at a ladies clothes shop, to pick up some items for herself and her sister. When Digger asked if he needed to check them over, she informed him quite firmly that he did not!

It took Bertie approximately two minutes in the gentleman's clothes shop, to select a shirt and a tie and it then took Cook a further ten minutes to change that selection to something she deemed more suitable. The ladies clothes shop was a lot more complex. The parcel was ready and waiting and Digger was halfway out the door when Cook (who had felt compelled to accompany him on the visit) asked him to wait while she just took a minute to inspect some new coats and hats that had come in that week.

Fifteen minutes later, Bertie arrived to see what the delay was, to find Digger slumped in a chair counting the number of hat boxes on the top shelf. Spying Bertie he jumped up, quickly explained the problem and both men turned towards the door, whispering to the lady assistant that they had to check something on the car. Digger was safely through the door and Bertie had almost made it, when he heard those spine chilling words that every man has come to dread, "Bertie dear," called Cook, "tell me which of these coats you prefer."

He, of course, pretended not to hear and kept going, but the sales lady was a veteran of thirty five years experience and there was no way that this potential sale was escaping, so she gently grasped his coat, in a grip of steel and said, "Excuse me sir, but madam would like your opinion on the choice of a coat and hat."

Reluctantly he released the door handle and turned back into the shop and walked towards the mirror that Cook was standing in front of, "You called Victoria, a new coat, you mentioned?"

She was standing there in a knee length coat of a browny/reddy flecked sort of material, with large buttons and a hat, which looked more like a discarded eagles nest than an actual hat, perched on the top of her head.

"I am so tired of always wearing navy blue, I think it's time to change my image, what do you think?"

Had he said what he thought, he knew perfectly well that this new friendship would have come to an abrupt end, but he had been married before and was well aware of the pitfalls of the situation.

"It will be easier for me to choose if I see all the choices at one sitting, so to speak," he replied.

"I knew you wouldn't like it, I try and change my image and that's all the help I get," she parried.

"I am not going to be drawn into giving you an answer Victoria, until I have seen all the other coats you have been considering, OK?"

"Oh men, all I want is an opinion, that's not a lot to ask," she said sulkily.

Now a lesser man would have made the mistake, at this stage of saying something like, "The coat's too young for you and the hat should be in the Natural History Museum," but Bertie was a seasoned campaigner and sat quietly in the chair.

Cook took off the coat and hat and tried on the next combination, which was a navy blue calf length coat, with big pockets and a wide collar and a neat blue hat with an upturned brim on one side and a bow on the other.

She stood there, glowering at him, daring him to say he liked it.

He coughed and then said, "Is that it, or is there a third choice."

"Well there is another one, but it is a bit more expensive than I wanted to pay."

"Ah hah" he thought, "so this is the real choice, thank goodness for that."

"Victoria, when was the last time you bought yourself a new coat?" he enquired.

"1936 from C & A's in Oxford Street and I am still wearing it," she replied immediately.

"Show me the third coat and I will give you an opinion," he said.

The last one was light brown with a fur collar, with a fur and brown hat to match, he sighed with relief, this was obviously the favoured combination.

"Well, there is a clear winner here Victoria, this last combination is just you, you look fantastic."

She smiled and cooed and turned up the collar and walked up and down and told the lady assistant she would have it, who then quickly asked if madam needed a new dress and accessories to match, which she was easily persuaded into believing that she did.

When they emerged from the shop, over an hour later, they found Digger curled up on the back seat, fast asleep. Just one more brief stop at the shoe shop and after only twenty five minutes and a dozen pairs of shoes later, they triumphantly drove back to Millstone House.

The rest of the day passed quickly and they all had an evening meal together, with Moira and Bertie joining them. With Mrs Duffy-Smythe's prior agreement, Cook informed Moira that she was welcome to use her kitchen while she was away, if she wished to.

Digger took Moira home and then went round Bertie's to collect his case, so he wouldn't have to carry it in the morning.

Everyone was up bright and early Thursday morning and Digger dropped Cook and Bertie at the Coach Station twenty minutes before it was due to leave. They had a cup of tea together and Digger waved them goodbye, dead on ten past and set off for the wood yard. He laid the old blanket over the back seat and managed to pile all the wood inside and arrived back home at mid-day.

He agreed with Mrs Black the chores he should do while they were away and that specifically, it would be a great chance to repaint the laundry, while Cook was absent. She said she would work out a list of jobs for Sissy, but a top to bottom Spring clean, should be completed while they were away and Digger would be required to assist in moving any heavy furniture for her.

She also asked if he would give the car a quick check on Friday morning, before they went on their trip.

On Friday morning it poured down and Digger checked the car over in the garage and cleaned the spark plugs again and gave the interior a good clean. He reported back to Mrs Black over elevenses, saying, "Everything seems OK, but if you have time, I would call in at the garage in Aylesbury and pick up a spare fan belt. I think it will last, but it's better to have a spare one with you." She thanked him and said she would do that.

They had lunch together and Digger brought their cases downstairs for them and loaded them into the boot and the ladies finally left home around one o'clock. Five minutes later they were back for their address book and to tell Digger that if there was a letter with a Worcestershire postmark, to open it and ring them at their friends with the details, as it would be from Ron's parents. They left again at twenty past one and this time did not return.

Digger and Sissy discussed the list of jobs and having assumed that they had till the end of next week to complete them, planned the order in which they would do them. Sissy suggested that it would probably rain Tuesday or Wednesday, according to the weather forecast and she would give Digger a hand with re-decorating the laundry, if he would give her a hand moving the furniture on Thursday and Friday of next week, "Who knows, Digger," she said smiling, "perhaps Cook and Bertie will take more than a week's holiday and that will give us plenty of time to work together!"

The two sisters were enjoying the scenery and happily chatting away when Mrs Black remembered what Digger had said, "Oh dear Penny, with all the confusion of forgetting the address book, we also forgot to call in at the garage and pick up a spare fan thingy, that Digger suggested."

"It was a fan **belt**, dear. Mind you, even if we had one, I wouldn't know what to do with it, would you?"

"I remember reading a story recently in one of the magazines, where a couple were out for a drive and the fan belt broke and he got his girlfriend to take off a stocking and he somehow used that as a temporary fix," Amanda replied.

"Well, you are the driver and you forgot, so if anyone's stocking is coming off, it is going to be yours, not mine," Penny laughed.

The rain had stopped by the time they had driven just north of Aylesbury and the sun was hazy behind the clouds and they agreed that it was good to be on holiday together. Around half past three they were feeling in need of sustenance and a loo, so stopped at a small country hotel on the outskirts of Fenny Drayton. They enjoyed afternoon tea and scones and continued on their way again just after four.

It was about five to five when Penny first noticed a strange smell, but said nothing to Amanda as she assumed it was a normal country smell. Amanda also noticed the smell and was not quite so sure about its origins and asked the obvious question, "Is it me, or is there a funny smell in the car."

"I am sure it is not you dear," quipped Penny, "but I was just wondering the same thing. We are just coming into Duffield, we can stop there and investigate."

As they stopped outside the post office and turned the engine off, they heard a loud hissing noise and a plume of steam billowed out of the engine cowling. They got out of the car and stood there looking at it, wondering what to do, when the postmaster joined them from the shop and advised them to stand away until the steam had stopped, which they did. Mrs Black undid the bonnet catch and the postmaster gingerly opened the bonnet, using his wife's oven gloves to protect his hands.

"I know nothing about engines ladies, but I think you need assistance with this, are you members of the RAC by any chance?"

"No we are not," said Mrs Duffy-Smythe, "we make so few long trips it has never seemed necessary. Can we use your telephone, we know someone who is knowledgeable and would like to give him a call?"

"It is against the rules," he answered, "but since this an emergency, I am sure it will be alright. This way, but I will have to charge you for the call."

They both followed him into the post office and behind the counter and into his small office. He spoke to the operator and explained that he would need to know the cost of the call, once it was completed.

The telephone at Millstone House must have rung twenty times, before Digger was able to answer it, "Hello, this is Millstone House, Digger speaking, can I help you?"

"Hello Arnold, this is Mrs Duffy-Smythe, we have a problem with the car."

She related the full story and all that had happened and then he answered, "At a guess I would say the fan belt has broken and the engine has over heated. Did you notice if the little red ignition light had come on?"

"Hold on Arnold; Amanda he is asking if we noticed if the ignition light had come on?"

"I don't know Penny, it may have, but I cannot be sure."

"It may have done but we are not sure. If we fill the radiator with water, can we get going again?"

"Did you get the replacement fan belt like I suggested?" he asked.

"No."

"There is a danger that you may have blown the head gasket when the radiator went, you will need to get it checked. Are you a member of the RAC?"

"No."

"I don't suppose you are anywhere near Derby, are you?"

"I will ask; excuse me Postmaster, how far is Derby from here. Four miles, thank you. Arnold, he says we are about four miles from Derby, why did you want to know?"

"My army friend Big Dutch, owns a small garage in Derby. At this time of night, no-one will want to come out and help you, but if I can contact Dutch, I am sure he would help, ask the postmaster if he knows the telephone number of Greenfields Garage please and also the number you are ringing from there."

"Excuse me again, but would you have the telephone number of Greenfields Garage and would you mind if my friend rings me back here, he is trying to sort out some assistance for us."

The postmaster checked the directory and wrote the number down, which she then read out to Digger along with the number of the post office.

Digger put the phone down on Mrs Duffy-Smythe and phoned his mate's number. They hadn't spoken since they were all de-mobbed in 1945 and he was musing on that, when a voice the other end said, "Greenfields Garage and we're closed. Call again tomorrow."

Without thinking, Digger was back into the army banter, "Hold on a minute you great hairy oath, this is Digger and I have a damsel in distress for you to save on your white charger! If you still have one."

"Digger, is that you, you cockney hooligan, where have you been hiding," Dutch responded.

They chatted for a few minutes and Digger explained that Ronnie Black's wife and sister had broken down at Duffield and needed to get to Hope in Derby for a few days holiday, but suspected that the radiator might be damaged or the head gasket blown. Dutch said he didn't carry a great many spares but could probably get all he needed on Saturday morning and would be happy to go and pick the ladies up and take them to Hope, but the only vehicle he had available was his breakdown wagon. He thought he could get to them in about thirty minutes, as he had to shut the garage and then take the week's takings to the bank.

Digger rang the ladies back at the post office and gave them the good news about being rescued by his army friend from Derby, but omitted the small detail that they would be travelling to Hope in the front of a breakdown wagon. They in turn asked him to telephone their friend at Hope and let her know about their situation. The postmaster had given them a cup of tea and a biscuit and allowed them to stay in the post office, even though he had closed for the night.

"Penny, it looks like Arnold's friend has arrived as a big red lorry with a crane on the back has just stopped outside. We had better go and say hello."

Dutch jumped down from the lorry and walked towards the two ladies emerging from the post office. He was a big man, six feet two inches tall, with wide shoulders and still had a mop of brown hair, which was fighting to escape from under his cap. He smiled and held out his hand to them as he said, "Which of you is Ronnie's wife?"

Mrs Black stepped forward and shook his hand as she answered, "I am, it's very good of you to came to our assistance Mr. err."

"Tulip, Mr Tulip, but please call me Dutch, everyone else does."

"Dutch, I see now, I am Amanda and this is my sister Penny."

Dutch smiled again and shook hands with Penny, totally unaware that no-one outside of Amanda and Cook had ever called her by that name.

"Nice to meet you Penny. I explained to Digger that I don't carry a lot of spares and I won't be able to get any until tomorrow, but let's have a quick look under the bonnet, shall we."

He opened the bonnet and checked the radiator and engine and then closed the bonnet again and turned towards them. "The fan belt has certainly gone and I think there is a split in the top hose, but apart from that, everything else is OK. I could probably bodge the hose for you, but the fan belt does need replacing. You don't happen to have a spare one with you, do you?" he asked Penny.

"I am afraid we don't Dutch ," she answered.

"Digger must be losing his touch, to let you ladies embark on a long journey like this, without a spare fan belt, I will have to have a very serious talk to him about this!"

The two sisters smiled at each other and remained silent, "Arnold did say you might be able to take us to Hope tonight, is that still possible and if so, how long will it take to go and fetch your car?" asked Penny.

"Arnold eh, gone all posh has he, wait till I speak to him, these fancy bankers! The good news is I can take you to Hope tonight and fix your car tomorrow morning and probably borrow a transporter to bring it up to you Saturday or Sunday afternoon. The bad news is that I don't have a car of my own, but the breakdown wagon has a wide bench seat and a storage box, so I can take you and your luggage to Hope, if you want me to."

With which he opened the door so they could look inside and were amazed how neat and clean it was.

Penny decided to accept the offer on behalf of both of them, "Thank you Dutch, we would be most grateful to accept your offer, it really is most kind of you to take such trouble over a pair of complete strangers."

"Ronnie was the sort of chap who would do anything for anyone, I learnt a lot about my fellow human beings from him, I owe him a lot and am only too pleased to help you both."

Dutch pushed the car round the corner and left it down the side of the post office where the postmaster could keep an eye on it for them. He then transferred all the luggage to the storage box and helped the ladies climb aboard.

It was gone seven when they arrived in Hope and following Lilly's instructions they turned down the road opposite the church and pulled up in the yard at the side of the old farmhouse. The journey had been very pleasant particularly when Dutch discovered that Penny was a writer and she discovered that he wrote short stories for the local weekly newspaper. It could have been difficult however, when Penny's right knee (for she was sitting in the middle of the bench seat) kept being touched by Dutch's left hand, when he was changing gear, but for some reason, neither seemed bothered.

He helped them down from the cab and un-loaded their luggage and then climbed back into the cab.

"Please stay and eat with us Dutch, you must be famished," said Penny.

"Perhaps tomorrow, when I bring the car back, I rang my mother from the garage and told her I would be late home, so she will have kept something for me. I can pick up your car tonight and work on it tomorrow morning, so all being well I could be back here around two thirty, if that suits," he said.

"That suits fine, perhaps we can book a table at the pub down the road, safe journey," Penny called out as he reversed out of the yard.

Lilly rushed over and gave her a hug, "It is so good to see you again, do come in before you get cold, mind your head particularly upstairs, there is a low beam by the bathroom."

Just then, there was a bump and a howl from upstairs, "Oops, looks like your sister has found it already."

Dutch hooked up the car to the breakdown lorry, after telling the post master what he was doing and towed it back to the garage. He rang his mother to tell her he was back and to ask her to heat up his dinner and then walked home. He was whistling when he went into the house and after washing his hands sat down at the table and related the day's events.

"Well Dutch," said his mother, "this is practically the first time in three years I have heard you whistling and seen you smiling, you should speak to your friend more often, why don't you invite him up for a few days, now you know where he is."

He smiled and nodded but didn't reply, he just ate his meal slowly, as he looked forward to Saturday.

It was Friday lunch time when Amanda's letter to Ron's parents dropped through the letter box onto the doormat. Mrs Black had been out to a committee meeting of the local branch of the WI (Women's Institute), where arrangements for the forthcoming month had been discussed. She had sat with the letter in front of her for about ten minutes when Mr Black arrived home. He was an insurance agent for the Liverpool Victoria Insurance Company and was to be seen most days walking his bicycle around different parts of town, resplendent in bicycle clips, raincoat and a trilby hat, collecting premiums.

"Hello Myrtle, my love," he said and kissed her on the forehead, "what have we got here then?" He removed his bicycle clips and placed them in his raincoat pocket, which he then hung on the hallstand, beneath his trilby hat, which he had already placed there.

"Who do we know in Oxford, Percy," she asked, "the envelope has an Oxford postmark."

"Didn't your cousin Florrie's son go to Oxford," he replied.

"That was five years ago and he got thrown out after the first year. I wonder if it could be that Mrs Peter's from number sixteen, she said she was going to work in a university down south, somewhere."

"Give it to me and we will find out," he said and she passed him the letter which he opened carefully with his penknife. "Well I'll be jiggered, who would have thought it, goodness me, fancy that, what are we doing towards the end of next week Myrtle?"

"Really Percy, do you do this just to irritate me, who is it from?"

"It's from Amanda, our daughter-in-law, she is on holiday with her sister and asks if she can drop in towards the end of next week to see us. Oh, it seems she has left today, but has said we can telephone one of Ron's army mates, Arnold, who is stopping with them at the moment and leave a message for her with him. I don't recall Ron ever talking about a mate called Arnold, do you?"

"Well I'll be jiggered," she said and read the letter for herself. "We could pop down to number thirteen and use their telephone, I suppose, or we could make the call tomorrow, there are a couple of phone boxes outside the Co-op."

He looked at her rather surprised, "I didn't think we were talking to number thirteen these days after the last time we used her telephone and the whole street wished us a happy holiday at Weston Super Mare, without us having told anyone."

"Quite right Percy, we will use the public call box, make sure you have plenty of change in your pocket and that you have your reading glasses with you," she instructed, "I have some food to buy and some baking to do, if we are to have visitors next week."

"Isn't it time we got your own glasses fixed dear, I swear you use mine, more than I do," he mumbled.

"Don't swear Percy and please don't mumble," she commanded, as she embarked on the planning of Worcester's version of the feeding of the five thousand.

It was raining lightly on Saturday morning when the Black's set out for the Co-op which was about a half mile walk from their house. Percy was carrying the two empty shopping bags and Myrtle was holding his arm and greeting the various neighbours as they walked down the street.

"This rain is getting heavier dear, pop back and get the umbrella will you," she asked.

He knew better than to challenge this request and briskly walked back to the house to find the postman had just pushed a post card through the letter box. He read the card, picked up the umbrella and returned to his wife, who was looking into the window of the corner shop.

"What on earth took you so long Percy?" she asked.

"We had a post card from Blackpool, your sister, dear."

"I don't believe it," she said, "the postal service these days is awful. She has been back home for over a week now and it was only a weekend trip anyway. Put the umbrella up dear, it's not for show!"

Percy did as he was bidden and they carried on to the Co-op to get the week's shopping. Laden with the two large shopping bags, filled to capacity and the string bag he carried in his pocket for emergency, they emerged from the Co-op and headed for the telephone boxes. One of them was already occupied but one was empty and as they walked towards it, Myrtle noticed another couple, also laden with shopping, heading in the same direction.

She prodded Percy and hissed, "We have to beat them to the box, make a run for it."

As a true soldier, used to obeying orders, he rushed for the box, not realising that there was a hole in the pavement just in front of the door and as he opened the door he put his foot in the hole and was surprised to discover that the puddle was over two inches deep and his foot was soaked. While he stood looking at his foot Myrtle pushed past and took possession of the box.

The other couple were extremely put out and the wife was heard remarking about the appalling manners some people had these days.

By now the rain was falling fast and he took down the umbrella and was about to step inside the box when Myrtle spoke, "No Percy, there isn't room for the two of us, you stay there, just pass me your glasses, I have the telephone number here."

He knew better than to argue and reached inside his jacket pocket for his glasses, but they were not there. He tried his other pockets but with no luck.

"I asked you before we left home this morning if you had your glasses and you assured me you did, so where have they mysteriously gone to? This box is not big enough for the two of us."

"I left them on the hallstand. I took them out to read the postcard from your sister and left them there. I am sorry, but you will have to step outside and I will dial the number dear."

"If you think I am standing in the pouring rain while you make the telephone call, you can think again. If I just stand to the back, I think we can both squeeze in together. Don't leave the shopping outside, pass it to me first and I will put it on top of the shelf here."

The shopping was stacked on the shelf, the umbrella lent against the side of the telephone box and Mrs Black squeezed into the corner. Now she was one of those ladies with what is normally described as having 'ample proportions' and Mr Black although quite fit from all the walking was used to eating large meals with plenty of homemade sweets and cakes, so he too was 'amply proportioned'.

He first tried to get in with his back to the telephone, to discover that he was unable to turn round. He then tried getting in facing the telephone, to discover that he couldn't raise his arms to lift the receiver, without having the door open, which meant the rain came in and soaked them. He eventually gave his good lady the ultimatum, you either get out and let me dial the number or we have to go to number thirteen and ask to use their telephone.

"Right, you get out and open the umbrella for me and then we swap over, do you understand Percy?"

"Yes dear."

They swapped over and he started to dial, only to realise that it was a long distance call and they would have to ask the operator to get it for them. He had the good sense to open the door and inform his beloved of this fact before continuing.

The operator made the connection and he fed his money into the box and pressed Button 'B' which gave him his money back. By now Myrtle had realised that glasses were not required and opened the door and hauled him out before he had a chance to repeat the operation.

She lifted the receiver and repeated the steps and actually heard Digger say hello, before she also pressed Button 'B' and got her money back.

"Which Button did you press Percy?" she enquired.

"Button 'B' dear, but you should press Button 'A' once you have put the money in and the person the other end has answered."

Third time lucky, she got everything done correctly and spoke to Arnold and was delighted to discover that he was the 'Digger' that Ron had mentioned in his last letter from France. She told him that they would be delighted to see Ron's widow and her sister and that she would be at home all day Wednesday and Thursday and after four pm on Friday at which point the money ran out and the call ended.

Percy's wet shoe squeaked all the way home and he had to change all his clothes and have a hot bath, just in case he caught a chill.

When Moira came over in the afternoon, Digger told her all that had been going on and they were still laughing about it as they walked to Bertie's cottage and checked things out. He too had received a letter, with a London postmark, which Digger guessed was from Deborah and melodramatically put it on the dresser using the fire tongs, in order to keep a safe distance from it.

Back at Millstone, Digger telephoned Hope several times and eventually spoke to Mrs Duffy-Smythe around ten p.m. He told her of his conversation with Ron's mother and that she would be delighted to see them both next week, from Wednesday onwards. She in turn related how Dutch had been so marvellous and that he had brought the car back earlier in the day and what a nice man he was. Digger thought she sounded different, but put it down to being on holiday.

Moira had cooked lamb chops for tea and afterwards they sat together on Cooks sofa and listened to the wireless while they held hands and chatted. He walked her home just after ten thirty and after kissing her goodnight on the doorstep he returned home, locked the house and went to the cottage to find Mac was fast asleep on his chair.

"Some guard dog you are," he said, but didn't notice Mac raise one eye to him as he walked up the stairs to bed.

CHAPTER FIFTEEN
SOMETHING ADVANTAGEOUS

The coach from Oxford stopped in Birmingham to pick up a few passengers and Bertie had time to jump off and get them a cup of tea and a piece of cake each from the kiosk. It had been raining all morning but as they left the outskirts of the town, the sun started to break through the clouds and the countryside looked green and lovely.

Later on they ate the sandwiches which Cook had prepared for the journey and chatted about the different places they were passing through and the various crops they could see growing in the fields. Bertie then asked her about the telephone call she had made to the solicitors in Kendal and as an afterthought enquired, "Which hotel are we staying in Victoria; I hope its somewhere posh. Did they offer to book it for you or did you have to book it yourself?" She did not answer him so he thought she had not heard him and repeated the question again. "I said, where are we staying in Kendal Victoria and who booked it, you or them?"

Cook was sitting there, with her hands raised and her mouth open, "I forgot all about it Bertie, I was so nervous at talking to the senior partner I just forgot. I suppose I was thinking that I was going home and of course would normally stop with my brother."

"Does he live near the town then?"

"No and he only has a cottage and he isn't very well." "I suppose that there are some hotels or guest houses in the town?" he asked, trying not to sound sarcastic.

"Oh, plenty, it's a very popular tourist area, there are at least two hotels in the high street alone, I am sure we will be able to get some accommodation at this time of year, but they will not be cheap, that's for sure!"

"The cost is not what's at issue here as we are not paying Victoria, remember, the letter clearly said, 'all expenses paid'. What is at issue is getting a roof over our heads; so when we stop in Manchester, I will pop out and phone the solicitor's office and ask them to book rooms for us. I can also confirm the time of the appointment for tomorrow."

The coach stopped for a 'convenience break' around three o'clock so they stretched their legs and had a cup of tea and located a telephone, where they rang the solicitor's office. Mr Belmont's secretary confirmed the appointment for eleven a.m. Friday and said she would book two rooms in The Highgate Hotel which was located on Highgate and very close to where the coaches normally stopped. If there was any sort of problem, she would leave a message with the porter at the hotel.

The rest of the journey was a lot more comfortable, knowing that they had accommodation for the night in Kendal and apart from a shower of rain while going into Manchester; it turned out to be a very pleasant Spring Day. As the coach came into the outskirts of the Lake District and the hills started to become more apparent, Bertie sensed that Cook was somehow changing, she smiled a lot more and started to point out landmarks to him, she was coming home!

Bertie had asked the driver if he could drop them outside the hotel entrance, which he duly did and was rewarded with a sixpence tip. They stood by their cases outside the hotel and waved to the driver as he drove off and a porter came and stood next to them and welcomed them to the Highgate Hotel. Bertie was about to refuse his assistance with the cases, when Victoria jokingly reminded him that he was no longer a fit young sailor in a strange port, but a gentleman on a business trip, so he should allow the porter to do his job and carry the cases for them into the lobby. The reception clerk was expecting them and informed them that the solicitor had reserved two fine rooms for them on the second floor and that a table in the restaurant had also been booked for them, for seven forty five p.m. that evening and he hoped that they would find that acceptable, which they did.

They both signed the Register and were escorted upstairs to their rooms which were spacious and well appointed with small windows that looked out onto the courtyard at the rear and had interconnecting doors, with a key in each. The bathroom was just down the corridor from their rooms with a toilet and hand basin next to that.

They unpacked their cases and freshened up and at seven forty precisely, Bertie knocked at Cook's door and the two went down to dinner. The restaurant was three quarters full and a table had been reserved for them between the fire and the window. They both decided on the venison with onion soup to start and the waiter recommended a red wine which they both enjoyed. Bertie was careful not to be too lavish with his praises for the venison, after Cook had informed him that it was one of her specialties. They enjoyed a fine Stilton Cheese for desert, washed down with a glass of port and followed by coffee and were both sound asleep by eleven o'clock.

The next day they had a full English breakfast at eight thirty, allowing themselves a short lie in after the tiring journey of the day before. After breakfast they got their coats from their rooms and then walked around the town until the time for their appointment with Mr Belmont, of Cliff, Banks & Belmont – Solicitors, whose offices were just round the corner from the hotel in Allhallows Lane. After the initial introductions, tea was offered and accepted and Cook produced the package that she had been sent.

"Tell me Mrs Owen, who are the boys in the picture that we sent you and do you have a copy of the photograph yourself," asked Mr Belmont.

"That boy there is Howard, my step son and the other boy is his friend, also named Howard, but for some reason he was always called 'Beano', after the children's comic. I am afraid that I do not have a copy of the picture, in fact I don't even remember my husband taking it, to be honest with you. Why do you ask Mt Belmont?"

"We have to be sure Mrs Owen, that we sent the package to the correct person. Beano is in fact a cousin of mine and knew you and your brother, so that's how we traced you, but we had to ask your brother to say nothing to you."

"Well he did that alright, not a word, I'll give his beard a tweak when next I see him. So this Mr Owen mentioned in the Australian newspaper, is Howard, I presume?"

"That's quite correct," replied Mr Belmont, "let me give you a brief history of what has happened and why we sent you the package and letter and you will see why we had to be certain we had the correct Mrs Owen." He then went on to tell the story of Howard Owen from 1925 to the present date.

"As you well know, Howard Owen sold the business, the house and everything else he had in England and immediately set out on a 'round the world' cruise. Towards the end of 1925 the ship called at Fremantle in Western Australia and while Howard was ashore, he got bitten by mosquitoes and contracted Ross River Virus. This is not a disease we are acquainted with in England, but I gather that it is a very real problem over there and is taken very seriously, just as Malaria is in India and such places. He was taken to a hospital in Fremantle where he was nursed for several months and of course, the ship had to sail on without him. When he left hospital, he was still very weak and a young nurse who had been caring for him, suggested he stopped for a while on her parents farm, which was situated just outside a country town, called Pinjarra.

Howard duly recovered and was invited to stay and work on the farm, which he did. It appears that he loved the life out there and when a neighbouring farm came on the market, he bought it and the two farms were operated together as one large unit. In September 1927 he married the nurse, who was called Winifred and they set up home in the farm which Howard had purchased, which they called 'Coniston'. Sadly, Winifred died in childbirth on the 6th October 1928 giving birth to their daughter, that he named Victoria."

Cook jumped up from her seat, "I don't believe it, he called her Victoria, he actually named his daughter after me!"

Bertie stood up and put his arms round her and just stood there with her for a few minutes while she composed herself and then they both sat down again.

"It is the daughter, Victoria, who has written to us, Mrs Owen. If I may continue, you will understand why."

Cook nodded and he began again to read from the document on his desk.

"Howard was a good father and became an excellent farm manager and ran both farms together when his mother-in-law and father-in-law retired, a few years before the war started. He never re-married and all was going well until he had a stroke last year. His wife's parents had both died by now and his daughter was far too in-experienced for the task of running the farm; so they promoted a farm hand to act as the manager for them. It appears that he has been running things for them quite successfully since then, while Victoria has continued with her studies and got to grips with the business end of the farm, as well as looking after her sick father.

It would seem that whilst Howard was paralyzed down his left side, which also affected his speech, he could still communicate and his mind was still clear. Victoria spent many hours talking to him and slowly pieced together his life in England and solved the mystery of who she was named after, namely you, his step-mother. It appears that it would have been too painful for him to call her after her mother and you were the only other woman he knew, who he held in high enough regard, to name his daughter after."

Cook looked as if she had been struck by lightning and barely mumbled, "Well that is astonishing, Howard having a high regard for me!"

As if by magic the secretary came in with more tea and biscuits and they all had a ten minute break before he continued with the story.

"It appears that around Christmas last year, Howard had another minor stroke and this prompted him to ask his daughter to fetch his 'Last Will and Testament' from their safe, which she did. He then told her to open it and to her surprise, discovered that it was not Howard's Will, but his father's Will, duly signed and witnessed in January

1924 and in it, his father quite clearly stated that half of his business and all his other worldly goods should go to his wife, Victoria Owen and the other half of his business to his son, Howard Owen.

Now some time previous to this, Howard had already told his daughter that he had inherited all of his father's estate and that he had sold the business and all the possessions and had used the proceeds to pay for the cruise and then to buy the farm and set up home at Coniston. She realised that something was seriously wrong with what had gone on back in Kendal, so she demanded to know what he had given to you by way of compensation, for not getting what the Will had stated. In the end he had to confess that he had given you £100 and nothing else and that he had cheated you out of your share of the inheritance. He told her that it was now 'water under the bridge' and to protect her own inheritance, she should burn the Will and forget it ever existed. She flatly refused to do this but in fact immediately contacted he own solicitors in Perth to arrange a meeting. She went to see them the next week and explained all that she had discovered and instructed them to write to us. This they duly did, explaining the whole matter and emphasizing Victoria's desire to put things right with yourself. They also included the newspaper and photograph which we then sent with our letter to you. I can also tell you, that we have received a banker's draft in our name, for five hundred pounds to pay for all of our fees and your expenses."

"I am speechless," said Cook, "this girl has spirit and seems to be a very decent young lady, but what would I do with half a farm in Australia, assuming I would be entitled to it?"

The solicitor continued, "The legalities are quite complex, as I am sure you will appreciate, but whilst Howard has not had a real change of heart if we are being honest about it, I certainly get the impression that the young lady would like to meet with you and will act fairly towards you. It is my opinion, therefore, that we should promote the idea of a non legal agreement between yourself and the daughter, rather than go down the legal route with your stepson, with all the vagaries and frustrations of the Australian and English legal systems. I think that this will prove to be the best path to follow, but of course that decision is up to you."

While Cook sat quietly contemplating this new information, Bertie turned to the solicitor and said, "This has all come as a bit of a bombshell Mr Belmont and Victoria will need to go away and think about things before she gives you an answer. Why don't we arrange to come back Tuesday morning and talk again, say eleven o'clock. I assume we can continue to stay at the hotel on the expenses you mentioned?"

Mr Belmont nodded and they got up and slowly walked back to their hotel, they called at the hotel bar for a stiff drink and chatted about the information they had just received. Bertie went to reception and extended their stay until Tuesday evening and after a light lunch they ordered a taxi to take them out to her brother's cottage at Burneside.

Eddy and his wife were thrilled to see Victoria again and to meet her new 'gentleman' friend. Victoria gave him a big hug and did indeed tweak his beard and teased him about keeping secrets from his only sister. He was suffering from another bout of pneumonia and appeared to be very weak, but his sense of humour was as robust as ever and he and Bertie were soon swapping stories and telling jokes; although Dolly, Eddies wife, did give the impression that she had heard all of his jokes once or twice before.

Victoria related the whole story of Howard, his daughter and the stolen inheritance to her brother and sister-in-law and they all spent hours discussing the rights and wrongs of the matter and more importantly, what Victoria should do about it. The taxi returned at eight o'clock to take them back to Kendal and they all bid each other farewell and promised to stay in touch. .

On Saturday they boarded a bus and took a trip to Windermere. After touring the town they booked a ride on a steamer and spent several hours cruising the lake, which they both thoroughly enjoyed. As a girl, Victoria had always wanted to go for a trip on the boat, but had not been able to afford it when she lived there and it quite naturally brought back seafaring memories for Bertie and prompted him into telling some of his maritime stories, which kept her spell bound for the whole of the trip and the rest of the day. On the ride back to the hotel in the bus, Victoria kept dropping off to sleep and then waking up with a start as she bumped her head on the window; so Bertie felt obliged to put his arm round her and to let her rest her head on his shoulder, just so she didn't hurt herself!

On Sunday they went to church and Victoria spotted Howard's old boyhood friend , "Look Bertie, the tall man with the green tie, it's Beano, Howard's friend, he hasn't changed a bit."

Beano came over for a chat and then invited them to his house for a spot of lunch and then tea, while they chatted over old times and remembered some of the happy occasions they had shared together.

When they returned to the hotel, it was almost nine o'clock, so they asked room service to bring up a hot drink and biscuits to Bertie's room, where they chatted and agreed to leave the adjoining doors un-locked, in case of an 'emergency'.

When talking about it years later, Cook was sure that Bertie had been the instigator of that first kiss and Bertie was far too much a gentleman to contradict a lady.

Back in Derby, Dutch picked up the transporter which he shared with another small garage and then proceeded to ring round all his usual contacts to try and find a fan belt and hose for the Morris Eight, after assuring himself that the cylinder head gasket was sound. Eventually he admitted defeat and was about to give up and ring Hope with the bad news when his mother asked if there might possibly be a garage in Sheffield with some in stock, since he was going up that way. He immediately rang the main dealer there, who had the parts he wanted and would have someone on site until one thirty if he could get there by then. Dutch replied that he would and asked if he could use their workshop to work on the car, which they agreed to.

He reached Sheffield by eleven a.m. and had the car ready by mid-day and was parked in the farmhouse yard by ten to one, to find the ladies sitting in the summerhouse, chatting to each other. Penny got up and walked over to the car and without thinking gave Dutch a peck on the cheek as she thanked him for all he had done and then asked him what had happened to his transporter?

"I wanted to try the car for myself, to make sure it was properly fixed, so I left the transporter at the garage in Sheffield. Since I have not had a holiday for a few of years, I thought I would book a room at the pub up the road for a couple of nights and do some walking over the weekend and then scrounge a lift back to Sheffield on Monday morning."

"We had planned a walk up Lose Hill this afternoon, Lilly says it is her favourite walk round here, why don't you come with us?" suggested Penny.

"What was all that about 'Lilly says'?" asked her friend who had joined them.

Penny explained what had just been said and it was agreed that she and Dutch would go and book his room, while the ladies got some lunch ready.

The walk to the 'Cheese' took only five minutes but unfortunately they had let the rooms to some soldiers who were looking for crashed plains on the hills around Hope in order to remove any munitions that they might still have in them. Dutch asked if there were any other places with rooms in the village and the pub on the main street was suggested, but the landlord did not sound hopeful. Penny then mentioned that the summerhouse did have a door on it and perhaps, if Lilly agreed, Dutch could manage in there for a couple of nights. To save any embarrassment, Penny spoke to Lilly privately and then reported back that Lilly said it would be fine, if Dutch could manage with cushions and blankets, as she did not possess any more spare beds.

The garden was beautifully laid out with shrubs and trees and all sorts of moisture loving plants and was on a slope which ensured it was well drained. A small gate right at the top led onto the footpath which slowly wound its way over the railway and then past a few farms up to Lose Hill. It took a couple of hours to walk up the hill and Dutch was given the rucksack to carry, with the box camera, groundsheet, thermos flask and sandwiches in it. There was a slight breeze all the way up but the wind was a lot stronger as they reached the steep section near the top, so Amanda and Lilly joined arms to support each other and Dutch and Penny did the same.

The view was breathtaking, with Win Hill in one direction and Mam Tor in the other direction; they had to agree with Lilly's assessment that it was the most beautiful scenery they had ever seen. After the picnic had been consumed and at least half a dozen pictures had been taken, they took the other path down which led round the foot of Win Hill and then along the road back to the farmhouse.

After taking turns to use the bathroom, they were all washed and changed and were seated at the pub by seven fifteen, ready for their meal. Lilly recommended the home made Cumberland Pie which they all ordered and enjoyed. Dutch got up half way through the meal to get another round of drinks and when he returned found a couple of drunken squaddies, attempting to chat up the ladies. When they saw Dutch standing there they both squared up to him and everyone expected a fight to break out but Dutch just leaned forward and said something quietly to them, to which one of them replied, "Oh, he's fine thanks mate," and they both wandered off.

"What on earth did you say to those two men Dutch?" asked Amanda.

"I just asked how my old friend Sergeant Major O'Hara was these days, that's all. We served together for a while in France and I recognized the unit these lads were in and knew they would most definitely not want to upset a friend of Sergeant Major O'Hara!"

The rest of the meal passed pleasantly and Dutch was made comfortable in the summerhouse and everyone went to bed around mid-night. Overnight there was a thunderstorm and Dutch discovered first hand, that the summerhouse had nine leaks in it, of which five were positioned directly over where he was sleeping.

A leisurely breakfast was followed by a walk to the village for the eleven o'clock service and after lunch they decided to drive to Castleton and if the weather held to walk up Mam Tor and back. The rain held off until they were half way up and then fell down, so by the time they got back to the car they were all soaked. The ladies drove back to the farmhouse and Dutch decided that since he was wet already, that he would walk back. By the time he arrived, they had all had a hot bath and were sitting in front of the fire in the lounge, so he could enjoy a long soak in the tub.

Lilly cooked one of her famous 'roasts' for dinner, which took the whole evening to consume and since it was raining again, Dutch was given permission to sleep in the lounge rather than the summerhouse.

On Monday morning the four friends drove into Sheffield and dropped Dutch off at the garage before visiting the local shops. Penny walked across the road to where his transporter was parked and after thanking him again for all he done for them said that she was sure he would want to meet up with Arnold again and suggested that he arranged a visit in a couple of weeks time, when everyone would be back from their holiday.

He smiled and said that he would love to see Digger and Penny and Amanda again and that he would ring Digger and arrange things. She smiled and going onto tiptoe, managed another peck on the cheek, before returning to the car.

When Digger got the telephone call on Monday afternoon he was surprised to find his old friend so good humoured and delighted that he was coming to visit them all in a couple of weeks time. He jokingly told him that he would have to sleep in the laundry in the bed-chair that he himself had to use when he first arrived and even this did not seem to reduce his enthusiasm for the visit.

As an afterthought, at the end of the conversation, just before hanging up, he asked, "You didn't tell them anything about me did you mate, apart from army stories that is?"

"I don't think so Digger, no I am sure I didn't, why is there a problem?" Dutch asked.

"No of course not, just checking, you know how it is, see you soon."

CHAPTER SIXTEEN

DECISIONS DECISIONS

Victoria and Bertie spent the whole of Monday walking in the hills around Kendal and stopped for lunch at a lovely old pub they found and where the landlord turned out to be an amateur poet, so they gave him 'a good listening to'. They discussed what they should do about the 'Australian Matter' as they had come to call it, how this would affect her position at Millstone House and how it would also affect Bertie and his future plans.

As they sat down on a low wall Victoria turned to him and said, "I would love to see Australia and to meet this young lady who has been named after me. As you know I never had children and Howard was more like a delinquent younger brother than a step-son and I somehow feel drawn to this girl. But when I look around here and breathe the fresh air, I just feel how good it would be to live in the Lakes again. Oh Bertie, tell me what I should do!"

He put his arm round her and just sat quietly for a while and then he said, "My last trip as a skipper was 'down under'. I had to take some machinery parts to Sydney and bring a load of wool back to England, but we also had to drop off various items at Melbourne and Fremantle. I just love the place and the whole coastal area around Fremantle has a great climate. I used to tell my wife all about it and promised her that after I retired we would go on a world cruise and spend some time in Western Australia, but as you already know it never happened, she became ill and I nursed her till she died. So maybe we should go, after all, it isn't everyday you are given the chance to see the world at someone else's expense!"

"Yes but I am sixty two and you are almost seventy, don't you think we are too old to be gallivanting half way round the world?"

Bertie smiled and said, "As my Great Uncle Harry used to say, 'Life is for living, not looking back on'. At the age of sixty six he volunteered to drive a bus as a troop carrier in the Great War over in France and right up to the day he died he was ready to try new things.

I remember going to visit him once and he had the most awful smell coming from his head, which was, by the way, completely bald. He could see I was having problems so he came over and being a lot shorter than me, thrust his bald head under my nose. I asked him what was going on and he told me that an old friend of his had read in a magazine that if you rub garlic into your head it would make the hair grow again. It appears he had been doing it for a week or so by then.

I informed him that it had made no difference to his baldness, but that I had noticed that all his neighbours were moving out and perhaps his old friend had played a trick on him. He just laughed and said that it had stopped the cat from next door, from coming in his bedroom window at night, which he always left open, so the garlic was not a complete waste of time.

The point is Victoria, if you never go you will never know and one thing that always saddens me is to here old folks wishing they had done something when they had the opportunity."

"Alright then, I will go, but on one condition, that you come with me Bertie," she answered.

"It's a deal," he relied and they shook hands on it, "we will tell the solicitor that if we can get our fares paid for us, we are both prepared to sail to Australia and meet this other Victoria and her 'bad egg' father and get what's due to you."

When they met Mr Belmont the next day they informed him that they wished to proceed with his suggestion of working through the daughter for a fair settlement, rather than pursue a legal course of action and that they were willing to travel to Australia to meet her and Howard, provided the fares were paid for them.

Mr Belmont said he would write to the solicitors in Perth with this information and keep her informed of all relevant proceedings.

Bertie raised the question of repayment of expenses and Mr Belmont gave Cook fifty pounds in cash to cover the coach fares and incidentals and said that he had already informed the hotel that he would settle the account, once they had left. Cook asked if it would be alright to stay until Friday as they still felt very tired from all that had been going on and were in need of a holiday. Mr Belmont confirmed that Friday would be fine but he had only been given five hundred pounds for expenses and since they were hoping to sail to Australia, advised them not to spend more than was necessary on this trip.

After a tiring day at the shops on Monday, Penny, Amanda and Lilly had a quiet day on Tuesday and just took a drive along the Snake Pass to Glossop in the afternoon. On the way home they stopped at a pub for a meal before returning to the farmhouse.

"Any idea how far it is to Worcester from here, Lilly?" asked Amanda.

"Well it's further than Birmingham and less than Bristol," she replied.

"How far was it from home to here?" asked Penny.

"Well it was about one hundred miles to where we broke down, just outside Derby, but I don't know how far Derby is to Hope. Lilly?"

"It's about forty miles from Derby to here, but how does that help you find out how far it is from here to Worcester," asked Lilly.

"Well I know that Worcester is about eighty miles from Aylesbury going to the left and we went virtually straight up to get here, so the most it can be is one hundred and forty plus eighty, so about two hundred and twenty miles, goodness, that's a long way," remarked Amanda.

"No, no," said Lilly, "Bristol is less than two hundred miles and Birmingham is half way and Worcester is somewhere between the two, so I doubt if it is any more than one hundred and fifty miles."

"Right dear," interjected Penny, "the point of all this being –is?"

"Well we do not have anywhere to stay tomorrow night, so if we are driving all the way to Worcester, it will take us at least four and a half hours and we need to be there early afternoon, so that means we should be away by just after nine tomorrow," replied Amanda.

"Well that's agreed then dear, anything else? How are we for petrol?" enquired Penny.

"We filled up in Sheffield on Monday so we have enough to get us to Stafford and there is bound to be a petrol station there."

Lilly had to be away before eight the next day as she was working and faithfully promised she would come and visit the sisters at Millstone House. They packed all their belongings into the boot of the car and were away just after nine and this time had only reached the village when they remembered they had left the address book by the telephone.

It was a nice day and the drive to Worcester was very pleasant with little traffic on the road. They stopped for about an hour to get some petrol and found a small café where they had morning tea and chatted with the lady who ran it. The car ran very smoothly with no strange noises or smells and they arrived in Worcester just after two o'clock and located the small family hotel just off the centre, which the lady in the café had recommended to them.

To their surprise they were welcomed by the manager of the hotel who said he was expecting them and had reserved two rooms for them, after receiving a telephone call from the self same lady, who was a regular guest at the hotel.

"Oh, wasn't that nice of her Penny, you should try and include her in your next book, she was such an interesting person," said Amanda.

The Hall Porter was able to direct them to the street where Ron's parents lived and commented that his insurance agent happened to live in the same street. The Black's had just sat down to listen to the Archers on the wireless, when the sisters rang the door bell.

"Percy answer the door bell please and I will go and put the kettle on, in case it's them this time," Myrtle said (there having been several times already when it was not them), " and if it is them, I don't want to hear any of your Insurance Collectors jokes, is that clear?"

"Yes dear," he said and meekly went to open the front door.

As the front door opened, the light from the hallway lit up Amanda's face and Percy instantly recognized his daughter-in-law, "Oh Amanda, love, you have hardly changed a bit and your sister, how nice to see you both again, do come in."

Myrtle had returned from the kitchen and was standing in the parlour when Amanda came through from the hall. She had gone over many times what she was going to say to her daughter-in-law when they met, because both she and Percy had been badly hurt by the way she had treated them after Ron had died. Amanda too, had spent many hours pondering what she would say to Ron's parents and had secretly dreaded this moment.

The two women stood facing each other and then Myrtle smiled and said, "I remember it as if it was yesterday, when Ron came home and told us about this gorgeous girl he had met and how much he loved her and wanted to marry her and how happy you made him Amanda, it's so good to see you again my dear," and she held out her arms and hugged her.

Thankfully in life there are some occasions when things go much better than you could dream possible and this was one of them for Amanda and Ron's parents. Explanations were not demanded or given, it was just good to be together and to laugh and cry together. The four met up again on the Thursday evening at the hotel where the sisters were staying and they had a very pleasant meal together. Percy was severely reprimanded by his wife for telling one of his 'Insurance Collectors jokes', but only after he had completed it and everyone had had a good laugh.

On Friday Myrtle took Amanda to the town's War memorial where they saw Ron's name carved in stone along with all the other sons and daughters of Worcester who had given their lives for their country. As the two ladies stood together, each remembering their Ron, they felt a peace and a oneness of spirit that was to bind them together for the rest of their lives.

Before they left Worcester on the Saturday, the sisters went round to see Percy and Myrtle and to invite them to visit them at Millstone and to meet Digger, Ron's friend from the army. They said they would love to and would write with dates once Percy had booked some holiday from work.

Since the weather had brightened up they decided to drive to Weston Super Mare and have a few days at the seaside, which they did, returning safely to Millstone House on the Tuesday.

Bertie rang Digger on Thursday to check on the cottage and to say that they would be leaving Kendal on Friday but that they had booked a few days at a hotel in Lancaster, as Cook wanted to look up some old friends. All being well they would return to Millstone next week and would ring again from Oxford once they had arrived. Digger told him about the letter from London, which Bertie guessed was from Deborah and that the cottage was still standing and to tell Cook that they had finished the Spring Cleaning and repainted the laundry and that Moira had not burnt the kitchen down yet.

"And how is Moira?" Bertie asked at the end of the conversation.

"Well to tell you the truth Bertie, I am not sure. She got a letter from her mother this week and has suddenly got a bit 'standoffish' if you know what I mean. She wants me to go to Scotland with her to visit her parents; I mean that's a fourteen hour train journey each way and it will cost a fortune in fares and we have only been dating a short while! What do you think I should do about it?"

"Digger my young friend, I fear the time has come for you to make a decision about your friendship with Moira. It would appear that she has already reached that point in your relationship where her feelings for you are more than just platonic and have become very serious and she has to know for certain that you feel the same way or your friendship will be coming to a very abrupt end, in the not too distant future. For someone like Moira, I suspect that her parent's approval is very important to her and if you care for her at all, you should agree to go to Scotland, it doesn't have to be next week, just some time in the next couple of months. If you don't care for her, then in fairness to her you should end the relationship now, before either or both of you get hurt."

"Oh goodness, Bertie, we have become good friends for sure, but I don't know how things could have moved this fast, I really don't think I am ready for another serious relationship right now, the last one left me a bit bitter, if I am honest."

"That's life Digger, sometimes things happen so quickly it leaves us in a spin and sometimes so slowly that we get bored and lose interest. Between you and me, Victoria and I have become extremely close friends and I can see us 'tying the knot' before very long, so if it can happen to an old codger like me, it can certainly happen to a young 'blood' like you. Anyway, times up, I have to go, bye and good luck," with which he put the phone down and turned to face Victoria who had just come up and stood beside him.

"So," she said, "who's an old codger and who's tying the knot quite soon and if that's a proposal Mr Bannister, I accept."

They embraced right there in the hotel lobby, much to the surprise of the other guests and were only disturbed by the manager, discreetly coughing behind them.

"This lady has just agreed to be my wife, isn't that great," exclaimed Bertie.

Everyone clapped and shook their hands and the manager led them into the bar for a celebration drink and to propose a toast to the newly engaged couple.

When Moira didn't turn up, as expected, on Thursday evening, Digger assumed she had just been delayed at work and heated up some pie and cooked himself a few potatoes and peas. He took Mac for a walk and sorted out some logs which he transported on the wheelbarrow from the woods to the garden. He checked the house was locked up properly and returned to the cottage and read for a while before having an early night.

When Moira failed to turn up Friday night he began to wonder if she was unwell and decided to walk round to her place and check up on her, he knocked at the front door but got no answer and was about to walk away when Sissy opened a downstairs window of her house and called out, "She's round the back hanging out some washing Digger," but was cut off somewhat abruptly by her mother who closed the window whilst commenting that only common people shout out of windows.

Digger walked round the back and sure enough, there was Moira hanging out her washing, who on seeing Digger, promptly removed several articles from the line and put them back in the basket.

"Hello Moira, I just knocked," he said.

"I thought I heard something," she replied.

"You didn't come round last night and I had to cook my own tea," he responded and immediately sensed he had said the wrong thing.

"Well I am sorry if you were inconvenienced Mr Smith, to the extent you actually had to cook for yourself for once, I will make sure that my monthly falls on a more convenient date in future," with which she turned and went indoors, but left the back door open.

Digger just stared in disbelief and thought to himself, "That settles it Bertie my friend, I am most definitely not ready for another relationship just yet," so he turned and headed off for the pub.

"Ello Digger, no Moira tonight, want your usual," asked Del the landlord.

"Hello mate, no to the first, yes to the second and any chance of something to eat please, I'm famished?"

The landlord pulled him a pint of best bitter and then wandered off into the kitchen and spoke to his wife, "Digger's in the bar on his own, miserable as sin, can you do him something to eat Luv?"

His wife prepared a big plate of cheese and pickles with a large chunk of bread and some salad and found Digger sitting in the corner of the saloon bar, all on his own. She put the plate down and sat down opposite to him.

"Thanks Sheila," he said, "but I'm not really in a chatty mood tonight."

Now Sheila had worked behind bars in pubs and hotels for more than twenty years and could quite easily have run courses for military intelligence, on extracting information from unwilling subjects, so needless to say within ten minutes she had obtained a complete understanding from Digger of the current situation between, himself and Moira. She sympathized with his confused state of affairs regarding the conversation he had just had with Moira but realized that urgent action was required by her, if this village romance was to last another day longer.

"Well Digger," she started, "if you want my advice (but didn't wait for any response) if you say that you really have no feelings for the girl, I would just walk away and have nothing else to do with her."

"I didn't say that I had no feelings for her Sheila, it's just," he got no further.

She continued, "I am sorry, I got the impression that since Moira was feeling unwell and didn't come round last night to cook your tea, that you decided that you didn't want her friendship anymore," at which point she fell silent and stared straight at him.

"No Sheila, that's just not fair, now you are putting words in my mouth, I never said that nor did I even think it!"

"You may not have said it in so many words Digger, but that's the impression you have given me and that will also be the impression you have given Moira; who incidentally is the best district nurse this village has had for many years and no-one will thank you for driving her away."

"Why don't you just blame me for the state of the roads, the power cuts and everything else that's wrong with the country today! All I said to her was 'you didn't come round last night and I had to cook my own tea,' you make it sound like I beat her over the head with the copper stick, for goodness sake."

"I like you Digger and I think you are a decent bloke deep down, so let me explain something to you. Each month, when a woman is feeling low and is often in pain, what she needs most of all is understanding and appreciation. She wants someone to care about her and to make a fuss of her, regardless of how she might look or sound. She does not need someone to speak to her as if she is a servant and trample all over her feelings, like you have just done."

"I never meant to, Sheila, honest I didn't. I thought she was all up-tight all about the letter she got from her mother, asking me to go to Scotland with her to meet them all."

Sheila smiled and put her hand on his and softened her tone, "Of course the two things are linked Digger, but let me assure you, right now she wants to know you care about her and that you don't just think of her as someone who cooks meals for you when Cook is away, but someone who likes her for herself and appreciates what she does for you."

"I am totally lost Sheila, tell me what to do," he almost pleaded.

Sheila got up from the table and returned in a couple of minutes with some flowers wrapped in paper, which she gave to Digger. "These are going to cost you a shilling, which I am adding to your bill, which you can settle with Del before you leave, which will be right now. Give her the flowers, tell her you are sorry and really care for her and that you would love to visit her parents in Scotland and don't ever mention this conversation to her or to anyone else. Is that understood?"

Digger nodded, picked up the flowers, paid his bill and walked back with some trepidation to Moira's house.

She had obviously been crying when she opened the door; she grabbed the flowers and then him and dragged him into the hallway where they hugged and kissed. After the flowers had been put in a vase, he apologized for what he had said earlier, told her how much he cared for her and that he would love to go to Inverness to meet her family.

When he finally got back to the cottage around midnight, he was mentally exhausted and quickly fell asleep, thinking all the time what a lucky chap he was to have such a fantastic girlfriend.

CHAPTER SEVENTEEN
MIXED REACTIONS

It was early afternoon when the sisters drove through the gates into the yard and pulled up outside the garage at Millstone House. Digger had been working on the vegetable garden and was busy weeding when they arrived and Sissy was doing a final inspection of the house, making sure everything was back in its place. As they got out of the car, Mac went bounding over to give them a big doggy welcome, for which he was well rewarded with lots of pats and fuss.

"Well you made it without further mishap then?" enquired Digger, "You both look very well, have you had a nice time?"

"We have had a marvellous time thank you Arnold, how has everything been here, is Cook back yet," asked Mrs Duffy-Smythe?

Digger picked up the cases which Mrs Black had taken out of the boot and carried them into the kitchen, "Everything has been fine here," he replied, "we have both finished all the jobs that you left us and as far as we know, Cook will be home later today or tomorrow."

Mrs Black looked round the kitchen and smiled at Sissy who had come in behind them, "I must say Sissy, you have done a great job here, the place looks and smells all fresh and new, well done and here is a small present we got you from Weston Super Mare," with which she passed her a box of fudge.

"Oh thank you Mrs Black, I will have to hide these from my mum, she loves fudge too," Sissy replied, "I wasn't sure what to do about food, so I put a casserole on the stove, knowing it would keep for tomorrow if you don't fancy it today."

"I will unpack my things and then perhaps, Sissy, you can show me what you have been doing in the house and laundry," said Mrs Duffy-Smythe, "and then Arnold, you can show me what has been happening outside."

"As you can see," said Digger, "I have repaired as much of the fence as was reasonable, but there are about five posts in that section that are completely rotten, so before I did any more, I wanted to get your permission to replace them. The wood yard in Oxford has plenty in stock, I just need to go and pick them up."

"Oh dear, more expense Arnold, I guess if they are beyond saving you will have to replace them, but until I get another cheque from my publisher or go into London and see the bank, we will have to tighten our belts I am afraid."

Just then Mrs Black emerged from the front door and called to them, "Cook is on the telephone and says that their coach has just arrived in Oxford. Do you mind if Arnold goes and picks them up Penny, OK I will let her know. About an hour from now, shall I say? You don't mind Arnold do you?" With which she went back into the house.

"If you leave now Arnold, you could go by the wood yard and get the posts, that will save a journey," she said and they both turned and went back indoors.

The posts were too long for the boot, so Digger put them in the front passenger foot well and tied them to the seat. Bertie and Cook were waiting for him at the coach station and did not seem to mind that they had to share the rear seat together.

"Am I allowed to ask how the trip went," asked Digger, fishing for information.

"Yours to wonder and ours to know," teased Cook.

"We do have some news Digger, but feel we should make Mrs Black and Mrs Duffy-Smythe aware of our plans first, since they are the ones who will be most affected," said Bertie, "but if you come round tonight I will give you a full briefing."

Cook then asked various questions as to what Sissy had been doing and whether she had turned up for work every day and seemed both surprised and pleased at the good report Digger gave her.

He dropped them at the front door and put the car away in the garage. In view of what had been said, he kept away from the house and started work on replacing the rotten fence posts with the new ones he had bought after dipping the basses in some creosote he had found at the back of the garage.

When Bertie and Victoria announced to the sisters that they had some news they wanted to share with them, Sissy was thanked for all her hard work and was sent home early. They went through to the lounge and sat down and all eyes turned to Victoria who cleared her throat and started to speak, "Before we went to Kendal, you were aware that I had received a package from a solicitor, which suggested that I might hear something to my advantage, regarding my step-son Howard Owen, who now lives in Australia. Well I did." She then proceeded to tell them the story in full and finished by saying, "We are now waiting for a reply from Australia, before we decide our next step, but it is only fair that I tell you now, since it does affect you both, that we are expecting to be asked to sail to Fremantle in Western Australia, some tome in the next five or six months."

The two sisters looked at each other in surprise, Mrs Duffy-Smythe spoke first, "You keep saying we, so am I right in assuming that Bertie will be travelling with you to Australia as well?"

Cook looked straight at her as she replied, "You would hardly expect me to leave my new husband behind in England, while I sail to Australia, would you?"

Mrs Black jumped up and walked over to Victoria and gave her a big hug, "Oh Cook, I am so pleased for you both, many congratulations, when is the big day?"

"We need to speak to the vicar about that, but the end of June or the beginning of July would suit, wouldn't it Bertie?"

"That's right," he said, "but we would ask you to keep it to yourself for a few days, as there are some more people we would like to inform, before it becomes local knowledge."

"Well excuse me," said Mrs Duffy-Smythe, "but I am not so sure that the end of June does suit me Cook," with which she got up and left the room.

"I was afraid of that," said Victoria, "but my mind is made up Amanda, I have looked after other people for long enough, and it's time I looked after myself. Bertie and I have discussed this possibility and if she is going to be unpleasant, I will move out of here a lot quicker than the end of June."

"I assure you that will not be necessary," replied Mrs Black, "I know my sister and once she gets over the initial shock of your news, she will be as pleased for you as I am. Just leave her to me."

While Cook and Bertie walked back to his cottage, the two sisters chatted about Cook's forthcoming marriage and journey to the other side of the world. Amanda pointed out that with one less member of staff to pay, the money would go a lot further and that Sissy had worked very well on her own while they were all away and that she herself, in all honesty, used to love cooking for herself and Ron, for she had been a very fine cook in those days.

"We also need to think about Digger too; we probably have enough work for another month or so, after that we will have to tell him that it is time for him to move on. I was thinking of looking for work in Aylesbury myself Penny, as I do get bored here sometimes, but with cook leaving, I won't need to."

Since Cook had not returned from the cottage, Mrs Black prepared the rest of dinner and the three of them sat down to eat around seven o'clock. Digger had told them of his conversation with Dutch and that he was expecting him to come down for the next weekend and had never known his friend so articulate. Mrs Black commented that she wondered why that was and Mrs Duffy-Smythe reddened slightly, but Digger missed all of that!

He had already told Moira not to expect him Tuesday evening so he walked to Bertie's cottage after dinner, but left Mac behind, just in case he caused problems again. Cook seemed relieved to hear that Mrs Duffy-Smythe had been in a good mood over dinner and assumed that Mrs Black had sorted things out. He was delighted with all their news and warmly shook Bertie's hand and ventured a hug and kiss on the cheek with Cook.

He then told them his news, that he and Moira were officially 'going out' and that he had agreed to visit her parents in Scotland, sometime in the summer or Autumn. He also mentioned that his army mate Dutch, was coming to visit him over the weekend, after acting the 'Knight in Shining Armour' with the sisters and their car during their trip north.

"That's a pity," said Bertie grinning, "the letter I received while we were away was from Deborah, she is also coming down this weekend, I was going to invite you and Moira round for dinner on Saturday."

"Oh dear, what a shame," replied Digger formally, "does she know yet of your forthcoming marriage?"

"No, I was going to wait until I see her and then tell her face to face. To be honest I have no idea how she will react, as she was very close to her mother, me being away so much of the time. By the way, you can tell Moira our news, but no-one else for the moment please."

Dutch telephoned Tuesday evening while Digger was at Bertie's to check it was still 'on' for the weekend. Since Digger was out he was quite happy to chat to Penny, who happened to answer the phone. They talked for quite a long time and Dutch was in an excellent frame of mind when he put down the receiver, which was located in the hall and returned to the parlour where his mother was listening to the radio.

"My goodness but your friend knows how to talk, that call must have cost a small fortune Dutch!"

"It wasn't Digger mum, it was Penny, the lady he is working for, you know the one whose car I fixed and took to Sheffield. She's a writer and a very good one, had quite a few books published, a really nice lady, we got on very well."

"Did you dear, Penny you say, what's her sister called 'Florin', what sort of a name is Penny? So who is it you are actually going to see this weekend, your army friend or this woman?"

"She's not 'this woman' mum and I'm going to see Digger and Penny and her sister. For goodness sake mum I'm forty one, I sometimes wonder if you don't want me to meet a nice girl and get married."

"Don't you raise your voice to me, my lad. Of course I want you meet the right person and get married, don't you worry about me, I have managed all these years to get by and I will manage long after you have left me and gone after your fancy writer!"

Dutch knew there was no point in continuing the conversation, so he got out his book and started reading.

His mother seemed fine the next day, back to her old cheerful self but happened to comment on Thursday evening that she wasn't feeling too good and had had one of her dizzy spells while he was at work and would he mind helping her up the stairs as she was frightened of falling. On Friday morning she felt too ill to get out of bed and asked him to call the doctor, who eventually came round to the house at twelve noon and whilst he couldn't actually find anything wrong with her, advised that she stay in bed for a couple of days and not be left on her own.

Dutch rang Millstone House as soon as the doctor had left and explained that his mother was unwell and he couldn't leave her and they agreed to reschedule the visit for a later date.

On Saturday afternoon mother appeared downstairs around three p.m. saying she felt a lot better and that some fresh air would probably do her good. Dutch helped her into the breakdown truck and they drove up into the hills to a favourite beauty spot and sat there enjoying the view. By the time they got back to Derby she said she could eat some fish and chips, which they bought in town and took home to eat.

Unfortunately mother had a dizzy spell the next time Dutch arranged to visit Digger and also the time after that and in the end, they never did manage to meet up to talk over old times!

Moira was thrilled when she heard the good news about Bertie and Cook and insisted on calling round to see Cook on Thursday morning to congratulate her. She was also able to tell Cook of their forthcoming trip to Scotland during her holiday at the beginning of June, which came as a bit of a surprise to Digger when Cook mentioned it over dinner that evening.

Mrs Black took the opportunity to mention another time frame to Digger, "Well that will pretty much coincide with your finishing all the work we have asked you to do, wont it Arnold?"

"Yes, I guess it will Mrs Black, I must start thinking about alternative accommodation, if I am going to stay in the area," he mused.

"I know one young lady who is going to be very upset, if you don't stay in the area Arnold," said Cook sternly. "I am sure Bertie won't mind you using his cottage while we are on our Australian trip, in fact he will probably be glad of someone looking after it for him, you should ask him about it."

"I will, thank you Cook, just the time between the two dates to fill in then!"

"No one said you had to leave the cottage Arnold, we just cannot afford to keep you indefinitely and I do sort of get the feeling that you are used to work that is a lot more mentally stimulating than we are able to offer," commented Mrs Duffy-Smythe. "But to change the subject completely, I had a call from my bank today to say I had to call in and sign some papers to do with some investments and they said the quicker the better, like tomorrow. The only problem is that they are in Princes Street in London and I hate driving in London, I always get lost, do you know where Princes Street is Arnold? Would you be prepared to drive me please?"

Arnold had now gone slightly pale as he looked at her in disbelief. "Yes I know where Princes Street is, which bank do you use?"

"Midland Bank, Mr White, who is my contact there, said that since it was urgent, he would arrange for me to park at the bank, it appears there is a small yard at the rear. Didn't you say once that you used to work around there, near London Bridge or something?"

"Of course I will drive you in, but the traffic is bad on a Friday and maybe you would be better going by train and I don't have anything smart to wear and I haven't checked the car over since your holiday," he blurted out.

"Good, that is settled then, we will leave after breakfast about seven forty, just go as smart as you are able and the car is running really well, your friend Dutch said he had checked it over for us," replied Mrs Duffy-Smythe.

It was nearer to eight o'clock when they left and then only after Digger had tried to persuade her again to take the train. The A40 was not very busy so since the appointment was for ten a.m., they stopped for a cup of tea on the outskirts of London. Mrs Duffy-Smythe was able to follow the route that Digger took for most of the way, but when they reached the Holborn area of London, she had to give up. It was about then that it started to rain and Digger drove down a maze of side streets and then suddenly it seemed that he just turned a corner and drove down the side of the bank and stopped in the car park at the rear. He opened the door for Mrs Duffy-

Smythe and was about to get back in the car when someone called out and started to walk over to them, she asked him to deal with it and said she would meet him inside, in the bank's reception.

He joined her ten minutes later and sat down next to her, without speaking and picked up a copy of the Telegraph, which he opened in front of him and started to read.

"What on earth took you so long Arnold," she asked?

"It appears we had parked in the wrong place, so I had to move the car," he said.

They sat in silence and he read the paper when she suddenly announced, "Here he comes now, Mr White, such a nice man, but with such a terrible taste in braces."

Arnold jumped up and said he had to go to the cloakroom just as Mr White appeared, "Mrs Duffy-Smythe, how nice to see you, that young man who left just as I arrived, was he with you?" he asked.

"Mr White, prompt as ever, it is so nice to see you again. Arnold yes, he is a sort of handyman come mechanic come driver, why do you ask?"

"Arnold you say, he looks just like a young man who used to work for me and his name was Arnold, mind you everyone bar me called him Digger."

"Tell me more," she said, as they walked into his office.

By the time she had finished signing the papers and discussing her other investments that the bank looked after for her, they had swapped 'Digger' stories and she had discovered that a young man with a wonderful banking career ahead of him, had walked into Mr White's office on Thursday 1st April that year and resigned. Furthermore he had asked that he be allowed to leave the next day, in lieu of the holiday he was due. He had come in the next day, cleared his desk, handed over all his accounts to his colleagues and had left the bank. He had not touched any of the money in his account and Mr White had grown very concerned as to his wellbeing.

They walked together back to reception, but Digger was not there, "He must be waiting in the car," she said.

"Maybe," replied Mr White, "but when Arnold went missing, he was normally to be found drinking tea with the messengers and swapping tales, I think we will try there first, for they are bound to have spotted him by now."

Sure enough Digger was halfway through telling them about Bertie's encounter with a roof tile, when they went into the messengers room.

"I thought we might find you here Arnold, it's very good to see you again," said Mr White as he held out his hand. "This dear lady has been bringing me up-to-date with what you have been doing, and I gather you have been doing the same with the gentlemen here."

Digger got up and shook the old man's hand. "It's very good to see you again too, sir," he said, "I knew you must have spotted me, nothing ever escapes you!"

"Mrs Duffy-Smythe has agreed to give us half an hour before she returns home, I am sure one of the gentlemen here will escort her to the coffee lounge, while we chat in my office."

They slowly walked to the office as word spread that Digger was back and all his old friends and colleagues rushed to say hello.

"You have been missed Arnold and not just for your work, but you were the life and soul of our office and things have not been the same without you. You can have your old job back tomorrow if you want it, or I can see what else is available around the country if you like. I am sure I recall an assistant manager's job in one of the branches near where you are now living."

He fished around in his cupboard and came back with a sheet of paper.

"Here, take this and think about it. I hear you have a young lady so maybe you should chat to her and let me know if you would like to pursue any of these, you know my number, but even if you decide not to, stay in touch Arnold, our friendship meant a lot to me."

"I don't know what to say sir, you always treated me well and I treated you badly, I don't deserve this, but thanks anyway and I will chat to Moira and let you know. I think my half hour is up and she is not a lady who likes to be kept waiting."

Digger discussed his conversation with Mr White on the way home and the offer of an assistant manager's job in the Oxford area, if he were interested. He said he would have to think about it and asked Mrs Duffy-Smythe to say nothing to the others until he had time to speak to Moira; but promised her that he would not leave her employ until he had completed the work she had asked him to do.

Deborah and motorbike arrived around ten and Bertie was on his own when he went through the garden to greet her. After the usual pleasantries, which being Deborah amounted to, "You get older and fatter every time I see you dad," Bertie sat her down by the fire, with a glass of port and told what had been happening in his life.

"So you see Deborah," he concluded, "Victoria and I intend to get married in a couple of months and then go off to Australia, for goodness knows how long."

"Dad, I'm so pleased for you, that you have found someone who can make you happy and bring a bit of purpose back into your life. Australia sounds great, I wish I could come too, but I guess having your daughter on your honeymoon, isn't the done thing, is it. You were not cut out just to sit in an armchair and grow old gracefully, you have always had an active life and that's what you can look forward to again, you were never meant to be a pumpkin grower, were you?"

"I guess not Deborah and I never thought of it as a honeymoon, I guess I had better start to get fit again," he laughed.

"All I ask is that you do not ask me to call her mum, mother or anything similar. We were more than mother and daughter, she was my best friend and I still miss her terribly," she said.

"I know love, Victoria has asked that you call her Victoria, but she is like you and hates to have her name shortened."

"Hey, I am warming to this lady already, when do I get to meet her?" she asked.

"I asked her to come round for lunch tomorrow, if that fits with your plans."

"That suits fine, the bike rally is at Leamington Spa Sunday morning, so if I leave early I will get there for the start and go straight home afterwards."

Victoria came round to the cottage just before lunch on Saturday and to Bertie's relief the two women hit it off immediately, going off to the garden to discuss female issues and returning to announce that Deborah had agreed to be bridesmaid and that they would both wear cream and would go shopping in Oxford in a couple of weeks time. They also announced that Bertie was to wear a dinner jacket which they would help him purchase, also in Oxford, which would come in useful on the cruise to Australia.

The three of them went out to the pub for a drink in the evening and bumped into Digger and Moira who were sitting quietly in the saloon bar. Digger and Deborah were polite, but kept their distance and only once did he call her Debs, which caused her to throw her bag of crisps at him, which he immediately consumed with a self satisfied smile.

CHAPTER EIGHTEEN
GETTING TO KNOW YOU

Somehow the pub did not seem the right place to tell Moira about the bank and the job offer and the end of work at Millstone and when Bertie, Cook and Deborah turned up it was certainly not the right place; so he decided to discuss the matter with her on Sunday, after church. Unfortunately for Digger, Bertie and Cook both went to church that Sunday, in order to speak with the vicar and inform him of their forthcoming nuptials and to arrange a time and date when they could meet. While the ladies were chatting before the service, Cook enquired as to the forthcoming trip to Scotland and mentioned that it would tie in nicely with Digger finishing the work at Millstone House.

Moira said she wanted to go home after the service since she had things to prepare for the various appointments she had on the Monday. On the way home she informed Digger that Cook had told her about his need to find alternative employment soon and asked what he was going to do about it.

"Did she mention anything else to you about me?" he asked, wondering if news about the bank visit had leaked out.

"No, why – is there something else I should know?"

"Actually there is and this is as good a time as any to talk to you about it."

"Digger, this sounds serious," she said, "we are almost at my home, come in and tell me whatever it is over a cup of tea," with which she gripped his arm a little tighter and walked a little quicker as they rounded the corner of her street.

Having made the tea they sat down around the kitchen table and she said a little apprehensibly, "Well, love, what is it you want to tell me?"

"Last Friday I took Mrs Duffy-Smythe to her bank in London and it just so happened that it was the self same bank where I used to work and who did I meet there, but the man who I used to work for."

She looked surprised but sat quietly, taking in this new information.

"He asked me if I wanted my old job back, which was very kind of him, considering I had left at very short notice."

"Why did you leave at such short notice Digger?"

"I had been going out with this girl since before the war had started, her name was Sarah, she lived just a few doors down from me. She wrote to me the whole of the time I was in the army and I thought of her as my sweetheart and it was always understood that one day we would get engaged and be married. When I returned from the war, I discovered that she had moved away from the area and now lived in Southampton and worked for the navy. We saw each other at weekends and I thought everything was still fine between us, but she had fallen for a marine officer during the war who had then been shipped overseas and had been severely wounded and had only recently left hospital.

He had spent some time in tracking her down and they met up again towards the end of March, this year. Sarah realized that she loved him and not me and rang me to say she was coming to London on the 31st March and wanted to see me. She was there, at my place when I got home and I knew something was different, as soon as I saw her.

She told me about the romance and that she had come to realize that she no longer loved me and wanted to end things between us. I was devastated and got angry with her and maybe said some things I shouldn't have done, so she just got up and left."

Moira reached across the table and held his hand, "At least she had the decency to tell you as soon as she realized the truth Digger, but that does not mean that it was any easier for you to accept. So why did you quit your job? And what happened about your lodgings?"

"I was living in my sister Vi's house in Clapham, South London. Her children were getting older and needed a room each anyway, so I just put my things in her cellar and told her I would be away for a while and would move out properly, once I knew what I was doing. She and her husband were really good about it, said I always had a home with them, anytime I wanted to return.

Suddenly work lost its appeal, making money for other people to get rich on seemed a bit of a waste of time. I worked in investments in the bank, you know stocks and shares and bonds and things."

Moira shook her head, "That is a world I know nothing about and do not understand, dad always said that as many fortunes were lost, as were made on the stock exchange."

Digger smiled, "Your dad was partly right, some people do gamble and can lose a lot of money, but there are ways to spread your risk and without the Stock Markets of the world, large companies and trade would cease to exist as we know it today. But anyway, I went in next day and just handed in my notice; poor Mr White, he was my boss, almost fell off his chair with shock. Two days later I was away and caught the train to a new world, got robbed while asleep and the rest you know."

"So about having your old job back and working in London again, have you made a decision about that, yet?"

"My reasons for leaving were probably correct, I did need to start somewhere new and meet new people and I am tired of living in a big city, so I certainly don't want my old job back. Mr White did say however, that there were some branch vacancies in this area, maybe Aylesbury or Oxford, he even gave me the 'Positions Vacant List' to peruse and since I did start out in a small branch in London and enjoyed that a lot, I thought that perhaps I would check things out. Tell me, what do you think Moira, could you see yourself going out with an assistant manager at a bank?"

"Well I do not know Mr Smith. I thought I was going out with a poor and lowly handyman come driver and now I discover that he is a 'City Slicker' who might become a bank manager, what is a poor simple country girl to make of all this?"

She stood up and walked round the table twice, scratching her head and then sat down again.

"It is the man that interests me, not what he does for a living, I care for you because you are honest and decent and hard working and you are good company and I love being with you Digger. You take whatever job you like and that will be fine with me."

She sat quietly for a minute and then launched into a string of questions, "Does this mean you will have your own car, because you will need your own transport if you are going to work in Oxford or Aylesbury. Or does this mean you will move away from the village, in which case, where will you live? Could you still live in the cottage at Millstone

House if you paid them rent? And when do I get to meet this sister of yours and her family, she sounds a lovely person?"

The rest of the day sort of just disappeared for them and it was gone eleven p.m. before Moira started to prepare for Monday's appointments. Digger got back to the cottage and re-read the 'Positions Vacant List' and felt the assistant manager's job in Oxford sounded the most interesting, since he would be dealing with all the local businesses and some of the Oxford colleges and their students.

He telephoned Mr White on Monday afternoon, who promised he would make enquiries and ring him back. True to his word he called back around five and said that the position was still open and that Digger should ring the manager and arrange an interview, preferably for that week. Digger telephoned on Tuesday morning and had the interview on Thursday morning, Mrs Duffy-Smythe allowing him to use the car to get to Oxford. At the end of the interview the manager told him in confidence that he had the job, but would have to wait for the official letter before he could start work and acquire some more appropriate clothing. Digger explained that he had committed to finish the work at Millstone House by the end of May and that he and his young lady had planned a trip to Scotland from the 5th to the 19th June, so the earliest he could start work would be Monday the 21st June 1948.

This proved to be a real stumbling block as the current assistant manager was leaving to take over a new branch in the middle of June and needed to hand over to his successor before then. A compromise was reached, whereby Digger would work at the bank all day Friday and Saturday morning, starting the following week.

"Well Mr Smith," the bank manager said, "will you require assistance in finding somewhere to live in Oxford?"

"My current employer is allowing me to stay in the cottage where I currently live, for as long as I need it sir. I think she and her sister enjoy the extra security of having me and my dog around."

"Indeed and how do you propose to travel to Oxford each day, may I ask?"

"I intend to purchase a motor car. I was trained as a mechanic in the army, so should be able to look after it myself. I spotted a couple of cars at a dealers on the way in this morning, so I will give them a look over, on the way back. Which reminds me, I need to draw some cash out of my account, is it alright if I see the head cashier?"

"Certainly, I took the liberty of checking your account before the interview Mr Smith, just draw what you need. My old friend Mr White has spoken most highly of you and I look forward to working with you, we will see you at eight thirty next Friday. Goodbye."

The two men shook hands and Digger left the office and went straight to the Head Cashiers desk and drew out some cash from his account. Next he went over and said goodbye to the outgoing assistant manager, just to get the rumour mill started!

As he pulled up outside the car dealers yard he was dismayed by the motley collection of cars on show, but decided to go and check things out anyway. As he walked into the yard and started to peer into the cars a middle aged man with a bright tie and wearing a trilby hat came out of the old hut, which served as an office and greeted him, "Good morning sir, have you seen anything you like yet, would you like a drive in one of them, do you want to trade in the old banger you parked over there?"

Digger turned round and smiled at the man, "Hello, no I haven't seen anything I like among this lot and that is not my car, so no trade ins today. Is this all you have on offer?"

"I'm afraid it is, second hand cars are very scarce at the moment, well that is apart from an Austin Seven Tourer which came in earlier this week, my mechanic was going to give it the once over for me, but has gone down with chicken-pox of all things and won't be back for another week or so. I can take you to see that if you like, I have a workshop about two miles away. Provided you are serious that is!"

Digger visualized in his mind his friend from the bank who had bought a similar car before Christmas and all the problems he had encountered. "I don't know, a friend of mine bought one a few months back and had a lot of problems with it, he took his dad for a ride and the old chap very nearly fell out when the passenger door flew open on a corner and the suspension was very 'cart like' for want of a better term. What are you asking for it, as I have a very limited budget?"

"Your friend probably bought one that had been neglected during the war, the Tourers can have the sort of problems your friend encountered when the bodywork becomes a bit slack, but this one has been regularly used and maintained and is a real snip at two hundred and fifty pounds."

Digger gasped at this news, "Two hundred and fifty quid, they only cost half of that when new, anyway that's way over my budget, I guess I had better look somewhere else."

"Hold on, hold on, if you were to take it as is, get someone else to service it for you, I could let you have it a bit cheaper, come and see it anyway, I am not exactly busy at the moment."

Digger agreed to see the car and the man locked up the yard for the night and drove his own lovely old Bentley round to where his workshop was situated. They both parked and walked over to lock up garage. Now love at first sight, normally describes the emotions of a young man for a young woman, but it also describes Diggers emotions when he first beheld the 1936 Austin Seven AAL Tourer. It was a deep blue with black mudguards and a black hood. It was dirty and had a few scratches and the seats were a bit tacky and the engine sounded awful when it was started, but he knew he had to have this car. To Digger's trained ear, the engine sounded like everything that could be out of tune, was out of tune, but he heard nothing which gave him a real concern.

They chatted and bartered and in the end agreed a figure of two hundred and twenty pounds, which both seemed pleased with. Digger left a twenty pound deposit, for which he got a handwritten receipt and said he would be back Saturday morning to pick it up and pay the balance. The man said he had a friend who handled car insurance and would get a quote for Digger and gave him the friend's telephone number.

On the way home he pondered how he was going to inform Mrs Duffy-Smythe of all that had transpired and in particular that he would require garaging for his car and would not be able to work for her for the remaining Fridays.

When he arrived at Millstone he parked the car and then went into the kitchen and asked Mrs Duffy-Smythe if he might have a word privately with her?

"Of course you can Arnold, but do you mind if my sister joins us?"

"Not at all, it's just that I look on you as my employer and I wanted to inform you, first of all, of what has transpired today."

"Quite right too, but I would like my sister to hear this as well, Amanda, will you join us in the study please."

The three went into the study and sat down, Mrs Black spoke first, "Well, how did things go in Oxford, did you get the job, what happened Arnold?"

"Yes I did, the interview went extremely well. I think Mr White must have put in a good word for me. I start on the 21st June after we get back from Scotland, but there is a problem though."

He went on to explain the need to go in on Fridays and Saturday mornings and said he would work longer in the evenings to make up for the lost time, which with the lighter evenings now, was both possible and acceptable to the ladies.

"But what are you going to do about transport Arnold, I won't be able to lend you the car every time you have to go into Oxford, I am afraid," said Mrs Duffy-Smythe, "but you will need your own transport anyway, unless you intend moving closer to your work."

"Well actually, I have put a deposit down on a car. I called in at a second hand car dealers on the way back and found an Austin Seven in pretty good condition. They do about forty miles per gallon so are a very economical little runner and I will be able to maintain it myself, if you would allow me to keep it in the garage, as it is a Tourer with a soft top. As regards accommodation, I would really like to continue living in the cottage and would be happy to pay you rent for it."

Mrs Black looked at her sister and got the 'nod' to speak on her behalf. "We anticipated something like this and have already discussed it.

Firstly, if you fix the garage doors and clear a space, you can keep the car in the garage, but since we have let you use our car, I would like the option of using yours from time to time when Penny is out and you are not using it.

Secondly, we assume you will have your own tools to keep your own car in good order and we would like you to look after ours as well.

Lastly, we still expect you to keep us supplied with firewood. If you agree to these conditions, we will not charge you rent but we will expect something towards the cost of your food, if you wish to continue eating with us. What do you think?"

"I think your terms are extremely generous and I accept them in their entirety. Just one last request, is there any chance either of you is going into Oxford on Saturday morning?"

"One of us will take you, provided it is not going to be too early a start," replied Mrs Duffy-Smythe, "have you told Moira your good news yet?"

"I have planned to go round after dinner; she will be thrilled about the car."

"A blue car you say, what colour are the seats, did you put the hood up, will I need a shawl, does it have a heater, can we go to Scotland in it?" responded Moira to Digger's news as she hugged him after he told her he had got the job.

"I think Scotland will have to wait for another time Moira, I need to get my tools from Vi's place first and then strip the engine down and if I find anything damaged I will need to get it replaced. We will stick with the train this time but I was thinking we could give the car a run on Sunday and go and see Vi and Mick. I need to pick up some tools from them and a few smarter clothes for the bank. We could leave directly after the service if you like."

"Oh yes, I would love to meet them. Will you be able to let her know we are coming?" she asked.

"Mick's a plumber and has a phone, so I will ring him. Which reminds me, I must ring a chap tomorrow about car insurance. Will you be able to come with me on Saturday to pick the car up?"

"Just try and stop me," she replied. "While we are in Oxford we can go to the station and book the tickets for our trip to Scotland, sometimes the overnight express gets fully booked, especially at weekends."

"Good idea, but remember to wrap up warm, even with the hood up, Tourers can be a bit chilly."

When he got back to the cottage Digger found Bertie outside playing with Mac, "Hello Bertie, keeping my dog amused for me, do you want a drink?"

"Hello Digger, I just called round to congratulate you on the job and a new car I hear, whatever next, I wonder? Austin Sevens, they can be a bit tricky on bends; accelerate into the bend and don't touch the brakes until you are well out the other side, if I remember correctly."

The two men and Mac went into the cottage and Bertie made himself comfortable while Digger brewed a pot of tea.

"You are very well informed car wise Bertie, they can be a bit difficult to handle, but are extremely reliable and economical, which is very important to me. Any news from Australia yet, or is too soon."

"Oh far too soon old chap. Probably another month before we hear anything. If my sources are correct, you were something of an investments wiz in a previous existence. Any truth in the rumour?"

Digger poured the tea and passed his friend a cup, "You are well informed, but not exactly a wizard, I just followed certain principles the bank taught me, like ' don't put all your eggs in one basket and don't put all your money into eggs' and other such pearls of wisdom and it worked out fine normally. Is there something I can help you with Mr Bannister?" he asked in his best bankers voice.

Mick was delighted to hear from Digger the next day and scolded him for not keeping in touch, "Vi has been really worried about you, where have you been, the kids have missed you too, especially little Brian, he really misses playing football on the common with you. Sunday, early afternoon you say, I am sure that will be fine. Give me the number of the place you are staying at and I will ring if it's not convenient."

As the pips started to sound, digger shouted that he would be bringing a friend, but was not sure if Mick had heard him or not.

"Bringing a friend you say," commented Vi, when Mick returned home after his day's work, "he didn't say lady friend or army friend, just friend."

"For the third time Vi, he said friend. What difference does it make whether it's a girl or a bloke?"

"What difference - if I thought you could understand the answer Mick, you probably wouldn't need to ask the question. Oh, and don't mention it to the children, just in case something happens and Digger does not come." With which she got up from the table and went into the kitchen to take stock!

In the end both Amanda and Penny took Digger and Moira into Oxford to collect the car. Digger had telephoned 'the friend' about car insurance and he was there in the office when the party arrived. All the ladies fell in love with the car, which had now been polished and was glistening in the yard and were horrified when Digger announced it was to be called 'Matilda' after his army lorry.

"Oh no Digger," protested Moira, "you can see she is a lady, not a duck, surely you can think of a better name than that?"

"If she is half as safe and reliable as her namesake was, I will be delighted with her," he replied, "Matilda it is."

The balance of the purchase price was paid and the paperwork checked and handed over, the dealer informing them that his mechanic had managed to give the car a quick service. When Mrs Black informed him that Digger was to maintain the car himself since he had been an army mechanic, the dealer began to wonder whether he had let it go too cheaply, but they all shook hands and went their separate ways.

The sisters went to the shops to look at this year's summer fashions and to inspect some new armchairs to replace the old worn ones in the lounge. Digger and Moira went to the railway station to book their tickets for Scotland and found that Moira had been correct in her concerns, for there were only four berths left on the overnight train for that Friday evening.

He first drove to the nearest garage and filled up with petrol and half a pint of oil and poured a drop of water in the radiator, ready for the trip to London the next day, as there would only be a few garages open on a Sunday. Moira wrapped the blanket round her knees that she had brought with her and they then drove the scenic route back home, the car performing faultlessly.

CHAPTER NINETEEN
SISTERLY LOVE

The church service finished promptly and after bidding everyone good bye they were safely on their way by twelve twenty five. It was a nice sunny day and Moira said she would like to drive with the hood down and was sporting a woolly tam-o-shanter and a thick scarf that her mother had knitted and sent for Christmas a few years ago.

They followed the A40 through High Wycombe and Beaconsfield into London and then picked up the South Circular which took them over the river, past Kew Gardens, Wimbledon Common and eventually into Clapham. There was surprisingly little traffic on the roads and they pulled up outside a three storey terraced building somewhere around two thirty.

"Goodness Digger, does your sister and her husband live in that big house? It must have a dozen rooms or more."

"The lady who owns the house lives on the ground floor and Vi and Mick have the middle and top floors. It's a great location, being near the common and there are a few shops just round the corner. The kids have a ten minute walk to school and the only down side, is that the old lady won't let them use the garden, but apart from that she is fine. But come on; let me help you out, not too cold I hope?"

Just then the front door flew open and his niece and nephew came bounding down the path and almost knocked him and Moira over.

"Uncle Digger, uncle Digger, where have you been?" shrieked Patty as she jumped into his arms and he swung her round and round like a whirligig.

"Uncle Digger, is this yours, what a bobby dazzler, can I have a ride please?" asked Brian as he rushed past Moira and jumped into the driver's seat.

As Moira looked on, not sure what to do, Vi came up to her side and said, "Hello, I'm Vi, Digger's sister, would you like to come in and warm up with a cup of tea, I'm afraid the children will monopolize him for a good bit yet. The chap with his head under the bonnet with Digger, is my husband Mick and there is absolutely no way Digger will get inside before Mick and the kids have had a ride."

"Oh thanks, my name is Moira, a cup of tea sounds great, I have so looked forward to meeting you and your family Vi."

Just then Digger looked up to see the two women heading indoors. "Hi Vi, that's Moira, look after her for me, we are just going for a spin round the common," he called out.

By the time they had returned to the house after a trip round the ring road of the common and a call at a petrol station they found open, during which stop the children persuaded him to put the hood up, Vi and Moira had got well acquainted. Vi was trying to evaluate the nature of their relationship, when Moira let slip that yesterday, they had booked tickets for a trip to Scotland to enable Digger to meet her parents. This confirmed Vi's suspicion that Digger was serious about this girl and that Vi was probably entertaining her future sister-in-law.

She in turn mentioned that their parents had both died in the Blitz but still had close ties with several aunties and uncles on both sides of the family. As the swapping of information continued, Vi laughed at the prospect of Digger being a handy man and fixing roofs and windows and such like and was totally surprised when Moira told her that one of the ladies where he was stopping was the widow of his old army mate, Ronnie Black.

"It's almost like Digger was fated to be robbed on that train and end up in that small village, isn't it Moira? I wonder if we would be allowed to come and visit him at the cottage, the children have never had a proper trip to the country. Do you think the two sisters would mind?"

"Well if they mind Vi, you can come and stop with me. I live in a little house in the village itself, but I could easily put you up for a few days if you wanted to come and visit. Once we get back from Scotland we will fix a date, how's that?"

"Oh Moira, that would be lovely, thank you," she replied.

"What's lovely Vi, what have you two been scheming, I said to Mick it was a mistake going off and leaving the two of you together," said Digger.

"You come here you," said Vi, " not a word for all these weeks, I've been worried stiff about you, haven't I Mick?" with which the two stood and hugged each other.

"I'm sorry Vi, I wasn't thinking straight, what's for dinner, I'm starving? No let me guess, New Zealand – half leg of lamb – knuckle end – am I right?"

"Listen to him Moira, mister wonderful, we always have roast lamb on a Sunday. Go and wash your hands children, before you eat," called out Vi as the children rushed into the bathroom.

They all sat down and enjoyed the roast lamb with mint sauce and roast potatoes and peas with a big piece of

Yorkshire pudding and gravy. Homemade apple pie and custard followed and since it was a special occasion, Mick had bought a bottle of Tizer from the off-licence, which the kids were thrilled about. After dinner Patty showed Moira her dolls and Brian showed her his collection of cigarette cards and taught her how to play 'fag cards' against his bedroom wall. They looked for an Austin Seven Tourer in his card set of 'Old Cars', but could not find one.

While all this was going on Digger and Mick went through his boxes in the cellar after getting permission from the old lady downstairs, who was also pleased to see Digger again and insisted on meeting his young lady. When she found out that Moira had come from Inverness she rushed to a drawer and pulled out a photo album containing pictures that her late husband had taken on a holiday to Scotland that they had undertaken in the summer of 1932.

Several boxes and a suitcase were loaded into the trunk and back seat and just after ten to seven, they set off back home for Upper Style. Before they left, Moira and Vi had swapped addresses and gave each other a quick hug before Moira got into the car and Brian was removed from the back seat where he had been hiding. They travelled home with the hood up, which managed to keep out a lot of the wind, but did not make the car much warmer.

"So, what did you think of my sister and her family," Digger eventually asked Moira.

"She was lovely Digger and her husband was very nice as well. The children are just adorable and so well behaved and they think you are Dan Dare, Tom Finney and Dennis Compton all rolled up into one."

"Yes, it's amazing how perceptive children can be sometimes, isn't it?" he replied.

"If your head gets any bigger we will have to trade in this little car for something bigger, Mr Smith," she replied.

"Vi said that she would love to come out and visit you at Millstone and give the children a bit of a holiday; you know the last time Mick was able to afford to take them away was before the war. A break would do her good. I said that if you were not able to put them up, then they could come and stop with me, I hope I did right?"

"Of course you did right, I don't know how Mrs Duffy-Smythe would respond to children, not having any of her own and since I am not technically 'paying rent' I will have to handle this delicately, but it won't be till after our trip north, so plenty of time to 'test the water'. But that was good of you, I can see that Vi liked you a lot and anyone who can beat Brian at 'fag cards' stands very high in his opinion."

The traffic was heavy along the South Circular, but Digger did not seem too surprised and in the end took a detour he knew which brought them out on the A40 a bit higher up. It started to drizzle around High Wycombe and the windscreen wiper just speared bird droppings all over the screen and Digger had to stop the car and clean it properly with a duster.

He dropped Moira off at her house around ten thirty and drove carefully down the lane to Millstone. He stopped in the yard and left the engine running while he opened the garage doors and put the light on, when he got back into the car, Mac was sitting on the back seat and seemed very disappointed when he only got a ride into the garage.

"Never mind boy, I'll give you a ride another day, it's too late now," with which they both went in-side and he had just put the kettle on, when there was a knock on the door, "Come in," shouted Digger, expecting it to be Bertie, on his way back home after seeing Cook.

"Digger, I am so glad you are back," said Cook, "Mrs Black has been in an accident, in Oxford. She and Mrs Duffy-Smythe were visiting a friend and got hit in the side by a bus. Mrs Black is in the Radcliffe hospital and the car is by the roadside, I'm to ask you if you are willing to go into Oxford with Mrs Duffy-Smythe, first thing tomorrow and have a look at it. She wants to visit her sister in hospital."

"Of course I will, what time does she want to leave?"

"Straight after breakfast. She thinks the car isn't too badly damaged and was wondering if you would be able to tow it home and work on it for her."

"There is a tow rope in the garage and I have brought my mechanics tools back with me, so it will just depend on the condition of her car. How badly is Mrs Black hurt, are there any bones broken?"

"She has certainly broken her left arm and may have broken several ribs as well, as she was thrown into the steering wheel. Mrs Duffy-Smythe was sitting in the back with the friend, so they were thrown forward and bruised, but not seriously hurt," replied Cook.

"Well thank goodness for that, anyway, bye for now, see you at breakfast," he said, as she turned and went back to the kitchen.

Breakfast was a fairly silent affair, with Digger giving a quick overview of his trip to London to see his sister and Mrs Duffy-Smythe, who was sporting a black eye where she had encountered her friends shoulder in the crash, telling what had happened in Oxford. It appears they had been invited to a garden party at one of the colleges and were driving along, minding their own business, when a coach on its way to Birmingham, had pulled out of the bus station and driven straight across the road and caught them in the side by the nearside rear wheel. A policeman on his beat had quickly appeared at the scene and had rung for an ambulance from a nearby police box. The ambulance did not have far to come and arrived soon after and took them all to the Radcliffe.

She said that she has given the car keys to the policeman who said he would have the car pushed to the roadside and locked and the keys held at the police station for her. Digger asked if she had spare keys for the car, which she eventually found in her desk drawer.

They drove into Oxford and found the car where the policeman had indicated and Digger used the spare key to unlock it and start it up. He put it into gear and gently eased the clutch and allowed the car to move forward a few yards. There was a rubbing sound coming from the rear and Digger found that the rear mudguard was touching the tyre. He bent this away from the tyre and slipping the car into gear, he tried again.

"Well I think the car is safe to drive Mrs Duffy-Smythe, if you feel up to it. I assume you will be claiming on the coach's insurance, but that could take weeks to settle. If we get the car back to Millstone, I can check it over and make sure it is mechanically safe, so you will not be without transport while the insurance companies deliberate."

"Thank you Arnold, if you think it is safe, I am prepared to give it a try. If we drive to the hospital first, that will give us a chance to see if anything is wrong. Do you know the way?"

"No, I always get lost in Oxford, I will follow you, which will give me a chance to see if everything on the car is working properly."

Digger got into his car and followed her all the way to the hospital. They parked the two cars outside and then made their way to the ward. The ward sister was not pleased at having visitors outside of the official hours, but Mrs Duffy-Smythe was able to persuade her to let them visit Mrs Black for ten minutes.

Her arm was in plaster, her head and chest were bandaged and she was drinking through a straw as they approached her bed.

"Oh Amanda, you look terrible, what were the results of the X-rays?" asked Mrs Duffy-Smythe.

"Well thank you Penny, you don't exactly look a picture yourself, you know, black eye and all. Hello Arnold, have you seen the car yet?"

"Hello Mrs Black, sorry to hear about the accident, yes, we have just driven it here. Considering you got hit by a coach, the car is not badly damaged, but it will need a new rear wing and possibly a rear door. How badly were you injured?"

"A broken tibia, that's the lower arm, two broken ribs and six stitches in my head. They say I will be in plaster for at least two months, so I guess your car is safe for bit longer Arnold. How was your trip yesterday?"

They chatted for another ten minutes before the sister arrived and told them to leave. She informed Mrs Duffy-Smythe that they would be keeping Mrs Black in for at least another four days, for observation, in view of the heavy blow to her head, caused by her hitting the rear-view mirror. It appears she had blacked out yesterday evening and the doctors were concerned that she may have seriously damaged her head.

Mrs Duffy-Smythe followed by Digger drove slowly back to Millstone House after calling at the police station and collecting her keys and signing a statement about the accident. Digger parked both cars in the garage and managed to rig up some heavy wooden boards and some large blocks to create ramps that he put the damaged car onto. He told Mrs Duffy-Smythe that he would be happy to transport her into Oxford each day to visit her sister, if she did not wish to drive her own car. She accepted his offer until such time as he had properly inspected her car and passed it 'safe' to drive.

At Bell Ringing practice on Thursday, Digger discovered that everyone seemed to know about his new job, the car and trip to London, Mrs Black's accident and their forthcoming trip to Scotland and afterwards the vicar said he and his wife would like to speak to the two of them. They followed the vicar into his kitchen where his wife had a cup of tea and a piece of fruit cake waiting.

The vicar cleared his throat, looked at his wife and then started, "I don't want to rush you two into anything you are not ready for yet, but I am sure you are aware that Bertie and Victoria are to be married." They both nodded agreement.

"They have asked that I marry them here and I have agreed to that on the condition that they attend the Marriage classes that my wife and I run."

"I bet Cook was not too pleased with that ultimatum," said Digger.

"Her reaction was interesting," said the vicar diplomatically, "but to cut a long story short, I will be running classes with them starting Tuesday the 25th and since there is a lot of work involved, I am asking other couples, who I think might be interested, if they would like to join the classes as well. There is a couple form Lower Style and another from here and we were just wondering if you two might be interested as well?"

Digger immediately stood up, "No Vicar, we have only been going out a few weeks and we are not engaged or anything and anyway Moira's home church is in Scotland, six hundred miles away, thanks, but no thanks. Excuse me but I have to go."

With which he got up and went to the door, "Are you coming Moira?"

"You go Digger, I want to stay and chat, I will see you tomorrow and good luck with the job."

After Digger left, Moira turned to the vicar's wife and said, "I am sorry if Digger was a bit abrupt just then, but what on earth made you ask us if we wanted to attend the classes, he hasn't met my parents yet and he certainly has not asked me to marry him."

"I am so sorry my dear," she replied, "Bertie and my husband hatched the plot between them, men, they can be so insensitive sometimes. I think Bertie just did not want to attend the classes, having been married before, but he has been widowed quite a while and Cook has been on her own for many years as well and we think it would be good for them to chat about marriage, before they tie the knot, rather than afterwards. He suggested that you were a lot closer than just friends and I am afraid my husband has just jumped to conclusions."

Digger was fuming as he walked back home, having assumed that Moira had 'set him up', so he wandered on to Bertie's to see if there was a light still on. He knocked on the door, "Bertie, are you up," he called.

"Well I am now, come in Digger. To what do I owe the honour of this visit?"

"You won't believe what just happened after bell Ringing practice," with which he related the incident in the vicar's kitchen.

"Oh dear, I fear I may have contributed to all that, my young friend. Victoria has set her heart on being married in the village here, but the vicar insists on these silly Classes that he runs. What do I need with classes, or Victoria for that matter, we have both been married before, it's a nonsense!"

"Fine Bertie, but why are Moira and I suddenly involved in all this?"

"I may just have said that I would only participate if you were there as well, thinking Victoria would give up on the idea and get married at a registry Office, saving us a whole lot of expense and of course, these classes. Sorry my friend, I should not have involved you in all of this."

"I still don't see how that could have induced the vicar to invite us to the classes though."

"Look, this is just between us, if Victoria finds out I told you she will be furious, but she implied to the vicar that you and Moira intended getting engaged on your trip to Scotland. I'm sure Moira hasn't said anything to her, but she has set her heart on a church wedding and it's just her way of getting me to the classes, I'm really sorry Digger."

"Look Bertie, your relationship with Cook is none of my business, but if she is manipulating people like this before you get married, what on earth is she going to be like afterwards. Seems to me that these classes might not be a bad idea, a chance to get these sorts of issues on the table and sorted before you make promises that you are going to regret."

"Hmm, good point, you may be right my friend," said Bertie thoughtfully.

Digger pressed his suit when he got back home Thursday evening and drove to Oxford on Friday and spent the day with the outgoing assistant manager, getting back into the branch routine. They worked in the bank all morning but went to see a customer together at one of the colleges in the afternoon. Slowly it all came back to Digger, reminding him of why he had enjoyed working in a branch so much. They discussed what they would cover on Saturday and agreed to meet at nine thirty as Digger wanted to pop into the Austin dealer and buy a new windscreen wiper.

After work he drove to the hospital and picked up Mrs Black who was being discharged at lunch time. He settled her in the back of his car and drove very sedately back to Millstone House, where he helped her to walk in-side after which her sister and Cook took charge.

During the morning Bertie spoke to Cook about the Marriage Classes and then went on to the vicarage to see the vicar and informed him that they would be attending the classes, but without Digger and Moira and also suggested one or two topics that he would like the vicar to include.

Digger and Moira met at the pub for a drink and had a great evening together, Digger telling her about his conversation with Bertie the previous evening and how his first 'day at the office' had gone.

CHAPTER TWENTY
SLEEPING ARRANGEMENTS

The next two weeks passed very quickly for everyone in Upper Style. Mrs. Black continued to get stronger each day and spent her time reading recipe books and magazines and planning the changes she wanted to make in the kitchen, once she was back in charge. Mrs. Duffy-Smythe was busy writing a new book and disappeared for several days at a time as the inspiration took her.

Cook and Bertie had several meetings with the vicar and had settled on a date of the 3rd July for their wedding and had found the 'Marriage classes' a lot more fun than they had expected. Cook had telephoned the solicitor in Kendal to see if there had been any news, to discover that Howard's daughter, Victoria, had telephoned the day previously to say that Howard's condition had got worse and that Cook and Bertie should sail for Australia as soon as possible. Bertie had suggested that Victoria instruct the solicitor to book a passage for them straight after the wedding, as they could then treat the trip as a honeymoon, which she immediately did. They had started to discuss the trip and the clothes and other things they would need to take with them and were currently waiting to hear back from the solicitor's secretary with definite boarding dates and tickets. He mentioned that he had often sailed the route that he thought the ship would probably take to Australia when he was a skipper, some years back and would enjoy exploring some of his old haunts with his new wife.

Digger was frantically working away at the remaining jobs at Millstone House, but every time he completed one, a new one was added to the list, which at least meant they would not be evicting him when he started full time work with the bank. The hand over with the outgoing assistant manager went well and Digger struck up a good rapport with all the other employees, apart from a senior clerk, who thought he should have been given the assistant manager's job. He was a big man, an ex-guardsman, with a small brain and a big ego and a particularly foul sense of humour. Digger was told that all the women were frightened to go into the filing locker with him, as he was anything but a gentleman.

Moira was busy with her rounds and had to go over everything in detail with the nurse who would be covering for her, while she was away on holiday in Scotland.

On Friday 4th June 1948 the doctor gave Moira a lift into the railway station at Oxford, where she met Digger at 6:30pm. He had driven his car to the bank manager's house on the outskirts of Kidlington, where he parked it in the double garage at the side of the house. The manger had then given him a lift back to the station. The train that was due at 6:45pm had been delayed due to points failure a couple of miles west of Oxford and had finally arrived at 7:20pm, which had at least given them a chance to have a cup of tea and a sandwich at the station buffet.

"It's a good job that the express from Euston doesn't leave until 10:10pm Digger, or we would have been in serious trouble," said Moira, as they settled into their seats, having put the suitcases in the overhead rack.

"We should be in Paddington before nine o'clock, so plenty of time to get round to Euston," commented Digger, who closed his eyes for just a moment, before reading the newspaper. He was woken by Moira gently shaking his arm and immediately noticed how dark it had become, "What is it Moira, I must have dozed off," he said.

"You have been asleep for almost two hours Digger; we have been sat here, doing nothing for forty minutes."

"What time is it then, goodness it's almost half past nine, has the guard been down the train at all?"

"He came past once and said there was something on the line, but that was ages ago."

Just then the railway engine let out a long hiss of steam and the train started to slowly move forward. As they passed under a bridge, they could see a gang of men at the side of the track and a large black object, badly damaged alongside them. As Digger looked back, he could make out an ambulance parked on the road over the bridge.

"Can you see what it is Digger?" asked Moira, "Is anyone hurt? This is a great start to our holiday!"

"I am not sure, lots of people; it could be that a billboard or something fell over the bridge. Anyway, we had better get our coats on and get the cases down as we will need to sprint as soon as we hit Paddington. I think a taxi will be quickest, provided there isn't a queue for them."

The train pulled into Paddington at 9:45pm and everyone had the same idea, for the platform was soon full of passengers running with cases, but they were young and fit and were only second in the taxi rank queue. When the lady behind them heard them say Paddington to the driver, she asked if she might share with them, which they agreed to, glad to have someone to split the cost with. They arrived at Euston at five minutes past ten and ran straight to the platform that Moira had used before to catch the overnight express. Their compartment was almost at the end of the train and they jumped aboard with just one minute to go. Moira had the tickets and soon located the two person sleeping compartment and sat down.

They were still sitting there, on the edge of the lower bunk when the train started to move forward and Digger stood up and looked around for somewhere to stow the cases. He turned round quickly as he heard the door open behind him and the lady who had shared the taxi with them entered the compartment and tapped him on the shoulder with her umbrella.

"What exactly do you think you are doing in this compartment young man?" she boomed at him, "get out immediately, or I will call the guard."

"I beg your pardon, but this is our compartment, now you get out or I will call the guard," he said back.

"Well unless you have undergone a gender change since we travelled in the taxi together, I will have to assume that you are illiterate, for it clearly says 'Ladies Only' on the notice outside the compartment," with which she turned towards the door and stepped outside.

Digger followed and discovered she was absolutely correct and stepping back into the compartment said to Moira, "She's right, have you got both tickets there love?"

Moira fished around in her handbag and eventually brought out both tickets and studied them, "I am so sorry Digger, I never looked at your ticket, your compartment is back down there, near the carriage door we came in by, you had better go and I will see you in Glasgow, they normally give us a call about half an hour before we arrive. Bye."

Digger took his case and walked back down the train and found his compartment, someone was already in the lower bunk, so he said hello and climbed up top and within a very short time was sound asleep.

The guard gave them a wake-up call about half an hour before they arrived at Glasgow and Digger was waiting in the corridor near Moira's compartment when the train stopped at Glasgow. She and the other lady emerged, deep in conversation and from what he overheard led him to understand that she too was in the medical profession. Since they had almost an hour's wait for the train to Inverness, they went into the buffet for a full 'English' breakfast.

"You seemed very friendly with the lady sergeant major; she didn't give you too hard a time then!"

"Oh no, we had a good laugh once you had gone and she realized it had all been a mistake. She is a mid-wife in Abingdon and asked me if I might be interested as there will be several vacancies coming up in the next few months."

"Abingdon, that's miles from Upper Style, why would you want to go there?" he asked.

"Abingdon is no further from Oxford than Upper Style is, what difference would it make if we lived south west of Oxford rather than north east. Anyway, nothing has been arranged, we just chatted about the possibility, that's all."

Digger was a little surprised by this revelation that it would make no difference 'if we lived south west of Oxford rather than north east', but said nothing, just made a mental note to be careful what he said to her on this holiday.

The train arrived at Inverness on time and as Digger got off the train and walked along the platform, he felt the air was definitely cooler than it had been in Oxford, but the sun was shining and everything seemed bright and clean. He had not given much thought to meeting Moira's parents and suddenly wished he had asked a few more questions and also wondered if he would be able to understand them, as he realised that he had just passed a couple of porters having a conversation and he had not understood a word they had said to each other.

"Hold on Moira," he said, "just a couple of questions before we meet the folks."

"Too late Digger, there they are, don't panic, you'll be fine," she replied and walked through the barrier and across to the middle aged couple waving at her.

"Och Moira, it's so good to see you, you're looking bonny, give your old father a hug," said Moira's dad.

Moira gave both her parents a hug, while Digger looked on and grinned, "It's so good to be home and breathe clean fresh air again; mam, dad, I would like you to meet my young man, Digger," with which she grabbed his hand and pulled him towards them.

Digger held out his hand and said, "I am very pleased to meet you Mr. and Mrs. Leith, Moira has told me so much about you."

"Well she hasn't told us much about you, but you are welcome anyway young man," said her dad and shook his hand.

"Behave yourself Dod," said her mother. "Welcome to Scotland Digger, I gather this is your first trip."

"That's right Mrs. Leith, I have never been further north than York before this trip, so I have been really looking forward to walking the hills and to seeing Loch Ness and the Monster," said Digger.

"Shame on you Moira," said Mr. Leith with a wide grin on his face, "what have you been telling him about your Granny!"

Moira started laughing and grabbed her dad's arm as they started to walk out of the station, "Don't pay any attention to him Digger, he and Granny are as thick as thieves but they always tig at each other like this."

Mr. Leith hailed a taxi and the driver got out and put their cases in the boot while they all got inside. Moira and her parents chatted away to each other on the journey and

Digger was pleased that he had managed to understand the gist of what was said, even if he did not comprehend every single word of the conversation. The taxi stopped outside the house and Mr. Leith took out his wallet and asked the driver how much he owed for the fare. Digger felt obliged to offer to share the cost with him and to his relief, Mr Leith declined the offer; so he decided that this was not a good time to joke about a Scotsman's reputation for being tight with money.

As they stepped out of the taxi several neighbours came up to say hello to Moira and to welcome her home and of course to give the new 'man' the once over. Moira was secretly quite pleased when she overhead one of the neighbours say to the other, "Well he's a awful fine looking boy and I hear he's a banker ye ken!"

The house was not quite like anything that Digger had seen before. It was an imposing building, built of a pinkish/greyish stone, which he assumed was granite, with the front door in the middle of the house and a large room either side of a central passageway, with a big double window looking out onto the street. Although it was a two storey house, the upstairs rooms were set in the loft with large dormer windows and a small window giving light for the stairs. There was not much of a front garden, just a few shrubs struggling to survive and he was surprised to see that the low front wall had railings on it, since in London, virtually all the railings had been removed in order to help with the War effort.

Digger was ushered in to the front parlour which had large comfortable armchairs and a settee that would take at least three people. A large display cabinet against the dividing wall contained an assortment of fine china, silverware and objet d'art. There were several pictures on the wall including the Boys Brigade picture of the 'King's Messenger' which he remembered from his youth and he was looking at this when Mr. Leith entered the room.

"Admiring my picture eh Digger? I was presented with that last year, for serving ten years as the Battalion President. I am very proud of that picture."

"I am sure you must be Mr. Leith, I only attained the rank of sergeant before I went into the army, but the training stood me in good stead. I knew my left foot from my right and how to keep a uniform clean, I look back on my days in the Boys Brigade with real affection and gratitude."

"Moira never said you were in the BB and a sergeant, well that is good to hear."

"What's good to hear Dod?" asked his wife.

"Digger here was in the BB before he went into the army."

"That's right, I thought I told you the other week," she replied. "anyway it's time for afternoon tea. While I think of it Digger, my sister Doris who lives round the corner is dying to meet you. One of her neighbours has a son who is going to London to work and wanted to ask you about life in the big city. Would you mind talking to him about it sometime, he has never been away from Inverness before and both he and his parents are a bit apprehensive about the move?"

"No, of course not, but London is a big place, I only really know South London and the City and West End, so my advice will be limited I'm afraid."

As he finished speaking, Moira came in carrying the tea pot which she put down on the table next to the pile of cakes and scones that Mrs. Leith had made.

"You'll have a piece with your tea Digger?" asked Mrs. Leith.

"A piece of what exactly, it all looks so nice," he said, "I have never seen so many different scones and biscuits on one plate before, are they all home-made?"

Moira came to his rescue at this point and said, "Yes, mam made them all, she has been very busy these last few days. Anyway, a 'piece' means any cake, scone or biscuit that you like, try one of mam's bannocks they are really good," with which she offered him a flat looking cake about the size of a small saucer. "I like them best with syrup, here try some."

Digger tried one and enjoyed it so much that he tried one again and every time he finished a piece, Mrs. Leith was up with another plate of something different to temp him with.

They talked about this and that and Moira told her parents what life in Upper Style was like and what a lovely day they had spent with Great Aunt Mary in Buckingham and how they had missed the last train home and Digger had spent the night on a railway station bench. To his surprise no-one mentioned anything about taking his case upstairs or which room he would be using or where the bathroom was, so he eventually decided to say something to Moira.

"Could you direct me to the bathroom please Moira," he said.

"Top of the stairs turn left and then the second door on your right," she answered.

Digger got up and left the room and climbed the stairs and found the bathroom where indicated but the toilet was not with it, so he washed his hands and face anyway and went back downstairs.

"Which way is the toilet Moira he asked?" as he entered the room and stood by the china cabinet.

"Right next to the bathroom Digger," replied her dad, so this time he found the toilet but it was still not at all obvious which room he would be sleeping in. On returning back to the front parlour he said to no-one in particular,

"I am feeling in need of a change of clothes, which is my room please?"

"Has Moira not told you about the sleeping arrangements Digger?" asked Mrs. Leith. "We have arranged a room for you down the road with Mrs. McKay our neighbour, she has a large spare bedroom and has agreed to put you up for your stay here, we thought you would be more comfortable there."

"You see, we only have three bedrooms here and the third bedroom is very small and I am afraid it is full of junk and old furniture," said Mr. Leith.

"I am used to roughing it," said Digger, "I don't mind sleeping on the settee, I wouldn't want to put your neighbour to any trouble."

"It's no trouble Digger," replied Mrs. Leith, "everything is arranged with Mrs. McKay and she is expecting you and looking forward to meeting you."

Digger glared at Moira and she quickly realized that the situation was about to turn difficult so she grabbed his arm and suggested that she and Digger take a walk in the back garden.

"I am truly sorry Digger; I honestly forgot that mum had made this arrangement with Mrs. McKay. Please don't make a fuss, at least stay with Mrs. McKay tonight and if you are not happy about it tomorrow, I will talk to my parents about it, but I don't want an argument on my first day home. Mum always says that Dad keeps the room full of junk so that Granny cannot stay here and she might well be right. We will go in now and get your case and I will take you down the road and introduce you."

Mrs. McKay was just two doors down and was expecting them. She was an elderly lady, well into her seventies with a twinkle in her eye and a pleasant personality and Digger could not help but notice that her back was as straight as a ramrod.

She made them both welcome and showed Digger to a large bedroom at the back of the house which had enough space for a table and two chairs as well as a double bed and a wireless, with a window that looked out over a very colourful garden.

She gave him a key and told him to come and go as he wished and said that Moira was welcome to visit as she wanted and gave her hand a squeeze as she left the room and told her what a handsome man she had found for herself.

Digger was amused by this little interaction between the two women and was beginning to feel a lot better about the arrangements Mrs. Leith had made on his behalf. He realised that he was better off here, in his own large room, where he could relax and be himself away from the constant attention of Moira's parents.

"I think your mum was probably right Moira, I would not have enjoyed spending our holiday crammed in a room with your dad's junk and Mrs. McKay seems to be a very lovely lady with excellent taste!" said Digger. "She obviously knows you very well and is very fond of you and I can't believe how straight her back is for someone her age."

"Thanks love, I am pleased to hear you say that," and she kissed him gently on the lips, "Mrs McKay used to be my dancing teacher when I was younger and is real fun to be around. I am sorry my parents have sprung this on us; I guess they are just trying to be considerate and a bit over protective. To be honest, it might prove to be a blessing in disguise and give us a way of having some time to ourselves during this holiday, as I have discovered that mum and dad have taken next week off work so that they are free to be able to take us around and show us places."

"Oh, that's just great, it will be like being back in school again, is there anything else I need to know?" he asked.

"Well actually there is. I counted that you ate six different pieces when we had tea and that will automatically give you a reputation for being a big eater. That means that wherever we go, people will expect you to eat a lot and every time we go and meet someone, they will bring out tea and cakes and will be most insulted if you refuse. I am afraid that you may well put on several stone in weight over the next two weeks Mr. Smith which could mean a whole new wardrobe before you start back at the bank. But don't worry; I am sure that I will still love you," with which she threw her arms round his neck and kissed him.

CHAPTER TWENTY ONE
'ON THE REBOUND?'

Digger quickly discovered that they spoke very good English in Inverness, it having been a garrison town for many years and that he had no problems in understanding everyone, that is, apart from Moira's grandma, Granny McDonald.

She had actually spent much of her life over in the north east of Scotland, thirty miles north west of Aberdeen and still had an accent that was distinctively different from the good people of Inverness.

Granny McDonald was already in church when they arrived with just a minute to spare; Digger having been woken by Mrs. McKay at 10:15am with the news that they would all be leaving for church in fifteen minutes and that if he wanted any breakfast he should make haste. As it was the others went on first and he and Moira followed after he had speedily downed some toast and marmalade.

Granny had saved room for Moira next to her and Digger sat on the end next to her father and mother. The service lasted about an hour and twenty minutes and Digger followed the proceedings with interest and actually knew all of the hymns bar two. As they filed out of church several people came to say hello to Moira and to welcome her back, which left Digger standing on his own, looking at all the fine granite buildings. He was deep in thought when Granny McDonald came over and looking up at him said something completely unintelligible to Digger.

"I'm sorry, but would you mind repeating that please," he asked. She made some comment back, the only word of which that he could understand was 'lugs' but had no idea what she said again. He turned to where Moira was standing and called out to her, "Moira, have you got a moment please. Your Granny just said something to me and I have to confess that I have no idea what she said. Perhaps you could translate."

She walked over and took hold of her Granny's hand and said, "OK Granny, what did you say to my young man?" This time Digger caught the one word 'Sassenach' and Moira giggled as she turned round and said to him, "I am not sure I should tell you what she said, but here goes. The first time she enquired as to whether your watch had broken and if perhaps that was the reason we were late for church. The second time she was asking whether people in London ever wash their ears and lastly she asked me what was so special about an Englishman who cannot tell the time or listen properly." When she saw the look on his face, she began to wish she had toned her words down a bit.

Digger scowled at Moira, then her Granny and replied in his quickest roughest South London accent, "Iadfreeharssleeplasni wia flaminowlriutsidemawinner sabakov Granny." With that he turned and walked away to where Mr. and Mrs. Leith were standing.

"What on earth did he just say Moira, the only word I picked up was Granny?" asked the startled old lady.

"I have absolutely no idea Granny, but I sort of suspect he was just getting his own back! Digger always gives as good as he gets, and it is important to me that you two become friends, so please take time to get to know him, he is a really nice man."

"Oh, I am sure he is dear, I was just tiging at him," replied Granny.

They all walked back home together during which time Moira discovered that what Digger had actually said to her Granny was ' I had three hours sleep last night with a flaming owl right outside my window so back off Granny'.

Moira laughed and said, "Well I think you made your point but please do try to get to know her, she is very special to me."

They went in and sat around the sitting room drinking tea before Mrs. Leith announced that dinner was ready. The roast beef was delicious and the fruit pie and custard went down a treat, but Digger remembered the warning of yesterday and declined seconds of both. Granny and Moira's dad sparred for most of the time she was with them and Digger was not sure if they really liked each other or not, but the old lady spoke slowly when she was talking to him and with a bit of help from the others, he was able to understand most of what she said and to appreciate her very sharp wit.

The first week passed very quickly and it only rained for three days, which Digger was led to believe was good going for June in Inverness. He and Moira escaped most evenings on their own for an hour or so and loved to walk hand in hand, along the banks of the river Ness. Since June the 21st is the longest day of the year, it hardly got dark at all and they really enjoyed the long summer evenings together. They all took bus rides to the Black Isle and Dingwell and went down to Drumnadrochit on the Wednesday and visited Urquhart Castle by the side of Loch Ness. The Monster was not spotted and Granny never got a mention either from Mr Leith.

The more the Leith's got to know Digger, the more they warmed to him and he in turn could appreciate what good parents they had been to Moira and how well they would have got on with his own mum and dad had they still been alive. They enjoyed listening to him talk about growing up in London and all the things that he got up to as a boy, especially the days he spent in the different museums in Kensington. He said his favourite was the Science Museum, but his sister preferred the Natural History, with all its dinosaurs and big animals. Moira learnt a lot about his early family life and what a close family they had all been.

During the second visit to Auntie Doris, Digger was introduced to the neighbour's son who was going to work in London and he was able to tell him what to expect in London and where to go and also what places to avoid. Digger suggested that he write and ask for a copy of the office internal bulletin, as often people used it to advertise for flat mates. The lad said he would do this and also took a note of Diggers current address, in case he needed help with anything.

On the second Wednesday Digger and Moira were interrupted on the front porch in their goodnight embrace, by her dad, who was coming home late from a church meeting. He had to cough three times before they were aware of his presence and before Digger could say goodbye, he was asked to come in by Mr. Leith who wanted a quiet word with him. Moira was firmly told to go through to the kitchen and the two men went into the sitting room and sat down.

"Digger, I want you to know that my wife and I really like you and are so pleased that Moira has found someone she really cares about. She has told her mother, however, that it was only in March that you parted company from your previous young lady, which triggered your move out of London, away from family and your work. We have to presume, therefore, that you were extremely upset by what happened and, I'm not sure how to put this tactfully Digger; but we are just concerned that Moira may have caught you 'on the rebound' so to speak and we don't want her getting hurt. I'm sure you understand our concerns."

"Well, that's pretty direct Mr Leith, I must say. Did she catch me 'on the rebound' as you put it? Whew!! I don't know. Maybe she did." He took a deep breath and then continued, "Coming up here to meet you all was her idea, not mine. This was her annual holiday and since I was a free agent, work-wise, it was easy for me to keep her company. Sigh!! I guess you're asking me if I care about her and are my intentions honourable? Grief, what do you think I am, some sort of monster? I've had it, say good night to her for me."

With which he got up and left the room and the house, closing the door behind him.

Moira heard the door close and rushed into the sitting room with her mother, "Where has he gone? What did you say to him dad? Tell me!"

"Don't speak to your father like that Moira, I won't have it."

"Listen both of you; I am twenty six, I am not a child. I have been fending for myself for eight years now and you have just scared off the only man that I have cared for in all those years. What did you say to him, I need to know?"

"I told him that we knew his previous girlfriend had broken their relationship in March and that she was the reason he had left London and that we did not want you to get hurt by someone who was still feeling bitter about what had happened. Moira, we care about you and you hardly know this man, of course we are feeling protective about you."

"Dad, I told you that in confidence!" Moira sank into the settee and started to sob. Her mother shooed her father out of the room and sat next to her daughter and held her close.

When she finally stopped crying she turned to her mother and said, "I know it's late mam but I need to speak with him and let him know how I feel."

"No dear. What's done is done and can't be undone. If he is upset, it's with your father and not you, so leave him to sleep on it and get his own thoughts together. If he really does care about you, then there will be no harm done, if he doesn't, then your father has done you a favour, although I will still be speaking to him about it!"

Digger did not go back to his room, but just walked and walked until he found himself down by the river and sat down on the bench that he and Moira sometimes used.

The little old man who often passed them with his Scottie dog came slowly walking bye and stopped to speak. "On your own tonight laddie?" he asked. "the lassie nae with you?"

"Look, I don't want to be rude mate, but I am not in the mood for talking. Sorry."

The old man sat down next to him, took out a hip flask and offered him a drink. Digger looked at him and said, "Didn't you hear me, I said I was not in the mood to talk."

The old man smiled and said, "Who said anything about talking?" and offered the flask again. To his surprise Digger took the flask and had a drink and passed it back to the old man. "Boy, that was good, what was it?"

"Have ye nae had a single malt whisky before laddie, your education has been sorely neglected. That was Glenfiddich, the finest there is, in my opinion, made from the best Scottish barley and the purest and softest moorland waters. This particular one was made in 1933, fifteen years ago, the year I retired, in fact. What were you doing in 1933?"

"Well I was twelve, so I was probably playing football on one of the commons or going to school or Boys Brigade. That was my life then. What did you do before you retired?"

The old man started to tell Digger about his life and travels and he listened spellbound and amazed at what this little old man had achieved.

At about 2:45am a policeman on his beat suggested that the two gentlemen on the bench and the little dog, should go home and be quiet about it. They bid each other goodnight and Digger went to his room and fell asleep without any effort whatsoever.

He woke at about 9:30am and went down stairs for his breakfast, to find Moira chatting with Mrs. McKay and looking at a photograph album.

"Moira, get the man some porridge while I show him some embarrassing photos of a pretty little girl in her dancing outfits. Sit down here Digger."

There were pictures of dozens of boys and girls who had been Mrs. McKay's pupils over the years and were shown wearing all sorts of different outfits that they had to wear for the different dances when they were competing in the Highland Games.

Pictures of Moira were carefully studied, whilst eating the porridge and they started when she was four and continued right up to when she was seventeen and acted as Mrs. McKay's assistant and took the youngest children for their lessons.

"So you could actually be a teacher, yourself, right now, if you wanted to Moira?" He asked. "Do they do Highland Dancing down south at all?"

She smiled at him and replied, "I suppose I could, if I had the time and the pupils and somewhere to do it. I think there are a few dancing schools in London and somewhere in Hertfordshire, I was told, but I don't know where exactly."

"Your hair has always been curly, by the look of it; I thought that you had to get it permed on a regular basis to keep it like that."

"I wish. No, me and my hair have fought many a battle over the years, now I just give in and let it have its own way."

At this point, Mrs. McKay got up and left the room, closing the door behind her and Moira sat down next to Digger and put her arm through his.

"Dad told me what he said to you last night. He said you just got up and left. I didn't know he was going to say those things, honestly I didn't. Mrs. McKay said you didn't come home while she was awake, what did you do? Where did you go?"

"Your Dad caught me off guard. He touched on matters that were deep and personal and that, to be honest, I have avoided thinking about. Sarah did hurt me when she told me she had found someone else, but it was the sort of hurt you get when someone steals your bike or football, not when you lose something or someone, that really matters. Thinking about Sarah when I was overseas, helped to keep me going, but deep down, I knew she was only a very good friend, nothing more. Your Dad suggested that I had met with you, while 'on the rebound' from Sarah, but when I thought about it, it just wasn't true. I had made the decision to start over, begin again and I think of you as part of that new life, that new beginning, not as a reaction to the past."

He stopped for a drink of tea and a piece of toast and then continued, "Your Dad was really asking me how I felt about you and that he was concerned that I should not hurt you. Well, I would never intentionally hurt you, I think you know that, you are a very special lady and I just love being with you, but at this stage, that's about all I am certain of. Is that OK?"

"Of course that's OK. Thank you for being honest and understanding and I do know that you would never hurt me and I would never hurt you either."

With that they embraced and were only separated by Mrs. McKay fumbling with her dustpan and broom, outside the door.

"Mum has invited a few people round tonight, as it's my last night here and I need to go and help her. Is that alright with you, do you mind?"

"Of course not and tell your Dad, no hard feelings. I want to walk into town and get Vi and the kids something from Scotland, so I will see you later."

He went into town and got the presents for Vi and the children and got Mick a bottle of something special as well. He took them back to the room and found a note from Moira to say that Granny was not well and she had gone round to see her and Digger was welcome to join her, but otherwise the party was due to start at about 5:30pm and she would see him then. He was contemplating his options when Mrs. McKay knocked on the door and offered some lunch, which he decided to accept and followed her downstairs to the big kitchen.

"Well Digger, I was wondering what happened to you last night, when I was informed that you had spent several hours blathering to ma faither, down by the river."

"The old man with the little dog was your dad! Well I never. What a great old man, you must be very fond of him. Such an interesting life he has had as well, all that time in South America with the Indians, gold hunting and that fight with the giant snake, absolutely amazing. I could have listened to him for hours."

"I hate to spoil the illusion, but he has never been outside of Scotland. He is an amateur fiction writer and often takes on the character of the main hero of his books to try out a story idea on un-suspecting people. No doubt he told you that his name was Dougal McNess and that he rides a black horse named Pedro and can fly a plane. I expect he is planning a new book and was using your reactions to what he said, to see if it sounded feasible."

"I thought he sounded a bit vague over certain points I asked him about, but assumed the whisky had just confused him a bit. Well next time you see him, thank him for me will you, he was great company just when I was feeling a bit down and needed someone to cheer me up."

Digger decided not to visit Granny but let Moira enjoy her time with her on her own. She was obviously special to her and he did not want to get in the way. Instead, he packed his bags ready for tomorrow's departure, changed his shirt and took a slow walk round to the Leith's house and arrived just after 5:30pm, to find that most of the guests had already arrived, with the ladies getting in each other's way in the kitchen and the men chatting together in the front room.

Moira's dad was standing in front of the fireplace 'airing his knowledge' when Digger walked in, so he immediately went over to him with an outstretched hand and said, "Good to see you Digger, I hope everything is OK?"

Digger took the hand and shook it firmly and replied, "It's good to see you too, Mr. Leith and everything is fine." The two men looked into each other's eyes for a second or two and smiled and both knew that nothing else needed to be said; and it never was.

The party went on till just after 11:00pm when, as if a gong had sounded, they all said goodnight to each other and left. Digger received more hugs and kisses from all the departing ladies than he had had in a long time and Moira explained afterwards, that it was their way of saying that they liked him and that he was welcome among them.

Mr. Leith had organized a taxi to take them to the station the next day, where they arrived with almost half an hour to spare. They had a cup of tea together and then boarded the train and said their goodbyes to each other, waving madly through the window as the train pulled out of the station.

They chatted and slept and had a buffet meal and chatted and slept some more. Although Moira was dying to ask what had happened between Digger and her father; her mother had advised her not to, so she did not.

They got a taxi from Euston to Paddington and only had to wait twenty minutes for a train to Oxford. They got a bus from Oxford to Kidlington and retrieved the car from the bank manager's garage, which started on the third turn of the handle. He first drove to Moira's house and popped in to make sure everything was alright and have a cup of tea and enjoy a quiet time together, with no watching eyes to track their every move.

"I don't know quite what I was expecting Moira, but that was a great holiday and I feel really refreshed and ready for work. I loved Scotland and all your friends and family and was made to feel most welcome. Thank you for inviting me to go with you."

She kissed him again and replied, "I had a great time too, Digger, it was so nice having you with me. My mother thought you were just wonderful and my dad said you were a very decent sort of chap and even Granny said that she thought you were a very handsome man, for a Sassenach!"

CHAPTER TWENTY TWO
MR. AND MRS. BANNISTER

The first full week at work went very well and Digger was glad he had decided to go back to branch banking rather than return to Head Office. On the Friday morning he was having a meeting with the branch manager when they both heard a woman scream and then a loud crashing noise, which came from the filing room.

They immediately got up and ran to the room to find the senior clerk on the floor surrounded by the contents of a couple of box files and a young female junior clerk, who had only been with the bank a few weeks, sobbing in the corner. The manager called for his secretary and asked her to take the young lady to the interview room and find out from her what had happened. He then instructed the senior clerk to accompany him to his office.

It transpired that the older members of staff had failed to warn the new member of staff about the senior clerk's antics and that he had attempted a kiss and cuddle in the filing room. She, however, was a spirited girl and had grabbed a couple of box files from the shelves and hit him as hard as she could over the head, whilst letting out the scream which had alerted everyone else in the office.

As soon as it was known that the young lady was happy to make a formal complaint against him, several other women also came forward with similar complaints and the man was formally sacked for gross misconduct, with no notice and no reference.

The manager asked Digger if he knew anyone suitable from the City, who might be interested in the position and he was able to suggest a very likeable young man who had been part of his team there, but was keen to work out of London. The manager phoned Mr. White who sent the young man for an interview and he then started work in Oxford a few weeks later.

On the Saturday, Bertie and Cook arranged a lift with Digger into Oxford, as they needed to pick up dresses and Bertie's suit and he happened to be working in the bank that morning. They arrived in town far too early for the shops to be open; so he dropped them off at the railway station, which was on his route, to get a cup of tea. They sat down at a corner table and started to discuss the sailing arrangements for their forthcoming trip to Western Australia. "What time again does the boat sail Bertie?" asked Victoria.

"It sails on the evening tide on Wednesday 7th July at 6:30pm, but the agent has advised us to be on board by 2:00pm."

"Are you sure Digger does not mind taking us down to the New Forest on the Sunday beforehand, you did tell him that we would pay for his petrol?"

"It was his suggestion. He didn't know what to get us for a wedding present, so that will be his present to us, the trip to the New Forest. He was disappointed that Moira couldn't come, but when I told him how much luggage we would be taking, he said that there would not be room for her as well. Stop worrying, everything is sorted. The hotel is booked as well as the taxi to take us to the ship on Wednesday. Anyway, by the time we have been to the loo and walked to the shops, it will be about time to pick up the dresses and hats for you and Deborah and my penguin suit from the tailors, so drink up and let's be on our way."

The wedding dress was tried on and apart from a few threads which needed cutting off, everything fitted perfectly. Victoria inspected Deborah's dress and was satisfied with the alterations that Deborah had asked for at the previous fitting. They next went to the millinery department and picked up the hats for herself and her maid of honour and also one that Moira had chosen for the occasion.

The Dinner Jacket fitted properly and the extra shirts and bow ties, they had ordered last time, were all ready. When Bertie mentioned that they were going on a voyage to Australia via the Mediterranean Sea and Ceylon, the outfitter asked if he had a suitable lightweight outfit to wear and managed to obtain an order for two such outfits. It was agreed that these would be delivered to Digger at the bank, during the week, along with the wedding suit that he was buying from the shop.

Laden with all their shopping, they arrived at the bank just before one o'clock and only had a short time to wait before Digger was ready to lock up the bank and drive them all home.

That last week, prior to the wedding, went so quickly, that Bertie had forgotten that Deborah was coming down on her motor bike Friday evening and was on his way out as she arrived at the cottage.

"Don't worry about me dad, I need to eat and then take a bath, so make sure that half-witted friend of yours does not turn up with his dog again, please."

"There is no need to go on about that Deborah, anyway, I am meeting him at the church for a quick practice and then we are off to the pub, so you are quite safe tonight. See you later."

The practice was fine and the pub was finer. Word had gone round that Bertie was buying tonight, so his 'Stag Night' was well attended. The two friends left just after eleven and slowly walked home. Fulfilling the duties of the 'Best Man', Digger saw his friend to the door and was about to enter when Deborah appeared before them, took hold of her dad, said, "That's as far as you are coming tonight Dimwit," smiled, and slammed the door in his face.

"What did you call me?" he said more to himself than anyone else and couldn't resist calling out, "See you tomorrow Debbie, don't be late!"

Unfortunately for him, she had anticipated such a foolhardy move on his part and to his surprise was struck firmly on his back by either an apple or a potato, which almost knocked him off his feet. Somehow he managed to keep his footing but he did step into a large hole at the side of the path. He considered it prudent to make no further comment and increased his pace, in case anything else was coming his way.

Deborah arrived at Millstone House just after noon and was horrified to find Digger was still having his breakfast. "What were your parting words to me? Don't be late! You were expected an hour ago; some Best Man you have turned out to be."

"I was knocked unconscious by a large rock, shortly after leaving your dad and lay all night on the wet grass. I didn't get home till six and have a terrible pain in my back and head; I am really not sure if I am fit enough to do my duties today."

"Just ignore him Deborah," said Cook, "I was still up when he came home and it was only just after midnight, but the service is not until three and we have plenty of time and Digger has washed both the cars this morning, so if you two could manage to get on together, just for today, I would be really grateful."

"C'mon Mac, we know where we're not wanted, let's go and get ready."

They wandered outside and Digger cleaned the windscreens and put the white ribbon on both cars, ready for driving the bridal parties to the church. Mrs. Duffy-Smythe was driving the bride and maid of honour and Digger was driving Bertie and himself. Mrs. Black was going a bit earlier to put the final touches to the church flowers. The reception was taking place in the pub, who was handling the catering arrangements.

Sissy and her brother were acting as Ushers and the vicar gave Bertie and Digger a very warm welcome when they arrived with half an hour to spare. As she hated to be late for anything, Cook broke with tradition and arrived early for the ceremony. To every one's surprise she was being given away by Dr. Bloom, who had been suggested by Moira and was delighted to act in this role.

The organist started to play 'All things bright and beautiful' which was Cooks favourite hymn and as the church clock struck three, they started their walk down the aisle.

Bertie and Digger turned round to watch them as they walked towards them and it also gave Digger a chance to smile at Moira who had moved into the pew behind him.

Dr. Bloom signified that he was giving the bride away and Deborah took Cook's flowers from her, so that the ceremony could proceed.

"Dearly beloved, we are gathered here together, in the sight of God, and in the presence of this congregation, to join together this Man and this Woman in holy Matrimony; which is an honourable estate, instituted by God."

The ceremony went well until it was Cook's turn to make her vows and suddenly she had a 'flashback' to her first marriage, all those years ago, when she had promised to love Dick for ever; and she froze.

The vicar was the first to sense that something was wrong, he squeezed her hand and smiled at her and said quietly, "It's OK Victoria, just take your time."

She smiled back at him, coughed twice and then repeated after him in a clear loud voice, her marriage vows:

"I Victoria Owen, take thee Bertie Wilberforce Bannister, to be my wedded Husband, to have and to hold from this day forward, for better for worse, for richer for poorer, in sickness and in health, to love and to cherish, till death us do part, according to God's holy ordinance; and thereto I give thee my troth."

The vicar prayed and then concluded the ceremony with the words,

"Forasmuch as Bertie and Victoria have consented together in holy wedlock and have witnessed the same before God and this congregation and thereto have pledged their troth to each other and have declared the same by joining hands and by the giving and receiving of a ring; I pronounce that they are Man and Wife together, in the Name of the Father, and of the Son and of the Holy Ghost. Amen."

The Groom kissed the bride, everyone clapped or cried or cheered, or a mixture of all three and Bertie led his new wife down the aisle and out of the church to a hail of confetti from everyone present.

There had been a short shower of rain while they were in the church and the photographer had to place everyone very carefully to avoid wet bushes and puddles. Mrs. Duffy-

Smythe drove the bride and groom to the pub where they were warmly welcomed by Del and Sheila who had laid out the whole of the public bar for the buffet meal and had arranged the saloon bar for receiving guests and serving drinks. They had hoped to use the garden as well but decided to wait and see what the weather was going to do.

Digger arrived with Deborah, Moira and Dr. Bloom who had sensed the tension between the two ladies and Digger and volunteered to sit in the back with Deborah and talk about motor bikes. The two ladies went off to powder their noses while the two men checked if there was anything they could do to help, before getting a pint of beer from the bar and sitting down near the window.

Moira was first to appear and was in good form and seemed very pleased about something which she was not prepared to discuss with Digger. Deborah appeared a few minutes later and went over to speak with Bertie and kept well away from Digger and Moira for the rest of day. It was in fact several years later that Digger discovered what had happened that day.

It appears that as they entered the ladies, Deborah had said to no-one in particular, "Well the village idiot managed not to lose the ring, I suppose we should be grateful for that!"

"I beg your pardon," said Moira, "I assume you are talking about my boyfriend, Digger?"

"Your boyfriend, you must be a lot thicker than I thought. I assumed that district nurses had to be intelligent and pass exams and things!" With which she pushed Moira out of the way to get to the sink to wash her hands and face.

Moira assured Digger that she did not intentionally put her foot out as she fell against the wall, it just sort of happened and Deborah just sort of fell forward and caught her head on the side of the sink and went down very hard on her backside onto the tiled floor.

"Well! How the high and mighty have fallen," said Moira, "It serves you right Miss Banister for being so unpleasant. This is your father's wedding day, for goodness sake, show some respect, will you." With which she left the room with a very undignified Deborah, still sitting on the floor.

The reception was acclaimed a great success by everyone who went and since Bertie had booked the best room in the pub for the night, they were able to stay there and enjoy it right to the end. Cook did make one or two comments about the food not being quite right, but conceded that they had done a very good job overall.

When Digger and Moira got back to the cottage after Church the next day, they found a note to say that Cook's bags were in the kitchen and she had gone round to Bertie's to help him pack and could Digger drive round there to pick them up, after he had eaten lunch. Mrs. Duffy-Smythe had invited Moira and Arnold to join her and Mrs. Black for lunch, which had given the ladies ample opportunity to discuss the wedding, the attendees, what they had worn and what they had said and done. All agreed that it had been a great occasion and Mrs. Black ended the meal with a toast for 'Good health and happiness' for Cook and Bertie.

Digger picked up the bags and filled the trunk of the car and put another bag behind the driver's seat. Moira drove with him to Bertie's and they walked down the path together, holding hands. Fortunately, Bertie only had two cases which fitted on the rear seat next to Bertie, Cook having said that she had previously felt sick in the back seat of the car. They all said their goodbyes to Moira and Digger promised he would drop in to see her on his return, if it was not too late.

They first drove to Oxford and filled up with petrol and then picked up the A34 which they followed to Winchester where Digger decided to fill up again, in case the garages were closed on his way back. Apart from missing a sign and getting lost once around Totton, they arrived at the hotel in Ashurst in good spirits about 6:35pm. The porter came and took the bags while Mr. and Mrs. Bannister signed the register and said goodbye to Digger. They went to their room and he drove home, arriving at Moira's around nine thirty, in time for a cup of tea and chat before returning to the cottage.

The two days at Ashurst were warm and sunny and apart from feeding the New Forrest ponies and a bus trip to Lymington for some last minute shopping, they passed quietly with the two newly-weds relaxing and getting to know each other.

The taxi arrived at 12:30pm on Wednesday and they arrived at the dock in Southampton an hour later. The taxi driver told them he was used to bringing passengers to Southampton docks and not to worry, he would organize their luggage, just to tell him which cabin they were in. As they boarded the Fair Ocean, their hearts skipped a beat when they heard several members of the crew talking in Italian and they wondered if they were on the correct ship, but the officer at the top of the gangway spoke impeccable English and welcomed them aboard and confirmed this was the correct ship and a steward would show them to their cabin.

Their luggage arrived about twenty minutes later and they unpacked everything and stowed the cases, before taking a tour of the ship. It had been used as a troop carrier in the war and still had the odd mark to prove it and could do with a coat of paint, but Bertie declared it 'shipshape' and said it would do very nicely and would give them a safe and smooth passage.

They were a little late in leaving port, something about a train being delayed and passengers not on board, so they finally set sail about 8:00pm.for the start of their journey to Australia.

CHAPTER TWENTY THREE
BACK TO SEA

"After seeing those tiny tourist cabins, Bertie, I am really glad you persuaded me to travel First Class on this trip," said Victoria, on returning to their cabin after she and Bertie had been on a tour of the ship. "The thought of being cooped up in a tiny cabin with bunk beds for a month or more with hardly enough room to 'swing a cat in', would have spoilt everything."

"Well 'cat swinging' was abolished in the navy many years ago and I am far too much of a gentleman to say 'I told you so', mind you there are some advantages of travelling 'Tourist Class'!"

"Really," she replied, "I can't think of any, what did you have in mind?"

"Well to start with the beer was a penny a pint cheaper in their lounge and the stewards don't expect such a big tip at the end of the voyage either." He wandered over to where Victoria was pulling on the foot of her bed and stood there for a moment smiling to himself, before saying in a slightly perplexed tone, "What are you trying to do with that bed Victoria?"

"I just though t I would re-arrange things in here. If we put the two beds together it will be a lot cosier and it will give us a bigger area of useable space."

"That's a good idea," he replied, "I'll ring for an engineer."

"What do you want an engineer for?"

"Well those beds are either bolted or welded to the floor and I don't think you are going to move them on your own," he quipped, as he sat down in the armchair in the corner of the cabin.

She turned round quickly and walked across to the armchair and sat down on his lap, put her arms round his neck and said, "No-one likes a smarty pants, Mr. Retired Sea Captain," and kissed him squarely on the forehead, leaving two big lip imprints from the new lipstick that she had bought for the trip.

He walked round like that for the next thirty minutes and she could barely stop herself from laughing out loud every time she looked at him. When he suggested getting a drink and a sandwich in the lounge bar, she was happy to agree and it was only because he had to wear a tie for the occasion, that he looked in a mirror and spotted the imprints on his forehead. "You artful minx! You wouldn't have let me go out like this would you?"

"Mine to know and yours to wonder," she replied and after wiping the two red marks off his head, she took his arm and went up to the First Class lounge bar, still chuckling to herself.

To her utter surprise she was woken at about 2:00am by Bertie being violently sick in the bathroom. She rushed to see if he was alright and understood that he wanted a glass of water, which she fetched him. She asked if he had eaten something, but he shook his head and finally managed to say, "Sea Sick".

"But you were a captain, surely you weren't always sea sick?"

"First night out and very calm seas; otherwise I'm OK. Go back to bed." That was all he could manage before he started to be ill again.

She was tempted to ask if he was related to Lord Nelson, but decided now was not the right time, so instead she put on her coat and went back on deck and managed to find an officer and told him her problem. She did not do it intentionally, but somehow managed to say that Bertie was a retired captain and often had this problem. The officer escorted her to the ship's doctor who gave her some pills for Bertie, which she took back to the cabin and gave to him. It took about forty minutes for the pills to start working and then she helped him back to bed where he stayed until just after twelve the next day.

Bertie said he could manage some soup and bread which the steward brought along to the cabin and the pair of them managed a couple of circuits of the ship before heading back to their cabin again. They read for the afternoon and the Ship's Doctor called to see how Bertie was and left a few more tablets in case the sickness should return. He mentioned that the Bay of Biscay could get rough, to which Bertie replied that he had never been sick before in the Bay and was sure that he was over it now. During the conversation he told the doctor that he had been in the merchant navy for most of his life and had often been this way before on his way to India and the Far East.

The following day they were both up early after a good night's sleep and ate a hearty breakfast before a walk round the ship. They sat down on some deck chairs and got chatting with a couple who came and sat down beside them. They discovered that the couple had been visiting family in Holland and were returning to their glass wholesale business in Ceylon. Their names were Samuel and Caroline Van Royt who turned out to be both interesting and pleasant to talk with, and although they were a good few years younger that Bertie and Victoria, the four seemed to get on extremely well.

"I have always admired the saltwater pearls which Ceylon is famous for," said Bertie, "perhaps I will treat my new wife when we get there."

"You make sure he does," replied Caroline, "in fact a friend of mine has a shop near the harbour which I will take you to Victoria, these men are too quick to make promises which they never keep."

"Oh I don't know about that, they sound awfully expensive and to be honest, we are not actually paying for this trip ourselves, but my step son in Australia is treating us, so we have to be a bit careful with our finances," Victoria said.

"Have you been allocated seats in the dining room yet?" asked Samuel, "if not, we have two seats spare on our table and would love it if you could join us."

"That would be great, I was not very well yesterday, so we ate in the cabin," said Bertie.

The two couples chatted for a while and had tea together and then went back to their cabins after arranging to meet again at 7:00pm for dinner.

"Victoria, can I tactfully suggest that you keep our financial status to ourselves on this trip. The Van Royt's are obviously nice people and it made no difference to them, but it may do to others; so whilst we have nothing to hide, please be a little more sparing with that kind of information in future. Besides, we are not exactly paupers you know. I have contacted a friend of mine in Gibraltar who is holding something for me and assuming he has not absconded with it; well enough said, you just wait and see!"

"What do you mean a friend in Gibraltar and I have to wait and see? Who is he or she? You can't leave me hanging in thin air like this. Tell me Bertie."

"It's a he, a friend from the war, but that's all you need to know, trust me."

"It's nothing illegal is it Bertie? You weren't a smuggler or anything, were you?"

"You really will have to trust me Victoria, but nothing I did in the war was illegal. I am just sworn to secrecy as other people's well being is involved. I only mentioned it because I will be going ashore as soon as we dock and will probably spend the first night ashore with my friend and I don't want you to worry or be surprised."

"Well you have surprised me and I am worried, but you do what you have to do and of course I trust you, how could you think otherwise Bertie?"

They both dressed for dinner and were introduced to the other two couples by Samuel Van Royt. There was a retired stockbroker, Major Edward Grant and his wife Isabel who were on a world cruise with a three month stay in Sydney to visit relatives and possibly start a new branch of his firm there and a middle aged farmer and his wife, from Gloucester, Dai and Gwyneth Conway, who had sold their farm and were going to buy land in Victoria to breed cattle.

Bertie told everyone that he was a retired captain and that he and his wife were travelling to Fremantle to visit relatives. No sooner had he mentioned Fremantle than the Major started on one of his war stories from the Great War, involving Australian mounted troops, many of whom had come from Western Australia and how they spearheaded the attack on Jerusalem. Everyone was fascinated by the story and thus encouraged, the Major managed to keep everyone entertained for most of the evening, apart from his own dear wife of course, who could repeat the stories in her sleep, or so she would claim to her friends.

They all enjoyed a glass of port at the end of the meal and went their separate ways to their cabins. "What a pleasant evening that was Bertie, such nice people, conversation is not going to be a problem with the Major present, although I felt sorry for Dai Conway who tried to interject his own comments once or twice, but was always out-manoeuvred by the Major."

"It was Isabel, I felt sorry for, she looked so bored, this must happen every time they meet a new group of people, but we will not have that sort of problem for a few years yet, will we," he said, and winked at her slyly.

The ship docked at Gibraltar late in the afternoon and there were only a couple of passengers disembarking, who followed Bertie down the gangway. He had put on his rough working clothes and a seaman's cap and had not bothered to shave that day either, all of which had started to worry Victoria, but she had said nothing. He had also taken an old gas-mask bag, left over from the War, with him, into which he had put a bottle of Johnny Walker Whisky, some cigars he had bought the previous evening and one of his spare silk shirts from the wardrobe.

"Now remember, if anyone asks you where I have gone, you just say, to visit an old shipmate who has settled here and you know nothing more and don't talk about this if you do not need to," were his last instructions to her before he left the cabin.

He turned left at the bottom the gangway and walked for a further quarter of a mile before he came to the road leading to Fishmarket Lane. The café, where they had agreed to meet, was just on the bend and he went in and took a booth near the back but facing the door. He ordered a pie and a coffee and sat reading a newspaper he found on the seat. After about twenty minutes a man dressed like a merchant sailor came in and sat down opposite him.

"I thought it was you outside, standing in the doorway opposite the café, as careful as ever David, it's good to see you," said Bertie.

"Just making sure Burt, even now I have to be careful, but it's so good to see you again, my friend; what did you tell the new wife?"

"The truth of course, I just said I was seeing an old shipmate, do you have transport?"

"No need, if we cut through the alleys we can get to my place in ten minutes, cars tend to draw attention. Are you ready to go?"

Bertie paid for the food and drink and followed his friend out of the café, through a maze of streets and passages and then up some stairs to a small flat over a shop.

"Is that your shop below, David? What exactly do you sell in it, or shouldn't I ask?"

"The shop is completely legit and it is actually in my wife's name. We have just carried on where we left off before the War and deal mostly in jewellery, gold coins, and antiques, you know, small items with a high value. We have a very good market here, it being a major port where hundreds of seamen and passengers pass through on a regular basis and no-one asks too many question or expects too much in the way of paper-work! As we agreed when I left you last, a third of all this is yours Burt. Without you I would never have got out of France alive in 1945 and certainly would never have managed to land here in Gibraltar. With the cash and those Gold Rands you gave me, we had enough to buy the shop and get the business started. I am forever in your debt, my friend."

"Look David, without you and your group a lot of our boys would never have made it home, so a lot of people are in your debt too. You just give me what you consider fair and I will be happy with that. By the way, do you still have the package I gave you when you landed here, as I might now have need of it on the trip?"

"Your third is worth a lot more than I have currently in cash Burt, is it all right if I settle with you from our stock of jewellery and precious stones? But if you just need a few thousand pounds worth, why not leave the remainder with me and it will continue working for you."

"That will be fine David; I will return to the boat early tomorrow morning and bring Victoria, my wife, out on a shopping trip. We will aim to be here about 2:0pm and I will buy her some really nice earrings and one of those Barbary Ape figures. I will leave it to you to make sure that the value of the earrings plus whatever you hide inside the figure will be in part settlement of your debt to me and I will collect the rest from you at a later stage. I suggest that you charge me a tenner for my purchases and then she will be none the wiser. Agreed?"

Bertie then produced the whisky, cigars and silk shirt and he and his old friend chatted to the wee small hours, about old times.

Bertie was back on board about eight o'clock and immediately went to the cabin and washed and changed, whilst Victoria asked a lot of questions about his mysterious friend and what he had been up to in Gibraltar.

"For the last time Victoria, I met David by a café I knew and went to his flat over his shop and his wife cooked us a meal and we chatted and drank the whisky. I was going to suggest a walk later on today, so I will take you to the shop and you can meet them. He and I had to part in a hurry at the end of the war and there was some un-finished business between us, which we cleared up last night. No fuss, no problems, just two old friends catching up, nothing mysterious and nothing for you to worry about. But I am worried about missing breakfast, so let's go and get something to eat and please don't discuss this in front of anyone we meet up there."

No sooner had they sat down and ordered breakfast than the Conway's came and joined them and asked Bertie if he had met up with his friend in Gibraltar, as Victoria had mentioned it last night at dinner.

"Yes thank you, I think married life is suiting my friend, I am sure he has put on at least a stone and a half since last I saw him. But tell me about these cattle you hope to breed in Australia, sounds fascinating," he said. Having thus diverted the conversation away from his exploits, they then had to listen to the good and bad points of at least four different breeds of cattle, three different fodder grasses and a selection of farm sites they had been considering.

"Will we see you for dinner tonight, or are you both slipping ashore this time?" asked Gwyneth.

"No, we will both be here tonight. Bertie is taking me to meet his friends this afternoon, but we will see you both at dinner. Goodbye," replied Victoria.

As they walked down the gangway after breakfast Victoria asked Bertie if he had ever seen the Barbary Apes which Gibraltar was known for and was it true that they almost died out in the war.

"No I haven't seen them and yes they did almost die out, but I believe new members were located in Africa and shipped over. Why don't we ask that taxi driver where we can see some?"

They were told that the best chance was somewhere up the Mediterranean Steps which wind their way up the east side of the rock and start from the Jew's gate at the end of Engineer Road. They were warned that it was a steep climb but decided to give it a go. The taxi dropped them near the foot of the steps and they started the slow climb up. Bertie had brought his bag with a drink of lemonade and some biscuits, so after about an hour, they sat down for a rest and a drink. He took out the biscuits, which were only plain old digestives and handed one to Victoria and took one for himself. While he had a drink of lemonade he put his biscuit down next to him, but when he came to pick it up again, it had gone. He looked round quickly, just in time to see a young monkey scampering away with it to some nearby rocks.

"Quick Victoria, over there, a monkey has just made off with my biscuit."

She turned round quickly and saw the monkey climb onto the rock and start to eat the biscuit. "Quick get the camera out Bertie, take a photo," she said.

He carefully took the faithful box camera out of his bag, rolled on the film to the next frame and took a photograph. He then took another, 'Just in case' and then took one of her standing to the side of the monkey, who may just have moved sideways as he clicked the shutter.

"Hey, look at the time," he said, "I told David that we would be there about two, so that gives us just over an hour. Let's get going, shall we?"

Going down the steps was no faster than going up and it was almost three O'clock when they arrived hot and tired at the shop.

"Burt, do come in and this must be Victoria, how lovely to meet you," said Esther, who opened a gate in the counter to come out and greet them. "David, our visitors have arrived and they are hot and tired and badly need a drink, sit yourselves down and rest, where have you been, we were getting worried?"

They explained where they had been and the 'monkey encounter' and apologised for being late. David came through with some tea and put the 'CLOSED' sign up on the door and locked it and pulled the blinds. He looked at Bertie and said, "I hope you are going to buy something from my shop, for your lovely lady wife, while you are here Burt. I will do you a very good deal and if you have seen the Barbary Apes, then you must take a china figure home with you, in case the photographs don't come out."

"Well I had been intending to buy some earrings for Victoria and I like the Ape idea, what do you have?" Bertie asked.

"Earrings you say, not my normal line, but I do have a very nice pair I could let you have and unfortunately I only have one Ape figure left as well, so I hope you like them."

Bertie turned to Victoria and quietly said to her, "Look dear, whether you like the earrings and Ape or not, please say you do, as David would be terribly embarrassed if you don't."

She smiled and said, "I am really excited David, I left my decent pair of earrings at home and feel very under-dressed at dinner each night. Please show them to me."

Her eyes almost popped out of her head and her mouth just gapped open, as she stared in disbelief at the earrings. Finally she managed to say, "Bertie, they are breathtakingly beautiful. Can we afford them?"

"I really don't know Victoria, but try them on while we find out. David, how much are they?"

"To you my old friend, since you would not accept payment for the silk shirt you brought me, four pounds fifteen shillings."

This was the code, by which Bertie knew that they were worth four hundred and seventy five pounds and the monkey figure would contain the rest.

"And what about the monkey figure, you mentioned, how much is that going to cost me?"

David produced the figure from under the counter and it stood almost nine inches tall and to put it mildly, was not very attractive. "Since this is the only one that I have left, you can have it for one pound five shillings, making six pounds all together."

Victoria was about to pull a face and say no, but saw Bertie shake his head at her and said nothing.

"You know David, my daughter Deborah would just love that, she adores animals, six pounds is a very fair price, thank you." He took out a big blue five pound note and a one pound note from his wallet and passed them to David, who put the money in the till and then wrote out a receipt and gave it to Bertie, while Esther took the earrings from Victoria and put them in a small box, which she then returned to her.

They chatted for a while longer and drank some more tea and finally decided it was time to leave. David and Esther walked them to the ship, pointing out places of interest on their way.

"Next time you are in port, you make sure Burt lets you can come and stay with us for a few days, we would love to get to know you and show you round," said Esther, who hugged them both and stood waving as they walked up the gangway.

Victoria said nothing until they were in the cabin and the door was closed and then she turned to Bertie and said, "I am not a complete fool Bertie, what exactly was all that about?"

Bertie wondered exactly what it was had triggered this reaction and carefully replied, "What was what about, dear?"

"These," she said, holding out the box with the earrings, "these four pound fifteen shilling earrings. Remember I said that I used to work in a grocers shop with my second husband, well the shop next to ours was a small jewellers' It was just the owner on his own and if he had to pop out, I would mind the shop for him and over the years he taught me a thing or two and I know real high quality diamonds when I see them! So then, I have been honest and open with you, now it's your turn."

"You never cease to surprise me Victoria; who would have thought it, you a diamond expert? Well, most of what I did in the war is covered by the Official Secrets Act and that includes virtually everything about David Josephs and his wife. When the War in Europe had almost finished, I helped him to leave France and come here, where his wife was waiting for him. Unfortunately, David left in such a hurry that he was almost penniless and to make matters worse, we knew his wife was not well. At the time I happened to have some of my nest egg with me in the form of some cash, gold coins and jewellery, so I gave most of it to him to pay for a doctor and to get him started in a new business. The deal was that someday I would come past and he would repay me. The earrings are part of that repayment."

"So why the charade back in the shop and how much are they really worth?" she asked.

"They are worth just under five hundred pounds and I was afraid that if you knew their real value you would panic and not wear them, and be forever worrying about losing them."

"I will certainly be very careful with them and only wear them occasionally but they are beautiful Bertie; I suppose I have to ask the other question, which is, are they really mine or am I just temporarily holding your nest egg for you?"

"A bit of both, I guess. The earrings are yours and the china monkey is mine, how's that? But if times should ever get hard for us, or we need a lot of money quickly, they will have to be sold, do we have a deal?"

"That sounds very fair to me, can I wear them for dinner tonight?"

"I would be disappointed if you didn't," he replied and hugged her tight.

Needless to say the other ladies noticed the earrings the moment that Victoria sat down and she explained that they were a surprise belated wedding gift from Bertie. She then quickly led the conversation into their encounter with the young Barbary Ape on the Mediterranean Steps at which point the Major remembered a war story about some steps in Italy and that was the last her earrings were discussed.

The boat sailed out of the harbour at Gibraltar just after ten on the morning of Monday the 12th of July 1948 with the passengers, all unawares, of what was happening at the other end of the Mediterranean Sea. For reasons which were not explained to the passengers at the time, the ship seemed to take forever to sail from Gibraltar to Port Said and it was early evening on Friday the 16th July before they dropped anchor some distance from the shore, opposite to a large white building with three blue domes.

"Look at this magnificent building Bertie, is it a palace?" asked Victoria.

"No dear. That is the headquarters of the Suez Canal Company, impressive isn't it? Had we been allowed to disembark, I would have taken you to see it, as I used to know quite a few of the managers who worked there and I am certain that someone would have remembered me.

But as the captain has explained, the current hostilities between the Palestinians and the Israelis make this whole area far too dangerous for us to venture ashore." "Are we in any real danger here, do you think?"

"No, we are quite safe on the ship and I am sure the British Navy has the odd gunboat or two in the vicinity. Anyway, tomorrow we pass through the Suez Canal and by this time tomorrow night, we will be sailing down the Red Sea on our way to Aden, where I will be able to take you ashore and show you the sights."

The evening passed without incident apart from some spasmodic small arms fire in the distance. The ship was third in line the next day to pass through the Suez Canal and Victoria was disappointed to discover that for the most part it was flat, sandy and not very interesting.

The journey from Port Said to Suez took about fifteen hours with the occasional RAF plane flying overhead and they did wave to some British servicemen who were relaxing in the waters around Fayid on the Great Bitter Lake.

"It seems incredible that thirty thousand people were working here at any one point in time, Bertie, where did they all live and how did they feed them?" she asked.

"Well it is thought likely that work first started here two thousand years before Christ, but most of it was done in the last century. The Canal has been opened for business since eighteen sixty nine, so as to how all the logistics worked and how they managed to feed and provide shelter for everyone, you will have to ask someone a lot older than me!"

They sailed slowly down the Red Sea, enjoying the warm weather but having to keep covered up from fear of mosquitoes, which could be particularly troublesome in the evenings. They got to know their knew friends a lot better and when Victoria mentioned that Bertie had been to Aden before, the Conways' asked if they might join them for a tour of the sights, as Gwyneth's elder brother had been there during the War. Bertie was pleased to agree but asked them not to mention it to the Major, as a whole day of war stories would have just been too much.

They arrived in the harbour late afternoon and were struck by how peaceful and still it seemed and how the reddish grey rock of the extinct volcano completely dominated the whole bay. There were many other ships of all sizes and ages in the harbour, with quite a lot of tugs moving them all around and Bertie explained to her what the tugs were doing and the probable cargoes of the different ships. It was a little after seven when they were finally settled in their anchorage for the night and they decided it was time to get ready for dinner.

"I have spoken with the chief steward who has promised to arrange a taxi for the four of us tomorrow morning at ten, so we will have the whole day to explore," said Bertie.

"It will be so good to be on dry land again," replied Victoria, "and will we be able to try some of the local food Bertie? I am getting tired of the ship's food and it would be really good to eat something different."

"Oh I think we can manage that, it just depends how different you want different to be!" he replied smiling.

CHAPTER TWENTY FOUR
WHALE SPOTTING

The chief steward had a quiet word with Bertie before they all disembarked and the ship's boat took them ashore at nine thirty. This gave them half an hour to stroll around Steamer Point before the taxi arrived at ten past ten. Bertie told the driver the different places they wanted to visit and to find them somewhere nice for lunch which served both Arab and western food and agreed a price for the day. The two ladies and Dai Conway sat in the back and Bertie sat in the front with the driver.

"What was the chief steward saying to you Bertie?" asked Victoria.

"He was giving me some idea of how much to pay the taxi driver and warning me that there had been some unrest here a few months ago but everything seemed to be quiet now, but to just be careful."

They drove out through Maala and past the airport and stopped by some large pits in a very flat area. "Look Dai a windmill, I didn't expect to see that here, what is it doing Bertie?" asked Gwyneth.

"These pits are used to produce salt by evaporation. The windmill pumps the sea water into the pits; the sun evaporates the water, leaving the salt, which is collected. A very valuable commodity in hot climates. They produce thousands of tons of salt every year. OK driver, Sheikh Othman."

The driver slowly drove through the town, avoiding the goats and pedestrians who just wandered all over the road and stopped so that Victoria could take a photograph of a camel pulling a cart with a large barrel on it, from which a man was selling water to people. He eventually stopped the taxi by a low wall and they all got out to discover the most beautifully laid out gardens; full of cannas, flowering shrubs, green grass and trees which gave ample shade.

"How wonderful Dai, a real Garden of Eden in the middle of a desert area, how do they mange it Bertie?" asked Gwyneth.

"This oasis is blessed with a plentiful supply of underground water, so they simply have to bore down and find it. There is over forty acres of gardens here, so we will only be able to see a small part, but this has always been a favourite place of mine. You can sit down, close your eyes and just imagine you are back in England. Well, I can anyway!" he laughed.

They wandered around the gardens for an hour or so and then got back in the taxi and informed the driver that they were all feeling hungry and ready for lunch.

The restaurant turned out to be the home of the taxi driver, who had taken the opportunity while they were in the gardens, to make the necessary arrangements with his wife and mother. They sat round an old wooden table in the garden which was shaded by two large date palms and were given a large earthenware jug full of cool fresh water and some pottery beakers. Bertie told them that the water was considered safe and he personally had never had a problem drinking it; so he filled everyone's beaker to the brim and encouraged them to drink as much as they were able.

"A toast," he said, "please raise your beakers, to new friends and new experiences."

"To new friends and new experiences," they all said and drank heartily.

A young Somali boy brought a plate with a large round flat loaf of bread on it, from which Bertie broke a piece off and gave to Victoria and then to himself, with the others following suite.

The main course was rice with chicken and mutton, which everyone loved, but the desert course of some sort of sweet cereals was not enjoyed by Victoria and Dai who both confessed to not having a sweet tooth.

Lastly they were offered honey, which was eaten with a small spoon from some sort of container and dates, which they presumed had been grown in the garden.

Finally they served tea, which arrived on a beautiful inlaid wooden tray. The tea came in elegant silver tea pots and was served without milk, but with sugar, into tall engraved glass tumblers and proved to be delicious and most refreshing.

After the meal, they all thanked the ladies for the wonderful food and climbed back into the taxi and the driver headed off in the direction of Crater, a small town which, as its name suggested, had actually been built in the centre of an extinct volcano.

The road to Crater climbed uphill for some distance and they could see that they were passing ancient cemeteries and were about to ask questions about them, when the driver announced that legend had it that Cain, the brother of Abel was buried in one of them. The road narrowed and the cliffs grew higher and higher on either side and they wondered if the road was going to run through a tunnel when they saw a small pass in the cliffs which the road went through, with fortifications built over the top of it.

The driver parked the car just before going through the pass and they all got out and looked back down the road to enjoy the view. Bertie pointed out Maala and the Dhow Harbour and Slave Island, where he told them that they still build dhows to the ancient pattern.

Having returned to the car, they drove through the pass and the road widened and gave them an excellent view over the town of Crater, which was much bigger than they had imagined.

"I will give you a choice of what we do first ladies," Bertie announced. "We can go to the museum and then the Tawahi Tanks and then to the Bazaar and shopping, or we can go to the Bazaar first. Which would you prefer?"

The two ladies looked at each other, both nodded and Victoria replied, "We would prefer to go to the Bazaar first Bertie and if there is time see the Tanks afterwards. Don't you men ever get tired of seeing guns and things?"

"They are not that sort of tank dear, but never mind, we will go the Bazaar first. Just a couple of pointers though. Firstly, everything is bartered for here and whatever price they first say, you should end up paying half or less. Secondly, make sure you hang on tight to your handbags and don't bring out a wad of notes. Just put a couple of pounds and loose change in a pocket. It may be better if I demonstrate to start with, to give you an idea. I want to get something for Deborah, my daughter here, so that will get us started."

The taxi took them through a built up area of housing and then past the Sultan's palace and finally stopped at the edge of the Bazaar.

"The driver will wait here for us but says if we want to see the Tanks we should not be more than a couple of hours. Is that OK everyone. Remember, if you get lost, we are parked by the police station and bank, but do try and stay together."

Bertie grabbed Victoria's arm and headed off down a narrow street with shops packed tightly on either side. He found the jewellery shop he was after and the owner made out that he had remembered him, but Victoria was not convinced by the performance. He found a silver filigree necklace he liked and started negotiations. He managed to get the price reduced from four pounds to two pounds five shillings, when to his amazement, Victoria made some comment about the other shop, grabbed his arm and started to walk away with him. He was too dumbfounded to argue and found himself outside with the owner holding the necklace in front of Victoria who seemed disinterested in what he had to say. She suddenly stopped dead and said loudly and clearly, "One pound fifteen shillings, that is our last offer. Yes or No?"

The man nodded, they went back inside, she then demanded a box for it, which was produced and Bertie paid the money.

Once outside Bertie turned to her and said, "That was amazing Victoria, where did you learn to do that?"

"Bartering isn't restricted to Arab countries you know, I used to do it a lot. The secret is in the eyes. I knew he was really pleased with the deal you were about to make, so I guessed there was room to manoeuvre. I think you men should leave it to Gwyneth and me, just tell us what you want and we will haggle for it, for you," she said laughing.

The two hours passed very quickly and they returned to the taxi with the necklace and some cufflinks, two shawls, a hat, several ladies garments, a cigarette case, an ornamental dagger, a silver teapot and a pair of pointed shoes, which curled up at the front, which Dai just liked the look of.

The driver took all the purchases and put them in a box he kept in the boot and locked the boot. "I will guide you at the Tawahi Tanks as the steps can be dangerous and we do not wish to leave your goods on show to everyone," he said, "I suggest we visit the museum afterwards, if we have time."

From the markets they drove straight to the municipal park which contained the museum and the Tawahi Tanks. The taxi driver stopped next to some other cars and taxis and the four friends got out and followed the driver down the path through the rocks to the start of the tanks.

Victoria waved to a lady she recognised from the ship and almost tripped over a rock. The driver grabbed her arm and stopped her from falling and then commenced his commentary.

"These tanks were built hundreds of years ago to trap the rains when they came, but we are not sure who built them or how successful they were. They were re-discovered under tons of rubble by an Englishman, about a hundred years ago and it is thought that they would hold twenty million gallons of water when filled," said the taxi driver. "Please be careful where you walk as there have been rock-falls recently and be warned not to stroke the dogs you see running around. I know how much you English like dogs, but these are wild and will most likely bite you."

They all went down the first flight of steps to get a better view, but Victoria said she was tired, so she, Bertie and the driver remained on the landing, looking out over the Tanks, while Dai and Gwyneth decided to go down two more flights of steps. They were close to the bottom of the first flight when a couple of the wild dogs started to run after them down the steps, barking wildly. The Conway's turned to see what was happening and one of the dogs crashed into Gwyneth's leg and knocked her off balance and she fell down the last five or six steps. Luckily the dog stopped at the bottom and looked back to see who was shouting at him and Gwyneth landed on top of him, thus breaking her fall.

The dog was not impressed and was about to bite her when she remembered the driver's warning and had the presence of mind to hit it very hard with her bag and moved her leg so that the dog could get up and run off.

The driver immediately set off down the steps and he and Dai ran to wear Gwyneth lay, to discover she had twisted her knee and ankle and that she was incapable of walking. They managed to lift her to the top of the steps between them and then carry her to the car.

The driver produced some water to wash her knee and ankle, which by now had swollen to twice their normal size and Bertie suggested that they take her to the main hospital at Steamer Point.

The RAF doctor on duty was very attentive and examined her knee and ankle and applied some ice, which brought the swelling down. He told her that nothing was broken, but the knee was badly torn and would take many weeks to heal. The ankle was not quite so bad, but she should avoid putting too much weight on it for a few days.

He then put a strapping on both of them and gave Dai spare bandages and strict orders that she rests her leg for at least twenty four hours and then gets the ship's doctor to examine it again. He also said that it was a good job the dogs had not bitten her, as they were wild and there is always the chance of rabies.

Bertie settled accounts with the driver to cover the day's journey and meal and then proceeded to give him a big tip for having been such a good guide and help to them and Gwyneth also hobbled over to thank him for assisting her.

The ship's boat took them back to the Fair Ocean in time for the evening meal, which Victoria thought was very bland, compared to the feast they had eaten for lunch. The Conway's decided to eat in their cabin as the ankle had started to swell again and had required another ice pack.

To everyone's surprise the Major had never actually been to Aden before and listened with interest to all the places they had seen and the things that they had done during the day.

The ship left Aden on Thursday morning and the passengers quickly got back into their on-board routine. Everyone was delighted to see Gwyneth up and about and the ship's doctor confirmed that nothing was broken but the knee had been damaged and would require rest and support. The swelling round the ankle had gone down and she was able to walk slowly with the aid of a stick, which another elderly passenger had offered to lend her.

Victoria had taken to sitting somewhere near the rear of the ship and watching the birds and fish that were diving and swimming alongside, aided by some binoculars which Bertie had brought with him. She decided to make a list of everything she saw but had to rely on the information which Bertie and crew members gave to her.

"Remind me to look for a book on birds and fish when we reach Colombo Bertie. The shark you told me was a Hammerhead has been called at least three other names by other people, so I am truly not sure if the names I have listed are really what I have seen. Apart from the ones you have told me, of course."

"I'm glad you added that dear and please put the leather strap round your neck when using my binoculars, I don't want them falling into the sea when you stand up suddenly to get a better view of something."

By Thursday evening it had come to the Captain's ears that Bertie had been a skipper himself, so he and Victoria were invited to join the Captain at his table. The two men swapped yarns and places they had both visited, but were unable to find anyone they both knew apart from a few shop and tavern keepers in Hong Kong and Melbourne. It was a late night by the time the dinner was completely finished and Victoria was feeling very tired when she got back to the cabin.

"You know Bertie, I found out more about your past, tonight over dinner, than all the rest of the time we have been together. What a wonderful adventurous life you have lived, don't you miss it? All those exotic countries and things you have seen and done, I would have thought that a cottage in the middle of a quiet English wood, just outside a small village, was the last place you would want to end up."

"Well it's funny you should say that Victoria, because I had not realized how much I had missed it, until tonight. During the war, all you dreamed of was going home and having a quiet life, which is what I have done until meeting you. That has all changed with a vengeance and I am really pleased; marrying you and travelling to Australia has sort of kick-started me into a new life. So thank you dear."

During breakfast on Friday, Bertie got a note from the captain inviting him to visit the Bridge, which he did as soon as he had finished eating.

"I don't suppose I will be very long Victoria and it would be rude to ignore the invitation," he said, "You don't mind do you?"

"Of course not, you go. I will still be here when you come back," she laughed.

Bertie wandered off to the Bridge and Victoria went to her seat at the back of the ship.

The day was hot and humid and everyone had been warned again about sun burn and to keep themselves covered up. Caroline Van Royt had found a book on fish in her luggage and she sat down next to Victoria to join her in fish spotting and identification.

When Samuel sat down besides them the two ladies were very excited as they thought they may have spotted a Finback whale.

"You look Samuel," said Caroline, "It is huge you can't miss it. Over there by that round shiny buoy thing."

Samuel grabbed the binoculars from her, almost breaking the leather strap.

"Hey be careful, that's my neck your pulling," she shouted.

Samuel focused on the round shiny buoy thing and let out a loud groan. A steward who had heard Caroline shout had come over to them, "Is everything all right Mrs. Van Royt?" he asked.

Before Caroline could say anything, her husband answered for her.

"No it most certainly isn't, you take a look, over there, just past the school of fish, do you see it?"

The man nodded. "Would you go and tell the captain sir and I will stay here and keep a watch on it."

By now a small crowd had gathered round them and another passenger with binoculars had also managed to see the round object in the water, "Oh my goodness it's a mine," he said, "Its huge and I'm sure it's getting closer. Do we need to abandon ship?"

"No we don't sir. Please be quiet everyone and do not panic, there is no need for alarm. I can assure you that the mine is definitely not getting closer, but now we have sighted it, we will have to do something about it, as this is quite a busy shipping lane that we are in."

When Samuel reached the Bridge, he found the captain and Bertie in deep conversation on maritime practice and was forced to interrupt them. He quickly explained what he had seen off the stern of the ship and waited for the captain's reaction, which was to stop all engines and order the ship's boat to be lowered over the side.

"You think it had spikes sticking up from it?" asked the captain.

"I am sure it did," replied Samuel.

"Sounds like a German floating contact mine to me," said Bertie, "Two hundred pounds of explosives, an evil device, it must have come loose from its mooring. We can't leave it there, it will be a danger to every other ship coming this way."

"I know we can't Bertie, but I do have to think of my passengers and crew first. Even at this distance if it should suddenly explode, the ship would be seriously damaged."

"I could take the ship's boat and one of the men and go and deal with it sir," said the first mate.

"And then what happens if the captain has a heart attack or suchlike, this is a very dangerous enterprise, my friend, who is going to take charge of this ship if something happens to you as well," responded Bertie. "Why not let me skipper the ship's boat and give me a couple of crew who can shoot at the mine. In the meantime, you move the ship to a safe distance."

The captain stroked his chin and pondered a moment. "I don't like the idea Bertie, but to be honest, I don't have a better one and we need to do something fast. I will get a couple of volunteers from the crew to go with you."

"I can go," said Samuel. "I was the .303 long distance rifle champion of my unit. Do you have an armoury on board?"

The captain gave the key to the armoury to the mate and told him to get two rifles and plenty of ammunition. The young crewman on the bridge said he had been in the infantry and volunteered to go with them.

The mate returned with two Lee Enfield Number 4 Mark 1 rifles and about a hundred rounds of ammunition. Samuel checked the action of the rifles and chose one for himself and gave the other to the crewman. Before boarding the ship's boat, they affirmed the exact position of the mine from the steward who had not taken his eyes of it. They agreed with the captain that he would fire a flare when he considered he was at a safe distance and that would be the signal for the start of the mine hunting expedition.

Bertie steered the small boat away from the ship and headed back the way they had come. The mine was harder to spot this time, as the boat was a lot lower in the water and it was in fact the Finback whale which the young crewman first saw, which allowed them to find the right area where the mine was lurking.

"Why couldn't we shoot it from the ship itself," asked Samuel, "Surely it would be big enough to withstand a large wave from that sort of distance?"

"Possibly, but you never know and the captain was quite right in taking no chances. For all we know there could be several more mines in the area or even chained to it, which could cause a massive explosion if several detonated at once."

"Well exactly how safe are we?" asked Samuel.

"As far as I understand these things, the mine is just as likely to take on water and sink to the bottom of the sea, as it is to explode," said Bertie, "And I have even heard stories of them being set off by large fish, so let's just stop worrying and do what we came for."

"That's the Captain's flare," said Samuel, "Let's find that mine."

They spent an hour looking for it with no luck and were on the verge of giving up, when something clunked against the side of the boat. Everyone froze and waited for the explosion, but it was only a piece of driftwood. As the crewman leant over to push it away, something caught his eye about fifty yards away and he called to the others, "Over there, something flashed, I think that's it."

Samuel trained the binoculars on the spot and confirmed they had found the mine. He then handed them to the crewman and picked up the rifle and settled it into his shoulder.

"Not yet, let me get a bit further away," said Bertie. "Fire off half a dozen rounds as quick as you can, as aiming in this sea is not going to be easy."

Bertie moved another thirty yards from the mine and set the engine on idle and told Samuel to start shooting with the crewman acting as spotter.

Only one of the first volley hit the mine and the crewman reported that it just seemed to bounce off the casing. The second and third volleys were no more successful and reluctantly Bertie agreed to take the boat nearer.

"This time we need to rope ourselves to the boat, because if it does explode we will definitely feel the effects and everyone is to wear a life jacket and that includes you Samuel. OK, let's give it our best shot," said Bertie.

Best shot it was. The mine exploded with the first bullet and a column of water shot a hundred feet into the air. The noise was deafening and although Bertie accelerated as fast as he could, he knew the giant wave would overtake them. It hit without warning and picked them up and made it seem like they were flying for a few moments and then the crash, as they landed back down on the water; which Samuel later described as being hit by an express train.

The engine had stopped working and a lot of the gear had gone overboard and Bertie was badly cut on his head where he had collided with the wheel. He got to his feet and untied the rope and went to find Samuel and the crewman. The first was lying in the back of the boat, still holding the rifle, which now had a twisted barrel and broken stock. The unfortunate crewman had been thrown overboard and was lying unconscious in the water. It took a great deal of effort from the other two men to pull him aboard and revive him. Luckily he had not swallowed too much water and was soon able to give the others a 'thumbs up', to show he was still alive and kicking.

The flare gun had been well strapped to the boat and Bertie found it and set off a flare to tell the ship where they were and to come and get them.

The Fair Ocean arrived about forty minutes later and the captain launched the second boat which took them in tow and helped them to come alongside. The doctor was there on the second boat and quickly checked the three for serious injury and cleaned and bandaged the wound on Bertie's head. He told them that everyone on the ship had been told about the mine and that they had all heard the explosion and seen the water column and been rocked by the wave; but fortunately, they were far enough away not to have suffered any damage to the ship or any incurred any personal injuries.

As they went back on board they were greeted like heroes and everyone cheered and clapped and Victoria and Caroline cried with relief and hugged them and insisted on accompanying them to the Bridge, where they gave a full report to the Captain, for his log.

The Captain in turn said he had been in radio contact with the British Navy and had given them the position of the mine, so that they could come and check the area out, to make sure there were no further mines there. He then produced a bottle of champagne and everyone drank and toasted the heroes; who then went back to their cabins and were finally able to rest and relax.

CHAPTER TWENTY FIVE
NEGOMBO LAGOON

By the time they sailed into Colombo on Monday the twenty sixth, Bertie had reduced the bandages on his head to a couple of sticking plasters and the engineers on the ship had managed to repair the engine of the ship's boat and patch up the damage to the sides. The Bannister's and Van Rout's had become firm friends and Victoria had accepted an invitation to stay with them at their villa in Negombo, a small town about twenty two miles north of Colombo, for four of the nights that the Fair Ocean was in port.

They arranged that Samuel and Caroline would return home on the Monday and make sure everything was in order and that Bertie and Victoria would catch the train up on the Tuesday morning; which is exactly what they did.

Victoria was fascinated by all she observed through the carriage windows and was constantly asking Bertie questions about the people, crops, trees, buildings and the way of life there. Bertie laughed at her and said she was more like a young girl than a middle-aged lady. In no time at all the engine, which was called the Pearl Princess, pulled into Negombo station and there was Caroline waiting for them on the platform. Bertie retrieved the case from the rack and carried it onto the platform, while Victoria went across to greet her new friend.

"Samuel sends his apologies, but he had to go into work, how was the journey?"

"Just wonderful," said Victoria, "what a lovely island, I can't wait to see more."

"Hello Bertie, can you manage the case alright?" asked Caroline.

"No problem and it's good to see you again, was everything in order with the house and things when you got back?"

"Oh yes, everything was fine, we have very loyal and reliable staff here. The car is just outside, this way." They walked outside of the station and there standing on the road was a gleaming 1933 Riley Kestrel, sitting there in all its glory.

"Wow, what a beauty," said Bertie, "I must confess that I was expecting a horse and carriage not a limousine."

"Well, we do have one of those as well, but I was saving that for the tour I had planned for tomorrow. The car is Samuel's pride and joy. He had had it shipped out before the war and it is the envy of most of the men on the island. Anyway, get in; it's only about twenty minutes to the villa."

The villa was situated a couple of miles out of town on the Negombo Lagoon. It occupied about two acres of land and was surrounded by a six foot high wall. They entered through a large iron gateway which was closed and locked after them. The villa itself was a huge single storey building which had been painted white with a roof of red tiles. The gardens to the front of the house were well maintained with neatly cut grass and colourful shrub and flower beds, with citrus and coconut trees providing some shade.

They all got out of the car and stood there admiring the scene.

"Oh Caroline, this is beautiful," said Victoria, "you must have plenty of help with the gardens to keep them looking like this."

"I certainly do," she replied, "there are three men who work on the grounds and buildings and their wives all work in the house. Samuel does all his business entertaining here, so we often have two or three events, as he likes to call them, each week. That is why I insist on going away for our holidays, or we would never get a real break from the business."

"Do your workers live locally, or do they have to travel?" asked Victoria.

"You may have noticed a couple of other buildings in the grounds, as we drove in, well two of the couples live in those buildings and the other couple who have a large family, live about half a mile away."

Just then a group of five dogs came bounding up to where they were standing and stood there barking at them. Caroline said something to them and they stopped barking and sat down. Victoria was about to stroke one, when Bertie stopped her.

"These are called Pariah Dogs," said Caroline. "The older brown and white dog is Lady, she is the mother and these are all her offspring. If you stroke Lady first, she will then acknowledge you and the others will follow suite," she explained. "They are more guard dogs then pets, so they have the freedom to roam all over the grounds, but are not allowed in the house."

Bertie bent down and let Lady sniff the back of his hand before he stroked her back. Victoria did the same and then stroked a young male dog, who had been rubbing against her leg, whose name was Duke. He tried to follow them into the house but before anyone could stop him, Lady barked once and he turned round and followed the pack, back down the garden.

The house had been built on a raised platform which was about two feet above the level of the gardens and had large arched windows and high ceilings, with fans slowly rotating in the centre. The roof overhung the walls by at least three feet all the way round, which gave some shade to the rooms.

All the floors of the house were tiled, as was the undercover seated area at the back, which was at least twenty feet deep with two beautiful white marble pillars, which supported the tiled roof.

"I will show you to your room and give you a chance to freshen up and then we will have lunch here on the veranda, in half an hour, if that will suit?"

The room turned out to be a private suite with a large bedroom with a sprung bed, complete with mosquito netting. A sitting room led off it, with a couch and two armchairs; with French doors leading off this onto a small balcony, complete with a painted iron table and two chairs. Another door led to a private bathroom, which boasted hot and cold running water.

"Oh Bertie, this is a palace. I have never been anywhere like this before. Look, someone has brought our case in and un-packed our things, I really like it here. Do you want some water, there is a jug over here with some glasses, I assume it will be safe to drink!"

"They will have their own well, so I am sure it is safe, just remember to keep yourself covered up and use that mosquito cream which someone has left by the jug of water, we don't want to get bitten while we are here."

They washed and changed their clothes and left them on a chair and walked back down the corridor to the lounge area and went through the big double doors to where Caroline was supervising the food.

"Was everything alright?" she asked. "Are you ready for something to eat?"

"Yes and yes," said Bertie, "we are famished. What a fine view you have of the lagoon and that must be the Gulf of Manaar in the distance. What are they fishing for in the lagoon?"

"Please sit down and help yourselves. They are mainly fishing for shrimps, we have several varieties, all delicious, try them," she said, passing a large bowl of seafood to Bertie.

"Do you have a boat Caroline?" asked Victoria.

"We have a rowing boat which we use on the lagoon and Samuel keeps a larger motor boat in the small port at Negombo. He loves to take it out to sea and catch something big. I am sure he will offer you a fishing trip while you are here."

"Not for me thank you," replied Victoria, "I was hoping to explore the island, if that's possible. Were you joking about your horse and carriage and going for a ride?"

"Not joking exactly, but we lent them to a friend while we were on holiday, we can pop round and see her after lunch and see what we can organize for tomorrow or Thursday, but do please help yourselves to the food."

Caroline and her guests walked down to the lagoon in the afternoon and then took their shoes off and paddled their feet in the shallow warm waters at the edge for a while. They then put their shoes back on and walked along the beach a bit further before entering the back gate of the friend who had been minding the horse and carriage.

The friend was called Anna and was nearer to Victoria's age than to Caroline's. She greeted her friend warmly and made Bertie and Victoria most welcome and gave them some refreshing Ceylon tea to drink.

"I can have the carriage ready by ten thirty tomorrow, if that will suit you and your friends Caroline."

"That would be perfect Anna, can we tempt you to come with us? You know far more about the history of everything than I do."

"I would enjoy that very much, thank you for inviting me. I have really missed you while you were away. Things have started to change since Independence in February, which was inevitable of course; but I find change so hard to deal with these days, I must be getting old or something!"

When they returned home they found that the clothes they had discarded before lunch, had been washed, dried and ironed and put on hangers in the wardrobe.

Samuel did not join them for dinner and it was gone eleven when he returned home, tired out from his day at work. He left early the next day but told Caroline to tell Bertie he was welcome to use the rowing boat on the lagoon if he wanted to.

Anna drew up outside the house, with the horse and carriage, five minutes early and Victoria and Bertie were surprised to see that she was the driver. "Anna is much better at this than me," said Caroline, "she has lots of trophies for carriage driving competitions. Why don't you sit next to Anna, Bertie and Victoria and I can pretend we are ladies sitting in the back."

They drove around for several hours seeing the sights and exploring several old ruined buildings, built by the Dutch many years ago. They stopped for a picnic lunch, which Caroline had prepared, somewhere on the edge of the Lagoon and paddled in the warm waters. They set off at a slow trot back to Negombo and stopped to watch the boats on the canal as they neared the town. Anna dropped them off just after four o'clock and said she would take the horse and carriage home, to save getting the car out.

Bertie and Victoria went back to their room and while Bertie was washing, Victoria lay down on the bed and went to sleep. He decided to leave her alone and went out onto the balcony with a glass of water. At about a quarter to six he decided to wake her and found she was still fast asleep and extremely hot. He shook her gently and she woke up and immediately dashed into the bathroom where she was violently sick. He told her to change into her nightdress and go back to bed.

Caroline was relaxing in an armchair with a book when he went through to the lounge. She saw the worried look on his face and asked, "Is everything alright Bertie, where is Victoria?"

"She is in bed with a fever and has just been violently sick. Do you have a doctor we can telephone, to come and take a look at her."

"Of course, I will ring him immediately. She seemed fine while we were out, although, come to think of it, she hardly asked any questions after lunch. I wonder if something we ate has upset her?"

The doctor arrived in his car at six thirty and by seven thirty Victoria was in bed in the hospital at Negombo, being treated for Malaria.

"Mr. Bannister, your wife is very ill, it may help us treat her if we knew where she was bitten by a mosquito, probably ten or so days ago," the doctor said.

"Well ten days ago we were sailing through the Suez canal and Red Sea, it must have been then, but she never mentioned it to me."

"OK, that is helpful, she is going to be in hospital for at least another ten days, probably longer, when does your ship sail?"

"It sails on Sunday, I will need to go and get our things and let them know we won't be sailing with them. Is she going to be alright doctor?"

"Your wife is fit and strong and there is every reason to think she will pull through, but Malaria can affect people in different ways, we will just have to do our best and wait and see. I can say nothing more at this stage."

Bertie took the train to Colombo the next day and went to the shipping office and explained what had happened. They were very sympathetic and said that if he was able to complete his journey with the same shipping line, they would be able to negotiate a discount for them, but could not offer any compensation for not completing the cruise.

Everyone he met on the ship seemed to know about Victoria and offered their good wishes and the purser invited him to inspect the store of ladies clothes that had been left by passengers in the past, to see if anything would be of use for Victoria during her enforced stay at Negombo. He selected a couple of lightweight dresses and some pyjamas which he thought might fit and thanked the man for his consideration.

The steward helped him carry the cases all the way to the train and wished him good luck, refusing the tip which Bertie offered him.

This time the train ride was not a happy event as he sat back in the seat and remembered the death of his first wife, Deborah in 1935, when his daughter was just twenty. She had died of TB and he had nursed her and watched her every day for over year as she fought and lost the battle.

He was alone in the carriage on this trip, so no-one heard him sob quietly as he thought on these things and as the lump in his throat grew so large that it almost chocked him. "Dear God," he prayed, "not again, please don't let her die, please don't let her die!"

At that moment, the train whistle blew three times and a gap in the trees allowed the sun light to come in and illuminate the carriage and for just a split second, it seemed he was not alone and at that moment, the despair left him and never returned.

Caroline had sent the car to meet the train and the driver helped him to load all the luggage into it and they then drove first to the hospital to visit Victoria and then back to the villa.

The doctor was wrong about the ten days as it was nearer a month before she was allowed out of hospital and during that time Bertie had moved out of the Van Royt's villa and had rented a small house which overlooked the port of Negombo itself and was a lot more convenient for the hospital. At Caroline's suggestion, he had engaged the elder daughter of the couple that worked for her but lived off site half a mile away, to be a housekeeper and she had agreed that he could borrow Duke to keep them all company.

Samuel tactfully asked Bertie if he has sufficient funds for a long stay in Ceylon and Bertie had to admit that it was going to be difficult and asked if he knew of anyone who could use a skipper for a few months. Samuel said that he thought he might and a couple of days later introduced Bertie to a friend of his who ran an import/export business between India and Ceylon. He had recently lost one of his most experienced skipper's to a competitor and was happy to give Bertie a job for as long as he wanted one.

He had sent a telegram to the solicitor in Kendal to inform them that they had left the ship at Colombo as Victoria had contracted Malaria and that he would let them know when they were on the move again. The solicitor immediately telephoned young Victoria in Australia and let her know that they would not be on the ship when it docked at Fremantle. Bertie also sent a telegram telling Mrs. Duffy-Smythe of their problems, asking her to let everyone else know and of course one to his daughter Deborah.

The young woman that Caroline had recommended turned out to be an excellent housekeeper and a wonderful nurse and companion for Victoria, although truth to tell, a day seldom passed without Caroline or one of her friends, dropping in to visit. Victoria joked that Caroline was just checking up to make sure she was not spoiling Duke, which of course she was.

Bertie loved being back at sea again and as time went on and Victoria got stronger, his trips away lasted longer and longer. On one occasion, sometime during October, he was away for more than fifteen days and gave no explanation apart from having had a spot of trouble somewhere in the Bay of Bengal. The owner of the company had contacted Victoria to say that the trip had been delayed and showed his appreciation by giving Bertie a beautiful string of saltwater pearls 'for his lovely wife', on his return to port. After that, he only worked three or four days a week as a rule and this was normally on a single trip to somewhere in India.

As Victoria got stronger they started to talk about resuming their journey to Australia, but she had a bit of a relapse in November so it was delayed again. Somewhere around the middle of December they had a telegram from Australia to say that Owen was getting worse and was not expected to last for more than a couple of months. Bertie immediately checked with the shipping agent in Colombo and discovered that the Fair Ocean was due to call in at Colombo on the 10th January and to leave again on Saturday the fifteenth, arriving at Fremantle on Thursday the twentieth. They were able to confirm that there was a first class cabin vacant for that leg of the journey, which Bertie reserved. The agent said he would negotiate with the shipping line for a reduced fair for them, as he had promised earlier.

As Christmas approached Victoria was delighted to receive lots of cards and letters from everyone back in England and especially one she got from Moira, "Bertie, listen to this from Moira, 'and I am thrilled to be able to tell you, that Digger and I intend getting engaged at New Year and plan to marry in Inverness at the end of August. We do hope you will be back in time to attend our wedding.' Isn't that good, I knew they were suited right from the start. I don't suppose we could be there for the wedding, could we?"

"Now is that a question or a statement? Let's get the trip to Fremantle under our belts and see how you are after that, before we even talk about a trip back to England. Does she say anything else in her letter?"

"Digger checks your cottage every week and says everything is fine and has cut the grass a couple of times but his work seems to be taking up more and more of his time, just like someone else I could mention! Oh, it appears that Mrs. Duffy-Smythe's latest book has done well in the United States and she is hoping to go there and promote it in the New Year. The rest is just small talk, you wouldn't be interested dear."

They spent Christmas day with the Van Royt's and a few other friends and had roast turkey and Christmas pudding for lunch, despite it being thirty something Centigrade in the shade. They all went to church together in the morning and enjoyed singing carols and exchanging presents. On Boxing Day they all went to visit Anna and her family and had a beautifully cooked Indian meal and played games in the afternoon and returned to their own house in the late evening.

On Monday the twenty seventh they were woken early by a hammering on their front door and Bertie went to find out who it was. Samuel stood on the front porch breathless and very agitated. "Fire at the other office Bertie. May need some support. Can you come and help, have you got a gun?"

Bertie quickly dressed and picked up his old gas mask bag from the wardrobe. "Problems at Samuel's office in the hills, he needs some help so I am going with him, see you later."

"What office in the hills, why do you need that bag, how long will you----,"

He was gone. She heard the car start up and roar up the road to goodness knows where.

They returned around six and Bertie came in on his own, covered in mud and with cuts and bruises to his arms and legs. He sat down and she made tea and took off his boots. "You are getting to old for this sort of lark, my lad, what happened?"

"No-one really knows, but someone deliberately started a fire among some of the houses up in the hills and Samuel has a second office up there. Look, I can't go into details, but he has another small business he runs from there and it has a lot of valuable stock in it."

At which point his bag which had been on the arm of his chair, fell off and hit the ground with a thud. Before he could stop her, Victoria picked it up and his pistol fell out. She stood there in a state of shock, holding the gun.

He took the gun from her and put it back in the bag and sat down and pulled her to him. "It's OK Victoria, the gun

317

is mine and it went everywhere with me during the war. It was returned to me by David, in Gibraltar, just in case we ran into any trouble. Samuel didn't know what to expect today in the hills, so I just took it with me to be on the safe side. When we got there, the fire was burning through some woods nearby and everyone was just trying to beat out the flames and stop the embers from blowing around in the wind. Some outbuildings belonging to the man who owns the company I have been working for were destroyed, but everything else was saved. The police are there at the moment and will stay overnight and guard the area and carry out a full investigation tomorrow."

Although she had a lot more questions that she would like to have asked, she realized that now was not the time and just let him rest, but did wonder what on earth Samuel's other business was and whether Caroline knew anything about it.

They had an invitation to attend the New Year's Eve Party, at the Officers Club in town and had a great night dancing and singing and welcoming in 1949. "I think this is the best New Year's Eve I have had since I was young," said Victoria, as they walked back to their house, "What a wonderful year 1948 turned out to be, I wonder what the New Year will bring us in the way of surprises?"

"I wonder!" mused Bertie.

The next couple of weeks flew past as they said goodbye to all their new friends and Bertie did one more trip, six days this time, to India and back. They gave their housekeeper a big tip and a glowing reference and actually helped her find a job with a new family that arrived on the Fair Ocean when it docked. The hardest thing was taking Duke back to Caroline and then having to say goodbye to the Van Royt's.

"Surely not goodbye," said Caroline, "But Aurevoir. We haven't booked this year's holiday yet, so maybe we will come to Australia and see you. I get tired of going back to Europe every time and fancy something different."

"That would be wonderful," replied Victoria, "I will write as soon as we know something and have somewhere to live."

"I have got you a little present to remind you of your time here," said Samuel and he produced a porcelain figure of a Pariah dog.

"Look Bertie, it's the same colour as Duke, oh thank you Samuel."

" Let me have it back a moment Victoria as I have a box for it in my study, just to keep it safe while you are travelling. Why don't you come through with me Bertie and we can get it packed up while the ladies say their goodbyes."

The next day, the Van Royt's insisted on driving them to the ship and stood there and waved till it was almost out of sight. "What lovely people Samuel, I do hope we will be able to meet up with them again and are able to continue our friendship."

"Oh I quite agree with you Caroline," he said. "Yes, I certainly agree."

CHAPTER TWENTY SIX
AUSTRALIA AT LAST

The shipping agent arranged a great 'deal fare wise' for Bertie and Victoria. When the captain heard who the passengers were that he was picking up in Colombo, he insisted that they only be charged an administration fee each, so for six pounds they got their passage to Australia. The cabin was very similar to the one they had before and was situated very close to it, so they were soon settled in and were the special guests at the captain's table on the second evening out of port.

When Victoria said she had just got over a bout of Malaria, the captain said he would mention it to the ship's doctor and ask him to drop by and see her. The previous doctor had left the ship in England and this was a younger man on his first voyage.

The ship docked at Victoria Quay Fremantle early afternoon on Thursday the 20th January after a quiet and un-eventful voyage. They said goodbye to the captain and thanked him for being so accommodating and by three pm were standing on the quay with all of their luggage. Bertie chose to wear slacks and a blazer and Victoria a lightweight summer dress.

"Do we know what this young lady looks like?" asked Bertie.

"Oh yes, she is brunette, aged twenty and is supposed to look a bit like Howard Owen when he was younger. She also said something about a big fawn coloured Chrysler car and I said I would be wearing my light brown coat with the fur collar."

"You are not wearing a coat Victoria," Bertie commented.

"Firstly, it is far too hot to wear a coat today and secondly it got packed!"

"You wait here with the luggage and I will pop over to the office to see if anyone has left a message for us," he said, and wandered off in the direction of some office buildings.

No sooner had he gone from sight, than a young brunette, aged about twenty, approached Victoria and said, "Excuse me, but would you be Victoria Owen?"

"I am and you must be Victoria Owen too, I am so pleased to be able to finally meet you, my dear."

There was a moment's hesitation as to how they should greet each other, but their natural emotions took over and they just stood there and hugged each other.

"Where has your husband gone, is he alright?" asked young Victoria (who we will call Vicky from now on, for clarity).

"He went over to the office for something, he won't be long. Is that your car over there?"

"Yes, I will give Ray, our farm manager a wave and ask him to come over and get the luggage."

She waved to Ray who got out of the car and went to the back and opened the tailgate. Even from a distance, Victoria could see that he was a big man, well over six feet three and broad with it. He was dressed in army shorts and boots, a green shirt and a bush hat, pulled down over his eyes.

"Goodness, he looks ferocious, I hope he is friendly!" said Victoria.

"He does have a reputation among the men and no-one argues with him, but we would be lost without him and he is always the perfect gentleman, where the ladies are concerned. So, no need to worry."

Just then Bertie came up and was introduced to Vicky, who gave him a hug and a peck on the cheek. No-one had noticed that Ray had also approached the group, saw the embrace between Vicky and Bertie and simply erupted.

"You POME's make me sick. You come over here in your fancy clothes and think you own the place and who said you can kiss our Sheila's, I'll teach you some manners! You need cooling off my friend!"

With which he picked Bertie up and held him over his head, like he was a sack of paper and started to walk towards the edge of the quay. Vicky and Victoria were dumbstruck, but quickly realized what was about to happen and raced after him.

"No Ray, this is Victoria from England," said Vicky, "who we came to meet and this is her husband. Put him down immediately. Don't you dare hurt him."

"Don't worry," he replied, "I know exactly who he is, I'll put him down alright," and kept walking.

Well, Victoria could see that words were not going to have any effect on this hulk of a man, so she took a three pace run up and kicked him as hard as she could in the back of his left knee, not knowing that this was the knee he had injured whilst playing 'Ruckman' in Ozzie Rules Football. His legs buckled and he went straight down, just three yards from the edge of the quay and Bertie went down on top of him.

The two men lay there in a heap, with the two women standing by, wondering what to do next. Bertie started to move and Victoria was shocked when she saw his whole body shaking and him sobbing. Vicky was even more shocked when she observed Ray was doing something similar.

"Are you hurt Bertie, is something broken?" asked Victoria.

"Haa-aah, haa-aah, haa-aaaahhh. I'm Okaaaaay, haa-aah, haa-aah, haa-aaaahhh." And that was all either men could say for at least five minutes. Eventually Bertie composed himself and stood up and said to Ray, "Well it's nice to see you again Ray. Not only are you built like a 'brick dunny', you now seem to have the brains of one." With which he held out his hand to pull him up, but found himself pulled to the ground instead, where they both laughed till they were hoarse.

Vicky gasped and turned to Victoria and said, "No-one would ever dare say anything like that to Ray, your husband and he must know each other already."

"Nothing surprises me anymore about Bertie. I thought I had married a nice quite old widower; to discover he was a wartime hero, he saved the liner we were on from a sea mine and a whole load of other things I will not go into. Bertie! How do you and Ray know each other? You two just frightened the life out of us. We want an explanation."

Bertie was still laughing, so Ray gave the first explanation. "I was mate on his ship for a single trip from Sydney to Broome, with a stop at Fremantle, a few years before the war started. While I was ashore, sorting out some business, he left port without me and abandoned me here. No money, no papers, no clothes, nothing. What sort of a man does that to his mate?"

Bertie had managed to compose himself again and proceeded to give his explanation. "The business he was on was personal business and had more to do with drinking and fighting than anything else. The reason he had no money was because he spent it and he never did have any papers.

I left his bag with the few things he did have with the gate keeper who promised to give them to him. I had already waited an extra day for you, before I sailed and you knew I had a deadline to meet, so that was it. I had no choice. Anyway, it looks like you have done alright for yourself!"

Ray stood up, held out his hand and the two men shook each other's hand warmly.

"To be honest Skipper, you did me a big favour. After I sobered up, I decided to stay and eventually got a job on the farm with Victoria's dad and married a local girl and here I am. No offence ladies, but we have some serious catching up to do and this man owes me a drink or three, so if you drive the car home today, the Skipper and I will chat over old times and get a lift out with one of the boys tomorrow. Let the missus know for me, will you love."

With which he loaded the cases in the back of the car, grabbed Bertie's arm and headed for his favourite local tavern.

The ladies were speechless at the way things had developed, but realized they were on their own so Vicky drove the big Chrysler to the family farmhouse which nestled half way up the Darling Range, about five miles outside of Pinjarra. The two Victorias' chatted all the way and it was just after five o'clock when they arrived at the house and parked the car on the dirt drive in the shade of a big flowering tree.

"Oh a blue tree, I have never seen one like that before, what is it?" asked Victoria.

"That's a Jacaranda and the flower is almost gone now, a couple of months ago, the whole tree was absolutely covered in blue flowers. I am afraid we have to take the bags in ourselves, with Ray still in Fremantle with your husband, is it OK if I call him Bertie, Skipper does not seem right for me?"

"To be honest dear, that was the first time I have ever heard anyone call him Skipper, so Bertie will be fine."

They carried the cases into the house and Vicky led the way to the guest bedroom and pointed out where the bathroom was.

"There doesn't appear to be a toilet in the bathroom," said Victoria, "I hope it isn't a long walk, as Bertie often has to make a call in the middle of the night."

"No, you just go through that outside door over there and you will see a small shed at the edge of the veranda, that's the dunny, err, I mean toilet. There is no electric light there, so you will need to use a torch or a paraffin lamp. We always have one on the table by the door, at night and don't worry about the frogs, they are quite harmless."

"Victoria, is that you, do you have your visitors from England with you?"

"Yes dad, it's me with Victoria, I won't be a minute." She then turned to Victoria and said, "Why don't you go and freshen up, while I see to dad, I won't be long." With which she walked away to the other end of the old house, while Victoria washed and un-packed her case and then went through to the kitchen and put the kettle on the range that was standing against the back wall.

"You took your time, it's almost six hours, I was getting worried," said Howard.

"I told you dad, Ray was driving me and he had someone to see in Perth first, you just don't listen to what I say to you. Anyway, it turns out that Ray and Bertie, Victoria's husband, actually know each other from before the war, so we left them in Fremantle to remember old times."

"Well, where is she then, bring her in so we can get this over and done with. I said I would see her, I never promised to be polite, the old money grubber!"

"Dad, don't you dare be rude, she has travelled all the way from England to see you and me and she has not been very well herself, so just behave yourself for once. I don't want another scene, OK?"

Vicky left the bedroom and went to the kitchen where Victoria was just making a pot of tea. "I hope you don't mind dear, but I was gasping for a cup of tea and I did bring a supply from Ceylon with me, which I have become very fond of, see what you think. How was your dad?" she asked, as she poured the tea out.

"Dad is not good, the doctors think he is down to days rather than weeks and I have to be honest and tell you, that it was my idea for you to come out here and not his."

"Don't you worry your head about me and your dad, I am under absolutely no illusions that this was all your idea and it was you I came out to see, not him. When can I see him?"

"Now if you like, no time like the present!"

They finished their tea and walked down the corridor to Howard's bedroom, which was more like a private suite, with its own sitting room and bathroom. Vicky led the way into the room and put a chair by the bedside for Victoria to sit on. She sat down and was shocked to see a man who was five years her junior, looking like he was twenty years her senior.

Howard turned to his daughter and said, "Get me a cup of tea Victoria, I am dying of thirst, lying here." She took the hint and went out, but turned round and pulled a face at him as she got to the door, which she left slightly ajar. She walked loudly for a half a dozen paces down the corridor and then turned around and crept back to the open door and stood just outside, where she could hear the conversation.

"Well, well, we meet again Step-mama, come here to watch me die, have you?" said Howard.

"Still the spiteful little boy Howard," she said, "I am amazed that someone as unpleasant as you can have such a lovely daughter, I can only assume that her mother and grandparents must have been wonderful people to cancel out your nastiness."

"Well on that we will agree, but please do not think I have any regrets in what I did twenty two years ago. You married my father for his money and it was all mine, not yours, you never loved him, you just wanted his name, money and respectability."

"In saying I never loved him, you are right. It was a business arrangement. He got my services as a wife, housekeeper, a mother for his son and an unpaid shop manager for twenty one years and I did get his name and respectability, as you so nicely put it. But just so you understand the facts, the shop was on its last legs when I took over. The previous manager was incompetent at best and a thief at worse and if it hadn't been for me and the changes I made, your father would have been declared bankrupt and we would all have been out on the street, with nothing!"

"You're lying, the shop was a goldmine, everyone said so. You fooled dad but you could never fool me, you would say anything to put yourself in a good light. I hated you then and I still hate you now. Get out of my room, let me die in peace."

"Suit yourself Howard. If you still have your father's books, you can see for yourself that what I am saying is the truth. For goodness sake you are about to die, let us at least part as friends, if only for your daughter's sake."

She held out her hand to him but he rolled over in the bed and turned away from her.

"Shut the door on your way out and don't bother to come and see me again," were the last words he said to Victoria and to anyone else either for that matter; as he died alone and bitter, about an hour later.

When Victoria got back to the kitchen, she found Vicky sitting there with a cup of tea in her hand; she was dying to ask questions but decided they could wait and in the end did not mention to Victoria that she had overheard the whole conversation between her father and herself.

"Your dad and I have said what needs to be said and he is resting now," Victoria said, as she poured herself a cup of tea. "Didn't Ray ask you to give his wife a message about not being back tonight, should we not telephone and let her know?"

"I had forgotten that, but their phone is out of order, so we will have to drive over and tell her, we best be going before it gets dark."

Ray and his wife lived in a small wood and metal house higher up the hill, about half a mile along a dirt track. There were some chickens running round the yard and they managed to park the car under some large Sheoak trees which provided some shade. Jenny came flying out of the house, when she heard the car pull up.

"Oh, it's you Victoria, I thought it was that good for nothing man of mine!"

"Hi Jenny, sorry, it's my fault, Ray asked me to let you know that he would be spending the night in Fremantle and will not be home till tomorrow. This is my name sake from England and it appears that her husband and Ray knew each other from before the war. In fact, it was her husband who skippered the boat which Ray was on, that went off and left him here, so you may have a few words to say to him when you meet him," she joked.

Jenny went over and gave both Victoria's a hug and said, "I am very pleased to meet you and thanks for letting me know, I hope your husband will be a good influence and keep him out of trouble, this time. Come in for a drink, I can only offer you beer or water and the water is not too good!"

Victoria was surprised to find herself drinking beer straight out of the bottle, sitting on the veranda, chatting to two ladies she hardly knew and having a really great time. Jenny found some cold meat and salad and some bread she had made earlier and it was gone eight thirty when they said their goodbyes and slowly drove back home.

"Why are we going so slowly, is there something wrong with the car?" asked Victoria.

"No, the car is fine, it's just a precaution in case a kangaroo jumps out in front of us. If one of the big ones comes through the windscreen, it will flatten us both."

They got home about nine and after putting on the lights, Vicky went to see how her dad was doing, knowing he would have been upset that they had been away for so long. She found him lying there, still on his side, with a funny expression on his face. She was neither surprised nor upset, as she had been expecting this moment for many months and had played it over in her mind a hundred times.

She found Victoria in her room and told her that her father had died and that they needed to phone the local doctor and to make arrangements for the funeral, as in this heat, it had to be carried out as soon as possible.

The doctor and the undertaker arrived more or less together. The doctor confirmed that Howard was indeed dead and wrote out the Death Certificate. The undertaker took the body away and suggested the burial take place on Saturday morning at 11:00am, which was agreed.

Once everyone had left, the ladies sat down on the old sofa and relaxed with a drop of scotch and just chatted about things.

"I am so pleased you are here Victoria, I feel you are like family to me," said Vicky.

"That's because I am family and I am here for as long as you need me," with which she put her arm round the young woman and let her weep silently on her shoulder.

CHAPTER TWENTY SEVEN
FUNERAL ARRANGEMENTS

In the ten or so years that Ray and Bertie had been apart, Ray had learnt to control both his drinking and his temper, thanks to the influence of his wife, Jenny. He had, however, a reputation to keep up and could not allow anyone to think he had 'gone soft', so occasionally he let it appear that he had drunk too much and sometimes had the odd bar fight, just to keep up appearances.

He took Bertie to a back street pub, where the landlord was a friend and sat down in a booth at the back and ordered some beers and food.

Bertie smiled across the table and started the conversation, "Tell me Mr. Raymond, how have you enjoyed being a free man? I assume it is safe to speak openly in this place?"

"Quite safe, but the name is Ray Thomas now and not Tom Raymond, just as you suggested, it worked like a charm."

"And no-one has ever come looking for you, Ray?" asked Bertie.

"No-one. Whatever you said about me must have been totally accepted. What did you say by the way? Were any of them there waiting for me at Broome?"

"Oh yes. They were there in force, waiting on the quay. They searched the boat from top to bottom and even found my secret cache of whisky, which they confiscated. I said that you had jumped ship somewhere north of Shark Bay, drunk out of your mind and that the sharks had probably done us all a favour. The other crew members all said they heard the splash, which was that bag of stones I had asked you to get for me. Remember?"

"Oh yes, that's right, very clever, I wondered what that was for. Did they ask about the gold?"

"Of course they asked about the gold! The crew knew nothing of course and I just kept to my story that I had employed you as a mate, on the recommendation of an old friend in Sydney; who, by the way, I had read in the paper, while in Fremantle, had died. Having found nothing in the boat, they had to let me go. But they did make it clear that I should not come back! So what did happen to the gold and why didn't you come to England as I suggested?"

Ray smiled and said, "I fell in love with the most wonderful girl, my Jenny. Having told her the story of being left behind by you, with nothing, I couldn't suddenly produce gold and tell her I was rich; could I? I have slowly traded it over the years for cash and it has helped us during the hard times but the rest is now in the bank, earning interest. We are hoping one day to be able to buy the farm we currently live on, but Mr. Owen, Victoria's dad, keeps saying 'not just yet', I don't think he will ever sell it, but he won't be around for much longer and we are hoping his daughter will be more amenable to us. Mind you, even if she is prepared to sell the farm to us, even with what we have in the bank we will need a mortgage for about half the value anyway."

Bertie nodded and replied, "I gather from the letters we have received that Howard Owen is not going to last another month, so maybe his daughter will sell you the farm; after all she is still very young and would not have the experience to run everything on her own. Who knows, she may sell the one and let you manage the other farm for her as well, while she goes off to see the world. Would that work?"

Ray scratched his head and replied, "That's funny, because Jenny was saying the same thing. She thinks Victoria wants to go to University to study biology; she is very interested in plants and animals and insects and such like and Jenny thinks it would do her good to get away from here and see somewhere different. So yes, once Mr. Owen has gone, it could be the opportunity we have been looking for, if I can raise a mortgage!"

Bertie nodded and said, "Talking of raising money, you said you were able to sell the gold without raising any unwanted interest. I may need to sell a few gems while I am here, do you know someone who would give me a fair price? They are mine, it's just that an old friend owed me a lot of money and he paid me in gems. I will also need to open two bank accounts while I am here, one for myself and one for a friend I met in Ceylon. Any suggestions?"

"The bank account for yourself should not be a problem, but I don't know about your friend, you will have to ask the bank manager about that. As regards the gems, if you are not in too much of a hurry, I am sure my good friend Blackie here, can organize things for you. Let's ask him."

The publican Blackie, proved to be most helpful and Bertie agreed to provide him with the first stones sometime next week. Since Bertie was a friend of Ray's, he would handle everything for a 6.5% commission and Ray assured Bertie that Blackie would treat him fairly.

They drank beer and swapped stories right through the night and Blackie drove them out to Pinjarra early the next morning. They arrived at just after seven to find the two ladies having breakfast in the kitchen and were quickly informed of all that had happened the night before. Vicky then drove Ray back to his place and then came home to continue the discussion about funeral arrangements with Victoria and Bertie.

The three then went to the undertakers together and discovered that Howard had made all the arrangements prior to his death. "He had even chosen the hymn to be sung at his funeral," said the undertaker. "A bit surprising, since he never went to church."

"Let me see," said Victoria and she read aloud the first verse, "'Abide with me: fast falls the eventide; the darkness deepens; Lord with me abide; When other helpers fail and comforts flee, Help of the helpless, O abide with me.' That's the same hymn that your grandfather had at his funeral, fancy him remembering that!"

"He has purchased a plot in the cemetery at the edge of town, I organized it all for him a few months ago," said the undertaker. "He has also left some money for a bite to eat and a drink at the hotel afterwards. He did not want you to be rushing around, worrying about all these things, Victoria. Do you want me to send a car for you tomorrow, or will you drive yourselves to the church?"

"No, we will make our own way, thanks. Ray and Jenny are coming with us and I am sure Ray will not mind driving. We will see you tomorrow, goodbye and thanks for everything."

They arrived at the church in plenty of time to greet the people as they entered and Vicky introduced Victoria and Bertie to the close friends who attended. It was a simple service which lasted only forty minutes and everyone then drove the few miles to the cemetery for the burial itself. Afterwards, they all went back to the hotel, who had laid out a cold buffet and a variety of drinks. As no-one present seemed to have been particularly fond of Howard and had turned up to support Vicky, the conversation was more about what she planned to do with herself in the future, rather than about Howard and the past. Bertie did his best to circulate around the guests and eventually found himself talking to an old friend of the family, known to everyone as Nugget, who happened to be Howard's bank manager, who was based in Perth.

"Can I assume that Nugget, has something to do with gold?" asked Bertie.

"It would be nice if that was so, but no, it's the' lollie' kind of Nugget. I used to eat a lot of it when I was young and invariably lost most of my milk teeth, through biting into it, so that was what they all called me at school, and it seems to have stuck. I guess there are a lot worse nicknames floating around these parts," replied Nugget. "Do you and Victoria intend staying in Australia very long Bertie, or are you rushing back to the snows of England?"

"To be honest I am not really sure. My wife would like to be back in the UK by the middle of August, as some young friends of ours are getting married at the end of the month, somewhere in Scotland I think and she would like to be there for that. Come to think of it, he is in banking too, just like you. Personally, I love Australia and the sunshine and would be quite happy to stay here."

"Mid August you say, well we might yet travel together. My bank is carrying out some interviews in London around then and I have been asked to be part of the team. You should let your young friend know, he might be interested in some of the vacancies, I will give you details and you can send them on to him."

"Certainly I can do that, but he has only just changed jobs, so it might be a bit soon. Talking of banking though, I need to open an account while I am here and get some money wired over from England, would you be able to help me with that?"

"I would be delighted, here is my card, just ring my secretary and book a time that suits you. If you want a joint account, remember to bring your wife along with you, as she will need to sign some papers as well and of course your passports and English banking details. We have an excellent restaurant in the building if you happen to come around lunch time."

With that, the two men shook hands and went off to chat to other attendees of the function. By three thirty it was all over and Ray drove them back to the farm where Victoria made them all a cup of tea and they sat out on the veranda and chatted about all that had happened and what they should do next.

"I will ring dad's solicitor on Monday and arrange to go and see him sometime next week, will you come with me Victoria?" asked Vicky.

"Of course I will, if you want me to, but talk to him first on the phone and see what he suggests, do you have any plans for your future or is it still too early for you?" replied Victoria.

"Well yes I do, actually. I won a place at University the other year to study Biology at a College in Sydney, but then dad became ill and it all got shelved. I would love to see if I can still take it up and go over there, but then what will I do with the farm? I did want to sell the farm dad bought originally, so that I could give you back what dad took from you, all those years ago, Victoria; but of course that is the farm where Ray and Jenny live now and I would hate making them homeless. This farm where I live used to belong to my mother's parents and I just love it here and could not bring myself to sell it, but I can't run a farm from the other side of the country. I just don't know what to do for the best!"

Bertie caught Ray's eye and an unspoken message passed between them and then Bertie spoke, "You are only young once, young lady and as my Great Uncle Harry used to say, 'Life is not a spectator sport – go out and live it'. I am sure that this fine figure of a man here (turning to Ray) could continue to manage both farms while you are off at university. But this is not the day for big decisions, they can wait till after you have seen the solicitor next week and I feel certain we can find something stronger than tea to finish the day with!" with which he disappeared to his room and came back with a bottle of fine old French brandy, which everyone enjoyed.

On Sunday they all went to church in the morning and afterwards Vicky thanked the minister for conducting the funeral service and then drove them down to Preston Beach, which was about an hour's drive away. Howard had bought a small wooden cabin many years ago, just a few yards from the beach itself and it was fitted out with all the usual home comforts including a small stove and a table and chairs. Vicky went for a swim while the others just paddled in the warm waters of the Indian Ocean and afterwards they all devoured a picnic which Vicky had prepared earlier. She was intrigued by the stories Victoria told her of the Lake District, Kendal, the shop and of the grandfather she had never known. It appeared that Howard had refused to talk about England and all these other things and she was delighted to find out so much from such a reliable source.

Towards dusk the kangaroos all congregated on the grass banks to feed, just as they were packing up their things to leave. No one was in a hurry and Vicky took plenty of time driving home.

When Bertie went through to the kitchen on Monday morning he found a note from Vicky, saying she had decided to go into Perth and see the bank manager and her father's accountant before contacting the solicitor. He made tea for himself and Victoria and went back to their room with the tea and the note.

"It looks like we will have to amuse ourselves today," he said, giving Victoria the note. "I think we should go into town and buy some more appropriate footwear if we are going to stay here for any length of time. Ray said he would come by sometime this morning for a chat, so I will get him to give us a lift into town."

"It's a real shame that one of us does not drive Bertie, as it would be good to hire a car and see the country for ourselves," said Victoria, " and what is wrong with our shoes that we need to go and buy new ones?"

"Snakes and ants dear. We need strong lace up boots to walk around the farm to protect us from snakes and ants. We must also carry a stick and beat the ground as we walk through grass to make sure the snakes know we are coming and get out of the way."

"You never mentioned snakes and ants before, are they poisonous, do they bite?"

"Some of the ants can give you a nasty bite and as regards the snakes, let's just say that if a snake should bite you around where we parked the car, you might not have enough time to make it to the front porch. They are very poisonous as are the spiders you see around, particularly if they have a little red spot on them. Do not attempt to remove cob webs, do not do any gardening and always tap your shoes up-side-down on the floor before you put them on. I am not trying to frighten you, just making sure that you understand that things are different here and you must act accordingly."

She smiled and nodded to him that she understood.

" Oh, and by the way I can drive a car and yes I did remember to bring my driving licence with me; I just chose not to drive when I was back in England. I have been thinking about buying a car when we go to Perth, so we can be independent, it will just depend on how much they cost over here."

She smiled at him and kissed him on the cheek as she said, "Mr. Bannister you never cease to amaze me. Not only are you a travelling encyclopaedia of all types of knowledge, but I discover that I now have my own chauffeur to boot. Just one thing though, cars do cost a lot of money and we are running out of funds, unless of course there is something else I do not know."

He winked and smiled and went over to the dressing table and picked up the china figure of the Barbary Ape that they had bought in David's shop in Gibraltar. He then took out a pocket knife and opened the large blade and proceeded to gently make a hole in the base of the figure.

"Can you get me a clean white handkerchief please," he said.

She went to the drawer and took out the handkerchief and spread it out on top of the dressing table. Bertie put the knife away and tipped the contents of the figure onto the handkerchief. Victoria gasped as she looked at the gems gleaming up at her, diamonds, emeralds, sapphires and a necklace of white gold with a single large ruby.

"Bertie, you never said that David owed you this much, there must be several thousand pounds worth there. What are you going to do with them?"

"He said he had done well, but I was not expecting all this; we will sell some through a friend of Ray's that I met the other night. The rest we will just hold for another time and just wait and see. We need to be careful though, not to

339

sell too many at once, as it will create unwanted interest and push the price down. We will try a couple of these diamonds first, just to test the market here and see how good Ray's friend proves to be."

He removed two small diamonds and put them in an envelope which he then put in the top pocket of his jacket; he then wrapped the other stones in some tissue paper and returned them to the china figure, sealing the hole up with some candle wax.

"There we are, as good as new," he said, "and just in time as I think I heard a car pull up outside, it will probably be Ray.

Ray had indeed arrived, in the most dented, dirty, pick-up truck that they had ever seen. He agreed to take them into town but when Bertie mentioned he would like to visit Fremantle and Blackie some time soon, Ray said that there was an excellent shoe shop not far from the pub; so they decided to drive there instead, with the three of them wedged together on the bench seat, once Victoria had cleaned it to her satisfaction.

They saw Blackie first and gave him the envelope containing the two diamonds and arranged to see him again on Thursday, when he said that he would have the cash for the gems. They sealed the deal with a drink and then Ray drove them to a very up-market shoe shop and bought some lace up boots for Victoria but Bertie could not manage to find anything he considered comfortable.

They left the shop and were walking back to the truck when Ray had a brainwave and took them to an army surplus store jammed from floor to ceiling with all things military. Victoria took one look at the shop and said she preferred to wait for them in the truck. Bertie tried on several pairs of genuine ex-Australian army lace up brown boots, until he found a pair that fitted him like a glove and then bought a couple of pairs of thick socks to go with them.

"But Bertie they are second-hand, someone else has been wearing them, surely we can afford a new pair for you, like mine?" said Victoria.

"That's the whole point dear, boots like these take months to break in, someone has already done it for me, they are perfect, don't worry," he replied.

Ray then drove them to a very smart hotel by the sea where they had a leisurely lunch and took the opportunity to discuss Vicky's dilemma about going to college and selling the farm.

"I would hate to think that our coming to Australia has in any way contributed to making you and Jenny homeless Ray," said Victoria, "would you want to buy it yourself or would you be happy to move somewhere else?"

"We just love it where we are and certainly have no desire to move but we could not afford to buy the whole farm outright without a really hefty mortgage, which I doubt that we could obtain," Ray replied. "Jenny has this idea about growing 'stone fruit' and setting up big orchards of plums, apricots, nectarines and such like. Another small-holder did it a few years ago and has done very nicely out of it, but that would cost a further couple of hundred pounds to set up, which again we don't have. What we really need is a partner rather than a mortgage, but everyone round here is in the same boat, so I just don't know what we will do."

Before the conversation developed any more, Bertie looked at his watch and then suggested that they should visit a local second hand car dealer just to see what was on offer and Ray drove them round to someone else he knew, who would give them a fair deal.

"Look Bertie, that car there, it looks just like the one Mrs. Duffy-Smythe drives back in England and Arnold would be able to look after it for us, too," said Victoria.

"Well spotted, it is a Morris Eight, just like hers, but I can't imagine Digger sailing half way round the world just to service a car for us," he replied smiling.

"May I say that the lady has made an excellent choice, the car only arrived here last week and it belonged to an old gentleman in town, who only used it to go to church and back every week," said the car salesman, "I could let you have it for say, three hundred and thirty pounds."

"I told you mate that these were friends of mine," boomed Ray, "let's try again on the price shall we!"

"Oh of course Ray," he quickly replied, "let me see, two hundred and ninety five and that really is the best I can do."

Bertie retrieved a screwed up piece of paper from the floor of the car and straightened it out before handing it over to the salesman. "I think your old gentleman may want his betting slip back," said Bertie with a smile, "and that nearside front tyre needs changing as it is almost bald and we expect a full tank of petrol and we would be most grateful, assuming it is convenient, to have a test drive right now please, to save us coming back another time."

The salesman asked to see his licence and then went and got the key from the office which he gave to Bertie. With Ray and Victoria in the back and Bertie behind the wheel with the salesman next to him, they had a leisurely drive round Fremantle and the car performed very well even when they had to stop suddenly for a dog which ran out in front of them. When they got back to the yard they shook hands on the deal and said they would be back with the money on Thursday or Friday, which the salesman agreed to and said he would hold the car for them until the end of the week.

Vicky had arrived back at the farm before them and was worried when they were no-where to be found and had not left a note for her. She rang a couple of the shops in town to see if anyone had seen them and then drove up to see Jenny who informed her that Ray was missing as well and that they had probably all gone out somewhere together.

When she returned home she discovered that they too had now returned and was quick to admire the new boots which Victoria had bought in Fremantle.

Over dinner Vicky told them what she had actually been doing during her day in Perth.

"I have to be honest with you Victoria and tell you that I was outside the door when you had your conversation with dad and I heard what you said about how he could check the books of the shop for himself, if he still had them. Well, he did still have them and today I took them to our accountant and asked him to have a look at them and tell me if what you had said was accurate or not."

Victoria's jaw dropped and she was about to respond when Bertie just put his hand on hers and gave it a little squeeze and signalled for her to say nothing and to let Vicky continue.

"I know it sound like I didn't believe you, but that really was not the case," Vicky said, "I just had to know for myself. Anyway the accountant got one of his senior clerks to study the books for me all day and when I returned this afternoon he told me that prior to your involvement, the shop had been losing money on a large scale and he suspected that someone had either been stealing the stock or had made bogus Journal entries and had simply taken the money.

He also said that the turn-round in the shop's fortunes had been immediate and concluded that it was all down to your ability and hard work, as the new manager."

Victoria relaxed and smiled at Vicky as she said, "That's alright dear; I understand you did what you needed to do and I am relieved that your accountant has finally cleared my name and given me the credit that I knew I deserved."

"Thank you," said Vicky, "for being so understanding and I am truly sorry that dad was so unpleasant to you when you spoke together. I telephoned the solicitor from the accountants and told him what I had discovered and confirmed to him that I wished you to own half of dad's original farm. I have arranged that we all go and see him on Thursday afternoon, if that is convenient?"

"Thursday is good for us, but we do have to go to Fremantle first," said Bertie, "we actually test drove a car today as we want to be able to see some of the country while we are here and told the car salesman that we would go back to pick it up later in the week, so perhaps you could drop me off, while the two of you go shopping."

"No problems, that will be fine, a new car you say, how exciting! I guess the only difficulty that I have now is how I break the news to Ray and Jenny that I am going to have to sell the farm and probably make them homeless."

"Well let's just talk about that for a minute," said Victoria. "I have never thought about being a farmer nor is it something I want to do at my age, but Ray was saying today that he could raise the money for half the farm and would like to have a partner in it so that he could diversify into some sort of fruit farming. We could be that partner couldn't we Bertie? And to be honest we don't desperately need the money either, we came here to see you Victoria and Howard and have already enjoyed a wonderful cruise, so what do you all think?"

Bertie was first to reply and said. "I think that is a very generous and workable idea Victoria. It means that Vicky will have sufficient funds to go to college and study Biology and that she can leave the running of this farm to Ray, while Jenny can look after the fruit farm and we can all live in luxury off the profits!"

"That's marvellous," said Vicky, "thank you both so much, I can't wait to see their faces when I tell them the good news."

CHAPTER TWENTY EIGHT
BUSINESS MATTERS

Tuesday turned out to be one of those hot humid days when you just want to sit in the shade and drink cool drinks and do absolutely nothing; which is exactly what Victoria and Bertie did for the first few hours of the day. Just after eleven they decided that they could manage a short walk to a field about half a mile from the house where Vicky kept a couple of horses, which, they decided would give them an opportunity to try out their new boots. As they approached the horses, they came trotting over to the fence to say hello and happily ate the sugar lumps which Victoria had in her pocket for them. Some kangaroos that were also grazing nearby, immediately looked up and then jumped off to the other side of the field.

They both had stout walking sticks with which they thumped the ground as they walked and noticed several reptiles rushing off to hide in the long grass. On the way back to the house Victoria stopped and pointed with her stick to a small creature about ten inches long with the head of a snake, but with short legs and no tail, "Look Bertie, do you know what it is, is it dangerous"

"I think it is called a Skink, Victoria and no, it is not dangerous. They say that if you have a Skink in your garden, you are unlikely to have snakes, but I don't know how true that is. But if you look over there, where those flat rocks are, you will see a snake sunning itself on that large rock. Now that is a Tiger snake and that is very poisonous, so we will just leave it alone and head back to the house. My shirt is soaked again and I could do with a beer so let's get going."

Vicky meanwhile had gone to see Ray and Jenny and tell them what she and Victoria had discussed the day before. Ray was astounded at their good fortune and slightly embarrassed, "I did say we wanted a partner but honestly had no idea that you were going to give them half of the farm Victoria, I hope they don't think I was just sweet talking them."

"I am sure they thought no such thing Ray and if you can raise the money to buy the other half, we could all go and see the solicitor on Thursday and get him to raise the necessary paperwork."

"Can I come with you on Thursday as well?" asked Jenny.

"Of course you can," said Victoria, "in fact it is essential, if you are going to be a partner in this venture. I was going to go shopping with Victoria, so why don't we three go straight to the shops at Perth and Ray can take Bertie to the car sales place in Fremantle and we can all meet up at the solicitors, what do you think?"

Ray called for Bertie at just after seven o'clock Thursday morning and the two men drove to Fremantle, discussing the arrangements for the farm, as they went. "Jenny has been going through all the catalogues again, pricing up fruit trees and basic equipment and has come up with a figure of just over two hundred and twenty pounds," said Ray. "Victoria has priced the farm well under what I was expecting, on the condition that I continue to manage her farm while she is away over in Sydney, so we have a bit more left over for the trees than I thought. If you and your good lady can contribute half the cost, one hundred and ten pounds; then we are in business."

"To be honest Ray, that will very much depend on how much Blackie gives me for the diamonds, so I will answer your question after we have seen him, but tell me how Jenny will be able to run the fruit farm on her own, wont it be too much work for her?" asked Bertie.

Blackie was waiting in the pub for them with a big grin all over his face. "G'day mate," he said and shook both of their hands warmly. "I think you will be very pleased with the deal I have made for you. The guy I sold the diamonds to had just been given a commission for some earrings for an anniversary present for a very wealthy lady and the stones you gave me were just perfect and I got eight hundred and thirty pounds, not bad eh? Less my commission and expenses, of course, which comes to sixty pounds, so I have here seven hundred and seventy pounds cash. He did ask me if I could find him a couple of emeralds for another pair of earrings that he has been requested to make, I don't suppose you can help out there, I said I would let him know."

"Maybe, I will get back to you early next week; but well done on the diamonds," said Bertie, "you have done very well for me Blackie, I am very grateful. A drink to celebrate I think."

Bertie took the money and separated it into two lots of three hundred pounds and four hundred and seventy pounds, so he had the correct cash to hand to pay for the car.

Ray and he then drove round to the car sales yard and paid for the Morris Eight after making sure that the bald tyre had been replaced and the petrol tank was full of petrol.

Ray then led the way from Fremantle to Perth and found somewhere to park on the edge of Kings Park. They walked into town from the park and found a small café off George Street where they had a bite to eat and discussed the morning's activities.

"Your friend Blackie did very well for me Ray," said Bertie, "I may just get him to sell one other stone that I have, but not just yet. Assuming that everything goes to plan at the solicitors this afternoon, you can count on the one hundred and ten pounds you need for the trees, but that is it; no more cash from us after that. We will also need to draw up an agreement as to how we run the farm and how we calculate and share the profits. As I am sure you have gathered, Victoria has never been well off and has worked very hard all her life, so I am expecting her to receive a reasonable income from her investment."

"No worries mate, Jenny and I are very grateful for what she has done for us and the chance she has given to us and we will see her all right, believe me!"

The two men had been sitting in the solicitors office for well over twenty minutes before the ladies arrived breathless and carrying lots of carrier bags.

"I know we are late," said Vicky, "but the time just went and we were having such fun, have you been waiting long?"

Just then the solicitor's secretary arrived and showed them through to his office. He was a middle aged man with a short beard and totally devoid of any humour, but he knew his job and everything was in order and just needed to be explained, signed and witnessed. Howard had left everything to his daughter as expected, but she was surprised to find out that she already owned half the farm that had belonged to her grandparents, something he had forgotten to tell her.

The papers for her father's farm were all drawn up, transferring ownership to Victoria and Ray and Jenny. Ray then handed over the bankers draft for their half of the deal after which everyone signed on the dotted line and the secretary was called in to act as witness. Bertie suggested that they see the solicitor in a week or so, once they had agreed how to manage the farm and divide the profits.

Vicky announced that she had arranged to see Nugget at the bank a bit later, so Bertie made a quick telephone call from the solicitors, to the bank, to find out if it would be possible for him to see Nugget after Vicky had finished; which his secretary confirmed, 'would be convenient'.

Ray and Jenny walked to the park to get the pickup truck and then left for home while Vicky pointed out where the bank was situated and suggested that Bertie could get the car from Kings Park and bring it round to the side of the bank building, while she and Victoria put the shopping in her car, which was already parked near the bank.

When Bertie arrived at the street by the bank half an hour later, he was able to park right behind Vicky's Chrysler and walked round the corner into the big entrance lobby of the bank. A young man at the Enquiry Desk was most helpful and told him that the two ladies had already gone up to Mr. Johnston's office. A bank messenger was called over and he led the way to the second floor where he found Victoria seated in a waiting area, reading a magazine and drinking a glass of cool lemonade.

He sat down next to her and was immediately offered a drink by Nugget's secretary, which he willingly accepted.

"What was all that about getting the solicitor to draw up an agreement with Ray and Jenny," asked Victoria, "surely we can trust them to do the right thing by us Bertie, it's not like we were relying on the money for anything, is it?"

"Thank you dear, I am fine and yes I did manage to buy the car and I got a good price for the diamonds and I am not too tired after walking back to the park in all this heat, thank you for asking," he replied. "Now what was the question again?"

"Sarcasm is the lowest form of wit, you know," she said, "I just wanted to understand why we need a formal contract, that's all!"

"We need a formal contract to protect their interests as well as our own. We have not yet decided whether we want to live in Australia permanently or just come for holidays now and then, in which case we will have to engage an accountant to look after your interests and he will need to have a formal contract to work to. Now do you understand?"

"Yes I do understand," she said, "and if this heat is going to make you so snappy, I think the quicker we return to England the better, so there."

They sat in silence for about ten minutes when the door opened and Vicky emerged, looking a bit down.

"Is everything all right dear?" asked Victoria, "you are looking a bit down."

Bertie stood up and moved away and Vicky came over and sat down next to her, she had obviously been crying. "I'm OK thank you. I had no idea that dad was in debt to the bank, so the money that Ray has given me for the farm has gone on settling that and I only have about fifteen hundred pounds left to do all the things I want to do. It's just so disappointing that my recent memories of him are all of his deceitfulness and his bitterness."

"Come now, he wasn't a bad man and he certainly loved you very much and you still have a beautiful home and your whole life is in front of you; so let's not get too far down in the dumps, there are millions who would gladly change places with you, my dear."

"I know Victoria, you are absolutely right, but Nugget is expecting you, so it's your turn now. I want to visit a school friend who works round the corner, so I will see you back at the farm later. Bye"

Victoria and Bertie were shown into Nugget's office and sat down at the other side of the big walnut desk that stood in the middle of the office. "How nice to see you both again, it has been really good for young Victoria to have you here, with her, during this sad and difficult time," said Nugget. "I gather that you were, in fact, her father's step mother and that she was named after you Mrs. Bannister."

"Yes that is perfectly true," said Victoria, "and it is all the more surprising since her father and I never really hit it off. But please call us Victoria and Bertie and we will call you Nugget, if that is all-right with you."

Just then a senior clerk knocked on the door and came in holding a pile of forms for them to sign to open a joint bank account. "I will require you to make a small deposit to get the account going, so to speak, five pounds will do, until you can get some more wired over," Nugget informed them after everything had been signed and the passports and bank information had been verified.

"Well actually I was going to deposit three hundred pounds," said Bertie. We did have funds made available while we were living in Ceylon, so if we can leave this with you today, I will deposit the rest of the cash, next time I come to Perth, if that will be OK? Are you able to give us a cheque book today, or will it have to be sent on?"

The clerk took the money and said he would write out a receipt which would be sent to them along with the cheque book in a day or two.

"There is another matter," said Bertie, "a good friend of ours from Ceylon wishes to start trading on a regular basis with Australia and has asked me if I would open a bank account for him. I can give you his name and address and you can write to him and tell him what information you need. He also has need of a safety deposit box as he sometimes trades in high quality pearls and gem stones. Will you be able to arrange all that for him?"

"Most certainly I can, it may just take a while to check everything out and set things up. I suggest that you put the safety deposit box in joint names, yours and his, until such time as he comes himself to Australia, when he can open one in his own name. Do you know when he intends coming here to set up business?"

"Not sure about that, probably the second half of the year, but perhaps when I come with the rest of the cash, I can set up the safety deposit box then."

Having concluded all their business for the day, they went back to the car and drove home to the farm, which gave Victoria time to ask him all the questions that were currently filling her head.

"So let me get this straight Bertie, you received seven hundred and seventy pounds for the diamonds and paid three hundred for the car and deposited a further three hundred pounds with the bank, leaving you with one hundred and seventy pounds, but you have promised Ray one hundred and ten pounds towards the trees and equipment, leaving us with sixty pounds in hand."

"That's about right," said Bertie, "I think I will sell the two emeralds next week and that should produce more than enough cash to keep us going and pay for a passage back to England, if you still want to go to that wedding in Scotland."

Over the next few weeks, the pace of life slowed down considerably for everyone at the farm. Vicky heard from the college in Sydney that she could start her course at the beginning of March and that they had reserved a place for her in the halls of residence. She booked her flight straight away and ordered all the books and things she needed to be delivered over in Sydney.

Bertie gave the one hundred and ten pounds to Jenny for the young trees and equipment and then he and Ray hammered out an agreement for the farm and they all went along to the solicitor who wrote out the legal document for them and was able to recommend a small accountancy firm who would administer everything for Victoria and keep the books of the new venture.

Blackie sold the two emeralds for Bertie which netted him another three hundred and sixty pounds of which he deposited a further two hundred pounds with the bank and opened a safety deposit box in his and Victoria's name, into which he deposited one china figure of a Barbary Ape. He then opened another box in his name and that of Samuel Van Royt in which he deposited a cardboard box containing a china figure of a brown Pariah dog, having assured Victoria that she would get the figure back at some later stage . He carefully labelled both keys which he kept in his wallet.

The bank clerk sent the cheque book and the receipt as promised and Nugget also sent details of the various vacancies that the bank wished to fill with staff recruited from the UK.

Having decided that they would return for Digger and Moira's wedding they wrote and let them know and asked them to book accommodation in Inverness for a few days before the wedding and for a week afterwards. They also sent the information about the bank jobs, just in case Digger might be interested.

They went to see the shipping agent in Fremantle and found that if they were prepared to split their journey they could catch a ship at the beginning of June which would take them to Ceylon and then at the end of June they could catch another ship that would take them all the way to Southampton, so this is what they went for. They wrote to the Van Royt's telling them of their plans and asking if they would be able to put them up for a couple of weeks, which of course, they said they would be delighted to do. Bertie also sent a message to say that the dog was in safe hands.

They discussed with Vicky as to whether they would be able to stay with her, next time they came to Australia, to which she replied that she would be very upset if they did not.

During the month of February they drove up to see Geraldton, which was a few hundred miles north of Perth and visited the Pinnacles en-route which were just an amazing site to see.

Vicky left for Sydney at the end of February and soon settled into college life and made lots of new friends very quickly. Her letters kept talking about someone called Sandy who turned out to be a young fellow from Adelaide who was also on the Biology course.

During March they had a long drive down to Albany and spent a couple of weeks there in a tin roofed 'Bed and Breakfast' which had wonderful views over the harbour.

April was a funny month with heavy rain and lots of wind, which made Victoria feel quite homesick for England and after a lot of pestering from Nugget, who had become a good friend to them both, they tried their hand at lawn bowls and even joined the local club in Pinjarra.

The trees Jenny ordered arrived in May and everyone gave a hand in setting out the orchards and getting them planted, ready for the winter rains. Their old tractor broke down just at a crucial time, so it was a case of going along to the local market and bidding on a second hand one that had been put up for auction. There was only one other bidder, so they got it for a fair price in the end.

Towards the end of May, they were chatting over dinner one evening when Victoria said, "What are we going to do with the car Bertie, I have grown very attached to it and would hate to have to sell it? Jenny was sort of dropping hints that we could leave it with them, but having seen the way Ray treats that old pickup truck, I am not sure I want to do that."

"I should think not," he replied, "in fact the undertaker asked me that same question after church the other week and suggested that we could lend it to him for funeral work. He said it would only be used once or twice a week on average and he would keep it in his garage and look after it for us, so it would be here ready and waiting for us when we come back."

"That's a much better idea," she said, "what did you say to him?"

"I said that I liked the idea and would let him know once we had discussed it, so we agree that is what we will do then!"

On the morning of the departure, Vicky telephoned to say goodbye to them and to say that she hoped to see them back in Australia very soon and to thank them for all they had done and for encouraging her to go to college. She said that she and Sandy had been talking about a trip to Europe, so she might yet see them again in England.

It was in fact the undertaker who drove them down to Fremantle, in their own car on Wednesday the eighth of June 1949 to catch the ship that was to take them to Ceylon. Ray and Jenny were also there along with Nugget who came to say goodbye. There were lots of hugs and tears and waving of handkerchiefs as the ship sailed out of the harbour.

"What lovely people Bertie, I will miss them all so much, they have become like family to us and all in just a few months. It seems only yesterday that Ray was holding you over his head and threatening to throw you into the water. He wouldn't really have done it, would he?"

Bertie just smiled and took her arm as they walked back to their cabin and it was only later that she realised he had not answered her question!

CHAPTER TWENTY NINE
THE INTERVIEW

"There they are Bertie, over there, just behind that big red thing," said Victoria, as she stood by the rail, waving furiously at Caroline and Samuel Van Royt, "I think they have just seen me, look Caroline is waving!"

They disembarked and greeted their friends and within the hour they were on their way to the house at Negombo Lagoon, exchanging news on all that had been happening during the five months they had been apart.

"So no more German mines to deal with this time Bertie?" asked Samuel.

"None whatsoever," Bertie replied, "the only thing I had to deal with was another bout of sea sickness during the first day at sea and another retired army officer and his good lady who seemed convinced that we needed to hear every single event that had ever happened to them in their long and distinguished service lives."

"Did you manage to get along to either of the test matches with the West Indies?" asked Bertie.

"I attended the first one where they beat us by an innings and a few runs and have to say they were superb, but the second one, which was a draw, I missed unfortunately, as I was away on business. By all accounts it was a much more even game and our team put up a good show. I have heard from the bank in Perth, by the way and am still in the process of setting that all up, but many thanks for seeing to it for me," said Samuel.

When they arrived at the house they were immediately greeted by the dogs and Duke in particular. He just could not contain his excitement at seeing them again and Victoria made a big fuss of him. Caroline had invited Anna and a few other friends to join them for dinner, so they were very tired but very happy when they finally got to bed.

The next day, Caroline took Victoria into town which gave Bertie and Samuel a chance to talk. The maid brought tea and biscuits through to the study for them and then closed the door to give them some privacy. Bertie took the key to the safe deposit box that he had opened in the joint names and gave it to Samuel. "Here we are my friend, this is yours. I had to open it in joint names, but there is nothing of mine in there, just the box you gave me with the china dog in it, which is still intact."

Samuel took the key and shook Bertie's hand, "I am deeply indebted to you Bertie, it would have been just great if you and Victoria could be back in Australia to show us around when we visit there at the end of the year. This man who sold the gems for you, can you give me a letter of introduction or do I need to involve this other man you mentioned, Ray?"

"I don't think either Ray or Blackie would appreciate anything in writing Samuel; I have told Ray that I am expecting you and Caroline to visit Perth on holiday later in the year and that you would want to speak to him about a certain business matter; so I am pretty sure he understands what you will want and will be able to set everything up for you."

"That's great and both men are trustworthy in your estimation?"

"Absolutely, just remember not to try and sell too much at one go, just drip feed the goods on to the market. The bank manager has also become a good friend and will be able to point you in the right direction as regards business premises and somewhere to stay in Perth. May I wish you good luck with the new venture and I really think you are onto a winner," said Bertie, "they drink a lot of tea in Australia and every lady loves to wear silk, so I am sure that the business will do very well, especially if you ship to the eastern states as well as to WA."

The two weeks in Ceylon passed very quickly and Victoria got very upset when Bertie was asked to do one more run to India for his old boss, but it only took two days and he was well paid for the inconvenience. During the final weekend that they were in Ceylon Victoria remembered that she had said in her last letter that they would telephone Upper Style and let them all know when they would be arriving back in England.

Mrs. Black, Mrs. Duffy-Smythe, Moira and Digger were still having Sunday lunch when the telephone rang at Millstone House. Mrs. Black picked up the receiver and excitedly told everyone who it was phoning them. She chatted for a few minutes and then passed the phone to Digger. He said that he would be happy to come and pick them up from Southampton since the ship would be arriving on a Saturday in the early afternoon. Bertie said that they did have a lot more luggage this time and it could be tight for space, so Mrs. Duffy-Smythe said that he could use her car. Victoria could not help herself saying that they had a car in Australia just like hers; which left everyone discussing which of them had learnt to drive.

When Moira got on the phone she asked Bertie why he had sent the information about the job vacancies with the Australian bank to them and that Digger had not stopped talking about them since their arrival and had even said he might go to London for an interview. She had obviously been upset by it all, so Bertie assured her that he had simply sent them to Digger because their new friend at the Bank had asked him to and that Digger might let some of his friends in Head Office know about them.

When they came to leave Ceylon it was as if Duke knew somehow that they were going and would not leave Victoria's side. "I wish we could take him with us Bertie," she said, "I am sure he knows that he may never see us again."

"Never is a long time and I am sure we will be back here again, so maybe next time we can make the right arrangements to take him with us, OK?" he replied.

"Did you see the replacement dog figurine that Caroline gave me?" she asked, opening the velvet covered black box, "she said she was so embarrassed when she heard that you had deposited the other one at the bank for Samuel that she got her friend who owns the shop to obtain a replacement for me. Isn't it beautiful. I will take it back to England with us and show everyone what Duke looks like"

"Wow, what a beauty," he replied, " the ear-rings from Gibraltar, the pearls from our first visit and now this, I hope you are not expecting expensive presents, every time we go on a trip."

They boarded the new ship on Tuesday the twenty eighth and once again the Van Royt's gave them a lift to the dock and waved them goodbye.

The ship called at Aden for fuel and fresh food but the captain said that there had been a spot of bother lately and would not let any of the passengers off the ship. Between Aden and Gibraltar, Victoria was on edge in case she got bitten by a mosquito again and had another bought of Malaria, but she kept herself well covered and put on a cream that the ship's doctor recommended to keep all insects at bay. The cream worked well and Victoria had no further problems from insects but both they and several other passengers had a touch of food poisoning while they were sailing in the Mediterranean Sea.

The ship was only in Gibraltar for one night but they were able to go ashore and meet up with David and Esther Josephs for a meal at a very fine restaurant, which Bertie insisted on paying for, in view of his friends generosity it settling their old debt.

"Do you mind if I leave my old bag and its contents with you David," asked Bertie, "I am not sure they will let me take it through customs with me." He was of course referring to the gun which had come in very useful during their stay in Ceylon.

"Of course you can, did you need it at all?" asked Samuel.

"Yes he did," said Victoria, "he frightened the life out of me with all his antics and I hope I never see the thing again. Tell them about the German mine Bertie."

Bertie told them about the mine and then quickly went on to tell them that Victoria was now a part owner of a fruit farm in Australia and that they really would have to come and visit them there one day.

The ship left Gibraltar next day and although the crossing back to Southampton was rougher than the journey out, they docked just around two o'clock on the afternoon of Saturday the 16th July 1949.

Moira had insisted on coming with Digger to meet them, which meant that the journey back to Upper Style was very uncomfortable for all the passengers as everyone had a case or several bags on their laps.

Digger drove them straight to Bertie's cottage which Moira and Mrs. Black had spent the previous week cleaning and airing and washing and changing sheets and pillow cases and Mrs. Black had left a joint of beef, slowly cooking in the oven, along with plenty of vegetables and some stewed rhubarb.

"Oh Moira thank you so much," said Victoria, "it was really good of you both to do all this for us, the cottage looks really great and stewed rhubarb, my mouth is watering already, isn't it funny the things you miss when you are away from home. You are going to stay and eat with us aren't you, you can't leave us now, we have so much more to tell you and I want to hear all about the wedding plans and have a proper look at that ring young lady!"

Deborah drove down on her motor bike on the Sunday and actually stopped a couple of nights with them and enjoyed the detailed report which Victoria gave, of all that they had done while they were away. "It is so good to actually hear what has been happening to you both," said Deborah, "normally dad just says 'nothing much happened' and that's about all we used to get. The pearl earrings came from Ceylon you say, thank you so much, they are lovely and the dog you had was called Duke and was a Pariah dog. I have never heard of them before, I will have to look them up. Do you have a photo of him?"

We have something better than a photo," Victoria said and went and got the figurine from the bedroom, "this is exactly what Duke looked like, isn't he gorgeous."

By the time she left on Tuesday morning she had already decided that she wanted to go with them to Australia when they next went out and was determined to save the fare, so that she too could travel first class and enjoy the trip."

Digger and Mac came round Tuesday evening to keep Bertie company while Victoria, for everyone was now allowed to call her by this name, except Sissy of course; paid an evening visit to Millstone House. He found Bertie, sitting in his favourite corner of the garden reading a book.

Mac bounded over and gave him a very warm and wet greeting.

"Hey Mac, you're a big dog now, my goodness you are," said Bertie, "what are they feeding you on? Hi there Digger, over here, just follow the wagging tail."

"Mac, get down, 'Sssit!' Good boy," commanded Digger and gave the dog a pat.

"I am sorry the garden is not in very good shape Bertie, but I have been working such long hours lately, that I have just not had the time, you know how it is."

"I do indeed my young friend, I am very grateful for what you have done, it will give me something to do for a week or two. Look, I am sorry if I have caused a problem between you and Moira over those job adverts, but it never really crossed my mind that you would be interested, I was just doing it for appearances sake, as Nugget had been so helpful to us."

"Nugget," said Digger, "Oh your banking friend. I actually looked him up and he is a very senior manager at the bank and one or two of these jobs look very interesting. I spoke with my old boss in London the other day and asked his opinion and he said that I had nothing to lose by going for an interview, so I arranged one for Monday the first of August; Moira went barmy when she found out, women!"

"Indeed," said Bertie, "choosing a new hat and coat are nothing to some of the pressures I have had to face in the last few months from my beloved. But I thought you were happy at Oxford and settled there."

"Bertie, I am twenty eight and between you and me I am feeling trapped. Don't get me wrong, I love Moira and want to get married but the thought of spending the next thirty seven years tied to a nine to five job in Oxford, is not what I had imagined for myself. I certainly do not want to go back to London or any other large city here; what I really want is a bit of excitement in my life, I want to see new places and do new things. I can do this job standing on my head, I need something different, I need a challenge! Surely you of all people can understand that!"

"Of course I can understand that," said Bertie, "and by the way, a lot of people are already going from here to Australia under the Assisted Passage scheme; they call them £10 Poms over there. I met a couple of men who were bricklayers here who have started their own building company and are doing very well. There are certainly a lot of opportunities for people with imagination and are not afraid of hard work. Moira too, would be in great demand as a district nurse; I would encourage you to look into it, even if you don't get a job with the bank."

"Thanks, I needed that bit of encouragement. Even if I only worked for the bank for a couple of years to pay them back and get myself established over there; I could then try my hand at something new if I wanted to. Just got to convince Moira now!"

"Don't worry about Moira, remember, she has already left home once. I am sure that she loves you a lot and that she can be convinced to give it a try 'Down Under', I will make a point of speaking to Victoria about it."

It was about ten days later, after Bell-ringing practice when Digger was escorting Moira back home that she mentioned 'the bank job' again.

"I am sorry if I have over-reacted about all this Digger," she said, "I guess, my thinking about how I would tell my mum and dad that we might be going to Australia, was what was really worrying me."

"That's perfectly understandable, I am sure that Vi and the kids will not be overjoyed either, but it is our life and we only get to live it the once."

She smiled and nodded and then continued, "Well, the doctor asked me to check up on Victoria, to see how she was after having had Malaria while she was away and I was talking to her about their trip and this fruit farm she has become part owner of. It sounds like it will be extremely hard work, but it all sounds so exciting and did you know that Bertie had some sort of adventure while they were staying in Ceylon?"

"No, but nothing surprises me about that old dark horse any more. So you don't mind if I go for the interview on Monday, is that what you are saying?"

"Yes, I guess that is what I am saying. You go and do your best at the interview and see what comes of it and I promise to be at least open-minded about what we do next."

"It is a long time since I had a proper interview for a job," he said, "I will try and get to the library in Oxford and see what I can find out about Perth and the bank, forewarned is for-armed, or something like that."

"What's this Mr. Smith, not having doubts about our ability to pass an interview are we?"

With which she opened the door to her home and ran in, before he could answer.

The interview was at eleven thirty and there were a dozen candidates for the various positions. It started with a written test covering normal banking procedures, some arithmetical questions and finished with a short essay on a town in Australia; which made Digger glad that he had chosen to find out about Perth, which he wrote his essay on.

All the candidates then went to lunch together along with one or two people from the bank. After lunch seven of the candidates had their names called and were thanked for coming but informed that they were not deemed suitable for any of the vacant positions and they left.

The five remaining candidates were then invited to meet with a personnel manager who briefly told them about Australia and what to expect there and frankly answered all the questions they wanted to put to him. He described the living conditions in Perth and the outback and talked about the dangers from snakes, insects and the environment. As a result of this session, two of the candidates decided that they were no longer interested in emigrating and left.

There were three final interviews for each candidate and it was made clear to them that they had to receive the go ahead from each interviewer to be accepted for a position with the bank.

The first interview was with a young man who introduced himself as Brian and said that he worked at the head office in Perth. He seemed more interested in cricket than banking and said he hoped to go to Lord's during his stay in England. Digger pointed out that the second test match against New Zealand had already taken place at Lords but that he might still be able to get tickets for the fourth test at the Oval. Digger remembered the name of the ticket agency he used for theatre tickets and said that Brian might be able to get hold of a ticket for the Oval game from them.

The second interview was with an older man who introduced himself as Don Davis and waited to see what Digger would do next.

"Good afternoon, Mr Davis," Digger said and stood there waiting for the man to reply.

"Sit down Smith, I see you work at a branch of Midland Bank in Oxford. Tell me about your job there."

Digger told him as much as he was allowed to but several times had to say, "I am sorry Mr Davis, but that information is confidential," which did not seem to go down very well.

At the end of the interview the man smiled and held his hand out to Digger and said, "Well done Smith, I like a man who can stand his ground and knows when to keep his mouth shut. Good luck."

The third interview was with an older man who introduced himself as Mr. Johnston. Half way through the interview the telephone rang and Mr. Johnston started to have a conversation with the caller. Digger stood up and intimated that he would wait outside, which he did. The secretary made him a cup of tea and said that the call was from Australia and would take some time. Eventually Mr. Johnston came out and apologised for the interruption. He invited Digger back into the office and had a quiet word with the secretary before returning to the office himself.

He came in and sat down and waited while Digger sat down and got comfortable again.

"Well Digger, that is what they call you isn't it?" Digger nodded in surprise. "You obviously have not realized that I am Bertie and Victoria's friend Nugget, that they met in Australia."

"No sir, I certainly didn't," Digger replied.

"Last Friday I telephoned the man you had put down as a reference a Mr. White with Midland Bank round the corner from here and he invited me over there to have lunch with him. What a charming man, one of the 'old school' of 'gentlemen bankers'."

Digger looked surprised but smiled and nodded again.

"If half of what that gentleman said about you is true, then you would prove to be a worthy candidate for this bank. Now, the interesting thing that he told me, is that in his opinion, he did not think that you would last more than twelve months at Oxford, before you realized it was not for you. He was not surprised therefore, to hear that you were applying for something different and challenging and said to give you his best wishes. He also warned me to only offer you a job that required a man of the highest calibre, if we wanted to keep you for the long term."

"Good old Mr. White," said Digger quietly to himself.

"The secretary has just informed me that you received top marks in all of your tests and that your essay on Perth was most satisfactory. Both Brian and Mr. Davis have given their full support to your application and I will be writing to you to offer you a position with the bank at the Head Office in Perth in Western Australia. I cannot be specific about the exact job, as we will need to see for ourselves, where your true talents lie. As part of the package, we will offer to pay the sea passage for you and your intended bride and in exchange, we will expect you to remain with the bank for at least three years or you will have to reimburse all of the bank's expenses. I will need to have your answer by the fifteenth of this month or the offer will be withdrawn. Any questions?"

There were lots of questions and several cups of tea and it was gone four o'clock before Digger left. He then went round the corner to see Mr. White and his old colleagues and to thank him for supporting him once again.

"Hello Digger, I wondered if you might drop by. What a wonderful opportunity for you, why if I was twenty years younger, I would want to go with you," said Mr. White, "I will ask my secretary to get us a drink and then you can tell me all about it, before you rush off home."

Moira had given a lot of thought to the subject of Australia and was delighted to find out that Victoria and Bertie really did intend going back there at the end of the year, but was not quite so pleased when she heard that Deborah had talked of going back with them as well. Digger parked the car outside her house when he arrived back in the village just after seven o'clock and knocked on her door.

"How did it go, the interview?" she blurted out. "How was it?"

He stood there giving her that 'I don't know what you are talking about look' which so infuriated her and then smiled and said, "They are going to offer me a job and pay all our expenses to go out there and find us somewhere to live for the first month, but I have only got just over a week to give them a decision, or I lose it."

"I spoke to mum today and told her about the interview," said Moira.

"And what was her reaction, histrionics I suppose!" said Digger.

"Surprisingly not," said Moira, "it appears that dad had a chance of a job in London soon after they were married and she refused to go with him and leave Inverness. She said it was the worst decision of her life and she has regretted it ever since. Dad was never given the same opportunity again and has had to do a job beneath his ability ever since, which explains why he got so frustrated with his work when I was younger."

"So is that confirmation that I should write and say yes?" asked Digger.

"You bet it is," she said, "but make sure you tell them we can't come till after our wedding on the twenty seventh and then boy oh boy, a six week honeymoon has got to be good!"

The following day they were invited to have supper with Victoria and Bertie who were thrilled to hear that Digger had been offered a job and had decided to accept it. They said that they had not planned to go back to Australia until the end of October, whereas Digger said that they had hoped to sail during the second week of September.

"Have either of you handed in your notice at work yet?" asked Bertie.

"Yes I did it today and the bank manager in Oxford was not very pleased," said Digger.

"And neither was Dr. Bloom," said Moira, "but we have to do what is right for us, don't we Digger?"

"They all have a month's notice and that is more than we have to give," replied Digger, "anyway, I am sure they will all get along just fine without us and the nursing and banking systems in England will just have to manage somehow."

"I think a toast is called for," said Bertie, with which he produced four glasses and a bottle of apple juice. "Here's to the future and all the adventures it holds in store for us."

"To the future," they all said and clinked glasses and downed the juice.

"Talking of adventures, Bertie," said Digger, "you must tell us the story of what happened to you during that very long boat trip out of Ceylon, that Victoria mentioned to Moira."

Bertie looked surprised and then smiled and shook his head, "Not now my friend, this is not the time, that story can wait for another day."

THE END

Epilogue

We walk the road of good and ill,
We sail the sea of loss and gain;
In beggars rags or rich man's silk,
Each one is made to play life's game.
How we respond is what decides
The person we turn out to be;
The tyrant feared and wished for dead,
The friend who's loved and sets folks free.
One life we have upon this earth,
So think dear friend what you will bring;
It's down to you and no-one else,
Blossom in Winter - Frost in Spring.

2nd July 2010   LS

Lightning Source UK Ltd.
Milton Keynes UK
07 October 2010

160891UK00001B/1/P